KEEP YOU

CHRISTOPHER M. TANTILLO

Keep You

Copyright © 2024 by Christopher M. Tantillo

This book is a work of fiction. Any references to historical events, real people, or real places are used fictitiously. Other names, characters, places, and events are products of the author's imagination, and any resemblance to actual events or places or persons, living or dead, is entirely coincidental.

All rights reserved. Printed in the United States of America. No part of this book may be used, including but not limited to, the training of or use by artificial intelligence, or reproduced in any form or by any electronic or mechanical means, including information storage and retrieval systems, without written permission from the author, except for the use of brief quotations in a book review.

Contact Info: christophermtantillo.com
Cover Design by: Nicole Hower
Cover Image by: Rosie Sun/Unsplash
Audiobook Narrated by: Eric Altheide

ISBN: 979-8-9867622-4-1 (hardcover) 979-8-9867622-5-8 (paperback) 979-8-9867622-6-5 (ebook) 979-8-9867622-7-2 (audiobook)

First Edition: May 2024
1 2 3 4 5 6 7 8 9 10

ALSO BY
CHRISTOPHER M. TANTILLO

<u>Novels</u>

The Night I Spent with Aubrey Fisher

Keep You

<u>Poetry Collections</u>

things never said Series

1. things i never got to tell you

2. things you never got to hear

3. things we never got to share

<u>Short Stories</u>

It's Not Christmas Without Aubrey Fisher

Aubrey Fisher's a Very Misfit Christmas

PRAISE FOR KEEP YOU

"...managed to create a novel that's mysterious, romantic, thrilling, tragic, hilarious, and does all of that so seamlessly the genre changes just seem natural."

— MASON CARLISLE, AUTHOR OF "THE ROANOKE RESISTANCE TRILOGY"

"These are tough pages to get through, but the pain within them is important to drag out into the light. We can't heal while still shrouded in darkness."

— WILLIAM GRANT, AUTHOR OF "WITH YOUR FRIENDS"

"It drew me in from the beginning and just kept getting better until the extremely intense ending."

— READER REVIEW

"This one gutted me."

— READER REVIEW

"Sometimes I read a YA book and 'am reminded just how much I love reading this genre. Tantillo is a new author to me and I am a definite fan."

— READER REVIEW

"The plot is unique, the pacing perfect, and the characters real."

— KARA RENEE, AUTHOR OF
"THE DESIGN OF GOODBYE"

"Another phenomenal book by Tantillo! It's twisty and just so hard to put down."

— T.M. LORE, AUTHOR OF "THE SECRETS
THAT THEY KEEP"

"My jaw was on the floor, literally."

— READER REVIEW

"I enjoyed the thought-provoking poetic prose and how well-written this book and its characters are."

— ALISHA GALVAN, AUTHOR OF
"AUTUMN"

"This author has such a poetic writing style, and it makes even the most heart wrenching tale beautiful!

— READER REVIEW

"This book takes you on a fun adventure, with dark themes and a great twist. It had me excited to see how the series continues!"

— READER REVIEW

AUTHOR'S NOTE

Reader, be aware, the below list of warnings will contain **some spoilers**. Read only if you need to. You've been advised.

This book contains and implies scenes/themes related to abandonment, abuse (child, emotional, inter-marital, mental, physical, sexual), anxiety, aversion to medication, brief mention of child pornography, bullying, CPTSD, crude language, depression, drug use, head trauma, mentions of BDSM and grooming, misogyny, neglect, PTSD, repressed memories, self-harm, sexual assault, suicidal ideation, and violence—all involving teens. Please practice self-care before, during, and after reading. Know that it's okay to put this down and come back to it later. Your health and safety should always come first.

If you or anyone you know is suffering with thoughts of suicide or self-harm, please seek a professional as soon as possible. Or call or text 988, the Suicide and Crisis Lifeline.

If you or anyone you know has survived any act of sexual violence, please visit https://www.rainn.org/. Or call the 24/7 hotline at 800-656-HOPE (4673).

For the ones who scream when no one is listening.

And for you,
I wish I'd known sooner.

This book has always been yours.

TUESDAY, NOVEMBER 12TH - THIRTEEN YEARS PRIOR

HADLEE

Age 5

THERE IS A MONSTER UPSTAIRS.

The ice cream is good. Creamy and slimy and yummy, but so cold. Daddy says good girls eat downstairs, so I do. Chocolate is my favorite.

Momma and Daddy are up there. I don't like being down here alone. I want Momma here.

But the ice cream is good. Daddy says not to go up there. There are noises. Monster noises.

The moon is out. I see it. I don't like it down here. See monsters crawling on the floor from the sky moon. Coming for me. To take me away forever and ever.

I don't like it down here. I'm scared and sit on my feet, so they don't grab my ankles.

I need to go upstairs. I just want them here. Need to be safe in bed.

I finish my ice cream and leave the bowl on the couch. Look up there. Voices. I think it's Momma and Daddy. But the floor has bad things that can grab me. I want to cry.

But I'll be a bad girl. I could watch a movie like I'm s'posed to. So I don't get taken away.

Then Momma cries, like I do when I fall down and get a scratch and need a Band-Aid.

Daddy talks, but I can't hear what he says. So I jump from the couch to stairs but hurt my knee.

"Momma!" I try not to cry. There is a lot of pain. I sit on the bottom stair, safe from the floor.

No one comes to help me.

There are noises here. Things in the dark I can't see. My body shakes. I freeze 'cause they can't touch me if I freeze. Count down like Nani taught me and stand.

I walk up the stairs. They make loud noises, so I stop. Close my eyes. Don't want the monster to hear and grab me. My knee hurts bad and something behind is watching me. I feel it. 'Cause I didn't watch a movie. 'Cause I left ice cream on the couch.

Nothing happens. I open my eyes and get upstairs fast to their bedroom door. Hall isn't safe yet.

Noises. Loud. I can't hear it.

Momma is crying even though Daddy doesn't like it.

He's talking but sounds funny.

She cries a lot when it's just us two.

My hand reaches for the door. Maybe it's too late.

Something is watching me still. More shivers. I need to go potty.

I turn the handle until it cracks open and stops. Press my ear to the crack. Stay in the dark.

Momma talks low in her voice. I don't like when she is sad.

I can't hear Daddy, but hear the monster, so I stay quiet. The monster is inside now. I'm too late. We are in the bad place. Where bad people go. I wait to be picked up.

Push open the crack wider until I can see. Too black.

Just dark things moving on the bed. Maybe they're both swallowed by bad things.

I lick dry chocolate from my lips but taste salt and gag.

Look at the dark for a long time. Knowing it will come for me. Waiting to eat little girls.

It swallows little girls with sharp teeth.

I felt the teeth once. They hurt me. Daddy was there at the end.

It stops. The noises and the movements. I hear Daddy again, but it's hard. He's alive! They need my help.

I feel it behind me. It will take me. I'm not 'llowed to scream or cry.

"...cleaned up. Don't...Hadlee se—..."

Then Momma: "Yes, okay."

Footsteps. Not sure who. I run into my bedroom like the game we play. The dark thing is in the hall, then the bathroom. The door is loud, and it hurts my head. I feel it in my knee.

Crying again, so I sneak out. Momma is in the bed. The covers are like mine when I wake up. I want to see her, but can't walk. I stare for a while. Scared to come out of the dark.

"M-Momma?"

She stops crying and looks at me. Rubs her eyes. "Oh, baby." She tries to sit but something hurts her in the bed and can't get up. She makes a noise I don't like and holds out her hand, so I go grab it.

"Is the monster gone?"

"Hadlee, sweetie." She rubs her thumb on my hand. I shake. We are in the bad place now. I'm too late. "Did you see us?"

I nod cause it's what I'm told to do when someone asks me something. I want to be good. "Did the monster hurt you, Momma?"

She touches my face and shushes me with a finger. "Tell me, baby girl. Are you happy?"

I nod again and bring my hair to my mouth and start chewing on it. The dark thing has me now.

"Can you keep a secret?"

PRESENT DAY

DEV

Age 16

I WAKE UP ALONE, SHIRTLESS, SHOELESS, AND LYING freezing in the woods. I have no idea how I got here. My hair is soaked, and my breath condenses in the chilly night air. It's completely black, minus the pinprick glow from the half-moon in the sky. The tall trees obscure any stars in the night. It's dark.

Eerie.

No. No no no.

My lungs seem to close up like they're suffocating—the vast nothingness. Tears well in the corners of my eyes, so I inhale a few breaths to settle my racing mind. I try and call out for help, but all that escapes is hot air, and then the thought:

You're going to die here.

It takes a moment for my ears to register the sounds of crickets playing their orchestra. There's the scent of pine, dead leaves, and moss. I extend an arm and feel something cold and wet before hitting a coarse vine.

My heels sink into soft earth, so I jerk my foot to fling off the clay and stand up. A light breeze licks the tops of my shoulders.

Heart skips a few beats. Breaths, shallow. Mouth, dry.

You're alive. You're okay.

I wrap my arms around my body, my teeth chattering, and look around to determine the direction I came from and to let my eyes acclimate to the dark. By now, it should be second nature. My mind should possess the map needed to find the way back to civilization. But, of course, this isn't the first time, and it won't be the last. It always takes a minute for the fog to clear from my head and for warmth to fill my body, my bones—my soul. But I'll find the right way and get back to the main road.

The woods. This place. Desolate and dreary—is always where I go when I'm asleep.

Mom and Dad used to be really worried about it, and eventually the occurrences became less frequent, and then after a while I just stopped telling them. I'd be back to the motel before they even realized I was gone.

It's better that they don't know.

SNAP

The breaking of a twig echoes from behind. Could be a few feet, could be a few yards. Instantly, my body stands alert, hairs on my neck rise, and my stomach lurches hard enough to make me gag. Just when I think I had imagined the sound, it happens again. Closer.

SNAP

Someone's here.

This isn't supposed to happen. I'm alone, practically naked. *No one* knows about this place besides my parents.

Dev. Run.

When my mind clears, and the tree bark looks familiar, I count backward from three and head to the right, careful not to make too much noise. A spider web drapes across my face, so I slap as much of it off as I can, feeling phantom spider legs crawling through my hair and laying eggs. I leap over one log here, a tree stump there. My shins brush past a few prickly bushes, but I continue.

Soon, I find myself on the dirt gravel outside the entrance to the trailer park. The cold stones hurt my feet, so I step carefully around them until I hit dewy grass. A shiver creeps up my ankles, and I dash in the direction of the motel, just a couple miles down past the trailer parks and River Road, past the abandoned gas stations and an old convenience store that was looted long ago.

I want to look behind me, worry that someone wielding a machete is going to be there, suddenly within arm's reach, but I don't. Ignorance is bliss. What I can't see won't hurt me. Snot leaks from my nose, so I wipe it off with the back of my hand.

The blood in my veins warms up with the movement of my body, my joints, and I'm invigorated. My breath quickens. My lungs burn in the cold harshness of night—of my body coming alive. I pump my legs harder, despite the pain in my feet when I hit a rough patch of earth. But the running warms me, wakes me up, takes away the fog and confusion. Like maybe it never happened. Like it never happens.

And I'm alone, always alone. Always that same place. Sometimes farther in, sometimes closer, but always the same woods. The same trees and isolation. The same throbbing in the back of my head like I have right now. The steady *thump thump thump*.

But never has someone been with me when I woke up. Never. I run.

It's not long before I round the bend past some of the poorer neighborhoods and run-down houses and spot the lights inside the motel's front office. I slow down and drop my hands on my knees to catch my breath. I'm sweating now and will probably come down with a cold, shivering again. Still, I don't look back.

But Dad is there, inside the front office that's half the size of a bedroom—a glass outer wall so anyone driving by can see we're open, see there's still vacancy. He's hunched over some books, probably looking at our funds and crunching numbers like he always is, or maybe doing a crossword. I can see him blinking his brown eyes, rubbing the stubble on his chin that's overdo for a shave, and I imagine that if he looked up and saw me right now, he'd dart, thinking I'd been shot.

For now, he rubs his temples as if he has a migraine and cranes his neck. From here, I can tell how rosy his puffy cheeks are, how pale his complexion is in the crude lights. He's put on weight over the years. Mom isn't anywhere visible, so she must already be in bed.

It's been two months since the last one happened, and almost nineteen months since my parents last found me.

I walk past the parking lot to the opposite side of the motel where there's a wooden fence taller than me that separates the road from our lot. Like usual, I back up, count to three, and dash for the fence until I get enough momentum to spring forward, grip the top, and hoist myself up and over. With a soft thud, I land on my feet like a cat and scan the courtyard behind the motel lobby. There's a narrow concrete walkway just beside the little laundry shack and a rotted iron fence that closes off the in-ground pool, which hasn't been operational in years. The bottom is littered with dirty, green water and garbage from kids who throw stuff over the fence. The concrete is cracked. Uncut grass and weeds sprout through and brush my shins as I pass.

I yawn, still unable to check the time because my mesh shorts pockets are empty, so I jog behind the building, along the lines of motel rooms. Each with a tiny window every few feet, and around the L-shaped design until I reach a second building perpendicular to the first. The one that hasn't been used in years. There's no key on me, so I go to the back window for

Room 13, crack it open, and crawl through. I step onto the toilet seat and close the window behind me.

Flicking on the dim yellow light, because the wirework was never updated in this building, I see that my curly hair is a mess, and my face is covered in dried dirt and grass stains. I'm too tired to clean up with the faucets that spit out nothing but black goo, so I shuffle out of the bathroom and into the main area with the beds.

Room 13 is exactly as I left it: the bed unmade, a pair of dirty jeans on the floor I need to take to the laundry shack to wash, and my Geometry notebook opened on the nightstand. The walls are adorned with old photos, trinkets, and drawings from the past few years. I shut the bathroom door behind me and find my phone and earbuds resting on the pillow where I had been sleeping. I put the earbuds back in and play the last song I was listening to.

In the far corner, propped next to the bathroom door, is the old 50s red Schwinn bicycle, dusty from lack of use. I don't ride it anymore.

Dirty, disgusting. As if my skin covers nothing but rot.

Unable to think about it, I tear my eyes away and my gaze drifts to the collage tacked up on the far wall, opposite the bed, at what has been collected.

I lay my head on the pillow and close my eyes, back in my "real" bed. Back at the motel where I live, that my parents own.

It's been years since I've slept in my actual bedroom; I much prefer this one. I close my eyes, letting myself drift off as "Come Fly With Me" by Frank Sinatra croons in my ears.

I can't let this keep happening. Not again. Not so my parents worry or coddle me.

I just wish I knew what it was or how to make it stop, make it go away.

The scar on the back of my head still throbs.

But mostly I wonder why, above all else, do I feel that as soon as I leave the woods....

I need to go right back.

MALEVOLENT BEAUTY AND THE RUNNING MAN

PART ONE

I can't breathe. Can't see.

    No matter how hard I try, nothing works but my legs.

    There is a man behind me.

    Chasing me.

    Closer

       CLOSER

          CLOSER

    From somewhere over my shoulder, there is screaming. A name over and over. A voice. No. A ringing. Over and over and over and over and over.

    The faster I run, the slower I get.

      Like my legs are being weighed down.

    The man is within arm's length.

    His **hand** *reaches out for mine.*

    Can't see——

      No face——

        He almost has me,

    *and the voice still cries out (**ringing**)... farther away.* _{*Clear.*}

Smokescreen.

CHAPTER 1

Hadlee Renee Morgan carries her camera everywhere she goes. In school, it's either hanging around her neck in the hallways or inside a case she keeps slung over one shoulder during class. Outside of school, it's in her hands and snapping anything and everything. Ever since freshman year, she's never been without one. Safe to say that the camera is part of her, and she's part of it.

Wasn't always this way, though.

Today is track day in gym, and I try to keep an even pace with my best friend Aiden as a few of the more athletic guys lap us. He's moving slower than I want to run, so it's a struggle to maintain our snail-like speed when all I want is to fly. *Clear*. To be alive for the four laps we're required to run. We have to complete the fitness test in a couple weeks. Everyone should be training, but most guys use this as a time to chat while running laps. Aiden's no different.

We have a track meet after school, and our gym teacher—Coach—doesn't want those of us competing on the team to exhaust ourselves too early, so a few of us take it easy.

The sun is set high in the cloudless sky, making heat waves

shimmer in what feels like ninety-degree weather. I wipe sweat from my forehead.

Aiden calls my name, begging me to slow down. I've barely advanced above a light jog and get ahead without realizing it. His arms flail uselessly, his knees bending at awkward angles—like limp tentacles—as he races toward me.

I slow to a walk and look at the bleachers behind the track fence to Hadlee. She's leaning against the guardrail that faces the field—the risers a few feet off the ground. Her elbows are tucked into her abdomen, one hand underneath the camera lens and the other on the grip, and her face pressed to the back. Every once in a while, she adjusts the lens, or she pulls her face back to look at something before repositioning herself against the rail.

But it's the way she squints, how her nose and forehead scrunch up in that adorable way, that makes—

"Dev, I'm cramping," Aiden calls from behind. He catches up to me, holding his calf and trying to run at the same time, which results in a strange hopping motion.

I think I mumble something in response, but not sure what.

Hadlee wears a red flannel shirt, unbuttoned, over a white tank with a dream catcher graphic printed on the front. The flannel shirt is rolled up to her elbows, and she wears a black baseball cap backward. Her chestnut bangs stick out of the Velcro strap. Black skinny jeans complete the outfit, with Hadlee's trademark red converse shoes to match.

A look, if you ask me, that no one can pull off at our school better than her.

Aiden looks over his shoulder to a couple of guys that have been trailing us for the last lap. He nudges my arm. "There's so much outline of dick today. It's insane."

"Dick outline, huh?"

"A plethora of sweaty, swaying, teenage scrotum in mesh

shorts. It's beautiful. Unfair, but beautiful." He nudges my arm again, groans. "Jesus. It's like a candy store out here, wondering how many licks each takes to get to the center."

I pick up the pace, shaking my head and chuckling. "Any particular flavors in mind?"

"Slow your skinny legs down and wait for me." Aiden gasps for air. "I wasn't done ogling yet."

I murmur something back as we round a turn past the bleachers by the football scoreboard. The track wraps around the endzone. As the lanes straighten back out again, Hadlee is still perched against the rail with her face in the camera. But one of the guys in class veers off course and runs up to the spot right below her, whistles seductively, and jumps—ruining her shot.

Travis Weathers.

Coach shouts his name from the yellow goalpost opposite the scoreboard. Travis hops down from the fence, hooting, and catches up with two friends.

Hadlee pulls the camera back, but I can't make out her face.

And moments like that make me hate Travis Weathers.

"Earth to Dev," Aiden says. "This is reality calling."

"I hear you."

"Then get back into your lane and stop creeping."

"I'm not creeping."

"Then slow down, Barry Allen."

"Do you ever think that maybe—"

"Dude, watch out!"

Hadlee points her camera in the direction we're running, but I have no idea what for. I turn to look ahead and see I'm nearly off the track. But when I pivot to adjust course, it's too late to stop the inevitable. The hurdle is directly in front of me.

In my mind, I attempt the jump, but in reality, my chest

smacks into the top of the hurdle. One moment my feet are on the ground, the next the hurdle falls forward, tugging me with it.

I crash face-first into the asphalt, scraping my cheek in the process. Sharp pain shoots up my chest, cheeks, and groin. My feet still want to move, so as I try to hop back up and continue as if nothing happened, my foot snags on the flat end of the hurdle, and I once again smash my face into the asphalt after I go down.

"Holy rutabaga!" Aiden shouts.

I'm too embarrassed to move. One leg is propped against the hurdle, the other sprawled to the side. When I open my eyes, Aiden and a couple guys in class hover above me—some of them laugh. Eventually, our gym teacher rushes over and helps me up, checking to make sure I'm not seriously hurt. I verify I'm okay after brushing dirt off my gym shorts. There are a few scratches on my forearm and a cut on my left elbow.

Only I would do something so stupid, especially with Hadlee watching.

Fan-freaking-tastic.

"I'm sorry, I wasn't looking where I was going," I tell Coach Odis, our gym teacher and track coach. "I didn't break the hurdle, did I?"

Coach Odis checks me out, shaking his head. "No, your face broke the fall. Eyes on the track next time, Landry. I was calling you, but your head was in the clouds. We need you in top shape for the meet tonight. And don't worry about the hurdle. Go see the nurse."

"I can still finish up the—"

"Nurse, Landry. End of discussion." He points to Aiden. "Have Brumberg escort you."

I nod and limp off the field with Aiden, whose eyes sparkle. Anything to avoid physical exertion is preferred with him.

We pass Travis and a few other boys on the way. One of

them snickers as we walk by, and I think Travis makes a farting noise. We ignore them and continue to the edge of the grass.

"Morgan!" I hear Coach shout from behind me. "This isn't a free period to get your jollies while the boys train. Where are you supposed to be right now?"

I look, and Hadlee stands up straight. She's silent for a moment before answering, like her mind is anywhere but here. "Study hall, Mr. Odis. I have a pass."

"I don't care what your pass is for. You can't be here."

She fidgets with her camera. "I'm not bothering anyone."

"Maybe your teacher's given you permission to not be in their class, but that's not an invitation to supervise mine. Get out. You're a distraction."

"It's for Yearbook."

Coach jerks a thumb toward the school. "Get back to class, Morgan. Yearbooks are already finalized for print. This isn't National Geographic out here."

Travis shouts from the far side of the field. "Have you seen her ass? That's nationally geographic."

A couple guys laugh in response.

I want to punch him right in the mouth.

Coach Odis reaches around his neck for the whistle and blows into it. "Everybody can drop and do twenty followed by one extra lap. You can thank Mr. Weathers for that." He blows his whistle at Travis. "And you can go directly to the principal's office. I won't have harassment in my class, Weathers. Or on my team."

Travis stops running. "It was just a joke."

"Good. Maybe the principal will find it funny when you tell him again. Now get out of my class, or I will be happy to escort you there."

"Coach, I'm the captain. Come on."

He blows his whistle again. "Make that two extra laps for

everyone here. I'll add more until Mr. Weathers realizes that I will not tolerate disrespecting women on the field or anywhere else. Track meet tonight or not."

A few guys in class groan, all of them panting and falling to the ground. One of his friends shouts for him to just leave before he makes it worse. Travis grunts and storms over the grass and past me and Aiden, muttering under his breath. He doesn't even look back at Hadlee to see her reaction.

Coach blows his whistle to signify each time the class is to do a pushup in sync. I'm not sure if we're supposed to drop or not too, so I signal to Aiden to sneak away before Coach has a chance to remember we're still here.

Before I exit the gate to the trail leading to the back of the school, I glance over toward the bleachers where Hadlee was snapping photos. I expect her to be facing the track again, but she's already moved from her spot—pointing her camera at what I think is the girl's gym class playing volleyball on the soccer field.

I wince with each limp, the cuts growing numb the farther we walk. Still, I can't help but feel like I deserve this. Just a passing thought.

Aiden huffs when he walks, still trying to catch his breath. Sweat beads the back of my neck, so I wipe it off. Coach Odis's whistle carries on the wind.

Aiden laughs. "You were like Superman back there for, like, a second."

I face forward. "More like Clark Kent, really."

"Right you are. But hey, sexy Clark gets feisty Lois Lane to go home to. What does Superman get? Overrated if you ask me."

"But you said I was more like Superman when I went over the hurdle."

"I did say that, didn't I? Weird."

"Yup."

I look over my shoulder at the bleachers, and Hadlee isn't facing away anymore. Her camera is in her hand, and she's looking at me. My stomach flips.

Or maybe she's just staring off into space, thinking.

We walk the rest of the way in silence, and I can't help but think of Hadlee and her camera as we enter the school.

I wonder if the world looks any different from behind the lens.

After the nurse cleans and bandages the scrapes, she gives us written notes to head to our next class. We return to the locker room to change out of our sweaty clothes, and we're the only ones here. I prop myself on a wooden bench and open my gym bag to get out clean clothes for the last few periods.

"I was just kidding about the Superman stuff back there," Aiden says.

"Yeah, I know."

"Okay, cool."

Aiden takes off his shirt and runs his hands through his short, gelled hair that he spikes up in the front. His skin is paler than most people's, and he has freckles covering his entire body. He's thin—frailer than I am, if that's possible. Aiden is the type who can eat an entire tray of pizza and not gain an ounce. We started hanging out freshman year, after he moved here from Maine, and we were both paired together for a Global assignment to create a map of present-day America. He traced out the states, and I cut out the pieces. We both took turns gluing them onto the poster board and coloring them. It felt like elementary school all over again.

We click because he's awkward, like me. And mostly friendless, like me. Even if Rosa at the motel says otherwise, I know it's true. That's why we get along so well. It was a fresh start for the two of us freshman year. And he's always geeking out about *Star Wars* or anything superhero or comic book related. I enjoy the movies, but they're his obsession. Every single medium. He even likes to get dressed in the morning to "The Death March" from *The Phantom Menace*. Like putting on his jeans and pullover shirt are preparations for battle.

Aiden applies deodorant and takes off his gym clothes, like it's no big deal to be naked and out in the open. I can't stand it. Feeling exposed. It just irks me. I always dress under a towel in the locker room. Never shower unless I'm home at the motel.

We finish changing, him into his jean shorts and Indiana Jones T-shirt, and me into khaki shorts and a striped polo.

"We're getting together tonight to play D&D at Greg's house," he says. "You should come."

"You know I can't."

"No, you can, you choose not to."

I lace up my sneakers. "I have to work front desk tonight."

"That's your excuse every time, Dev. Your parents can manage one Friday night."

My chest tightens. It's not that I wouldn't want to hang out with Aiden's other friends. I've met them before. But it's just a nagging thought that terrifies me. Like something bad will happen—I hate big crowds. I'm only good one-on-one. Consider me quirky.

Plus, my parents count on me to help on weekends, and they don't like me straying too far away from home. Plus-plus, my parents would never allow it. Not ever.

I always work front desk Friday nights. Always.

"You guys can move the game to the motel."

I hope he gives an excuse, like always.

"You know we can't," he says, like he's guilty. "Greg has to answer the phone for pizza orders."

"Maybe another weekend my parents will let you guys come over."

Aiden sighs obnoxiously. "Fine, if you want to be Han *SOLO* about this."

We're both silent as what he said sinks in.

"That was a terrible joke."

"Yeah," he says, ashamed. "Not my finest hour."

"George Lucas wouldn't approve."

"I just Jar-Jar Binksed myself."

We laugh, and I ball my towel and throw it at him. He catches it and throws it back. Once we're done, we grab our bags and head in the direction of our lockers in the junior hallway. We pass the display of athletic achievements and then zip past the cafeteria and the science lab rooms. We turn down a corridor and find our lockers just as the bell to signal the end of the period rings. Doors open, and dozens of kids file into the hallway chatting away, carrying books, and looking at their phones.

Guess you don't need the nurse's note after all.

After we put our gym stuff away and grab our books for next period, Travis and Hadlee round the corner together, him following behind. Her straight, chestnut hair falls halfway down her back—her camera in a bag slung over one shoulder. He tries to grab her ass, but she smacks his hand away. When he leans in to whisper in her ear, she hunches her shoulders and ducks away.

I ball my fist against my pant leg.

Travis has his black hair in the undercut style, with the sides of his head shaved but leaving a long poof on top. He has a tattoo on his upper shoulder trailing down into his shirt. He's muscular and lean, mainly because his dad owns the only successful gym in town. That's where Travis started training for competitions last summer and came back to school a new man. He used to be skinny, the best runner on our team, but already his clothes are a size bigger—his biceps bulge out of the shirt-sleeves, his chest sticks out, and the veins in his forearms are pronounced.

I can beat him this year. I *will*.

His family is rich. Or rather, rich for our town, and well-respected. Even when Travis is acting like a jerk, he still gets off the hook thanks to his parents and the donations they've made to the community and school. His mother is some kind of defense attorney, so their family is always who you go to when you're in legal trouble.

Travis has been harassing Hadlee since the start of our junior year, when he bulked up. But every time he tries to force himself on her, she denies him over and over. Like he's a puppy begging for a treat.

Hadlee doesn't date. She doesn't flirt. She doesn't fool around. But most of all, she doesn't do friends. Not anymore.

"You're being a creeper again," Aiden whispers. "You could, you know, just say hi or text her or something."

"She wouldn't want anything to do with me."

"You could not speak on her behalf and actually go up and ask her. See for yourself."

"You don't understand, Aiden. I'm not even on her radar anymore."

"Blah blah, same sob story. Heard it before. And yet here you be, still in creep mode. This is how villains are born, you know."

I hate it when he's right.

Hadlee continues to ignore Travis until he finally takes the hint, sneers, and flips her the middle finger before slapping her ass and passing to meet a group of guys down the hall. She tries to swing at him with a fist, but he ducks away. Amidst the commotion, none of the teachers standing outside saw. Travis points his thumb over his shoulder to Hadlee as she stops midway down the hall to access her locker—a few feet over from mine. They all start laughing.

I'll hurt you one day. Keep it up.

For a second, just a second, I think Hadlee's eyes flicker to mine. I want them to. Something, anything. A moment of recognition. And I get a close-up of her alabaster skin and long, thin legs. The mole just below her left collarbone. Her thick eyebrows and pierced septum.

She never had those clothes or that piercing before our freshman year.

It seems unfair that luck or fate or Hadlee's parents could create someone as beautifully perfect as she is. At least, to me. Even before she changed, she was always beautiful. She could always light up a room. Her giggle, smooth like velvet, was like a prize you never knew you wanted until you had it. I'm not sure if I'm smiling, but I know my mouth is open, because Aiden takes his finger and pushes up my chin until my teeth meet.

What a cartoon cliché.

"You know," Aiden says, a hint of a laugh in his voice, "I'm not really into that kind of thing myself, but even *I* would have sex with Hadlee Morgan if she asked. That girl is easily one of the hottest, most disturbed girls I've ever seen up close. Even if she has one of those, you know, vaginas." He shudders.

"I wouldn't get my hopes up. She's not really into guys that are into other dudes."

"That's discrimination."

"You don't even like vaginas."

"Ew, don't say that nasty word here!" He slaps my arm.

"You said it first!" I slap him back.

"So, you have no excuse not to just go up to her and say,

'Screw Travis,' and plant a sloppy kiss on her lips." He pauses, smirks. "The ones on her face, of course."

I roll my eyes. "Then watch as I get my butt kicked by him and his friends, or denied when Hadlee slaps me."

"They're tools, and everybody knows it. Hadlee knows it. They're hot, sure. And Travis can pose shirtless with kittens any time he wants to now that he's a meathead. I won't complain. But maybe she's waiting for a big romantic gesture from someone else willing to save her from her dark, disturbed life. You could be her awkward wittle Peter Parker."

Hadlee bends down to reach for a book in her locker. Her butt in those pants... I try not to be that guy, but it's just not fair.

"No slinging webs today, Aiden."

She closes her locker and heads in our direction. As Hadlee starts to walk past, I think she's looking right at me so, unsure what to do, I nod my head in acknowledgment. Hadlee doesn't act like she notices, so I quickly pretend as if I'm looking past her to someone else, but find myself staring at the butt of some girl bending into a locker across the hall. She is wearing a skirt, and one of her friends notices me accidentally staring and snaps her fingers.

"Grow up, pervert."

I divert my eyes away. "I'm sorry, I didn't mean to."

"What's going on?" The bent-over girl stands straight and faces her friend. Shauna and Mackie Hill. Same biological father. Different biological mothers. My parents used to talk to their family before things got bad.

Shauna points to me with a Mickey Mouse pen. "Dev Landry is being a pervert. He was staring at your ass."

Mackie faces me, her nostrils flaring. "Ew, I have a *boyfriend*, creep."

I exhale. "I wasn't——"

She reaches out an arm to shove me back, and I nearly trip in the process.

"Get out of here before I text him to kick your ass after school," Shauna says, pushing me too. "Run along to class, *coma boy*. I know brain-damaged people do things different over on the side where you live with your shady parents, but over here we don't——"

FLASH

We all look over. It's Hadlee, pointing her camera from a few feet away. And I feel so ashamed.

Mackie says, "What the heck....

An interesting thought:

What the heck is going on!?

Shauna says, "What are you doing?"

Mackie's eyes go wide. "She's gonna post this on her freaky website, I bet."

Hadlee looks away, past them, as she mumbles.

Shauna and Mackie exchange a look and shake their heads. I'm not sure what goes through their minds, but we all know this: If Hadlee plans to expose you on her website, she will expose you, and there is no stopping her.

Last year, some teacher at another school was caught selling weed to a student. Hadlee caught it on camera and posted it online. Considering the massive controversy and legal repercussions, the teacher was let go within a week.

Shauna and Mackie give me dirty looks, not saying anything else to get on her bad side. You never want to piss her off if she has dirt on you.

Aiden laughs behind me, because he always gets a kick out of how I manage to get myself in trouble. No one has to do it for me; I somehow find a way. But everyone is now looking at us. Everyone but Hadlee, who keeps her focus on the girls.

"Sorry, Dev," they say in unison.

Unsure what to do, I say, "Th-thanks." But I'm not saying it for them.

I sense my cheeks growing hot, so I close my locker and start walking in the opposite direction to our next class before anyone can speak again.

From behind, Shauna says, "We, um, *love* the corpses on your blog, by the way."

Mackie adds, "We really do love it so much."

Aiden slaps me on the back. "Oh yeah. You definitely have Han Solo luck, champ. Also, ignore what they said. Rude and uncalled for."

Over my shoulder, Hadlee stares at the girls until they close their lockers and walk away. She looks to the side, staring off into space again, thinking about who-knows-what. She takes her camera in both hands, goes into her typical stance, and adjusts a few dials on the lens, pointing it down the hall where Travis and his friends stand. I'm not sure what exactly she's focusing on, but she's still for a while, pointing it at something, before a teacher flags her down and tells her to put it away, hesitant, not wanting to get his picture taken.

I guess that's how it is with the local freak, so to speak. Not a term I'd choose.

Coma boy and the freakish girl.

She hugs her camera closer to her body and turns her head in my direction. A boy walks past, his backpack slamming into my shoulder. She stares stoically. Unmoving. She finally snaps out of her funk when the bell rings to signal the start of class.

But there was something in the moment, like out at the bleachers that seemed so different from the girl that usually walks the halls carefree and in control.

What's going on in your head, Haddy?

Despite knowing it's useless, I text my Mom and try anyway.

ME

it cool if i go to Aidens after school?

MOM

Your father and I would prefer if he came here.

ME

just 1 night, please? 4 a change

MOM

Your father said no.

ME

but what r u saying?

MOM

Don't do this. I'm Fun Mom. Don't make me lay
down The Law. Fun Mom defies The Law.

ME

it ok, just thot id ask

MOM

Here's your father.

ME

wait what?

MOM

(as The Law) No.

ME

parentheses doesnt make this any less corny

MOM

(The Law has spoken) They come here or it's
a no.

ME

fine

MOM

(The Law rests) Now put away your phone, you're in school.

ME

ok

MOM

Okay, honey, I'm back. I'm sorry. It's just the weekend. It's a bad neighborhood. But be rebellious like me and text all you want, just don't make us come down there if you get caught. And make sure you come home promptly after track ends. Plus, Ramone is missing. Plus-plus, have a great meet! Wish I could be there!

ME

Ramone your wrench?

MOM

You borrowed him then lost him. I want him back.

ME

u r so weird. i luv u but ur weird

MOM

Have you looked in the mirror?? :-D

ME

-_-

not funny

i'll tell u how track went when i get home

MOM

(as Fun Mom) We love you! Get first place!

ME

luv u 2, and thanks

still not funny

MOM

0

ME

OMG!

Hadlee Renee Morgan is the girl other girls stay away from. She's the daughter most parents are glad they never had. And the girl most boys make fun of and harass. She just came in one day at the start of freshman year: new clothes, new hair, new style, and her new camera. She started taking pictures—started a blog that eventually garnered local and then regional recognition for her graphic photography, poems, and sketches. Even won some local contests and awards.

Like maybe she sold her soul to the devil.

But I don't buy any of it.

Ask people in school at any given time, and they'll say she can be disturbed, a loner, misunderstood, depressed, suicidal, weird, freak, hipster, etc. Not many people I know like her website, at least, none that I see comment on it from our school. Maybe some of the artsy students do, but when she stopped talking to people, they stopped caring in return.

But to say Hadlee *became* a hipster would be lying. Hadlee is her own person, and in a way, she always has been. Hard to pinpoint. Never boring. Always charismatic toward others who are wronged. Never afraid to speak her mind via her photography, to show injustice or right some wrong, like she's a virtual vigilante. She's all over the place. I guess that's why so many people don't like her. She's beautiful in a unique way, a fashion sense that might seem cliché, and maybe it is, but it's also just *Hadlee.*

I exit the school, most kids filing to the buses in the drop-off circle—the seniors heading to their cars in the parking lot. The sun still makes the heat liquefy in the distance, and I have to shield my eyes from the light.

But she's there, perched on a picnic bench off to the side on the grass. I hook my thumbs under the straps of my backpack and watch her across the sidewalk. Kids brush past me. Hadlee has her elbows on her knees for support, the camera to her face. I look to where I think she's filming, and all I see is an empty candy wrapper that didn't make the trashcan. But Hadlee focuses the camera with such intimacy, such careful precision.

And I get it. I get what makes that tiny wrapper off to the side, the one that never made it to the trashcan where all the others are discarded, so special. I focus on the wrapper bundled up and wait for someone else to notice like me and Hadlee do.

No one else does.

It's moments like this that let me believe Haddy is still there somewhere.

I just wish I knew what she was looking for. What she sees that others don't. What she thinks about. Why the lens seems better to her, safer to her, than reality. Why she doesn't talk to anyone, and why she hides herself away. Even from me.

A girl in a red and yellow cheer outfit walks past Hadlee, carrying a water bottle. She chats into a phone and tosses the bottle toward the trash but misses. She continues walking.

Hadlee pulls her face back to look at the bottle rolling with the wind. She frowns, and then looks over at me. Just a moment, maybe not even that. My stomach flips again.

She leans her chin into her palm, holding the camera with the opposite hand. Her left wrist has a double-faced watch. She doesn't smile, but after a moment, she turns off her camera and puts it back into her bag. She jumps down from the bench and picks up the water bottle and walks it over to a separate bin for recyclables. But after she's gone, I see she left the wrapper in the grass where she found it.

What's going through your head?

I make my way to the trashcan and pick up the gum wrapper. And there, by the blue bin for recyclables, Hadlee is staring at me. I stand there and stare back for what feels like minutes, hours, days. I'm still holding the wrapper.

Aiden locks an arm around my shoulder from behind, breaking my trance, so I put the wrapper in my pocket before he can see. I accompany him to the sidewalk, so we can do our usual walk-and-talk before the meet after school.

"What were you doing?" he asks.

"Nothing."

"That's a lie. I saw you watching her again."

"Why do you think she took a picture of those two girls earlier?"

Aiden sighs, pulling out his phone to answer a text. "You're lucky you're my best friend, otherwise I'd have left by now. The pining is super annoying."

"I know it is."

"But you're cute, so I keep you around so I can stare at *you*."

I laugh. "You're ridiculous."

He's quiet before continuing. "I don't know why she did that. It's the first time I've ever seen her come within three feet of you, let alone that close to photograph, specifically I might add, about you being bullied by two girls for fake perving."

We reach our spot on the edge of the sidewalk where a patch of grass meets a wooded area. We turn around and head back in the opposite direction.

"It's weird, right?" I ask.

"Hence why you should, you know, actually *talk* to her."

"Tell me the right words to say, and I will."

"Comment on her blog that you stare at every night."

"I can't."

"You're hopeless."

"You're probably right."

"Ughhhh, you're not supposed to agree!"

I stare out my window and search for Hadlee. But when I find her, she's already walking off, past the buses and cars. Heading toward the road to walk home, like she does every day. Alone. Just her and the camera. I'm still filled with a million questions.

Most of all though, I want to ask her why, after we kissed that one summer night before freshman year, she stopped being my best friend.

CHAPTER 2

Out of all the athletics in late spring, track is one of the least popular. If we're the same day as baseball or any other home game, our bleachers are always the emptiest. Usually parents and friends, maybe a few faculty members, but rarely a turnout like the football players get in the fall.

I don't mind; like I said, I dislike big crowds.

It's the running that helps me focus and block it all out.

After I dress in my red shorts, yellow tank, and green Asics—the red and yellow being our school colors—we do our usual pre-meet routine:

- Dynamic Warm-up: (to prevent cramping/injury)
- 800m jog
- Toe, heel, inside & outside walks
- 20m lunges
- Walking hamstring, quad & butt stretches
- Light, high knee & power skips
- Side swipes
- Stride out
- Etc.

- Coach Odis's pep talk (brief)
- Individual hype-up (necessary)
- Run your butt off when it's your race or event (self-explanatory)
- Cheer on your fellow teammates (recommended)
- Go home a winner or loser (choice is an illusion here)

The track is eight lanes and 400m of polyurethane. Facing the scoreboard for football, the bleachers are to the right, where there is a gravel walkway from the back of the school to here. The concession is next to the stands, a few people in line getting hamburgers and hotdogs and fries.

I'm distracted by the flow of people, antsy, fearing that all their eyes are on me, waiting until I screw up or fail. To whisper things unheard. To steal some part of me I can't get back.

Too much——the crowd. I have to tear my eyes away before panic ensues.

"Landry," Coach barks.

I jump. "Yes?"

"Is this the day we lose you to cloud nine?"

"What?"

He frowns. "Pay attention. Get psyched. We're counting on you today."

"Yes, Coach."

Travis shakes his head, nudging Connor with a shoulder, and says, "Yes, Coach."

Coach sneer-frowns. "Weathers. You're batting zero today with me. Final warning. As acting captain, knock it off."

Travis lowers his head. "Sorry, Coach."

Coach Odis doesn't say anything new this time around, besides describing today's meet with Danbury Prep. So, when he's done, the sprinters all head with Coach O'Donnell, the female instructor, to go over their individual list of events. The field performers go with Coach Driscoll. Coach Odis leads the long-distance runners. Our team has twenty-one kids in all, guys and girls combined. I'm one of four runners that run in the 3200m race.

And then there's also Travis Weathers.

I walk over to Travis and the other boys on the team who are busy laughing at some joke one of his best friends, Connor Mailey, said. Connor has bleached hair that curves in a widow's peak, so he always wears it a fraction above buzzed. But like Travis, he's built, though not as bulky. His face is covered with acne scars.

We all kneel as Coach Odis goes over our list of events. The 3200m run is up sixth, the last of the individual races.

"We only have two more meets after today," Coach Odis says. "This could be the year we make it to States and show what we're made of. Now, here is where you guys need to stay focused and...."

He goes on, but mostly I tune him out. In the stands, playing a game on his phone, Aiden sits alone. He won't even look up until my race is called.

And then, below the bleachers and against the fence separating the track from the crowd, is Hadlee. Her camera snaps photos of the team. Hair blows in the wind. Her eyes look around but don't stay on anything too long.

The sun beats down on my shoulders, burning them. I air out my tank until I feel a nudge in my ribcage. When I look up, Coach is walking to the center of the field. Travis and Connor are right next to me.

"I bet she gives great head," Connor says. "The quiet ones always tend to be freaks in bed."

Travis hoots. "You think you can beat me, Landry?" He

wraps an arm around my neck, and I shove it off. "Want to show off for your girlfriend over there?"

A dozen thoughts go through my head, but I choose not to say anything. Travis talks crap, and silence is what will usually shut him up. I learned that a while ago, since I first joined the JV team during last spring for the outdoor track season. For some reason, he's never liked me, especially now that we're on Varsity. But he's always been the fastest on the track—always first place. I'm the second fastest on the team. Connor usually finishes behind me—he's the bigger jerk, but Travis is always the one to make jabs at me. Conner just talks crap about everyone and everything.

Travis lightly smacks my cheeks, and I fight the urge to punch his mouth.

"No one likes a second-place loser." He grins. "Prove me wrong, Landry." He and Connor walk away, laughing together.

Embarrassed, I turn to Hadlee. She's looking at me—or somewhere past me—intently. Aggressively. It gives me the chills, but when I blink to shake away the thought, her eyes don't leave. They're just there, following me.

If only you knew how a look can kill, Haddy.

I walk over to my blue gym bag on the field to find my phone and earbuds. I put on "Surfin' USA" by the Beach Boys, followed by "Tequila" by The Champs. Two must-haves on my running playlist. I close my eyes and listen, drown out the noise, the crowd, and focus on one thing only: the track. I envision it. The sun goes away, the breeze, the touch, the smell of vinegar fries and ketchup from the concessions stand. It's like all my senses shut down, and all I see is the red polyurethane.

Coach Odis taps me on the shoulder when it's time for the 3200m. Eight laps around the track. Just me and it. Nothing else.

I pull the headphones from my ears and walk to my place in

the third lane, shaking out my limbs as I place myself on the blocks. I look up to the stands one more time and spot Aiden, who is now looking and waving, a goofy grin on his face. Then I look to Hadlee, snapping more photos, adjusting her position by the fence and subsequently her boobs that press against the interlocked metal.

Jesus.

And, finally, I scan the crowd for my parents, who I know aren't here and never have been here. Because then who would be back at the motel to take care of it? Or working to pay the bills. But it doesn't stop me from hoping that one day—

Deep breath.

I close my eyes, breathe in, hold it, focus on the lane, and breathe out. My eyes now open. No one is next to me. No one is in the crowd. My entire world is like a giant void. There is no Travis or Aiden or Coach Odis. No Hadlee. As if from some distant galaxy somewhere, breaking through the silence, the starter announces us to take our positions.

"On your marks."

I do three high-knee jumps in a row, bouncing on the balls of my feet on the last jump.

"Get set."

I back into the blocks and suck in a deep breath.

The gun sounds, a cracking *BANG* that never fails to startle me. But I fall out of the blocks, think of my turnover, and exhale.

And I soar. It's getting as far away from the blocks as I can, needing to get to the end, wherever that is.

I start on my pace—find the right tempo, calculate internally the amount of times my feet will hit the ground. Breathe in and out. Once I get to a straightaway, I shift my focus to keeping that even tempo—stay in my lane. Run past the burning in my lungs and legs. Control my breathing and strides. Let my mind clear.

Clear.

Clear.

Around the third lap, it takes over, like it normally does. The sense that I'm running from something dark—some black cloud trying to eat me from behind. Some monster that will wrap its talons around my ankles and drag me back. To the woods. Some dark entity I can't shake. And I push myself harder. Pump harder. Breathe deeper. I focus on my mark and go as if I can't escape fast enough.

Lap four.

Lap five.

Lap six and—

FLASH

A camera to my right. Hadlee's.

And then she's there. In a world full of void, she's there with her camera poised. Adjusting the lens.

FLASH

The bright light blinds me, and I feel the heat of it, of her camera. Like a flame licking the side of my face. And there's something behind me. The darkness closing in on my heels, like a monster from deep in the bowels of the woods.

Lap seven something happens. I'm zigzagging. My head keeps snapping back and forth. The heat of the sun on my shoulders. The cheering of the crowd. The pounding of my feet on the track. Lost count of the amount of times they hit the ground. There is the beating of my heart in my chest—the heaviness. Like I can't escape it. I can't reach the finish fast enough. Can't get past the trees.

So, I sprint. On the seventh lap, I sprint with all my might. Sometimes it's lap five or six. Sometimes I've given up long before or blow it on lap two. But it's lap seven where I sprint, and already I know I've lost the race. Coach Odis preaches negative splits, but it's never worked out. I've lost focus of my stride and turnover.

The Wall.

Clear.

Darkness.

Clear.

The heat of the sun and my feet dragging. My nose twitches, and I smell smoke.

Smoke?

Travis is beside me, coming from behind. I'm in the lead. I was in the lead. And then Travis passes me, followed by a kid in red and black from the other school.

I'm back running half-naked in the woods.

Clear, Dev.

From the crowd:

"Run, Travis! Go, Travis! GOGOGO!"

"Ohmygod last lap!!! You got this baby."

"Pick it up, Greg! Pick up the pace on the straightaway."

"What are you doing, Dev? What are you doing?"

"He's going to win!"

"You're gonna lose, bro!"

Shhhhhh

The shouts and encouragements and heckling continue. By now, I've fallen too far behind. I'm in third, the runner from the other school only a few paces ahead. On the final lap, after the first bend, I push as hard as I can go to catch up, but all the energy is depleted. The oxygen gone from my lungs. I should've eaten more carbs earlier.

By the time we round the last bend and head for the finish, I've solidified third place. The crowd cheers and claps for Travis. Coach Odis does a weird hop-sway to celebrate, and

Hadlee snaps various photos as the stadium announcer calls out the time.

> 1. Travis Weathers (Brooke Meadows): 9:02:13
> 2. Gregory Keenly (Danbury Prep): 9:03:27
> 3. Devon Landry (Brooke Meadows): 9:05:42

Travis, amidst his win, nods his head at me, grinning proudly. He mouths:

"Maybe next time, pussy."

I grab my bag on the field and sit on my butt. Pissed off and disappointed. I'll have to train more at night. Get those negative splits down.

After the rest of the meet ends, Coach Odis tells us we'll go over the results at practice on Monday after school. He lets everyone go ride home with their families, then he motions for me to stay behind. With a dirty look from Travis and Connor, I sling my gym bag over a shoulder and wait to be told how much I suck.

Coach rubs the bridge of his nose. "What happened out there, Landry?"

"I don't know, Coach."

"You were in the lead. You were right there. You were graceful, like you owned this event. Then you got sloppy, lost focus, and pushed before it was time."

"I know."

"This happens every meet."

"I'm sorry."

He sighs. "I will not have this on the team. Rest up this weekend. Come back Monday ready to give it your all. You're a talented runner, Landry. You're one of our best, if not *the* best. You just run with fear. It's fear holding you back. Figure out what you're afraid of, conquer it, and own the field. Got it?"

Not really....

"Absolutely, Coach. I promise it won't happen again."

He takes his clipboard and taps it on my shoulder. "Go shower up, Landry. Shake it off. You still put up a somewhat impressive time."

"Just not enough for States?"

He offers a pained smile. "We'll get there."

I thank Coach and walk off the track where Aiden is waiting.

"That was..." Aiden trails off.

"Amazing?"

"I mean, if you're going for shit, then it was fantastic."

"Thanks."

"I'm just kidding. You know I love you."

I playfully punch his shoulder. He punches back.

"My parents are waiting to drive us home," he says. "Maybe we can convince them to stop for ice cream or something."

From the stands, looking over my shoulder, Hadlee is staring at us once again. The camera is hanging around her neck. I think there's a frown on her face, but I can't be too sure. The sun slowly sets in the distance behind her, and like a picture, it lights up her chestnut hair, making it glow as if on fire.

My eyes grow heavy, and the scar on the back of my head pings twice in a row. I feel nauseous, but it goes away as soon as it appears.

Then it comes back: the quickening beat of my heart, almost as if the sickening sensation was never there.

With my mind, I tell Hadlee I miss her. I love her. I understand her. I'm still the same kid I was three years ago, even though that feels like a lie.

She must not hear, because soon she's off again, meshing with the crowds and dashing from the back of the school to the front parking lot, like she can't get away fast enough.

Looks like you're not the only one running.

CHAPTER 3

I wait until Mom is asleep and Dad has to go to the bathroom before I reach below one of the ledges of the front counter for the master key ring. On it is a key for every lock on the property, including Room 13. Mom and Dad can never find out the room exists. I made a promise not to tell.

So, after I grab my cheap, hand-me-down laptop off my wooden desk, I sneak away with it—shut and then lock the door to my "fake" room, climb out of my window to the back court-yard, and make my way along the concrete.

"Landry," a voice hisses from above.

I stop, afraid it's one of my parents, but turn and find no one. My heart hammering, I look at my shut window, and then the bathroom windows for each room on the first and second floor. But no lights are on besides in the laundry shack, and no one is out here with me. I'm alone.

Weird. Hearing things now?

I make my way around the building to the parking lot and sneak into Room 13 without anyone noticing. I plop myself on the unmade bed, turn on a dim lamp on the bed table, and open the computer to search the web, even though our Wi-Fi here sucks. I lean back against the wall and cover my feet with the blanket, the computer in my lap.

It takes forever for my browser to boot up, but I go to my favorites and find her website. www.MalevolentBeauty.com. Her page and all the graphics load, one by one, and it feels like I'm there for hours. It starts off as a bright blue background up near the header, but the more you scroll down the page, it fades into purple, and finally into black toward the very bottom. Like the deeper you go inside the rabbit hole, the more you'll be consumed by the darkness.

I scroll a few of her more recent blogs that I've already read. Pass some of her verse and prose poetry. Pass a few photographs of profile or nature shots she's taken. Some are static, others are fuzzy or hazy. Some have wracked focus, others unaligned or tipsy. I don't understand it at all, but it's breathtaking. How talented she is. How she manages to capture a story in a moment. Captures life itself. It's impossible to explain without seeing it, so I won't even bother.

The most recent post from today is just one single photo, and I notice it's the gum wrapper from after school. There's no caption—there rarely ever is. Just the photo in mostly black and white. The gum wrapper is off-center, slightly toward the right edge of the frame. It's out of focus while a single blade of grass stands next to it, in vivid green, caught in the moment a breeze must have ripped through, making it bend at an odd angle. It catches the gleam of sunlight on the blade's tip, which causes a crescent flare of light on the camera lens. Somehow encompassing the gum wrapper, as if protecting it.

Beautiful.

On one of the sidebars are news updates, and the other side is a list of the contests and awards her work has won. I go to her collected albums and scroll through most of them: graveyards, sparrows, crows, maggots, dead grass, barren trees, tombstones, empty beer cans, shredded up sleeping bags, a bonfire that rages, a bonfire that smolders, trees, a tent, rocks, logs, abandoned flower petals, missing child posters, an abandoned campfire, more trees, grave markings, a house on fire, a chalked outline of a body, a man who's been shot in the leg, a woman being loaded into an ambulance, bruises, cuts, wounds, pills, festering pus, babies crying, people lost and unaware they've had their pictures taken, shadows, different shades of the moon, a drug deal mid-exchange, a looted train station, dismantled train tracks, road carcass, gloomy skies, overcast skies, cairn stones, a teddy bear with an eye poked out, a couple kissing, dead bodies, the trailer park behind our motel, and the woods where I wake up at night.

I have to stop. I always have to stop. It's intense. The back of my head is heavy, so I shut the lid to my laptop and rest against the cool headrest.

I will myself not to pull it back up. Not to force myself to watch the slideshow of pictures Hadlee takes. All so dark. Disturbed. Yet so beautiful, just like she is. It's after midnight, which means she's most likely already streaming if she's still awake. I open my computer and go back to her website, to the tab where she streams live for her fans. Sometimes she might give photography tutorials online, which are most popular for younger kids looking to get into the hobby. Sometimes she'll showcase herself editing pictures, drawing, or reading her poetry. All popular amongst fellow artists looking to trade tips/tricks/info. Sometimes she listens to oldies music, which only a select few older people enjoy. Other times, she just sits there and does nothing, which means I'm usually the only one still logged in. None of her members like when Hadlee just sits there and does nothing.

I, however, love it. It's almost like it used to be, when we'd have sleepovers before we got old enough for our parents to find it weird. It's just... *intimate.*

One day, Hadlee was my best friend, and then she wasn't. After she started getting into photography, her website followed soon after. It started off as a domain page where she posted pictures. Then slowly she added to it. Graphics, widgets, subscription/RSS feeds. She added weekly blogs, poems, art, sketches, and interviews with other local artists/photographers. Once a month she even hosts guest blogging/Q&A's. Her streams and video tutorials came after, when she was featured on the local news about a year ago after winning some award for Fresh New Voices. She's won a few others since.

I'm not really sure how she got to be semi-locally and regionally famous. It just happened gradually.

One day you're friends with someone, the next day you're not.

It doesn't stop the kids at our school from making fun of her though. She's still considered a hipster freak that doesn't talk to anyone, especially after she got that teacher fired for selling weed to a minor.

NightRunner13 has logged in

It feels weird, watching Hadlee. Even after all this time, like I'm spying on her. A voyeur or Peeping Tom. But she's there, even though the view is grainy because my computer can only process the lowest resolution possible, and sitting on her bed with her legs crossed underneath her butt. I can't make out much of anything else, as there's only enough dim light to see her figure on the bed, almost silhouetted.

It's silent. There's no music. She's not doing anything or reading anything. She's just sitting on her bed and staring at her webcam, dressed in baggy, gray sweatpants and a plain, white T-shirt that's three times her size. From what I can make out, her hair hangs loose, wrapped behind her neck and around to the front so it rests above her left breast.

There's a small chat box where members who watch can post live comments that she can respond to, but besides a few derogatory and sexual remarks from earlier, which is typical for internet scumbags, most anyone who tunes in has probably logged off if it's been like this the entire night. Hadlee hasn't typed at all yet. I almost think she's asleep before she reaches behind her to set a MacBook on her lap.

MalevolentBeauty: Welcome to the party, NightRunner13. Looks like it's just you and me tonight.
I thought you almost forgot about me.

We are the only ones here, and I shouldn't be afraid to talk. Shouldn't be afraid to answer back. And even though the screen names are anonymous, she might know it's me if I say something. But in all the times she's done this, all the nights she's let others into her world, in her bedroom, I've never had the courage. It makes me so disappointed in myself. Like I'm just a helpless, worthless boy in love with a girl but too afraid to act on it. We usually sit here in silence on the nights like this where it's only us. Maybe she appreciates my silence, maybe it allows her to just be herself: no fronts, no walls, no fake faces.

Just her.

MalevolentBeauty: Can't sleep either?

Luvs2SpoojBoy has logged in

Luvs2SpoojBoy: if it aint my fav girl. watchu doin up this late babez?
ill tie u up and spank u if u want

You have activated Invisible Mode
MalevolentBeauty has flagged Luvs2SpoojBoy

MalevolentBeauty: First strike, Luvs2SpoojBoy.
Luvs2SpoojBoy: was there sum1 else here? scare them off?
cummmmm on
u like that freaky shit, right?
flogger, paddle
butt plugs
nip clamps
im down for n e babez
MalevolentBeauty: Strike two, Luvs2SpoojBoy.

What I love about Hadlee is how graceful she is. She doesn't act out or retaliate. She doesn't give in to whoever is sick enough to type the worst things imaginable to her. She just gives them three strikes before booting them. I used to want to step in and defend her; I still do. But she can take care of herself. Hadlee doesn't need saving. So, I stay invisible until Spooj gets himself blocked.

But ever since she started her webcam, I've always had a feeling that whoever it is that got blocked keeps making new names and coming back. I think Hadlee notices it too, which is why she always warns him with three strikes.

Luvs2SpoojBoy: such a fukin cock tease
u bitch
u fukin bitch
ur loose as shit

MalevolentBeauty has blocked Luvs2SpoojBoy

I get so mad that I ball my hand into a fist and bash it into the wall behind me, which only causes me pain. I cry out and hold my hand against my chest while the waves of pain subside.

I'm so sorry, Hadlee. You don't deserve this. You don't deserve any of it.

MalevolentBeauty: Thanks for staying with me, NightRunner13. Moral support. :-) Better get going to bed. I just wanted to wait until you came.
I'll see you here tomorrow afternoon?

You have deactivated Invisible Mode

We're silent for a while, neither typing anything. But then she slides off the bed with her MacBook in hand and walks over to her webcam across the room. Most likely a camera running from her iMac on her desk. She steps into a closeup, allowing the pixel resolution to register her pretty face better, despite still having terrible light. She doesn't smile, just stares, blinks, stares, and then backs up to wave. She starts typing with one hand.

MalevolentBeauty: Check the homepage. Goodnight. Happy running. :-)

The webcam shuts off, plunging the chat into darkness. I exit the page and click on the home button. There, as if it had been waiting for me the entire time, is a photograph of a camp-fire. There are empty beer bottles and cans strewn about, but no depicted people. Just the smoldering bits of the pit after the fire went out, the embers still burning underneath. And from out of frame a figure stands, casting a shadow over the pit in a creepy way. As if the figure is waiting for something or someone. It gives me a funny feeling in my stomach.

Clear.

Shhhhhh

Below the picture is the verse she wrote:

> *The last bonfire*
> *of a youth burned*
> *to a crisp*
> *smoked away*
> *ashed anew*
> *revived*
> *still alive*
> *stoking the flames*
> *waiting for the guillotine to drop*

CHAPTER 4

Dev's Saturday To-Do List
Written by Dev

1. Rooms with Rosa... (9:00 AM – 1:00 PM)
2. Lunch with Mom & Dad... (1:15 PM – 2:00 PM)
3. Refill ice machine... (Clark Day request)
4. Do laundry... (3:00 PM – 5:00 PM)
5. Dinner with Mom & Dad... (6:00 PM – 7:00 PM)
6. Front desk shift... (8:00 PM – 11:00 PM)
7. Hadlee's website... (what else do you have better to do?)
8. Study for upcoming finals (??? - ???)

I've gotten quite good at cleaning rooms when I help on the weekends. Stripping the beds and snatching the towels, vacuuming, dusting, etc. I don't like doing the bathrooms—usually that's Rosa's job. But what would normally take twenty minutes to do, we can accomplish in ten. We've got a solid plan to attack the rooms, even though my parents can't afford more help. I don't get paid to clean. But I don't mind, because times with Rosa were the best growing up. Even now, my parents don't know me like she does.

I wipe sweat from my brow and let the noon sun shine into Room 22, heating up the cotton bedding. I tug the cover sheet under the mattress, realize I once again folded the wrong side underneath, and tear it out to try again. Never fails.

"That cost us a *minuto*, Dev," Rosa calls from the bathroom, her voice resonating with the Mexican accent.

"What?" I ask, even though I already know what she means.

"*Once minutos*. Be lucky to finish all rooms at this rate. Follow bed tags."

"Rosa, I swear you have superhuman hearing. But we're fine with time."

"*Chamaco*, you wanna be down on knees scrubbin' toilets all Saturday?"

"No, ma'am."

"*Bien*. Hush now. Less talk. More work." She mutters other words in Spanish.

I mumble under my breath and finish putting clean sheets on the bed and pillows, and then I wipe down the lamps and smack the curtains with a hand towel to knock free the dust. I'm vacuuming the rug when Rosa exits the bathroom carrying several dirty rags, all color coded to indicate the different cleaning chemicals I used. We deposit the dirty rags into the hamper underneath the cart, put the cleaning supplies back in their proper places, and look at our masterpiece.

This room, like every other one here, is drab: a maroon carpet with yellow spots freckled everywhere, and cream-colored walls that are bare to match the cream cotton sheets and pillows. One painting hangs above the master bed—two paintings if there's more than one bed. Usually an ocean or a lake or idyllic countryside—all in watercolor. Take your pick. Each bed is accompanied by an oak night table with a round lamp on top and a phone to call the front office. A Bible is tucked into the top drawer.

In the back, past the dresser with the outdated tube TV, are two faded armchairs, long overdue to be trashed. Not a table, just two chairs. The fabric is torn in some of them, and they aren't comfy to sit in at all. Even though Mom and Dad don't say it, I know we can't afford to get newer furniture, so we work with what we have.

I sniff and note a hint of bleach above the usual musty smell.

Rosa glances at her watch. "*Diez minutos y curarenta y siete segundos.*"

"That's not bad at all."

"We did last room in *trece segundos. No cuarenta y siete.*"

I roll my eyes. "Better than twenty minutes, though, right?"

She grins, pats my shoulder. "Take break. Work too hard."

We shut and lock the door, depositing the key into the cart. Rosa tightens the bun in her black hair—straightens her peach-colored uniform the Sacred Keepers have to wear. Rosa hates to be called a maid or cleaner; she prefers "Sacred Keeper."

I look at the age lines on her face. Crows' feet in each corner of her eyes, her cheeks rosy and sagging. Her skin bronzed. She's still in great shape, always on her feet day after day, but she's gotten slower over the past couple of years—since freshman year. She hobbles sometimes, occasionally needing to rest when walking up to the second level of rooms. So, I always help out on the weekends. It's almost like I'm doing all the work myself with Rosa overseeing.

We walk from Room 22 to 16 and begin the next cleaning. But before we start, I stop to lean on the iron railing, looking over the ledge of the second story and down into the parking lot. Stairways lead up to the second level on both far sides. The motel is divided into two two-story buildings—the buildings shaped like an "L." We have a total of thirty rooms between both buildings—each floor has fifteen. The building we're in is the only operational one, and it has sixteen rooms to rent.

Floor One: Rooms 1-8. Floor Two: Rooms 16-23.

No one's been in the other building in years.

There are four cars—one of them is ours, one is Rosa's, one is Clark Day's, and one belongs to the actual guests we have. On a regular day in winter, this would be good, but I know that we'll be in trouble if things don't pick up soon.

I try not to think about it, about the empty rooms that haven't been occupied in months. We still clean them regularly because Rosa won't stand for a lackluster job. And we always check on Room 1 ever since the complaint of bed bugs. Still none, thankfully. But Rosa has me re-spraying the bug killer at least once every other week to make sure. Dad had to refund a night's stay to the man who threatened to sue after being bit.

We don't let any of that stuff slide. Not anymore. Especially after Dad had to let go of all the cleaning staff four summers ago. We can't afford any insurance or benefits for employees.

Rosa, however, never checks on the second building, or on Room 13. She hasn't in years. Not even my parents have stepped inside.

"Dev," Rosa calls from the walkway by Room 16. "Where is your head at?"

I inhale a breath and hold it in my chest before exhaling. Sweat runs down my cheek, so I brush it away. Past the entrance to the front office, a few boys on skateboards rush by, shouting at each other as they do kickflips in the air. I squint, shielding my eyes from the sun. A few girls in short-shorts, sunglasses, and tank tops walk by after, holding melting ice cream cones. One of them looks over in the lot of our motel, licks the cone, and whispers to a friend while pointing to us.

They're out of view before I can determine what reactions the other girls have.

Outside the office, Mom hunches by the front door with a toolbox. Her curly strawberry hair is tied in a ponytail. She's dressed in khaki shorts and one of Dad's cutoff shirts from college. She opens the door slowly and watches as the bottom hinges come loose. Wiping the back of her hand against her forehead, she pulls out a screwdriver.

I try not to think about it, about this or the other night, but I can't stop. Rosa must pick up on it because she has her arms around me in a second. It's why I love Rosa. She just knows.

"Why long face?" She pulls back and nudges my shoulder. "You have beautiful face hiding in frown." I don't respond to her. "This about the woods?"

Every time. My parents never like to talk about it, but Rosa isn't afraid to.

"It happened again Thursday night." I rub the back of my head just as a phantom throb surfaces, like I intuitively knew it would happen. My fingers find the indent next to my right ear. I trace the scar. "Woke up freezing." I decide not to tell her about what I heard after I awoke.

Rosa blinks two times, breathes out. "Do *tus padres* know?"

"You know they'd worry."

"You need to tell them. Maybe you get back on—"

"I'm not taking pills again."

She shakes her head, but then examines my face. "Cuts? Scrapes? Infection is *desagradable*."

"Terrible?"

"*Sí.*"

"No. Just dirt, that's all."

Rosa wraps an arm around my shoulder and squeezes it. "And no worry about me. Lips sealed. You tell them. One day I no be around to take care of you."

"Don't even joke about that, Rosa. I won't let you go anywhere else. This is your home as much as it is mine."

Rosa grins, her eyes widen. "You sure you're *no mi hijo?*"

I pretend to contemplate the thought. "Would I need to be fluent in Spanish?"

Rosa nudges me again and walks back over to her cart. "You know what *mi* Luis tell me would clear away gray?"

I walk over with her. "Chocolate."

She smiles and reaches into her cart and pulls out a Hershey's Kiss. I instinctively open my hand so she can place the silver-wrapped candy inside.

"*Mi* Luis give me chocolate when I gray too. Eat. You feel *bien.*"

"Does this really count? Because you give me chocolate even when I'm in a good mood."

She crosses her arms. "You want, I take back."

"No, I'll take it. Don't be greedy, Rosa." She unfolds her arms and ruffles my curly hair. "But I'll only eat this if you have one with me."

Rosa pats her stomach. "Does it look like I need chocolate?" But she reaches into her cart to grab one anyway. "I really gave you so I could have some myself. But you let me give you haircut. Too shaggy. The girls want to see beautiful face."

"Maybe Tuesday when you're back from your days off."

"I pick you up from school and take you to *mi casa.* We bake. I set you up *con mi* Gabriella. She need good, smart, handsome boy in her life."

"Rosa...."

"*Ella es bonita.* You two make beautiful *bebes* together."

"Oh, God. Rosa." My face grows hot. "We've talked about this."

She smiles, enjoying herself, even though I know she's absolutely serious. "You deserve girlfriend. You come to *mi casa* and take break from all this. Get clean haircut." She indicates our surroundings. "You need a life that's *no tus padres*."

From somewhere beyond the motel, burning rubber wafts over to us.

The scar on the back of my head phantom pings again, so I massage it. "You know I can't. My parents won't let me go, anyway. They need me to help when I'm not in school."

She starts to frown, then nods like she understands. "I bring *mi* kit Tuesday."

I feel bad, like I've disappointed her again. Without thinking, I wrap my arms around her waist, pressing my head to her chest. She embraces me back, and we stand like this for a second before both pulling away.

We unwrap the Kisses and pop the candies into our mouths. I savor the chocolate. "Mom would have a fit if she saw you giving me these again."

"It's a *bien* thing *tu madre* is no around to see." She winks.

"Preach. I don't know what I would do without you and your obsession with chocolate."

"I can keep secret between us. Deal?"

I lick my lips when I'm done and wipe the excess melted chocolate on the back of my hand. But, like always, I instantly feel a little better.

"Deal."

"So, want to make visit to *mi* Gabriella?"

"Not at all."

"I have *mi hija* make banana chocolate enchiladas."

I squint my eyes. "You play cruel, Rosa."

She grins. "Food is way to any boy's heart. I'm just practical."

Mom is still outside working on the office door when I finish up with Rosa around one. I hop down the stairs until I reach the ground level. Below the stairs is the ice machine, something ancient that Dad scooped up from an abandoned gas station a couple miles down the road. I unlatch the metallic door to peer inside, but instead of being greeted by a whiff of frigid air, I'm met with rising steam. There's no ice. It's all melted. I look behind the machine and find it still plugged in. The temperature gauge inside isn't working, and kicking it doesn't help.

Broken again. Mom is going to have a fit.

I shut the door, re-latch it, and walk across the parking lot to kneel next to Mom on the scalding concrete. I wince as my bare legs touch the ground.

To the left of us, on a patch of grass next to the opening into the parking lot, is the white and red sign that stopped working five winters ago. Mom hasn't gotten around to fixing it yet. A red arrow wraps around the sign and points to the front office. Written in missing and shattered light bulbs on the sign: Brooke Meadows Motel.

A car drives past, its horn honking as the driver flicks a cigarette butt into our parking lot. The bass from some rap song blasts from blown-out speakers, then drifts away.

"The ice machine is broken again," I say.

Mom stops fumbling with the hinge on the bottom of the glass door and puts the screwdriver down. She falls back onto her butt and pinches the bridge of her nose. Mom sighs and looks back at me. Her brown eyes, like Dad's, seem painted on, like they'd be closed in any other reality. But I just stare back. Her cheeks and petite nose are red from the hot sun beating down on them, and Dad's navy-blue college cutoff hangs loose on her bony shoulders and lithe frame. I take after Mom in that way—can't gain weight or muscle to save our lives.

"Have you told your father, Dev?"

"I just found out now."

"I can't get a goddamn break around here."

She pinches the bridge of her nose again and mumbles something I can't make out.

"Do you want me to finish the door?" I ask. "So you can clean up for lunch?"

She places her hand on my chin and forces a smile. "You mean you haven't worked hard enough yet cleaning?"

"I've almost broken the ten-minute record. Maybe another week or two. Rosa taught me well."

Her eyes flash with something, just a brief moment, and I know she feels jealous. I'm not sure what about, but she always has this look when Rosa and I spend time together.

I clear my throat. "If you tell me what to do, I can try to fix the ice machine."

She shakes her head. "You and your father will never touch one of my tools again. You boys just weren't cut out for manual labor. And I still can't find Ramone. Leave it to me." She sits up on her heels. "Fun Mom's got this."

Mom leans in and wraps me in a hug, and my hands slap into the back of her damp shirt. We stay like this on the ground for a little bit, and I can smell sunscreen and sweat—her signature summer scent. When we pull back and polite-smile one more time before she gets back to fixing the front door, I realize how beautiful Mom still is. How the sun illuminates her natural features, makes the beads of sweat glisten. How her soft, tanned skin and long legs catch Dad's attention. Lately she's been stressed, both my parents have, but then there are times when no one laughs harder than her. How fearless she is to get down into a problem and fix it. Always independent. I can see why my father fell for her.

And even after all these years, she is still utterly breathtaking to look at.

"I love you, Mom."

She stops and looks at me through the reflection of the glass door.

"I love you too." She gets back to work. "Now go clean up for lunch and, please, don't tell your father about the ice. He's been in a mood all day. I'll get to it later, okay?"

I hate lying to my parents; I'm never any good at it. But I nod anyway.

After standing back up, I step past Mom into the humid front office. Two stationary fans try their best to air out the room with little success. My breath catches in my throat, and I grab an outdated tourist brochure on the rack by the door to fan myself. Dad is behind the front desk with a stack of papers and a calculator, dressed in a white and blue button-up with sweat stains in the armpits. His reading glasses rest on the tip of his nose, the black cord on each end wrapped around the back of his neck. He doesn't glance up when I walk in, so I go to the water cooler next to the brochure rack and fill up a cup with water, but it's not enough to cool me off.

A ratty loveseat sits next to the jug, and in front of it is a coffee table with a few magazines and local newspapers no one ever reads. The floor is a dirty gray carpet, and the walls are lined with more watercolor paintings of nature. A tube TV hangs in a far corner of the room, but it's turned off to save electricity costs. We only turn on the lights in the office for the night shift, so the natural daylight filters through the glass windows by the door. Taped on the end of the front counter is the sign:

No pets

Hadlee and I once brought a stray Beagle here that we found on the street years ago, unaware he liked to chew and devour everything in his path. My parents turned him in to a dog shelter shortly after.

We don't talk about the Room 6 Valuables Massacre anymore. It's still a sore subject with Dad.

Across the room, opposite the loveseat, is a vending machine for snacks, a soda machine, and a small rack of toiletries for guests to purchase.

I swig the last of the water and face the counter.

"How does pizza sound right now?" Dad says, typing numbers into the calculator. "Busy day." He points to the papers.

It's not hard to know what kind of mood Dad is in. When business is good, he's peppy. When it's bad, he's quiet. And anytime he pitches pizza for dinner, things are really bad. Dad normally does most of the cooking, and he's actually not bad, having grown up with Grandma who used to own a bakery. But pizza days usually mean lie low, don't give any bad news, and everyone eats separately so Dad can crunch numbers. You just learn his moods and go with them.

"Sounds good," I say, filling my cup with more water. "Want me to order?"

Dad mumbles what I assume to be a yes, so I pull out my cell phone and find the pizza guy in my contacts. We're regular customers, so when they answer, we always address each other by first names. You get used to it growing up in the motel business. Everyone has a first name, and people appreciate it more when you go out of your way to use it.

That, as Mom and Dad say, is how you get repeat guests.

And that, as Rosa says, is how you get extra pepperoni on the pizza for free.

And that, as Aiden says, is laying the pipe work for a booty call.

The phone rings and a young man's voice picks up, clearly

uninterested and annoyed at what he's doing. "Thank you for calling Frankly, It's Pizza. We're running a special on choose-your-own-topping pies all week. How can I help you today with all your pizza needs?"

"Hey, Greg. It's Dev."

His voice instantly perks up. "Dev! How's it going, buddy?"

"You know. Dad is busy doing the taxes. How about you?"

"Pops has me answering calls but doesn't realize I'm in the middle of an intense D&D campaign with Aiden and Davey, let alone babysitting my annoying little brother. Like, don't interrupt the game, you know? Lives are lost that way. Why aren't you here with us?"

"Wish I could, but have to work today. Maybe next time when you guys can come here."

"Will do, buddy. So, taxes tonight for Mr. Landry... Regular? Extra toppings? For delivery?"

"You got it."

"I'll throw in a liter of Mountain Dew for free."

"Thanks, Greg."

"Anytime. Tell your parents we say hi, too. And get them out of that motel. My dad has been calling your dad for months to play cards, but he never shows up."

"Yeah, he's been... busy."

It's silent on Greg's end, and then I can hear a few boys shouting, one distinctively Aiden's high-pitched tone when he gets defensive. Greg shouts something back, which hurts my ears.

"Have to go, I think Aiden's cheating. Pizza will be there in thirty minutes."

"Alright, take care, Greg. Good luck with your campaign."

"Yep. Definitely going to need it. We're down a player, and Davey is moping around. I'm sure Aiden will tell you later. But peace, bud!"

We hang up, and I smile. I always liked Greg. He would come around often with the delivery guys when they drove to the motel when I was younger. Me and Hadlee made friends with him quick. But he hasn't been around in a while, not since he took over in the kitchen with his dad. He graduated high school last year, and he's been working at his dad's place ever since.

Mom walks in shortly after, testing the door by swinging it open and closed until she's satisfied with her work. She gives me a thumbs up, so I do the same. She walks over to the front desk and hands her toolbox to Dad who, without looking, places it onto a shelf below him. He leans over the counter just enough so Mom can kiss him on the cheek.

So predictable.

"Did I overhear you say something about pizza for lunch?" she asks.

Dad pulls off his glasses so they fall against his chest, dangling from the cord. "I know, you're right, honey. Just got caught up with paperwork. No time to cook."

Mom rubs the back of his neck, and Dad closes his eyes. It's his weak spot. I get uncomfortable on the couch, so I pull out my phone again and text Aiden but don't expect a response. He and the other guys might still be deep into whatever argument they're having.

ME

just ordered pizza. not a good day. heard ur cheating?

"I can't trust you boys to fix a thing or cook a thing." She looks to the both of us, and the left side of her mouth turns up. "I think we all deserve a night to go out and see a movie as a family. We haven't done that all year."

"Joanne, you know one of us has to be here. When would we have time to go see a movie?"

Mom wipes sweat off the back of her neck and takes her curly hair out of the ponytail. It falls halfway down her back.

"I just think it would be nice to do something as a family that doesn't involve this motel."

"This motel is our legacy."

"Your family is your legacy, Joe."

Dad stares, unblinking, like he's waiting for Mom's punchline to a joke she never told. She returns the same expression mockingly. Eventually, they both break at the same time and do a quick kiss on the lips.

But I know the discussion isn't over. They'll talk about it later, when I'm not around, like they always do.

Dad stares at the ground intensely and places his hand over his chest.

Mom turns to me. "Dev, did you make sure to—?"

"Half pepperoni and half anchovies, pineapple, and mushroom. Yes."

"Well I'm going to take a shower." Mom pats Dad's shoulder, trailing a nail across his neck. "If anybody wants to know."

Dad straightens up, his face red, and they both exchange a quick look, Dad fixing some papers and coughing into his palm. Mom slowly walks down the narrow hallway and into the personal bathroom we all share. Immediately, I wish I was anywhere but here.

"Dev, I think I have to check on something." I feel my face grow hot. "Can you stay here and—?"

I nod, which shuts him up.

Dad places the papers on a shelf below the counter and tries hard to be nonchalant when he walks back into the hallway.

Mom and Dad can be really gross sometimes because they never try to hide their affection for each other in public.

Even after all these years, they're just as horny as half the kids in my class. Even when they fight, it's like foreplay.

So-freaking-gross.

I get up and walk to the counter and glance at Dad's monkey calendar taped to a support beam: June 3rd. Important for several reasons:

- My junior year is almost over
- I'm turning seventeen soon
- Our track team, the Barons, might make it to States this year for the first time in nearly ten years
- Business usually picks up over summer, which makes my parents less stressed
- The summer regulars will be back to hang out with
- Rosa is at work more when more guests stay
- Aiden and I get to hang more
- A whole summer without school, which also means another summer without Hadlee Morgan.

Also known as the season that beauty takes a sabbatical.

CHAPTER 5

I'T'S SOMETIME AFTER SIX WHEN THE SIRENS GO OFF. WE'RE
eating the leftover pizza from lunch for dinner because Mom
and Dad both forgot to get groceries. We're in the small kitchenette, eating on the plastic table that tilts because of the broken
leg that we duct-taped back on. I've learned never to lean on it
with my elbows.

That's how we ended up with the Bundt Cake Massacre
years ago.

Dad hasn't made one since.

We all get up and make our way to the front office just in
time to see a police cruiser barreling past our motel to the bend
at the end of the road. Dad is the first out the door, and we all
walk across the lot to the road.

A few police cars chase after the first cruiser, the sirens
echoing off the abandoned buildings around our place. The sun
is starting to set in the direction the chaos is heading, and from
somewhere to the side of our motel a set of firecrackers
explodes, followed by laughter.

Run

Shhhhh

From behind, I hear a couple doors open as the two guests we have walk outside to see what the commotion is about.

Our motel is one of the few remaining businesses still active in this part of town. It used to be the section where everyone went years ago, according to Dad. The motel had been around for years operating as some kind of boarding house or boys' dormitory back in the day. I guess it was shut down after some bad stuff happened in the 80s, back when this side of town went to crap. That's why the motel only has one working building.

It's also why Rosa refuses to go into Room 13.

As if this entire motel has been cursed.

"What do you think happened?" my mother asks, wrapping her arms around her body.

I snap out of the daze I'm in.

"Must be down on River," Dad says, glancing back at us. "Better get back inside."

I run into the middle of the street and watch the cop cars disappear around a bend, but their sirens still linger in the distance. And for some reason, I get a bad feeling in the pit of my stomach.

"Dad, do you think—?" I start before he is on me within seconds, grabbing my wrist and jerking me back toward the front lobby like a bratty little kid throwing a temper tantrum. It's embarrassing, so I shake him off.

"We've told you not to wander off in the street, Dev," he says. "What if a driver didn't see you? There are no streetlights here."

And just like that, Over-Protective Parent Mode kicks in.

Mom motions for us to get inside, and I can't help but try to look past the turn even though it's impossible. I can't see anything odd or even hear any gunshots. And after a while, even the faraway echoes of the sirens seem to be nothing more than on the edge of my imagination.

"Let's go inside," she says, her one arm open for me.

I turn into Mom's embrace as we walk across the lot. My foot catches in a crack in the cement, which almost causes me to lose my balance until Mom steadies me.

From above, the man in Room 17 shouts down to us through a crack in his open door; he's draped in what I think is a camo bathrobe. "What in the world is going on with the ice? It's been two days, Landrys."

Dad gives us a quizzical look, not sure what he's talking about. Mom shakes her head, caught in the lie.

She calls up to him. "Tomorrow, Mr. Day. You'll have your ice tomorrow."

"My glands are swelling, and the AC is busted again. I need that ice, Joanne Landry."

Mom's eye twitches. She hates when people call her by her full name. She grits her teeth. "Anything for your glands, Clark Day. They are my utmost priority when I wake up Sunday morning."

Dad shoots her a warning, so Mom releases a breath through pursed lips.

"I'll be following up with your son tomorrow after breakfast. Seven-thirty a.m. sharp?"

Mom flips him the finger by her side, where Mr. Day can't see it. Dad and I suppress our laughter.

"Our son?" Dad asks.

"Yes, I'd prefer if Little Landry delivered it this time around."

Weird.

"Sure thing, Clark," Dad calls up. "Whenever my son wakes up for breakfast."

I shoot Dad a look because he knows how much I don't like

Mr. Day. How uncomfortable he makes me and Mom. It's like a betrayal. All Mr. Day does is stare at me, like I've done something wrong. Crapped in his coffee or something. But we have to be nice. He's the main reason, possibly the only reason, we can still afford to keep this place.

Clark pauses, seems to frown, though it's hard to make out his face. "Whenever you wake up then, Little Landry."

Mom clenches her teeth for the both of us. "Goodnight, Mr. Day."

Clark breathes in deep, holding it in his chest, and ducks back inside his room. And Mom, promptly after, raises both fists to give him two middle fingers.

That's my mom: such a badass.

Dad leans over me to kiss her on the cheek. "You sure showed him."

"Cuckoo Clark is as much of a pretentious prick now as he was in grade school."

"Joanne...."

She puckers her lips. "I know, I know."

Something is exchanged between them, but I can't figure out what.

They peck a kiss again as we start to head back to the office. I decide to change the subject.

"Do you think we can go drive down there? Someone might be hurt."

"Leave it to the police." Dad opens the door for us to walk back inside. "It'll be all over the news later tonight."

"Can we at least just go down there and see if there's—?"

"Dev, please." Dad groans, closing his eyes. "Didn't we have this discussion before?"

"But—"

"You can't go around saving everyone all the time, son. It's not safe."

You never argue with Frustrated Teetering on Anger Parent Mode. Ever.

"Okay."

Mom pats my shoulders. "Your father's right. It's a bad neighborhood. Let the police deal with it."

"Your place is right here," Dad says. "We need you. It's not to punish you, kid. It's because we love you, and you don't know what kind of sickos are out there."

I force a polite smile, but Mom's eyes register sadness again. It's a look I hate.

I've learned to just go along with it. The same spiel I've heard for years now. There was a time when they'd let me go anywhere I wanted—random adventures with Hadlee. But it's been a while since they've let me go anywhere unless they're with me. Not since the incident. Like I'm still a kid that needs protecting. Sometimes I get annoyed, frustrated. Like they don't trust me to make the right choices. But other times, I feel like it's more for their benefit than it is mine. That they need me being here more. So, I always give in.

"You guys are right. Might as well go do some homework, I suppose."

Dad ruffles my hair, relaxing. "You know we love you, right?"

Mom and Dad both wait, like they can't breathe until I say it, so I do, and their eyes relax right away. After they hug me, I walk down the narrow hallway past the front counter and back to where we live. On the right is my parents' bedroom, then the kitchenette, the bathroom, and then at the very end of the hall is my "fake" room.

On the ledge of one of the wooden doorframes, I run my finger over the etching where Mom and Dad record my height every year on my birthday. Each notch a little higher than the last.

Inside my bedroom, my laptop is back on my desk from when I brought it back over in the morning. I grab it and jump on my bed, scooting until my back is against the wall and my head is pressed against the cool glass of the window above it. My feet dangle off the edge of the bed as I settle the computer on my lap.

NightRunner13 has logged in

The chat is already flooding with previous comments from the same handful of people. There's only us logged in, and I'm appalled by what I see coming in from members.

Hadlee, much like last night, is back on her bed. She's in black sweatpants and some kind of tank top with a graphic on the front. She's wearing another baseball cap backwards, her hair sticking out of the Velcro strap. I try to locate the mole above her left collarbone but can't make it out because of the terrible, grainy connection.

She starts typing something, and when she stops, her dialogue shows up in the comments section.

MalevolentBeauty: You going to say hi this time, NightRunner13?

I look around me, paranoid someone else is here that would know my username, but no one is. I hate doing this in my "fake" room. I don't answer but shift my attention from the chat to the live stream. Chat to the live stream. A few people respond back, but most of it is sexual slang, which Hadlee ignores. I hate that this personal thing she created herself, this website, is subject to such cruel torment.

Hadlee takes off her cap and runs her hands through her hair, looking at her camera and waiting for a response. She squints, which makes her nose and forehead scrunch in that adorable way, and puts the cap back on. I almost hit the log off button, but I don't.

You have activated Invisible Mode

Hot2Trot69: babez can say hi 2 me n e time
LiquidSuicide0003: what I would give to see your vagina honey mmm
StantheMaaaAAaaannnnn: cum right in between those breasts right Hot2Tro69?
MalevolentBeauty: One strike, Stan and Liquid.
Cowsgomoooooo: Really, Hadlee? Just sitting and staring? Maybe I'll come back next week. This is pointless.

Cowsgomoooooo has logged off

She starts typing again, and I hold my breath.

MalevolentBeauty: If you want to keep staring at me in secret, NightRunner13, I can do that right back.

Why is she calling you out now? Of all times? Defend her or kill yourself.

Hot2trot69: fuk NightRunner.
fuk em!
Princessgabby: You guys are SO gross. Grow up.

MalevolentBeuaty has flagged Hot2Trot69

MalevolentBeauty: Your first strike of the night, Hot2Trot69.
No bullying.
Hot2Trot69: really bitch?

MalevolentBeauty: Two strikes.

StantheMaaaAAaaannnnn: down for a 3-way. Get em loose princess!

LiquidSuicide0003: are you a cutter, Malevolent? just show me a scar. one scar!

MalevolentBeauty: Strike two, boys.

Princessgabby: You all need help. This is beyond disgusting, and I'm sure Hadlee would NEVER look your way twice. She has CLASS.

I love ur artwork girl!

MalevolentBeauty: Thank you, Princessgabby! :-)

StantheMaaaAAaaannnnn: take your preaching elsewhere unless it's on my face Princessgabby

MaelevolentBeauty has blocked StantheMaaaAAaannnnn

Princessgabby: Screw YOU! This is why she's not doing anything tonight. A$$holes!

And ha! Thanks girl.

MalevolentBeauty: I won't let anyone talk to you that way. Don't worry.

<3

I want to jump in. Want to defend them both. Tear these jerks a new one. But this happens every Saturday; I'm almost positive they are the same people. Maybe Travis and his friends always log in as different names when they're blocked. But who knows?

LiquidSuicide0003: just show me your self-mutilation. if your art is any indication. your one screwed up girl.

shit that kinda rhymed.

go me.

Hot2Trot69: bitch I fuxkin strangle you till face is blu, then ill fuk tha
shit outta u
now I rhymed 2
cum right in that emo-cutter mouth of yours
gutter slut
go make a fuxkin suicidal poem again

MalevolentBeauty has blocked Hot2Trot69 and LiquidSuicide0003

Princessgabby: Don't listen to those losers Hadlee.
Ur gonna go somewhere and get out of this town with ur art
They'll be flipping burgers or in jail.
MalevolentBeauty: <3 Thank you so much! Don't let those guys talk
to you like that either. We're strong, and we stick together.
I've got your back.
Princessgabby: Right!
Well g2g, but I'll ttyl
Stay strong!

Princessgabby has logged off

It's now only the two of us in the chat. I'm still in Invisible
Mode, even though Hadlee stares at her webcam for a long time,
waiting. I don't come out of hiding.

MalevolentBeauty: Looks like it's just us again.
Thanks for staying with me through that.
…
I don't bite. You can come back.

You have deactivated Invisible Mode

There you are. What should we do with the rest of the night?

...

I think I have an idea, NightRunner13.

Your silence somehow gives me all the answers.

Thank you. :-)

Happy running.

Maybe I'll join you tonight in spirit.

And then she waves into the camera, making the pixels in my resolution strain. That's when the screen goes black, and the live stream ends. Leaving a stark coldness on the web page. I click the home button and see a new blog update from a few seconds ago. Again, as if waiting for me specifically.

It's a single sentence with a black and white closeup of her eyes staring. The pupils contracted with the light. Just below the photo is a hand-drawn sketch of a man in shorts running along the road. There are outlines of trees in the far distance, and a destination that is marked on the very edge of the paper. It looks, oddly enough, kind of like me, but then again, a pencil sketch can look like anyone in shorts. And just below that are the words:

Now I see you too

CHAPTER 6

The images of Hadlee's sketch don't leave my mind as I take a shower. They're there. Every time I blink or close my eyes. It's in how similar it is, like I've seen it before. Maybe not that sketch specifically, but something just like it. And it might be crazy. It might be insane to think, but I've seen that outline before. Of that man with the shorts.

I shake away the phantom sensation of tiny creatures crawling over my skin and dry off with a towel before heading outside. The tube TV hanging in the corner of the lobby is on the local news channel, and when I walk out fully clothed, an older woman holds a microphone on the screen while police escort two men in handcuffs from the trailer park.

A news anchor talks over the image on screen, "...police investigators are looking into a possible drug ring with connections to the town of Brooke Meadows. The supply of illegal substances has become a local concern for...." I find the clicker and turn off the TV.

Mom and Dad are in their bedroom with the door closed, talking. I don't bother knocking or letting them know I'm done. I take out my phone and see it's time for my front desk shift. I get my Biology binder and review the notes for the upcoming Regents tests in a couple weeks. But it's not working. Distraction doesn't work.

Do you think Hadlee knows it's you? And where have you seen that sketch before?

My heart beats faster, and I think I'm about to panic before the front door opens, signaling a chime from the bell hanging above it. I look up and see a man in his early twenties stroll in wearing sunglasses, red basketball shorts, and a black beater. He has a drawstring bag hanging against his back, and he flashes his teeth at me—a large gap in between his two front incisors.

"What's going on, motherfucker?"

I smile back. "How many nights, Rory?"

"Right to the point. My man!" He claps his hands together and removes his sunglasses. His eyes are glossy and bloodshot. "All-night cram sesh." He slides the drawstring bag off his shoulders and holds it in front to show me. "I got books, I got notebooks, I got pens and pencils, I got Charlie's notes after I begged her to let me study from them tonight, and I got enough Adderall to kill fuckin' Free Willy."

I go to the computer and begin to pull up his file. It makes us look more official and professional than we really are. There are never any issues with overbooking or reservations. But it does help keep everything organized for the repeat guests. Like Rory Tonkin. He's been coming here for the past three years during finals and midterms. Always for a week or two before a major test. Longer than necessary, but I think he likes to just get away for a while and be on his own, maybe get high. I really don't know. But it's always nice having him around to hang out with, especially when Aiden's busy with D&D.

"Is Charlie the one you tried to ask out back during Thanksgiving when...?"

He rolls his eyes. "Bitches, man. Amiright?"

I nod like I understand, even though I really don't. I can't remember the last time I was able to talk to a girl without freezing up, acting awkward, or doing something foolish.

"I'm just kidding. Don't call girls bitches." He looks me up and down. "But I don't think I have to worry about you, my man." He points to me. "You're the fuckin' Godfather of this place, you know?"

I place him in his usual: Room 6. After I update his file and book the room, I look up and his credit card and driver's license are already on the counter. I slide his card through the reader we have and wait for it to print the receipt. After he signs the receipt, I make a copy of his license, even though we don't need it from his previous stays. I hand him back the information. Rory, for some reason, likes it when I follow protocol.

"Is it just you working again?"

"Yep."

"Lame."

"You want a slice of leftover pizza? Mushrooms, pineapple, and anchovies."

Rory puts back on his sunglasses, slips the bag over his shoulders, and makes a gagging noise. "Had myself a bad experience with mushrooms, man. Like PTSD type shit. I'll get wicked flashbacks. Thanks, but I'm good."

I nod and reach to the rack on the wall and hand him the key to his room. "Just call if you need anything."

Rory takes the key and runs a hand through his bleached blond hair. He leans into the front desk. "Can you say it for me please? That thing you guys say here? That shit is hysterical!"

"Do I have to?"

"Yeah."

Dammit.

I groan and reiterate in my monotone, "Enjoy your stay at Brooke Meadows, where our family is your family. The one-stop pit-stop for your hospitality needs." I throw on an exaggerated, if somewhat pained, smile to show my contempt for the outdated phrase my parents haven't used in nearly a decade. Rory, however, gets a kick out of it.

He breaks into laughter, slapping his palm on the desk more times than is necessary, and right away I know he's already on something. "That shit is so fucking bad, man."

"Have a good night, Rory."

He continues to laugh as he stumbles out the front door and toward his room. And like it was planned, my cell phone starts ringing. I pull it out and see it's Aiden, so I answer it.

"How was D&D?"

"I don't want to talk about it, and for the record, it wasn't me who cheated. Greg was the DM this time, and he went all Norman Osborn on us. Greg got all pissy because the cleric laughed when he killed an orc—said that it demanded an alignment check—and Davey failed the roll. So, you know what happens?"

"I don't, but I know you're going to tell me."

"An ancient red dragon shows up. I mean, for the one second Davey didn't role-play his character right, for one stupid saving throw, there went the whole campaign. Nearly two months of playing, and it's all wasted."

"This all goes above my head."

"Sorry I couldn't get back to you sooner." He mumbles under his breath.

"It's alright. Most of the day was typical Saturday work."

"You could have, I don't know, actually gotten away from the motel and hung out with a group of very handsome guys that know how to have fun. And, incidentally, they slay dragons in their spare time."

"Of course. What better friends are there?"

"Next time there will be no excuses, okay? Tell your parents you have plans with friends for a change, and then we will fight crime or something. I need a week off from D&D. Time away from Greg and Davey."

I doodle on a blank sheet of paper in my biology notebook, leaning into the counter. "We've been over this, Aiden."

"Can't you even pretend to be a normal, attractive teenage boy?"

"Very funny." I yawn. "Did you hear about the arrest or drug raid or whatever that happened out on River Road?"

"Aww, someone's sweepy. Wait, there was a drug raid over on River?"

"Yeah. I don't know much about it, but it was on the news."

"By the trailer parks?"

"Yup."

"Nice! My parents were just mentioning how this intern they hired the other month had an OD from some stuff that's been going around."

"Yeah, I don't know what happened. But in other news, I logged into Hadlee's livestream chat."

"Of course you did."

"Of course I did. She messaged me directly again."

"WHOA! Like SERIOUSLY?"

"Sarcasm noted. Yeah, it's really weird. But then guys started harassing her, so she blocked them and then said she'd run with me in spirit tonight before signing off."

"That's what I'm talking about! Someone should make the first move, and if not you and your passive, puckered little asshole, then it better be that little minx. I kid, of course."

"Of course. But nothing happened. I didn't answer back."

"Oh, Dev... you're so hopeless sometimes. Just be into dudes and get on with it already."

"Screw you."

Aiden pauses a moment, and I can hear a microwave

beeping in the background, followed by a man—presumably his dad—shouting at the TV. "Just saying. You'd make a killing batting for the other team, my friend. Also, in other news, did I tell you I've been chatting with a new boy for the past month?"

"Ummmm... No!?!? A month?"

"Yeahhhh, my bad. It was just online, and no hookup, so I didn't feel the need to tell you sooner."

"I hope this is followed up by a very long explanation. You never keep secrets from me."

"I don't, do I?"

"Aiden...."

"Dev...."

A bedroom door behind me creaks open, so I look and see Dad walk into the front office to get a cup of water from the jug. He takes a few sips and points to the phone.

"Dad is here. I think I have to go."

"Alright, text me tomorrow?"

"Yeah. But we're not done talking about this. Night."

"Sure thing, handsome."

Dad points again. I shake my head like I don't understand, so he points again.

"I think my dad wants me to give you a message?"

Aiden hums. "Well, does he, or doesn't he? You're being super non-exact right now."

Dad says, "Tell Aiden that *DC* is better than *Marvel*."

I raise an eyebrow because Dad is once again trying to be cool and hip, but it just comes across as awkward.

"Um, my dad said—"

"Oh, I heard him, Dev." He coughs. "I'm not even going to dignify that with a response. Your dad is not cool. Not at all. But I respect him."

I look at Dad. "Aiden says you're right."

"What!" he shouts into my ear. "I never said that! Those

words never left my mouth! You go and tell him—" I hang up before he can finish. I'll be getting angry texts for at least the next ten minutes until he gives up.

Dad crumples up the cup and throws it into the trashcan. He's wearing his same outfit from earlier.

"I didn't mean to be on my phone," I say automatically. Because I always feel like I have to explain myself with him.

He waves it off. "I don't care about that. You'd have better luck watching paint dry than doing actual work tonight."

And there's something in his voice, almost bitter humor.

What's going on?

"They'll come, Dad. We always manage over the summer months."

He runs his hands through his thin, wispy hair. "It's not the motel, Dev. You know I love you, right?"

I swallow saliva, even though my mouth is as dry as sandpaper. "Of course."

And we stand here, neither knowing what to say next. Dad is a man of few words. But I can tell he tries; I know he does. We always find ourselves stuck together, alone. With Mom, it's different because she controls the conversation between us three. But without her, it's like we're a boat without an oar.

How can two people who've spent their entire lives together, a father and son, be so completely related but so utterly different? How can we not know what to say? Why is it easier with Mom? Easier with Rosa?

"Do you resent growing up here?" he asks, looking at his monkey calendar.

"No. Why would you think that?"

"You don't wish you grew up somewhere normal? With friends? Outside of this motel?"

"This is our home. Why would I want to be anywhere else?"

He nods unconvincingly. "Your mother and I feel bad about missing your meet again."

"It's okay. I know you guys would be there if you could."

He concentrates hard on something, maybe to find the right words. "You're never going to get these years back. And we're not even there to support you."

What's happening here? "It's fine, Dad."

He strokes his chin, clears his throat. "How has your head been?"

Does he know about Thursday? "It's been fine. Why?"

He taps a finger on the counter, seeming to contemplate something. But he doesn't say anything else. Again, I think how sad he tends to be. Like he's masking something he can't tell.

He steps closer. "Your mother and I were talking and—"

Rory bursts through the front door, practically jumping on the water cooler. "Forgot to get some of that sweet aqua."

How convenient.

Dad raises his eyebrows cartoonishly, which makes me laugh, though I can tell he's annoyed that Rory interrupted whatever he was going to say. One minute he can be reserved and stoic, sometimes standoffish. And then, like the flip of a coin, he's the opposite. He folds his arms over his chest.

"Hello, Mr. Tonkin," Dad says. "*Studying* again, are we?"

Rory keeps his back to Dad. "You know it, Mr. Landry." He takes a few sips and fills up the cup again, swallowing a pill in the process. "Diligence is the key to success."

Dad raises one eyebrow. "Is it now?"

"Pretty sure, yeah."

Dad mouths, "*Stoned?*"

I mouth, "*Definitely.*"

Dad licks his bottom lip. "Good thinking, Mr. Tonkin. You're about to graduate college, right?"

"Next year." He finishes the cup and reaches for one more fill.

Dad pats my shoulder and gives me the We'll Talk Another Day look.

"You boys have a good night." He points to Rory. "No more meds tonight. You'll retain more without that crap in your system. And you don't know the kind of sickos out there pushing that stuff."

Rory brightens and pushes the sunglasses farther into his face. "Sure thing, Mr. Landry." They stare at each for a beat too long, and I feel like there is an inside joke I'm not privy to.

Weird.

Dad walks back to his bedroom and closes the door. Rory lets out a breath he'd been holding in.

"I almost shat myself."

"He's right, you know. They just busted two dealers out in the trailer parks."

Rory clears his throat. "I need it to study, man. I have ADHD."

"Be careful."

Now you sound like your parents. Why do you care?

He finishes his cup of water and throws it out. Just before he's about to leave again, he peeks over the top of his sunglasses. His eyes dart from side to side.

"I think there was someone hiding out in the parking lot, creeping in the shadows. I saw them when I came back in."

"You saw who?"

"I don't know, motherfucker. Some person just hiding behind one of those support beams, just staring at this office. Creepy as shit, man. You sure this place isn't haunted? I can't study with prowlers and shit."

I roll my eyes. "You were just seeing things, Rory. Go back

to your room, lock the door, and study. You'll forget all about this."

He pushes the sunglasses back to his eyes. "You might be right. Probably was my imagination. This place is creepy at night. No?"

Room 13. The woods.

"It can be."

He accepts the answer and swiftly disappears outside. But before I get back to the counter, I walk to the front door and glance into the night. There is no one in the parking lot or by the cars. I open to peek out and crane my neck, but there's no one waiting in the shadows, not by Room 6.

With a chill, I close the door and jump back to the counter to resume studying. I pull out my phone and turn up the volume as I select the *Ghostbusters* theme from Ray Parker Jr., smiling to myself despite the bad taste in my mouth.

It's nearly 11:30 p.m., and Dad should be waking up soon for his overnight shift. I'm exhausted, and my head bobs up and down. I stopped studying Biology an hour ago, and now I have my laptop with me on the front counter, scrolling through some of Hadlee's older posts to figure out where I last saw the pencil sketch of the running man. There's no way it could be a coincidence. I nearly have the post I'm looking for when a shadow passes by the glass front door. I look up, but no one is there.

I go back to Hadlee's site when I hear a cough from outside, followed by shoes scraping against cement. The hairs on my neck stand on edge, and immediately I remember what Rory said.

My feet move before my mind has a chance to process what they're doing. My hand pushes open the front door, and I peek out again, looking around. It's cool out tonight; the air has a dewy scent to it. There's one light pole in the middle of the parking lot, and then another few lights outside of every three rooms. But they're all dim and orange. The one light fixture outside of the abandoned building, next to Room 13, blinks a steady, bright red. Something Mom never got around to fixing.

I start to duck back inside, and then I hear it.

Breathing.

Right on the other side of the office, past where I can see.

My heart flutters; my knees wobble. Everything is happening so slowly, like whoever or whatever it is will get to me before I have a chance to shut and lock the door. Dying isn't on the top of my list. There's so much I haven't done, so much in life I've yet to see and experience. And my parents would lose it if I were gone.

What if it's the person from the woods?

I'm frozen like a statue. Can't move even though I want to. The worst possible scenarios come to mind: a burglar, a ghost, a serial killer, a monster with three heads and five sets of razor-sharp teeth, a sex offender, Darth Vader with the way the breathing continues. It's even. In sync.

And I hate Aiden for making me afraid of Darth-freaking-Vader.

Then there's a bright *FLASH*, and white light fills my eyes. I squint, blinded temporarily. I throw my hands up, cry out, and flee back into the office. But somewhere between all of this and being blind and trying to accept the fact that the person, or thing, is now closer than before—practically right next to me—I trip and fall on my butt.

I rub my eyes and open them back up, but the phantom flash lingers in my view. And that's when I see her kneeling in front of me with an extended arm. Shock has taken over, so I don't take it right away but instead stare dumbfounded, like I've never seen a hand before, let alone one wearing a two-faced watch, let alone attached to a wrist that's attached to an arm that connects with a body with boobs.

I see the blue converse shoes and let my eyes travel up. Black tights on long, slender thighs, then a white T-shirt with the words: "Gluten Free." I don't know what to say; I don't know what to do with the hand or the girl it's sprouting out of. God, this is stupid. Why am I so stupid? There couldn't be anyone else less stupid than me right now. I stare at her T-shirt, aware I'm also staring at her breasts, and point to the graphic. Only one thing comes to mind to say, so I say it.

"Isn't that an oxymoron?"

She smirks for a split second, but then her face drops, like it's frowning.

Kill me. Just kill me now.

I get myself up, ignoring Hadlee Morgan's hand, and brush off my butt. She's wearing a blue beanie on top of her chestnut hair, and her cheeks are rosy, like she's been running recently. Her camera hangs from her neck and rests in front of her stomach.

We just stare at each other, unmoving and in silence. She breathes in and out, and I do it opposite her so it's like this weird pattern we have going on.

And ohmygod, this is so awkward.

Finally, she says, "I need a room."

Oh?

My eyes widen. "Y-You need a room?"

"Yes." She looks around her, like other people are in the office, but we're alone. My parents are still asleep, and we can't afford a security camera. "I'd like a room please, Dev."

She just said your name. Shejustsaidyourname. OHMY-GODSHEJUSTSAIDYOURNAME!

Why are you being such a weirdo about this?

OMG! What if your parents hear her voice and come out here?!

I nod, swallow a mouth full of nothing but stand and don't move. "You want a room... here?" I point stupidly behind me.

Hadlee smirks again for a second, then frowns deeper. She looks behind her. "You're being really weird right now. I-I just need a room. Please. Um, I don't have much cash, but..." She slides a backpack off her shoulders and unzips one of the front pockets. She pulls out a few crumpled bills and thrusts them into my hand. "Will this be enough for a night? Have you guys changed prices since last time I was here?"

It's $75, which is more than enough for one night's stay. But it's the rushed way she does it, how agitated and nervous she appears, that gets to me, and I snap out of whatever funk or daze I'm in.

"It's only $50 for a night," I say. "Same as always."

"Right. I knew that." She straightens the beanie on her head, zips up the pocket on her backpack, and swings it over both shoulders. She looks around again, chewing on her lower lip, and right away I know something is wrong.

Hadlee Renee Morgan doesn't just spend her Saturday nights at cheap no-tell motels. She doesn't act like she is right now. And she doesn't talk to me. Not since we were thirteen.

She hasn't stepped foot in here in nearly three years.

But why is she here when earlier she was at home on her camera?

She can't know it's you.

"Is everything alright?"

She pulls the beanie lower on her forehead, trembling. "Yeah, um." She blows air through her lips. "I just need to stay here for a night, and if you're not okay with it, then I don't have to stay. I'll go. But please don't say anything to your parents."

I get nervous, and the room gets hotter.

Dev, one of your parents could wake up any moment.

I stare at her, look down at the money and back up at Hadlee. I make a decision, one I'm not sure I fully understand, and hand her back the cash. She looks just as confused as I feel, like I'm denying her sanctuary. And she looks so... *lost.*

Her russet eyes are beautiful and pleading.

I walk to the counter to reach over and grab the key for Room 1.

"Just go," I tell her as I hand her the keys.

"Dev, I'll pay."

"Just go."

She looks confused and grateful and tired. So many things I haven't seen on her. Ever. I nod and point outside to indicate where her room is.

"No one will know you're here if you don't want them to."

She closes her fingers around the key and hooks her thumbs under each strap to her backpack, looks behind her. "Thank you."

I nod, not sure what to say. I just stand there and wait for her to do or say anything else, but she doesn't. She heads toward the door and pushes it open, moving quickly, trying to beat some unseen force to the room. But before she disappears around the side of the building, she faces me.

"Can you, um, can you not tell anyone I was here? Not even Aiden."

I force a smile to show her I understand, when really, I don't at all.

She hesitates, appearing to contemplate something. Chewing on her lower lip again.

"Can you visit me tomorrow?"

My breath catches in my throat.

"Visit you... in the room?"

"Yeah. Just, when no one will see you. Just stop by sometime in the morning. Please? It's important." She looks around again.

None of this makes sense. Hadlee Morgan is beautiful and shut off and dark and doesn't just ask former best friends to visit her in motel rooms. She hasn't talked to me in almost three years, and now I'm giving her a room for free when it's the last thing we can afford.

But there's so much desperation and *fear* there. Like she needs me to check on her, like her safety depends on it.

Something is very, very wrong here.

"What time?" I ask.

"Does eleven work?"

"Of course."

She forces a smile and then runs out of the front doors, disappearing from view. I'm left standing by the counter, the music from my phone still playing in the background to "Jeepers Creepers" by Frank Sinatra.

And left wondering what the heck just happened.

CHAPTER 7

Not long after Hadlee leaves, I focus my efforts on her website. Part of me is concerned she saw I had it pulled up, but part of me is hoping she did. Maybe she'll realize how much I still care, and how much I love her work. Maybe she'll want to be friends again.

Or maybe she'll think I'm a stalker and a loser and want to stay away forever.

Regardless, I continue my scrolling, the page taking forever to load, and eventually find a post she left nearly two months ago.

I was right.

It's a pencil sketch of a man in shorts from behind. There is a crescent moon drawn out, and behind the outline of the man, his back turned, is the woods. A clearing. I can't make out what it's of, because she never sketched in too much detail. But it's obvious that the man is standing before the circle, blocking out whatever is inside. My indented scar hurts.

Chills.

And just below the picture is a verse. I almost hate myself that I never thought much of it the first time I saw it. But when I compare it to the one today, it's clearly the same person. One running toward something, the other having found it. Then the words:

> *Terrors of flight*
> *Gates of Hell*
> *Open and find me*
> *A story; a tell*

TUESDAY, JULY 22ND - THREE YEARS PRIOR

HADLEE DOESN'T TELL ME WHERE WE'RE GOING WHEN SHE bikes her way to the motel. My parents are busy trying to fix a flooding issue in Room 3 with Rosa, so it doesn't register when I tell them I'm leaving. I go to the laundry room in the back court-yard to get the old, red Schwinn bicycle that was left behind from the previous tenants of the place. It was Hadlee who convinced me that retro was cool, so of course the bike had to be. It was from the 50s.

We pedal our way out of the parking lot and down the road, passing a few blocks and some of the poorer neighborhoods—toward the trailer parks in an enclosed lot. The wind blows Hadlee's chestnut hair behind her, and I get a scent of lilac. I pump faster to catch up to her, and she's smiling—the sun shim-mering on her cheeks and in her eyes. There's a single dimple, her right one, which comes out to enjoy the weather.

A little girl sits outside of the entrance to the trailer park with a lemonade stand. She perks up when I ride past, so I wave to her and keep going in the direction Hadlee is leading me. But when I face forward, she's not next to me anymore. She's circled round and stopped by the lemonade stand, the girl pouring her a cup from a plastic jug. I ride back until I meet them.

"You wanna cup too, mister?" she asks in an adorably cute voice. Her hair braided and twisted together behind her. There is a bruise on her neck. "Only fifty cents."

"Fifty cents for a Dixie cup?"

"Yessir! Momma said if I sell it all today, she'd buy me a Popsick-cull when the ice cream man comes back."

Hadlee smiles as the girl pours a cup for me. "I love Popsicles! Green apple is my favorite. What is yours?"

The little girl sticks out her tongue and makes a gagging sound. "Gross. Cherry's my favorite."

Hadlee gulps down her lemonade and wipes her mouth with the back of her hand. She reaches into a pocket and gives her five dollars. "This is for us both, so maybe you and your mommy can both have a cherry Popsicle. What's your name, and how old are you?"

"Sadie. I'm nine."

Hadlee bends down so they're eye level. "That's such a pretty name. I'm Hadlee." She points to me. "This is Dev. I'm fourteen, but he's only thirteen." Hadlee reaches out to touch one of Sadie's braids as they both share a laugh. "I love your hair. Do you think you can braid mine when we come back again?"

Sadie's eyes light up, like she just gained a new friend. And knowing Hadlee, she had. She always knows how to make everyone around her feel important.

"Yeah! Momma taught me how." Sadie reaches out and runs her hands through Hadlee's hair, giggles. "It's soft, not like mine. Maybe you come back when the ice cream man comes?"

Hadlee laughs, but it's a sweet one. She reaches into her pocket, finds another dollar, and hands it to the girl, winking. "That's a tip. And you betcha we'll both be back. Won't we, Dev?"

"We sure will," I say.

Hadlee scrunches up her nose, like two friends sharing gossip I'm not allowed to know. But she runs her hands over Sadie's hair, and I can see her pause on the bruise around Sadie's neck. The dark spot like a black mark on Sadie's sienna skin. Hadlee looks, for a moment, like she wants to cry. But she doesn't. She just smiles instead.

"You wait for us out here, okay?" Hadlee asks.

Sadie nods, exuberant.

After I gulp down my lemonade, which is 90% sugar, we say goodbye and bike away down the road until we meet a dead end and turn onto a dirt trail that leads into the woods. I don't ask where we're going. I don't ask if we really will go back when the ice cream truck makes its rounds—doesn't make sense why it's important. I don't ask Hadlee if she wants me to repay her the money because she won't take it.

But with the midday sun beating on the backs of our necks, I'm grateful for the silence. To be right here, next to the only person I'd ever want to be around. My best friend.

My beautiful best friend.

After a mile or two on the trail, far away from civilization, the man-made path ends, and we have to walk our bikes the rest of the way. Through tall weeds and tree branches. Past ferns and thorn bushes. The music of cicadas all around us. It feels like we're at it for hours, and I want desperately to turn back, but Hadlee keeps going, like she's been here before. Like none of it fazes her. Like she walks the woods every day. I've been on her excursions enough times that the travel doesn't get to me anymore.

We're a team.

"Where are we going?" I ask. "You're not leading me out here to 'Blair Witch' me, are you?"

Hadlee lets out a single giggle. "Just a little bit farther. Trust me. This is amazing."

And I know that for Hadlee to be this cryptic, it must be spectacular.

We travel through twists and turns. Over rocks and under branches. The sun glimmers down through the canopy of emerald and sapphire leaves. Eventually we leave our bikes against a large ash tree. A pair of squirrels scurry up the bark when my handlebars hit the trunk.

And it's the rhythmic sound of our feet crunching the dirt and leaves, how birds call from above the canopy, and beams of light illuminate plant life in a beautiful, golden hue. Some of them occasionally land on Hadlee's hair, making it sparkle.

Just when I think she's leading us nowhere, we come to it—a clearing. A circle. Nearly perfect. Out here in the middle of the woods, without any visible path leading up to it.

Brushing the pollen and alfalfa that cling to my clothes, I take in the sight before me—the air leaving my chest. To what has been placed here, inside the circle. And I realize Hadlee was right.

It's the most amazing thing.

A CHERRY IN A PIT OF PLUMS

PART TWO

I'm in the wardrobe. I can't find my way out.

There are coats everywhere. One still dripping wet, another warm with feathers.

I like the feel of it as it tickles my cheeks.   Mothballs.

I think I find the door to get out, but I hit a wall, then another, and another.

A

Pinball

Stuck

In

A

Machine.

Can't get out.

Can't get out.
No matter

How hard I try.

The coats morph into one, like a giant fur. My throat closes up.

Fingers emerge from the coat's opening. Coming for me. Reaching. **A hand.**

I just want Mommy and Daddy.

The **hand** clamps around my wrist.

He has me.

CHAPTER 8

There's a bright white light, gone almost as soon as it appears, and I wake up to something crawling on my chest. Hairy. Eight legs. It's a spider, and I scream and fling it off. Scrambling to my feet, I slap the bare skin of my arms, legs, face, and chest. Anything else that's exposed and might have some creature dangling off it. There's nothing on me. When I gather my bearings and look around, I'm here again.

The woods. Farther in than before.

No. Nonononononono. It's only been two days.

I take a few deep breaths and calm the beating of my heart, but my head spins.

I'll find my way back; I always do. The trees are taller here—the ferns and weeds thicker. My knees and shins itch from lying in the grass, and I pray I didn't get into any poison ivy.

The cacophony of crickets avalanches its way to me, and the rustle of leaves through the canopy of branches above bring me back to the present moment. I turn in the direction I know is home, but when I do, a shiver overtakes me. I'm once again shirt-less and shoeless, but this time my shorts are off too. I'm in only my boxers. Goosebumps rise to the surface of my arms, and I rub my hands together to create warmth.

SNAP

Just as I'm about to walk, I hear it. Footsteps. A twig snapping and a shuffling of leaves. It's coming from behind.

They're back. Fuck, Dev. FUCK!

Instinctively, I close my eyes and count backward from three before turning around and opening them to find nothing. My feet are rooted in place, and they won't move yet. Not until something else happens, like they'll only work if there's another sound. I don't call out, because even I know that would be beyond stupid.

But I can't help the tears that pool in my eyes. I just want to go home; I'm so sick of this shit.

You're going to die in here. Remember?

After what seems like minutes, I suck air into my chest, and just as I do, I hear footfalls from somewhere. Another snap of a twig, as if carried on the wind—a whisper. Undistinguishable, barely audible, but there.

Chills wrack my entire body, my blood bubbles, and I get the courage to move my legs and run for the road. I hop over branches, fern thickets, thorn bushes, and a rocky stream. The burning in my legs and lungs kicks into gear, but I ignore them as I see the distant lights of the trailer park and the bend past River Road.

Leaving it behind. Leaving it all behind.

Must. Get. Away.

My feet slam onto a rocky trail before veering into the grass. The cool air outside hugs my chest, thighs, and shoulders. I pump my arms opposite the pattern of my legs. Take steady breaths in and out to get oxygen to my lungs. I do this until I calm and push away the fear.

Somewhere amidst the trailers up ahead, the lingering scent of firewood.

"Find that bitch."

The scar on the back of my head pulses.

I round the bend past the abandoned buildings, lopsided houses, a car that drives past on the opposite side of the street, and then to a stop when the parking lot of the motel comes into view. No one is outside, and inside the glass window, Dad is hovered over the front desk. His glasses are perched on top of his head, and he's rolling his shoulders back and forth, his face scrunched like it hurts him to do so.

Don't. Look. Back.

My feet sting, and both are scraped up from the rocks on the trail. Blood is smeared alongside the dirt and grass stains. I limp my way to the fence behind the motel. I brush my hands through my hair and run and jump over the fence. The walkway is empty, and the laundry shack smells of lavender detergent. A gust of wind blows past, and I hop along the concrete.

"Landry!"

There it is again. The hiss from somewhere. Just like I heard last time. It scares me because when I look, no one is around. No one is peering out at me from the bathroom windows. It's just me and the voice in my head. Because maybe I'm going crazy. Waking up in the woods twice in one week, someone following me, hearing someone call my last name. And now less clothing than before.

I wait until I get back to the window of Room 13 to crawl through. Once in the bedroom, I grab my phone. It's a little after two in the morning.

What if they got to you before you woke up?

I try not to think about it, so without rinsing off my damaged feet, I flop onto the bed. The clothes I was wearing are in a heap on the floor. My phone is paused on the last song I was listening to, like my unconscious mind knew to pause it until I got back here to press resume.

It unsettles me.

A lot.

I put the earbuds in and play the song I must have been listening to when I shed my clothes and walked to the woods.

"Wake Up, Little Susie" by The Everly Brothers.

CHAPTER 9

Dev's Sunday To-Do List
Written by Dev

1. Breakfast with Mom and Dad... (9:00 AM – 9:30 AM)
2. Clean room (the real one)... (9:45 AM – 10:45 AM)
3. Shower... (10:50 AM – 11:05 AM)
4. ~~Study for Trigonometry... (11:10 AM – 1:00 PM)~~
5. Give Mr. Day his ice (???)
6. Visit Hadlee... (!!!!!!!!!!!!!!!!!!!!!!!)
7. OMG
8. OH. MY. GOD.
9. OMIGAWD!
10. <3

I sit at my usual spot in the kitchenette. The floor's white tiles are scuffed and chipped in a few areas, and the wooden cabinet behind me is worn and faded. There's a green Philco fridge behind Mom's chair that came with the motel. It breaks more often than not. But it's usually up-and-running in no time once Mom works her magic.

She's still dressed in Dad's cutoff college shirt from yesterday and a pair of orange sweatpants. Her hair is in pigtails, and her eyelids droop. After our morning breakfast ritual, she'll take over the front desk so Dad can sleep. They trade off on working the overnight shifts, so someone is always sleeping at odd hours—usually every other night.

It was her night off. Why is she tired?

Dad is in a plain white T-shirt and jean shorts. His glasses rest on the top of his head, the black cord dangling behind his neck. He turns off the stove and delivers us each an omelet with bacon, cheese, buttered toast, and a glass of orange juice. Dad gives me a separate plate of toast with peanut butter melted on top. It's the only way I'll eat it.

Dad kisses Mom on top of her hair, and she closes her eyes and slouches in her seat—a corner of her mouth turns up.

He sits down on the opposite side of the table, which is really only half an arm's length away, and forks omelet into his mouth. "You look tired."

Mom rubs her eyes, not even bothering to take a bite. "Just had a bad dream, hun."

Dad frowns. "Do you want me to bring you breakfast in bed? So you can lie down?" Dad points his fork at me, and a piece of omelet falls off a tong and onto the table. "Dev can give Clark his ice and watch the front desk so we both can eat in bed." He stabs another piece of omelet and brings it to his mouth before thinking twice and putting it back down.

"I can't," I utter before I have time to think about it. "I'm busy."

How original. No seriously, Dev. Truly genius.

"Let him have today to himself, Joe. I think I just need to lie down and nap before I take over out here. Is that okay? Can you man the station a bit longer?"

Dad nods and pushes Mom's plate toward her. "You haven't touched your food."

Mom pushes it back. "Refrigerate it for me. I'll have it when I wake up."

Dad says to me, "Your mother always has to be difficult." To her, "Honey, please eat. I don't like when you go to bed on an empty stomach."

Mom winks at him. "Now you're just trying to fatten me up."

He rolls his eyes. "Not this again."

Mom taps my wrist. "Did you know your father once told me when he was younger—"

"I'd prefer we not bring this up again." Dad's cheeks go red.

"—that he loved watching me eat. He even loved hand-feeding me."

"Oh, no," I say. "I don't need to hear this."

"Oh, you do." Mom grins. "See, your father...."

Dad picks up the dropped piece of omelet and chucks it at her. She cries out laughing and chucks it back at him. Dad opens his mouth, where it lands perfectly, and swallows—smug.

"You're so *bad*, Joe."

I wish I were anywhere but here. Once again, my parents can't keep it in their pants for longer than twenty-four hours. I must have the weirdest family in the entire world.

I scarf down my omelet and toast as Mom gets up to kiss us each on the forehead. Dad scoots his chair back and pulls her onto his lap before she can walk away. He doesn't make romantic gestures often, it's usually Mom that initiates, so it's always a spectacle the few times he does. But he places his hands on each side of her face and plants pecks up and down her neck until Mom squirms away from him. She is ticklish.

She squints at Dad playfully. "I will be unconscious, so no funny business."

He shrugs his shoulders as if he doesn't know what she means, but there's a smirk on his face. Mom, content with what just transpired quite unnecessarily in front of me, walks back into their bedroom and closes the door.

It's a wonder I don't have psychological problems from all the PDA I've seen over the years.

Dad and I are left in an awkward silence. I play with a few leftover scraps of egg on my plate just to have something to do. I stick a finger in my mouth to scrape some of the melted peanut butter off my palate. My phone reads a little after nine, and I don't know how to compose myself, waiting until eleven when I can check on Hadlee. But the thought of what we'll say or do makes me nervous. We haven't been alone in a room together since....

Dad motions to my leg, which is bouncing up and down so much that it vibrates the entire kitchenette. I hadn't realized I was doing it.

Dad offers a polite smile. "You're shaking the table, son."

"Huh?" A beat. "Sorry." I stop, but then my other leg starts bouncing.

To most people, Dad looks like he has Resting Asshole Face, or RAS. Rarely showing emotion and usually full of dry humor that no one but Mom gets. I'm not sure what Mom sees in him.

Dad isn't a bad father. He was always there when I was a kid, always did his best to provide for us. But Mom was more fun—wanting to joke around, get muddy, go on adventures.

Maybe on some level I kind of understand. Mom keeps Dad from sinking, and he keeps her from floating away.

I can't help but wonder if either one of them thought they'd be raising their only son in a motel that is barely staying profitable. Would they do anything else if given the chance? Be with anyone else?

Would they still choose to have me?

"Son." Dad interrupts my thoughts. "You're doing it again."

I realize both of my feet are bouncing rhythmically now, and the rickety side of the table looks ready to give, so I slap my hands on my knees and push my heels into the tiles.

"Sorry. I'll just go and clean my room." I get up. "Want me to do the dishes?"

"I've got them. Don't forget to give Mr. Day his ice so you can relax."

"What were you going to say last night?"

He has a mouth full of toast. "Hm?"

"Last night, before Rory came in."

Dad takes a while to finish chewing and swallowing, like he's trying to formulate the perfect sentence. He wipes his mouth with a napkin. "Just wanted to make sure you had everything you needed before I headed to bed."

"That's it?"

I don't know why I know he's lying, but for some reason I just do. Dad doesn't ever talk unless it's something important. But he doesn't give his tell. He just raises the corner of his mouth and crinkles his lips.

"Yeah." He takes a sip of orange juice. "I have to do some running around, and I don't expect anyone will be checking in or out, so if I'm not home when your mother wakes up, just tell her I'll be back for dinner."

"You're going to leave the desk alone on a Sunday?"

"Yeah. Just some errands I never had a chance to do this week. Your mom won't be asleep long."

"Oh, okay."

Dad and I stare at each other for a while, but nothing more

is said. That look that says, "Case is closed." I just accept it, and after I realize we're done, get up and leave.

ROSA

Got kit! The hair is gone Tuesday, hijo!

ME

cant wait!!! love u Rosa!!

AIDEN

I couldn't sleep last night. I was sooooo disturbed from what your dad said about DC and Marvel...

ME

still on this, r u?

AIDEN

I'm tearing down random strangers in Vid-Hub.

ME

u know half those webcams r robots, right? most of the people on that site r old, foreign, or fake porn accounts of mens penises

AIDEN

Why do you think I'm drowning my sorrows on here...

ME

y r u on there if ur dating a boy?

AIDEN

He doesn't do dick pics. :'-(

ME

ill see you tomorrow in school. enjoy ur phallic pleasures

Sry about no dick pics

AIDEN

Me too.

Ooohh, I like that. Phallic Pleasures. I should start like a clothing line or something.

Lots of dudes n dicks.

ME

D&D, amiright???

AIDEN

Holy rutabaga…

I could kiss you.

ME

wut about dick memes?

AIDEN

This is brilliant. I'll go think up some good dick memes and get back to you.

Heh.

Drawing a little guy now.

What a veiny masterpiece.

ME

have 2 tell u something tomorrow, cant talk now tho

AIDEN

Sounds good. Cya bright and early. I'll get you to get away from that motel yet, boy. Mark. My. Wordssssssssssssssssss. :-)

Researching pictures for our clothing line now.

Holy scrotum!

Multiple scrotums!

Scroti?

Scrota?

ROSA

Yo también te amo. <3

ROSA

.

ME

?

ROSA

??

ME

u sent a blank txt

ROSA

Michelle es baking enchilada now. Es
delicious. Learns from her madre.

ME

stop hooking me up with ur daughter!!!

lol

ive never met her

ROSA

She says hi.

ME

OMG!

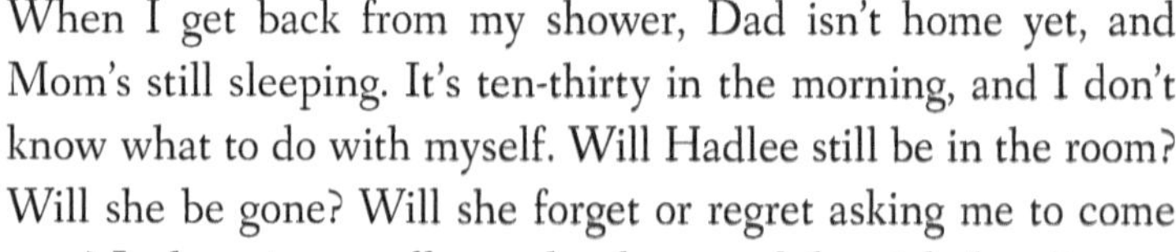

When I get back from my shower, Dad isn't home yet, and
Mom's still sleeping. It's ten-thirty in the morning, and I don't
know what to do with myself. Will Hadlee still be in the room?
Will she be gone? Will she forget or regret asking me to come
over? Is she going to tell me why she stayed the night here?

So many questions, and none of them have answers. Not yet.

I open the single-door wardrobe that rests against the wall. It, like everything else here, is either a hand-me-down or something we acquired from the building before Dad purchased it. Because of that, everything we own feels like an artifact from a long time ago. Like each piece of furniture has a history of its own. Like someone else's life is still here. Their presence, their *being*.

When I was little, the wardrobe in my room used to scare me. I'd lie awake at night, terrified the door would open or close by itself—I could hear the hinges creaking. For a while I'd stay up all night or fall asleep on the couch in the lobby, or crawl into my parent's room when they were sleeping. It was Rosa who came in to bless the room with sage bundles when my parents tried everything else imaginable. And ever since she's always been there when I needed her. Sometimes more than Mom or Dad.

It was Rosa who found me inside of it when I first started sleepwalking.

My breath catches in my throat when the wardrobe opens, until I can see my reflection in the mirror, then I run my hands through my damp hair. It's matted to my forehead and flattened over my ears. But it'll curl right back up within the hour if I let it air dry. The light from the window above my bed catches the moisture still clinging to my chest. I turn to my side and try to flex a muscle I don't have.

"Definitely don't go sleeveless," I mutter to my reflection. "Polo or button-up?"

I rifle through a collection of a dozen shirts I've owned since the sixth grade, but none seem right. A bead of water drips from my hairline, so I wipe it off with the back of my hand and run my fingers through my hair until it stands on edge.

"You really do need a haircut," I mumble.

I mess up my hair until it's sticking up every which way, and then I try to flex my chest muscles, which just embarrasses me. Finally, I settle on a pair of khakis and a blue-striped polo. My hair, as expected, is already curling above my ears. I check my breath in my palm, recoil at the stench, and grab a few mints from the night table beside the bed and chew on them like candy. I recheck my breath and decide to chew on a few more for reassurance.

I look back at my reflection and straighten out my clothes, plastering on my best movie-star smile. "Hiya, Hadlee!"

No, definitely not.

"Hey there, friend."

Dev, seriously?

"So... what brings you 'round these parts?"

Do you WANT to come off as a creep?

"You're overthinking it." I shake out my hands. "You used to be friends... just knock on the door and...."

This needs to be thought through. With Dad gone it's easier, but Rory and Mr. Day are still in their rooms and not going anywhere, and Mom could wake up at any minute. There are guests in Room 22, but they'll be checked out by tomorrow and moving on to somewhere else. I either need to sneak in through a window, which is beyond an invasion of her privacy, or get a spare key to unlock her door and slip in without anyone noticing.

"This is never going to work."

I close the wardrobe and take a few deep breaths. It's no big deal. At least, it shouldn't be. Hadlee was my best friend. We grew up together. She knows more about me than even Aiden does. It's not going to be that bad. How much could talking to her have changed? How is Hadlee randomly showing up at my motel asking for a room after ignoring me for three years any different?

And then it worries me:

What *IS* different now?

When my phone reads 10:59 AM, I grab the master key ring and head over to Room 1. My heart jackhammers in my chest, and I have to remind myself to breathe.

Step, breathe in, step, breathe out. Repeat.

The room seems to get farther away the closer I get, like tunnel vision. Nothing else matters except that red door. My surroundings blur, and the door wobbles, like it's moving to the side.

This is beyond cliché, Dev. She's a GIRL. You're a BOY. And she just happens to have been your BEST FRIEND. Man the hell up!

Clouds blot out the sun, but the humidity is just as bad as yesterday. I air out my shirt, check my breath one more time, and look up at the second row of rooms. No one is outside, and there appears to be no movement. I take a few shaky steps forward and fumble for the key to Room 1. And without a second thought, I unlock the door and step inside.

Just a boy meeting a girl in a vacant room. Unsure what to expect.

Once I'm inside, I close the door behind me.

And I find... nothing.

CHAPTER 10

The room is empty.

It's dark except for what little light sneaks past the closed curtains by the front window. I turn on the light switch by the door, and the room sheds a dim, yellow glow. The double bed against the right wall is still freshly made. Nothing is on the dark green carpets. Nothing is on the night tables. Nothing is on the two chairs near the back wall. My heart sinks at the reality that she probably snuck away early this morning after she woke up, or maybe even late last night when she realized what a mistake it was to come here.

But I try anyway in a whisper, "Hello?"

No answer. I call out again, but still nothing.

That's when the door to the bathroom opens, pooling bright light onto the carpet, and I see the backpack stacked stealthily in the corner. My body stands alert, and my fingertips tingle. I'm frozen in place as a shadow appears, growing bigger as the person steps into the main room.

I see the figure from bottom to top: bare feet with black nail polish and a bracelet wrapped around a right ankle, the alabaster skin that travels over shins, past the knees, and up long, slender thighs. My eyes pause on a birthmark on the inner left thigh and then rest just below the navel.

Her navel. Hadlee's navel.

She wears blue underwear with white lace that hugs her hips.

My eyes stay focused. My heart stops. Breath ceases. Sweat beads my forehead, and my face gets hot. She's here. She's standing right before me. In her underwear.

In her blue-freaking-underwear.

There's a pink, horizontal scar just above her belly button that I don't remember being there.

"Stop."

I know I should look up, take my eyes off the scar. This is both really creepy and a complete invasion of privacy. But it takes her scream to bring me out of my trance. And it's shrill, high-pitched.

I jolt, my entire body on edge like I'm going into cardiac arrest. And I see Hadlee's hands fly up to her bare chest.

Oh. My. God.

Her bare-freaking-chest.

But her hands cover them in time before I can see anything.

She screams again, and then I finally look into her eyes. Her hair is bundled up in a towel, and perspiration clings to her neck and upper chest. I'm here, in Room 1. With Hadlee Morgan. And she's practically naked. We lock eyes, both silent. Hers are wide, in shock. And I feel horribly embarrassed. And... *empty*.

"Dev?" she squeaks.

"Ye-uh-ya-um-yes!"

She clutches her breasts tighter, and I don't know what I'm supposed to do. Leave? Say hi? Wave? Apologize? Give her privacy? Tell her I really like the lace? Tell her how beautiful her skin looks? How seeing her here brings back good memories?

"What are you doing?" she shouts. "Turn around!"

"Ohmygod! Yes! I'm sor——"

"Turn around!"

"Right!"

I whirl around and face the door, closing my eyes and cursing myself for being the most awkward, creepy person ever. She is standing here exposed, and all I do is stare at her like a horny pervert.

This is so much worse than anything I could've imagined, and it leaves a really unsettled taste in my mouth.

A *really* unsettled taste.

She snaps me out of my thoughts. "What are you doing here so early?"

I take a deep breath before answering. Clutch my chest and wait for my heartbeat to slow down. "I was coming to check on you."

"You were?"

"Yes."

It's silent before I hear the sound of fabric shuffling behind me. A zipper.

"Is it eleven already?" she asks, her voice an octave lower and calmer.

On instinct, I turn around to answer her. "Yeah, it's actually two minutes aft——"

"I never said to turn back around!"

"Ohmygod! I'm sorry. You're right." I whirl back around again, cursing myself.

So-freaking-embarrassing.

"I should go," I say. "I shouldn't have come like this."

"I'm almost done."

"This was a bad idea. I should have knocked." I reach for

the door handle.

"Don't open the door yet, Dev."

I freeze in place. "Ahhhhh! I don't know what to do."

"Just stop moving and don't do anything."

"So, you just want me to stay here?"

"Yes."

"What do I do with my hands?"

"Why are you asking me?"

I look from my hands to my legs. "They're just dangling in front of my chest."

"Then put them down by your sides."

"Okay."

"Good." She sighs.

"I can leave if you need me to."

"I'm fine, Dev."

"I didn't mean to—"

"It's fine. Just be cool. If you freak out, I'm going to freak out. Are you cool?"

"As a cucumber." A pause. "I did not just say that."

There's a single giggle from behind me. "You did." A pause. "I don't know why I'm giggling."

"I think I should leave right now before I make this worse."

"Dev. Wait for me to get my shirt on. Your anxiety is giving me anxiety."

"Okay. Sorry."

I relax and take several deep breaths as I wait for my body to return to normal. But my cheeks are heated, and I can't get the image of her blue underwear out of my head. The white lace. How they hugged her curvy hips....

This is beyond uncool, Dev.

"You can look now."

"Are you sure?"

Another single giggle. "Um, not really. I don't know.... Now I'm freaked out."

After I prepare myself, keeping my eyes squinted just in case she's lying, which in hindsight really makes no sense, I do. She's back in her typical Hadlee outfit: ripped green leggings, plain white shirt with a black inkblot on the center, and a cutoff denim jacket. Her hair is straight, falling down in clumps behind her back. There are a few wet spots on her shirt where it caught her hair. The scent of berries wafts over to me. The motel shampoo she must have used.

And it's now that I realize that I have no idea what is supposed to happen. Do we just stand here and stare awkwardly at each other until one of us leaves? Do we hug and exchange pleasantries or past experiences? Do I ask her what she's doing or let it go unsaid?

Hadlee bends downs and pulls out her camera bag stowed in her backpack. She glances up at me quickly and fumbles with the strap before shouldering it. It's unnerving for a while, neither wanting to be the first to break the silence. That is, until she eventually does.

"Thank you for, um, letting me stay here."

"Of course." I make a gesture like it's no big deal, even though she doesn't see it. So, I add, "Anytime."

She pulls the camera strap closer to her body. "You don't understand, Dev. I can't even repay you."

"It's okay."

"It's not, though."

"Why?"

She bites her lower lip and sits back on the bed, letting her hair fall in front of her face. "I'll be out of here later today. I don't want to cause any trouble for you. Or your parents."

"Why would you cause us trouble?"

"You don't have to be nice to me." She fidgets with her nails.

It's so odd. Strange. How casual yet alien two people can be after years of not speaking. Two days ago, I never would've thought this moment possible again. But now that I have it, I'm not sure what to do.

"What's going on, Hadlee?"

And just the sound of her name as it leaves my tongue—so foreign. Unfamiliar. Yet smooth like butter. Like it deserves to be there.

She doesn't answer, so I take a step and repeat the question. Hadlee exhales and looks back at the door before glancing at me with bloodshot eyes. Not sure if I should continue or retreat. Some things you just don't go into with people.

Everyone has walls. This is hers.

That's when I hear her stomach growl. She doesn't acknowledge it at first. Not until it happens a second time.

"When's the last time you ate?" I ask.

She shrugs.

"Do you have any food with you?"

Again.

I frown. "You need to eat."

"I'll be fine. Really." She closes her eyes. "I shouldn't have come here. This isn't fair to you."

"What isn't fair?" I take another step.

"Stop." She holds up a hand and looks around the room at the bare walls, lands on the floor. "Do you feel weird seeing me here again?"

You should lie to her to make her comfortable.

"It's weird as hell."

So much for being subtle.

A corner of her mouth twitches. She raises her head, which makes the corner of my mouth twitch too.

"Yeah. For me too."

Hadlee runs a palm over her face. Her stomach growls again. *I've had enough.*

"I'm going to get you food. You need to eat."

"Dev...."

"Stay here. I'll be right back."

She hugs the camera case in her lap, like she's afraid it'll escape. Or be taken away. Without asking, I slip out of the room and head toward the front office.

Within seconds after I walk outside, I hear "Little Landry!" as Mr. Day barks from the ice machine, still presumably broken. "What are you doing?"

"Mother of pearl!" I shout, thinking I'll die from yet another heart attack. My entire body jumps and lands rigid, like a board.

Did you really just say 'Mother of pearl'?

"What was that?" He raises his nose——like he can sniff the lie I'm about to tell.

"What was what?"

Mr. Day stands in some camo getup and boots. A 12-gauge shotgun strapped over a shoulder, and a dead turkey hangs upside down in one hand.

It's the sight of the gun and the turkey that make me nauseous, like something is rotting in my intestines. *Isn't it off season for hunting?*

In the time I've known him to be at the motel, ever since I was a kid, Mr. Day has always been here. This motel is his home. But I've never stepped inside Room 17, where he stays. He doesn't let anyone in, not even Rosa. He cleans and fixes his own plumbing. He pays us to shop for his groceries and what-ever else he needs. And he hunts all season round.

He's a weird guy.

"You forgot about my ice, Little Landry." He peels away from the machine to cough. His chest hair sticks out from the V cut in the front of his undershirt. There's dried blood on his camo pants. "What are you doing in there?" He points over to Room 1.

I can't take my eyes off the gun or the blood. "Bed bugs, sir. That's all."

He grunts. "That's all, huh?" He looks at the room again. "Bed bugs...."

My heart thumps. *Does he know?*

"I c-can get the ice right no–"

"No, no that won't be necessary. Carry on with your gallivanting. Sometime tonight would be most preferable."

"I p-promise, sir."

"Very well." He frowns and starts to walk away but stops. The dead turkey in his hand sways with the momentum, and there's a hint of body odor that emanates from his clothes. I feel like I'm going to be sick. "Did you sleep well?"

What?

"Umm—"

He stares at me too long.

I REALLY don't like this at all.

"Good day, Landry." He stomps up the stairs to his room, limp turkey in hand.

All I can think about is that 12 gauge and how much I really don't like guns.

I arrive back a few minutes later, totally stealthy, with two packages of brownies and a bag of chips from the vending machine in the front office. I also sneak into Rosa's cleaning supply in the laundry room and grab her package of Kisses. I find Hadlee lying on her stomach on the bed, and I perch on a corner edge.

Hadlee tries to turn down the food, but after I insist, she devours the chips faster than I can blink. She takes extreme pleasure eating the first brownie as slow as possible. They were always her favorite. By the time I hand her some Hershey's Kisses, her eyes open wide when she sees I'm staring at her.

"Let me guess," she says. "Rosa's old cart in the supply closet?"

She remembers.

"Never changes."

She closes her eyes and licks her chocolate-stained lips. "She used to slip these to you in secret."

Still does.

"Yeah."

She finishes the last kiss, and I can almost hear a moan in the back of her throat. Suddenly, I wish Rosa had already delivered that chocolate enchilada her daughter had made so I could enjoy eating it with Hadlee. She grins, which makes me reciprocate.

Maybe the first time she's genuinely smiled since school on Friday.

Her cell phone rings, which makes both of us jump, so she puts it on vibrate without a second thought before glancing at the door, as if she expects someone to kick it down.

It kind of creeps me out.

Hadlee grabs the second packaged brownie and starts to eat it, stops herself, breaks it in half, and gives me the larger portion.

"I didn't know if you were still eating the chocolates. Does your Mom know? Thought she was worried you'd get fat like Rosa's husband."

"No, and I still do." I sniff the brownie. "You can have all of it. I already ate."

Hadlee licks brownie off her finger. "It's yours. It's only fair that I watch you stuff your face after you watched me stuff mine."

I get an image in my mind of my parents I don't want, so I shake it away.

"I don't mind," I say.

"Well, I do. It'll almost be like old times."

She says it automatically, like it came without thought. But I can tell it catches her off guard 'cause she looks straight ahead, like she doesn't believe what just happened.

"Sounds good to me."

Hadlee shakes her head and mushes her brownie against mine in cheers. "To totally getting fat and not caring for the consequences."

"Or the ripped jeans when we get too big to fit into our old ones," I add.

"Screw the calories."

"Screw being healthy."

"Screw shallow people who think plus-size is unattractive."

"Screw people who *are* attractive."

Except you.

"Except us, right?" she asks.

"Naturally."

She licks smeared brownie on her finger. "Screw 'em all!"

We wait a second before popping both halves into our mouths at the same time. Instantly, my entire body relaxes, and my mouth waters. I don't realize I've let out a sound until Hadlee starts laughing. And I forgot how much I missed it. So pure and natural. Unforced. Like it effortlessly floats above the air in the room. Contagious as hell. And I find myself laughing despite my mouth being full.

"Yeah." Hadlee pats my knee. "Ditto."

We stare at each other, trying not to choke as we alternate between laughing and chewing.

What is happening?

Her camera bag is tucked under one arm on the bed. This is all so random and weird and strange. I wish I could call Aiden so he could spit out his various theories, but I know I can't. For whatever reason, Hadlee needs me. In ways I can't understand or comprehend, she needs me. So, I'm not sure why the exact words come out of my mouth, but they do.

"Do your parents know you're here?"

Hadlee sits up and crosses her legs, bringing the camera bag in her lap. She fidgets over the zipper. "No."

"Are you in trouble?"

She runs her hands through her hair, which still sticks in wet clumps behind her back. "No, it's nothing like that."

"Do you want to tell me what's going on?"

She nods her head, still not meeting my gaze. But for some reason, my mind, or my heart, won't let it rest. There are too many unknowns and variables and questions.

"Why did you come here, Hadlee?"

"I shouldn't have."

"But you did."

She locks eyes with me. "I'm sorry."

There's a lump in my throat. "Sorry for what?"

"Everything. Abandoning you."

Chills.

I'm not sure what to say, if anything is appropriate. In all the time we've been in high school, this is the most we've ever talked. It's also the first time she's said those words to me. Things I thought for the longest time I would never hear. Didn't *deserve* to hear. Maybe her admitting fault would somehow make me feel better about entering high school alone and friendless. How she never called or texted again after that day over summer break. How I went all this time thinking it was me that did or said something wrong.

And it doesn't make me feel better, not at all.

It makes me feel worse, like I knew it would.

Unsure how to respond, I say, "How are your parents doing?"

"They hate each other."

"Oh."

"They hate you, too."

I swallow, hurt. A little angry too. "That was blunt."

"I don't want to keep skirting around your questions. My parents are miserable, and they make everyone around them miserable. I just want to get as far away from them as possible. Our house hasn't really been home in a long time, you know?" She caresses her camera. "And they hate you. If they knew I was here, they would lose it." A corner of her mouth turns up. "Is it weird that I kind of wish they'd find out I was here?"

I try to process everything she just dumped in my lap, but I can't. "Tell me how you really feel."

Hadlee frowns. "That was mean of me."

"It's good. We're just catching up, right?"

"Right."

I chew on the thought before speaking. "My parents hate you too."

We lock eyes. Silence.

"Is this awkward to you?" she asks.

"Totally."

"Cool." She nods. "Same."

Part of me feels relieved she's here, but there's a tiny ping too. Frustration? Resentment? I can't tell, and I'm not sure if I want to know.

"I'm going to redirect us somewhere less awkward. Small talk. That okay?"

"Totally."

More eye-locking, only this time she squints, and her nose and forehead scrunch, making my heart fall.

I take in a deep breath. "How's Maggie?"

Hadlee cracks a few fingers and wipes at her face. "She's amazing." She gives me a wan smile. "Just had her birthday last month."

"Oh, yeah. She's twelve now, right?" I inch closer to Hadlee. "Is she still doing gymnastics? I remember she'd always have a new move to show me when I'd come over."

And bringing this all up again, the memories of our old life, makes me want to cry.

"Dancer now," Hadlee whispers. "She's so beautiful and graceful when she's up on stage competing." She seems lost in thought. "She's suffocating at my house."

I lean in, not sure how to respond to that last comment, so I pretend she never said it. Maybe it was an accident. "I can see that. She's probably phenomenal." I clear my throat. "Too bad I never got a chance to see her perform." I let out a breath. "She always wanted to go on the trampoline when I was there." A laugh bubbles up. "Remember that time I tried to do a backflip and bounced right off the trampoline and went into your mom's garden?" Full, nervous laughter.

Hadlee giggles. "Yeah. Landed right in the petunias. Got petunia juice all over your back and hair."

"Ugh, it was the worst. I had to take two showers."

She puts her palm on my knee. "My mom was so mad about that."

I look down at her hand. I don't like it being there. "How do you think I felt about the petunia juice? It's really sticky. My clothes were stained."

"That's why she hates you, ya know. You ruined her petunias."

"I'm the worst, aren't I?"

We laugh awkwardly, letting it taper off into silence.

"You never had the best luck."

"Still don't. It's embarrassing. Everyone laughs at me, as if they didn't have reason enough."

She frowns. "People don't laugh at you."

"Yes, they do. It's okay, I'm used to it now."

"I don't laugh at you."

"That's 'cause you pitied my terrible luck."

She squeezes my knee. Or maybe it was just a twitch of her fingers.

I get a weird feeling in the back of my neck, and my head starts to pound.

"It was never pity." She takes time, seeming to chew on a thought, looking away. "I thought it was, um, kind of adorable." The air releases from her chest on the last word, making it an almost hollow whisper.

Chills. Heart skips. Head pain stops.

"I-It was?"

Hadlee locks my eyes again, taking her hand back. "Maggie still asks about you, ya know."

"She does?"

"Mhm."

"What do you tell her?"

As if on cue, a knock comes from the door, and Hadlee and I both jump up alert, looking from each other to the door, willing it to be in our heads. Just the wind that sounds curiously like knuckles. Just when I think it wasn't anything, the knock comes again, more forceful.

Shit. Shitshitshit.

Hadlee's eyes grow so wide I'm afraid they'll pop out. She cradles her camera, hops to the ground, and rolls underneath the bed before I even have a chance to think.

"I know you're in there," the voice shouts. "Open upppp."

You're dead. You're so dead.

Cursing myself, I hang my head and trudge to the front door, my hands shaking, and open it up.

"Well, well, motherfucker."

It takes me a while to realize I'm staring at Rory. He's dressed in the same shorts from last night, but now in a gray beater. Sunglasses rest over his eyes, and in the light, I can make out his athletic physique. In this exact moment, I want to steal it.

"Rory!"

Oh God. He's going to tell your parents. Is he high?

His head jerks back a little, and he rubs an ear. "I'm right here. No need to yell and shit."

"S-sorry." My eyes dart to the floor, praying he won't be able to hear or smell anything.

Did she leave her bag out in the open?

Rory turns around to cough up what sounds like a lung and a spleen. I glance over my shoulder just as a hand darts out from underneath the bed and pulls a backpack with it.

Oh Jesus.

Rory turns, and we stare at each other for longer than is comfortable or necessary.

"What are you doing?" he asks.

"Nothing.... What are you doing?"

He pushes past me looking around and flops on the bed. The springs make a groaning sound. I'm terrified he's going to squish Hadlee, but she doesn't make a peep.

"Going to get some coffee and stuff for my head. Also meeting a client. Charlie ignored my texts last night. She was at a party and said she was going to stop by here to crash, but then she never responded, and now I'm just worried something happened, but she would have called me, right? Unless she passed out, I mean…. Not that she has to call me, ya know. I just thought she would have." He stops himself. "My head is seriously pounding, and I need a pick-me-up."

"Sounds like a plan." I clear my throat. "How did you know I was in here?"

"I watched you walk right in. Duh."

"Oh."

He raises the sunglasses above his eyebrows. "You alright? You're acting all weird and paranoid and shit." He looks over both shoulders, and his eyes grow wide in recognition. "You saw something last night, didn't you?"

"No."

"Yes."

"No."

"Alright, if you want to keep it a secret, I can dig it. You're Don Corleone. I don't wanna sleep with the fishes." He smirks and lowers his sunglasses over his eyes. Bounces up and down on the bed.

I don't know how to respond, so I say nothing. I suck at lying. This is going to be *so bad*.

"We should probably go. Hope you feel better, Rory. I'm sure Charlie is fine."

And just those few simple words, even though we both know I couldn't possibly have any knowledge she's really okay, makes his features loosen up. He pounds his chest with a fist and throws out a peace sign. "Word. I'll be back later." He bounces up and down again.

From underneath the bed, there's an audible *humph!*

SHIT!

"I was just checking on the bedbugs in here," I blurt out.

Rory removes his sunglasses, his eyes burning into mine. "There are bedbugs?"

"Just in here. Not in yours."

He jumps up and swipes his butt, letting his hands swat his entire backside. "Dude, I can't have bed bugs crawlin' on me. Shit man, now all I'm going to be thinking of is those little bastards with their little teeth, and then I won't be able to sleep or study, and it's all a snowball effect from there. My mind goes a mile-a-minute, and it's *way* too early and my head is *way* too messed up and I'm *way* too upset about Charlie to process this." He hops to the front door and out into the sun, patting down his entire body. Mother-effing a storm.

"I promise you don't have bedbugs. And I bet she'll call you first thing when she wakes up. That way you can stop worrying."

He shifts the weight from one foot to another, rubbing his face with his palms. He groans, and I know I've just dug myself a hole.

"Can't say I wouldn't have it coming. Her ignoring me."

There's something about the way he says the last few words, maybe the inflection of his voice. But I can't put my finger on exactly what. I feel... uncomfortable.

Please leave.

"Do you want me to check your room for bugs while you're away, so when you come back it will be all clear? At least for when Charlie comes around?"

Rory perks up. "Can you?"

I nod.

"That's why you're The Godfather, man."

Despite how nervous and disappointed I am, I crack a grin. We wave goodbye, and he puts back on his sunglasses and walks to his truck.

I close the door, fall against it, and release air through my mouth. It's a while before Hadlee crawls out from under the bed, flinging off some cobwebs, shaking. I've never seen her scared before. Never.

We don't say anything, both rigid and alert. I lock the front door and look out the curtains to make sure no one else is out there.

Idiot. That could've been your mom or dad that saw.

We hesitantly resume our position on the bed. Hadlee hugging her camera for dear life.

When my heart calms down, it's almost peaceful, just sitting here. Like we used to do when we were thirteen years old on days when she would bike over from her house just to spend time on the weekends. Before things changed between us. Before she took me to that hidden place behind the woods and I kissed her.

"Do you want me to leave you alone?" I ask, still out of breath from near-cardiac arrest.

When she doesn't answer right away, I start to get up, but then her palm rests above mine on the comforter. Her hand is warm and clammy, and the hairs on my arms prickle.

"Please don't go." She flashes me those pleading, russet eyes again.

I sit back down on the edge of the bed, while she stays seated with her legs crossed. And we keep each other company in a vacant room, at a vacant motel, on the vacant side of town.

Her hand on top of mine.

Just a boy and girl alone in a room. Former best friends. The only place I'd choose to be.

CHAPTER II

Hadlee and I don't really do much for most of the day. She stays in Room 1 to do homework, while I distract my parents in the front office. It seems pointless, her being here. Almost. But I still wouldn't trade it for the world.

I eventually sneak over dinner for her, and later, I raid the fridge and take out the last piece of leftover pizza from yesterday. Hadlee sits on the bed, looking at her camera, scrolling through pictures and scarfing the pizza down in a few bites. Every now and then she'll appear to want to say something, but she never does. When it's late enough, and Mom and Dad call my cell to ask where I am, I tell Hadlee I'm going to bed.

"Are you staying the night again?" I ask.

"I have to get back home. My parents are kind of freaking out."

"Do they really hate me?"

She wipes her mouth with a napkin I've given her. "I shouldn't have said that. It was a bitchy thing to say."

"You were just being honest."

"Still. Not cool on my part."

I nod, and she places her fancy, digital camera in her lap.

"What happened to us?" I ask. "Three years ago."

She frowns. "What do you remember?"

"We went out to the woods, that hidden place."

She moves to the edge of the bed, like I'm about to reveal something huge. "Then what happened?"

The scar on the back of my head pounds—a steady thump. I clasp the back of my neck.

"I kissed you. You freaked out. Everything else is fuzzy. I just remember waking up in the hospital. They said I had an accident when we were out there. You and I were messing around with a pile of junk, climbing it. But I fell off and hit my head."

Hadlee's gaze seems to float away from me and this room. She clasps her hands in her lap and slouches over. I think her shoulders shake. She looks down into her camera.

I ask, "Are you okay?"

Goddammit. You upset her. She's going to leave again. For good. She's not telling you something, but change the subject anyway. Choose between her or the truth.

I point to her camera. "Did you take more photos for your website?"

The question catches her off guard, but when it clicks she shakes her head. "Yeah, um, want to see?"

"Of course."

Hadlee scoots over and holds out her camera, scrolling through a menu window to get to the slideshow mode. I can feel her eyes on me, but I focus on the pictures. The camera, I notice, says Olympus E-M10.

"This is part of a new collection I'm doing. I want your opinion on some of the photos."

"Okay."

She flicks through them. They seem typical. Similar to what she's posted before. The first one is of a young couple taken from afar. The boy is passed out against the girl's shoulders on a bench outside of an ice cream parlor while she licks a chocolate cone. Her free arm cradles him to her. Keeping him warm while he sleeps. Another one is a set of abandoned furniture in the middle of a vacant lot. A loveseat is left in tatters, and there is a single lamp with broken shades standing up to the right of the frame. Next is a roaring bonfire; a camera flare spans the lens. Next up is a group of what I think are college-aged guys huddled outside of a gas station, one of them holding a 30-pack. It keeps going on. Random images of small-town life—of summer days and nights.

But then the images get darker. A trail leading into the woods. A short man with long, greasy hair, slightly out of focus, lighting up a cigarette next to an old 1967 Chevy Camaro. Another shot of the same man with his back turned as his shoulders arch when he brings the lighter up to the end of the cigarette. A third of the man exhaling a plume of smoke—the cherry visible in the dark. After that, pictures of a crime scene. Like the police raid that happened Saturday night when the two drug dealers were arrested. The two men are being hauled away in one photo and are staring directly into the camera lens in another. Last is an unmarked grave.

She looks at me. Waiting for a reply. "What do you think?"

They are all so beautiful, and they seem to progress from intimate to detached. I don't get the connection from scene to scene. My scar still throbs. "I really like it."

She waits for me to continue, but I don't. "Anything specific? Like... did you notice a theme? Any details? Specific pictures that really, I don't know, *spoke* to you."

"I really liked the one with the guy sleeping on his girlfriend while she was eating an ice cream cone."

Hadlee pauses. "What makes you think they're a couple?"

"I just do."

We lock eyes. A hint of lilac emanates from her.

"Anything else?"

"You're so talented, Hadlee. Honestly. I know nothing about that stuff. It's beautiful though. All your pictures and poetry and sketches."

She tries to hide her smile, and I think she might even blush, but I can't be sure.

"What do you call it?" I ask.

She pushes a lock of her hair behind her ear and pulls the camera back into her lap. "Untitled for now. It's still in progress. But it's all about youth and innocence." She breathes air from her nose, and it tickles the hairs on my forearm. "You really liked the couple the most out of all of them?"

"Yeah."

She licks her lips and moves across the bed, away from me. Under her breath: "Of course you would."

I cock my head. "What does that mean?"

She inhales a breath and holds it in her chest. Tries to compose herself but fails. "You're happy, right, Dev? You're honestly happy?"

I shrug. "I-I guess so, yeah."

Hadlee wipes at her face and sucks snot up her nose. I hadn't realized she was crying, so I move to hug her, let her know that it's okay. That I'm okay—we're okay. But she's up and across the room before I can reach her.

You hurt her. You said the wrong thing.

Hadlee grabs her camera, turns it off, and stows it back in the case. "I should get going."

She's never coming back.

She puts her camera case into her backpack and zips it up, stares at the ground.

Do something! Now or never, or lose her all over again. Man. The hell. Up.

"I-It's me," I utter and stand up.

Hadlee busies herself, still not looking. "What's you?"

I take a deep breath.

"NightRunner13."

She finally stops and looks up, furrows her brows. "I know."

I shake my head, confused. "You knew?"

"NightRunner13. Of course I knew it was you. I've always known." She raises her head, and we lock eyes.

My scar stops throbbing.

The left corner of her mouth turns up. "Would you hate me if I said I've been wanting you to talk to me all this time?"

I blink, several times to be exact, before I open my mouth. Pretty sure my stomach jumps into my throat. Hadlee smirks and throws her backpack over one shoulder.

"Why didn't you ever say anything?" I ask.

"Why didn't you, NightRunner?"

I fumble for words but choke on each one. Hadlee must notice, because the smirk splinters, and she chews on her bottom lip. Unsure what to say, I turn around and sit on the edge of the bed to catch my breath. I drop my head to my hands and exhale.

Inhale. Exhale. Inhale.

The bed dips with added weight, and I can feel Hadlee's hot breath on the back of my neck. But something happens, in the moment before I know her hand will place itself on my shoulder, upper back, my neck, or back of my hair... a sharp pain springs from my scar, like it's been chiseled with a pickaxe. I close my eyes, my heart jackhammering. I feel like I'm going to be sick.

And then her hand touches my neck. A finger brushes past my hair before her hand is on my shoulder. In a flash, I fling my body up from the bed and smack her hand away as I see black. I can taste copper like blood in my mouth.

I turn around, dizzy, and steady myself against one of the

night tables. Hadlee is still on the bed. Her eyes wide, hands up like they were the catalyst to some horrible devastation. I don't even realize that I'm breathing heavy until Hadlee's mouth forms words that I can't hear. Everything is silent, muffled. I clutch at my chest.

Not again. Control it.

After a moment, Hadlee stands to walk my way, but I shoo her away. She looks terrified. Guilty. Remorseful. I'm scaring her.

"What did I do?" Her voice is barely above a whisper. "Did I hurt you?"

I shake my head. "No. Just... I don't... like when people touch me. From behind."

She's still holding up her hands, like a surrender. "Okay, Dev." Her eyes dart around the room, and she eases her way to the door. "I think it's best if I leave."

I close my eyes, hating myself. "Please don't."

Something in her just breaks. I don't know what or why, but it just breaks.

Hadlee tries to compose herself. "It's okay. You need to be alone right now. I get that. I won't come up from behind you. Not ever. Are we okay?"

Why is she worried about you when you're the one going all Jekyll and Hyde?

"Don't leave."

She stops. So much remorse. "I need to go, Dev."

"No." My breathing finally calms down. I sit on the bed, my body still shaking.

Fuck this shit.

"I want to start talking again," I say. "I don't care how or where. I... I want you in my life."

Hadlee freezes. A statue. It feels like forever before she

answers. I don't realize I've been holding my breath the entire time.

"Will you be up in, like, an hour?" she asks.

"Yeah."

"Log onto my website. Private session. I'll be on there. I'll wait for you."

I nod.

She grabs the doorknob to the room but stops herself from turning it. "And Dev?"

"Hm?"

"I never wanted you to leave my life either."

The rest of my body relaxes. Like those words were the magic ones to take away the pain. Like she used to be able to do years ago when we were kids.

"I thought your parents would freak out," I say.

"Oh. They will. Maybe they'll kick me out." A corner of her mouth turns up. "I can hit the road with my camera and never look back." She frowns. "But I'd miss you." A pause. "I do miss you."

"I miss you too." I think for a moment. "My parents can't find out either. We have to keep this a secret."

"What are you thinking?"

I don't know why I say what I do or where it even came from. But it's the only thing that feels right.

"You can't come here, and I can't go to your house. Not in the daytime at least, right? So, um, we can sneak behind our parents' backs." I snap my fingers. "Yeah! You can sneak over here sometimes... you can stay here anytime you want." I clap my hands. "I'll, like, have a room or something waiting for you whenever you want, uh, as long as you're okay with it. Right?" I look to her for validation, but she's not reacting. "So, like, we can text, or, talk on the phone, or, we can video chat on your website... now that you officially know it's me. Oh, this is embarrassing." My cheeks get hot.

"But we can't be seen hanging out together. Not even in school."

I know I shouldn't be angry, shouldn't open my mouth. I just got her back, and the last thing I want is for her to leave again. But then I open my mouth anyway.

"Why not?"

"You know why."

"I don't, though."

Hadlee shifts the weight on her feet. "Because if we're seen talking together—"

"It's because I'm *Lazarus* who lives at the motel with his perv parents, right?"

Hadlee scowls. "Stop."

"It's what you're thinking. I get it. I've heard it all before. Why be seen with a loser like me?"

Losers that have full-blown panic attacks when touched. How could you possibly think any of this was a good idea?

Hadlee closes her eyes, pained. "I don't want to fight with you."

"We're not fighting. I asked you why."

She groans, opens her eyes, lost in some distant sadness. "If people saw us together, it would eventually get back to both our parents. Then what do you think would happen?"

I open my mouth to refute it, but she's right. It's a small town. Secrets don't stay secret for long here.

"I'm sorry," I say. "This is just a lot, you know? It's been so long."

Hadlee pushes a lock of hair behind her ear. "You can hate me, Dev. I probably deserve it."

"No, you don't. I could never hate you."

"Well, you should."

I rub my eyes, suddenly exhausted, and fight to keep them open. "Three years, Hadlee." I hold up my fingers for emphasis. "Three years and now, all of a sudden, you're here." I clear my throat—remain calm despite my racing heart. "It just doesn't make any sense to me. At all."

"I promise that I'll explain everything to you. And I promise I'll make it up to you. The lost time, the questions you have, whatever. But this is bigger than just me and you."

Bigger?

"We have to be careful, Dev. We could lose each other forever."

Forever?

"Just for now, just a little while longer, we have to keep us a secret from *everyone*."

I try not to be hurt that she doesn't want to be seen with me. But I get why. I do.

"It'll be like when we used to have Room 13," I say.

Hadlee stares at me, but I can't read what she's thinking. Her face is blank. She whispers, "Exactly like it."

I can't help a small smile. "I haven't told anyone about that room."

Hadlee shifts the weight from one foot to the other. Scratches her nose, which makes her septum piercing catch the overhead light. "Me either." She pauses. "How come you didn't give me the key to that room last night?"

There's a lump in my throat again, and my eyes water. But I won't let myself get emotional, not now, not in front of her like a little kid.

I also don't answer her question. How can I possibly explain to her what I've turned it into?

She just nods at my non-answer and grabs the knob and turns until the door opens, letting in the nighttime. If anyone can sneak out without being noticed, it's Hadlee. She taught me all I know about being stealthy.

"You were really amazing in the track meet on Friday," she says.

"You mean when I came in third place?"

She taps her palm against the doorframe. "What do you run from? In your head."

"I don't know what you mean."

Yes, you do.

"I've never missed a single meet since you joined the team."

"I know." My cheeks get hot. "I look for you every single time I race."

She blushes. "I'll see you in an hour, NightRunner13. You can tell Aiden if you want someone to talk to. NO ONE else though."

I smile now, making a cross over my heart. "I'll see you in an hour, MalevolentBeauty."

"Seeing as our alter egos will still be up, the real us will pretend to be asleep so... goodnight." She does a half curtsy, lets out the giggle that I adore so much, and steps outside.

I laugh. "Goodnight, Haddy."

Frozen in place, horrified at what just escaped my mouth, I look and Hadlee is staring at me with wide eyes. Her lip trembles, and my cell phone vibrates in my pocket. I ignore it, but we both heard what I said. The name that hasn't been spoken in years. The one she always used to love hearing on late summer nights spent hanging out in random rooms, or bike riding at night, or outside swimming in the pool when it was still operational.

And right before she closes the door, a tear escapes her eye and crawls down her cheek. It's an unspoken agreement that she doesn't want me to talk any further. In my head, I go over to comfort her, but in reality, I just wait for her to leave. A few minutes later, I go deliver Mr. Day his ice and then walk over to my "fake" room to "go to sleep."

CHAPTER 12

ME

HUGE NEWS!!!!!!! HUUUUUGE!

ANSSWER ME

ANSSSSWER MEEFREWEEWEEEEE

AIDEN

I have to have my beauty sleep for school.
What do you want? My phone is blowing
up, boy.

ME

hadlee morgan is what happened

AIDEN

Wet dream?

ME

-__-

AIDEN

Lol, just kidding. You're so cute when you're
upset.

Go ahead.

Spill the beans.

ME

she slept over the motel last night

AIDEN

I'm sorry
WHAT?!?!!!?!?!?!?!!?!ASLKDNERIOJEIUFNOB

ME

thats all 4 2night. more 2morrow. night! zzzzzzz

AIDEN

Tease!

ME

u luv me

AIDEN

I hate when you're right!

Ugh!

Lame AF!

Ew!

Me wrong?

EW AF!

ME

trying 2 sleep

STFU :-D

AIDEN

I'm spanking you when we see each other…

I kid.

But all right, going back to get my beauty
sleep.

See you tomorrow so I can hear this riveting
story of teenage angst.

Hmmm...

Wear blue tomorrow if you can.

Blue looks good on you.

That one shirt that almost looks like a size too
small because it was shrunk in the wash...
yeah. THAT one.

I may be saying this because I love that shirt.

Probably going to steal it next time we change
for gym.

Make you walk around shirtless.

Hadlee, and probably every guy or girl in the
vicinity, will straddle you in the hallway. That
scrawny build and lack of any muscle definition
whatsoever.

Every man's dream.

ME

> trying 2 sleep and my phone is BLOWING UP
> AF, yo!!!

AIDEN

-_-

Sometimes I hate-love you.

Whereas you just love me.

Phallic Pleasures Inc.

ME

> well always have dudes n dicks

> 8===D 0-:

AIDEN

Amen.

...

Scroti, plural?

Like as in multiple scrotum(s)???

Like Platypi... You know?

ME

(is asleep)

AIDEN

Now I'm wide awake.

DAMMIT!

I HOP OUTSIDE THE WINDOW OF MY BEDROOM, LANDING ON the concrete in the back courtyard. A humid breeze licks the back of my neck, and from somewhere over the fence closing off our property, a dog barks on repeat—echoing in the wind. Making my way around both buildings, I inch against the wall to hide in the shadows.

Across the lot, the blinds to Room 9 are half open. The TV is on, illuminating the room in flickers of images and color. It wouldn't be out of the ordinary for Rory to be skipping his studies and watching TV or doing whatever else he does. But from the light of the TV, Rory sits on the edge of the bed, a mess of binders and books scattered around, and his face in his hands. When he pulls his head up, he takes a book and chucks it to the ground. Tears stream down his cheeks, and he checks his phone every few seconds.

He slaps his face once. Twice.

What the hell?

I don't feel comfortable watching, so I sneak behind the second building and slip inside Room 1 3, shutting the window behind me. Wondering what's going on with Rory.

That's the thing about working at a motel: people come here with secrets. Things they don't want the normal world to see. Like a storage locker of hidden desires.

It's amazing what people are really like when they're by themselves—so different from the versions they show the world.

My bed is still unmade, and half a chocolate chip cookie from earlier in the week rests on the night table. I eat it, despite it being stale, and reach into my pocket for the gum wrapper Hadlee was photographing. I still haven't washed my jeans from Friday.

So simple. So normal yet extraordinary. It belonged to a stick of gum that came from a package that came with other packages. But it never made it to the trash. It was left to the side, abandoned, alone. Just like everything else in this room. Remnants left from previous guests, from the boys' dormitory before it was converted to a motel. Different garage sales or things found in the world no one else wanted. That everyone else forgot.

I take another tack and pin it to a wall with the other wrappers. Around the room, each of these items have a story:

- A single walkie-talkie that Mr. and Mrs. Cartel left when their son Roger was having a temper tantrum
- A New York Mets baseball cap left in the bathroom when Chris Dodge from upstate New York was going on a road trip down to Disney World
- A Trac-fone (whatever that is) from before my time that Dad kept in the Lost 'N Found
- An abandoned book from the time that traveling author, Chris Driscol, tried to write about Mom and

Dad's profession. He scrapped it after two months with us

- The red Schwinn bicycle
- The silver pocket watch that hasn't worked in years, found at a garage sale four years ago on the opposite side of town. The image of an old 1800s locomotive etched into the face. An engraving on the inner lid:

Sylvia,
My platform when the tracks go dark
So you can count the days until I'm home

Love, Reggi

Hadlee picked it out with me.

All of these things and so much more—all here in this place. A room of the lost and tossed aside. The ones left behind but brought together.

I pull my MacBook to my knees and open it so I can log into Hadlee's website and wait for her to come on. When I bring it up, it says she's still offline.

I flip down on the bed and put in my headphones to search for "I'll Remember (In the Still of the Night)" by The Five Saints. Closing my eyes, resting my head on the pillow, I hum the melody and let it carry me away into the night while I wait.

Just a forgotten boy amongst his treasure of forgotten things.

CHAPTER 13

MalevolentBeauty: I'm really glad that we're friends again. :-)
NightRunner13: r we?

MalevolentBeauty set off fireworks

MalevolentBeauty: Do you realize this is the first time you've ever talked in my chat before?
NightRunner13: hold on
lemme try somethign
somethign
something**
darn autocorrect
MalevolentBeauty: Don't blame autocorrect. :-0

NightRunner13 threw confetti
NightRunner13 took a bow

MalevolentBeauty: Now you're having fun. :-D
NightRunner13: u smile a lot :-D
MalevolentBeauty: I'm just really glad I came over last night.

NightRunner13: me 2

wut does this mean 4 us?

MalevolentBeauty: It means we can't grow apart ever again.

You're too important to me.

NightRunner13: i am?

MalevolentBeauty bumped fists with NightRunner13

NightRunner13 accepted

MalevolentBeauty: I have to get to bed.

555-743-0270. That's my cell.

If you ever wanted to text or call.

I'm pretty awesome at app games too.

NightRunner13: i call shenanigans

we'll c about that

… does this feel weird 2 u?

us talking so casually?

MalevolentBeauty: Yeah, it does.

If it's too much for you, we can cool it off.

NightRunner13: NO!

not what i meant

i just dont want u 2 leave again

MalevolentBeauty is typing…

NightRunner13: 4get i said anything

it was stupid

MalevolentBeauty: I don't expect you to believe this, Dev, but I

never left you. I was always there keeping an eye on you.

I'm sorry; I'm just tired.

Can we talk about this another time?

MalevolentBeauty yawned

NightRunner13: will i see u 2morrow?

MalevolentBeauty: Text me!! :-)

We WILL see each other. Promise.

Just not at school, okay?

I can explain why another time, but just pretend like nothing is

different.

I'm sorry.

NightRunner13: no worries :-)

goodnight Hadlee

MalevolentBeauty: Goodnight, Dev! Happy running!

:-D :-D :-D

NightRunner13: :-D :-D :-D

:-p

:-o

MalevolentBeauty: Are you making fun of me?

:-o

NightRunner13: :-)

never

;-)

You have logged off

AFTER I HIT THE HOME BUTTON TO HER WEBSITE, THERE IS
an updated post from a few minutes earlier. It's a new photo
album she created. I click on the link, and it's all the pictures she
showed me on her camera. I'm drawn to the couple outside the
ice cream parlor again, but the photos unnerve me, viewing
them by myself without Hadlee. The two men arrested, the guy
with the greasy hair lighting up a cigarette.

I don't know why they're weird.

On the top of the screen is the title for the album:

A Cherry in a Pit of Plums

TUESDAY, JULY 22ND - THREE YEARS PRIOR

IT'S THE MOST AMAZING THING.

Hadlee steps forward and twirls her arms in the air like she's the ringleader. There are cable lines hung in the air tied to various tree trunks, crossing over one another. From them dangle pairs of shoes kept in place with laces. Shoes, sneakers, sandals, flip-flops, winter boots, combat boots, boat shoes, slippers. They all hang like tree ornaments. Scattered around are different items of discarded furniture. To the very back is a ratty loveseat, and closest to us are two ancient wooden desks from decades ago. Faced upright, planted in the grass as if ready for ghost students to attend their ghost lecture.

There are a few lamps scattered about, all upturned. Some are broken in half or cracked, others dusty, some are overtaken with weeds and moss. There are empty cigarette packs littering the ground, a few beer bottles and cans. A shredded mattress.

In the center of the circle is a two-seater go-kart. The red paint is chipped and faded on the body, and the white lettering on the side is peeled off, leaving a filmy residue. The one side is riddled with bullet holes.

"What is this place?" I ask.

"I don't know," she says breathlessly. "But isn't it amazing?"

She walks up to the go-kart, jumps, and plops her butt on the tiny door, letting her feet dangle off the side and swing back and forth.

"How long have you known this was here?"

Hadlee reaches below her and produces a plastic bag. She pulls out a cheap throwaway camera.

"Last week. I've been coming out here every single day since Sunday. It's just... perfect."

She places the camera to her left eye and points it at me. I raise my hands to cover my face on instinct, but the white flash blinds me momentarily. She lets out her trademark giggle.

I try not to be hurt that she's been out here more than once, six times to be exact, without me.

"How did you even know to find this?"

Hadlee raises an eyebrow and the camera jokingly. "I heard some high schoolers talking about it. I think this is the place seniors used to come to years ago. Pretty cool, huh?"

I mumble, "Yeah, pretty cool...."

Hadlee hops off the go-kart and grabs my hands in hers. Mine are clammy, but she doesn't seem to mind as she pulls me close and then spins me around. I latch onto her fingers and forget to let go, so when I start stumbling away, I take her with me and we fall. It hurts at first, as I land and bash my head into the hard ground, but when Hadlee giggles, I do too.

Hadlee helps me to my feet, brushing dirt from our clothes. I tag her on the shoulder and start running around the circular clearing. Hadlee attempts to chase after me, but she's not nearly fast enough. The wind is cool as it blows past, tickling my cheeks. Hadlee stops after a while and hunches over to catch her breath. I keep running; I don't stop. I do this for a while until Hadlee reaches into the seat of the go-kart and pulls out a few wrapped PB&J's.

"How did all this stuff get here?" I grab the one with grape jelly, 'cause Hadlee knows it's my favorite. She has strawberry.

"Brought stuff over the other night." She sees me eye the sandwich. She playfully slaps my arm. "Not these, silly. I had Mom make these this morning, and then I came by to drop them off before getting you."

We both take bites, and it's delicious. Hadlee reaches down again to pull out two juice boxes. We outgrew them years ago, but they just taste so darn good.

"Has anyone else been out here?" I ask.

"Not since I've come up." She exhales and looks up at the dangling shoes. "It's beautiful."

I look at her. "Yeah, it is."

My heart beats faster, and the sounds of the birds chirping and cicadas singing fade away until all that's left is the sound of her steady breathing in and out. The rise and sink of her chest. What I would give to be the reason she breathes. To feel it. Taste it.

"Dev?"

"Hm?"

"You okay?"

I snap out of the daze and can't see anything except her lips. At the tiny piece of crust stuck to the corner of her mouth. Without thinking I reach over and rub it away. Her eyes grow wide, her back stiff as a plank. I see her swallow slowly, and my stomach drops.

"Um, thanks." She blushes. Her eyes squint, causing her nose and forehead to scrunch, and I didn't realize something so strange could be so magnificent.

Hadlee clears her throat and pats my knee. "This could be our new spot."

"What about Room 13?"

She takes another bite of her sandwich. "They can both be

ours. But—" She extends her arms again, as if trying to gather the world around her and pull it close. "Look at this place, Dev! No other freshmen know about this but us. I haven't seen anyone come out here all week."

"Soon-to-be freshmen."

"Right! Just you and me. No rules or parents or school or chores. We can run away. We can make a home here. How cool would it be?"

I purse my lips. "You're not serious."

"Devy."

"Haddy."

We both chuckle.

She points up. "Take off your shoes."

"Why?"

"Just do it."

"No."

She pushes me until I fall on my butt. Laughing, she dives down and grabs at my sneakers. I try to fight her off, but she tickles me. I laugh until I cry, and just when she takes off one shoe, holding it behind her back as I try to get it, I tickle her until we're both laugh-crying. Eventually, she caves, and I steal my shoe back, taking off one of hers in the process. She flashes an evil grin.

"Devon Markus Landry." She stomps her foot. "I'm going to take your shoes if it's the last thing I do."

"Come and get them, Hadlee Renee Morgan."

We charge at each other until she ducks and gives me a wet willy.

"Ahhhh, that's SO GROOOOOOOSSSSSSSS!"

Hadlee tackles me from behind, and she falls on my back, re-stealing her shoe. I get leverage to roll over on top of her until she's pinned under my legs. She tries to get up, and despite my *scrawny build, she can't escape. Her face is red—breaths big. She wipes sweat off her forehead.*

When we calm down, neither of us moves, as we just stare at each other. I'm not sure how long we're like this, but when I let her up, we both take off our shoes in some kind of silent pact. We tie the laces together and both count to three before flinging them up to snag on a rope. They both catch, making the entire tapestry of cords and shoes sway with the added weight. And it's alive and beautiful.

We shield our eyes from sunrays that filter through, and then look over at each other. She's smiling—her teeth so white and gleaming, and my mouth is on hers. A gasp escapes her throat and sends shivers down my chin and into my chest. She smells of lilac and sweat, and her lips close around mine until we're pressed together. Her breasts push into my body; her hips dig into my waist. She pulls back slightly, but then her lips are pressed together more firmly. Almost perfectly. My bottom lip snuggled tightly between both of hers. And I'm lightheaded, dizzy. Not even sure if my feet are on solid ground.

We pull apart, breathing deep, our lips slick, and hold each other. My eyes are closed. I'm afraid it'll be over if I open them.

But then I'm stumbling back as her hands push me away. Her eyes are open—mouth a tight line. Her arms are shaking.

"What was that?"

"I-I don't know."

She pulls a clump of her hair to her mouth and chews on it. "We're friends."

I look at my feet. "I know."

"Best friends."

"I shouldn't have."

"Friends don't kiss friends."

"It won't ever happen again."

"Look at me."

I do. She's right in my face, inches apart now.

She runs her palm across my cheek and whispers, "Run away with me."

Everything stops. Everything.

"Where?"

"I don't know."

"Sounds perfect."

And then her lips are on mine again. Our tongues meet somewhere in the middle, and then we're kissing. REALLY kissing. Like they do in movies.

It's like this for a while; I'm not sure how long. I breathe her in and stand with her in this clearing.

This most amazing clearing.

And then from behind us I hear it: clapping. Whistling. The POP of a beer can.

And then a sneering voice. "Lookit who we found in our spot, boys. Two trespassers."

THOSE THAT KEEP THINGS HIDDEN

PART THREE

CHAPTER 14

Mom is watching the morning news about another drug bust across town when I step into the front office. She rests her chin in the crook of her arm while leaning on the counter. The newscasters transition into the story of a string of abuse cases in the surrounding districts.

Jesus.

A middle-aged couple stands off to the side and watches with her, each carrying luggage, cashing out. The Duffies. They stayed with us for a few nights while visiting relatives. We were the cheapest option available.

After the news story breaks for commercial, Mom takes their keys and processes their checkout on the computer before handing them a receipt and a form to sign. She wishes them goodbye as they walk out, and then she mutes the television.

"Heading over to Aiden's?" she asks.

Because the bus doesn't come here, I usually walk a half-mile down the road to Aiden's house and wait for it there.

"Yup, just getting us some breakfast." I point to the vending machine, trying to act cool despite the events of last night.

"We'll add it to his growing tab here." Mom reaches for the vending machine key and throws it to me.

I catch it. "He doesn't have a tab, Mom."

"Tell that to The Law."

"This joke is beyond expired by now."

Mom smirks. "Fun Mom doesn't think so."

"I'm gonna go to the vending machine now."

She studies my face as I walk over. She follows. "There's something different about you this morning...."

I freeze. "What?"

"It's weird."

"So, I'm naturally weird?"

Mom goes into the Is That Really A Question mode. Of course, the answer is obvious.

"Thanks, Mom. No wonder my self-esteem is terrible."

"Oh, hush, you." She laughs and ruffles my hair, walking back to the counter. "You do look different though. Call it Weird Fun Mom Syndrome. I can tell these things. You came out of me."

"Jesus, Mom. Stop. It's too early."

I unlock the vending machine for a couple packets of Pop Tarts as she busies herself. I throw her back the key when I'm done.

"Have you seen your father this morning? He wasn't out here when I woke up."

"No. You mean he left without telling you?"

Mom frowns, although she tries to hide it. She cranes her neck until it cracks and pushes herself from the counter, heading back to her bedroom.

She calls, "I'm sure he's fine, I'll call him. Have a great day at school. Tell Aiden he owes us a Pop Tart. We'll charge interest for every day it's late."

"I'll tell him."

"Love you, honey."

"Love you too."

But something feels weird, different. First Dad disappeared almost the entire day yesterday, and now he's not around this morning. Hadlee is suddenly talking to me, yet I can't tell anyone about it.

What else will be different today?

We step off the bus by the main drop-off circle. Kids make their way from other buses or from their cars in the parking lot. There's a horde stationed outside the doors talking, and just inside are a group of cheerleaders in red and yellow uniforms. Beside me, Aiden wears a T-shirt with the picture of a TARDIS that says *Doctor Who*.

We reach his locker, and I wait for him to grab his books for the first few periods. I scan the hallways looking for Hadlee, even though I tell myself not to. She is, obviously, not going to just walk up to me pretending to be best pals.

"So, we all met up yesterday to grab a few sodas after the campaign," Aiden says, bending down, "and Greg mumbled something about how he was sorry, and we agreed that Davey just likes to hack-and-slash and slay all the Orc dick possible. He's going to be a promiscuous barbarian warrior in the next game, 'cause, gross. Greg'll be a Druid. Kind of feel sorry for him, 'cause as soon as he's alone in the game, I'm doing a *Night of the Living Dead* thing to him."

"And why is that bad?"

Aiden stands straight and shuts his locker. We proceed to walk down the hallway until we reach mine. He has a devious grin on his face. "Because Druids can't do a single thing about the undead. He's *so* screwed." He raises his eyebrows and flashes his teeth.

I get my books and shut my locker, scan the hall again. We both rest against a bulletin board. "I still don't understand D&D."

"Then play with us, dammit. The guys ask me every weekend why you never come around, and Davey broke up with his girlfriend, who used to occasionally play with us, so now we're down one player. Do you know what it's like playing with a no-good cheat like Greg and a depressed heterosexual teenager in a basement?" He exaggerates a movement with his arms. "So. Much. Straight-boy drama."

"Yeah, I can really see the appeal now." I playfully punch his shoulder.

"I've told Davey that I know a few guys from online forums who would love to take away all that angst and heartache. But, you know, Davey likes those *female* parts and everything." He pretends to shudder.

"You mean vag—"

"Rutabaga, Dev. Rutabaga!" He punches me back. "We don't say that word here unless you want me to throw up in my mouth. Only I can say it when I deem it necessary, which is basically never."

"Right."

"And because we're friends and talking about this, that guy I've been seeing. So, I met him on VidHub months ago, we talked, and I got his number. He's older, like nine years older, as in twenty-six, as in sexy-as-hell older." He pulls out his phone to show some of their sexting, which I only pretend to be interested in. "I told him I was eighteen and never once mentioned my D&D fetish, so he wouldn't freak out. But can you believe me dating an older guy?"

"Sounds really weird. Are you sure he's not catfishing you?"

"Not at all. We've been on a bunch of dates already. He's really funny and sweet. He does volunteer work for troubled youth, and works in some kind of doctor or dentist's office as an assistant. Not sure which. We're going out again sometime this week." He sighs. "We haven't even had sex yet 'cause he wants to wait." He flutters his eyelashes to be stupid. "So romantic. I'll corrupt him yet." We both laugh.

"I'm happy you found a guy, Aiden. Really. But he sounds like a perv. Twenty-six-year-old? Volunteer work? Really?" I make a face. "Just make sure he's not using you."

"What a boner killer that would be."

"I still can't believe you never told me sooner."

"You hate when I talk about my sex life."

"You're not even having sex."

He ponders. "Fair point."

I scan the hallway again, and a few classroom doors down, Travis Weathers strolls the hallway. Notably by himself. He pulls out his phone, types something into it, and stands by a locker. Hadlee's.

Move along. She wants nothing to do with you.

Aiden waves his hand in front of my face. "Are you going to tell me what the heck happened last night with Hadlee?" He looks at my shirt, purses his lips. "I see you didn't wear the blue one."

"I did not." I clap my hands together. "But let me tell you about my night!"

I tell him the details as we walk down the hall to get a drink from the fountain. By the time I'm done, Aiden is practically speechless. He starts going off about what to do and say next, and asks for proof that we talked online. He's about to compose the perfect cherry-popping first text to her when, as if on cue, she rounds the corner of our hallway.

Taken by surprise, I step back and snag the shoe of someone

walking behind me. I try to pinwheel my arms for balance, but I fall backwards. My books slip from my hands and crash to the floor. My head hits the coffee-colored linoleum tiles with a hard *THUNK.*

Taste of blood in mouth
Beer bottle shatters
Crackling fire

Just like that, I'm back in the moment, on the floor of the hallway. My head throbs, and I don't realize my eyes are closed until I open them to fuzzy light. Everything comes back into focus after a minute, and Aiden is hovering above me with a teacher. A few kids stand to the side and look at me like a freak while most others glance down as they walk by on the way to homeroom.

From somewhere above: "Landry trying for coma number two."

And also: "That was literally super insensitive."

Hadlee stands off to the side. I can't see her, but I can feel her there.

"You all right?" the teacher asks, holding out his hand.

"Yeah," I say, rubbing the back of my head before grabbing it so he can pull me to my feet. "I'm sorry."

"Nothing to be sorry about, but I think you should take a trip to the nurse's office. I'll walk you down there."

I shake my head and tell him I'll be okay. Hadlee is behind the crowd as the few people who stopped walk away, chattering. Travis steps in our direction and mouths something I can't understand before abruptly changing course.

What?

The teacher pats Aiden on the shoulder. "See to it he gets there okay?"

Aiden responds, but my ears are ringing, so I can't make it out. I pick up my books and start to walk away. But before I round the corner for a new hallway, I look back and Hadlee has her camera pressed to her face. There's no flash, but I can tell she's taking my picture.

When she's done, she lowers it to her side and flicks her free wrist in a wave only I can see. I flick mine back.

Talk to you later, too.

The rest of the day is uneventful until track practice after school. Hadlee, true to her word, treats me like she always has. Aiden, as usual, offers up different ways to win her over. I wasn't expecting much by the time practice came.

We do our usual routine, just like before meets:

- Dynamic Warm-up: (to prevent cramping/injury)
- 800m jog
- Toe, heel, inside & outside walks
- 20m lunges
- Walking hamstring, quad & butt stretches
- Light, high knee & power skips
- Side swipes
- Stride out
- Etc.
- Coach Odis's pep talk (brief)
- Run your butt off (self-explanatory)
- Cool off (necessary)
- Go home (also self-explanatory)

Coach Odis doesn't say anything new this time around besides describing the upcoming track meet on Friday. We talk briefly about the meet we had last week, our times and what to focus on to prepare and improve. Usually, this late in the season, practices are lighter than in the beginning.

The team is divided by events, so we head off with the long-distance runners to the edge of the grass, by the goalpost.

Coach Odis wraps his hands over the clipboard. The sunlight reflects off the whistle dangling around his neck. "You know the drill, boys. One hour. Only stop if you absolutely need to. Three meets left this season. Let's make 'em count if we want State." He nods to our captain. "Travis will lead you guys along the trail behind the school and end on the track. Everyone stay together and keep an even pace. Focus on endurance today, not speed." He points to me. "Word, Landry, before you start."

I swallow a knot in my throat but follow him off to the side as Travis begins some motivational speech that he doesn't really care about or believe in. His eyes shoot daggers before turning back to Connor and the other guys.

I'm not even sure why I continue to do track. Coach saw me running one day after school to catch the bus when I was late. He said I was a natural, and I've always loved running at night, especially when Mom and Dad are asleep. It calmed me when nothing else did. Still does.

But you do enough running when you sleepwalk, don't you?

Coach leans up against the fence that closes off the track. I stand there in my red shorts and yellow tank top. Past him, sitting in the bleachers, Aiden hovers over a binder doing what appears to be homework. Hadlee is a few rows down. She has her camera, snapping photos. Somewhere behind the bleachers, a whistle and shouting voices echoes on the wind.

Coach Odis scratches an itch on his head. "I don't give praise often. Don't like it. Never did. Hate favoritism. Only causes problems, Landry."

He pauses, leaving me the option to respond, so I nod. "I agree, Coach."

"Good. That said, you're the most talented distance runner we have, but your race times are terrible. 9:05:42 on Friday. Stop holding back."

I continue nodding, fully aware I probably look like a bobblehead, but also not sure what he means. "I know."

"Don't know. Fix it." He points to Travis and the other runners. "You'll be a senior next year, and I'm open to new captains." He puts a hand on my shoulder and squeezes it, enough to make me wince, though I try and hide it. "You have so much potential. Whatever you have to do, do it. The next two meets are against 2A schools. They only have a handful of runners. You'll be up against their fastest both weeks, plus you'll have your teammates."

The wind picks up and gusts through my hair. I wave it out of my face. "You want me to be a team captain? If I win?"

Travis glances over our way, clearly waiting on me to begin our run.

"It's not about winning, Landry. It's about putting all you have into it and facing obstacles head on. But captain is anyone's game. You have heart, so does Travis, despite your differences. It would be good for Travis to have to cooperate with someone else, show the other guys about teamwork. I think it would be good for you too. Help you to win the respect of this team and yourself. Isn't that what you want?" He squeezes my shoulder again and motions for me to join the group by the bleachers. Coach steps into the sunlight; I have to shield my eyes to see him. "I won't tell you again that you need to push yourself more. No fear this Friday. Understood?"

I nod.

"Now go practice. No stopping, Landry. And for the love of God, eyes ahead of you, not wandering the surroundings."

"I promise, Coach."

I walk over to Travis and the other boys on the team, who are busy laughing at something.

"Please, take your time," Travis says. "Can you keep up with us today?"

"I'm fine," I say. "Let's go."

He grabs my forearm and leans close to whisper. "What was that about? You and Coach."

I shrug, not answering.

He rolls his eyes and lightly pats my cheek with his palm. "You'll never be better than me. But I welcome the challenge."

Travis walks away and starts by jogging backwards and shouting out inspirational quotes he probably stole from some movie before we all call back responses like boot camp. We run for an hour straight, Travis keeping time, and no one stops. Not even to pee or go to the water fountain. We run around the soccer and volleyball fields, then circle the school twice before running along the dirt trails to the side of the school that leads into a thin stretch of woods, which is what the cross-country runners do.

An image flashes in my mind of Mr. Day holding the dead turkey upside down, his clothes drenched in blood, the 12 gauge resting against his hip, just waiting for me in the woods, a feral growl coming from his throat despite his mouth not moving.

I can't do it—enter the trail. I shudder and run along the outside until I meet up with the other guys at the exit to the field.

By the time we reach the track again for the last eight minutes, Connor dares everyone to a race to see who can run the most laps. But before Travis can shut it down, they notice Hadlee on the bleachers; a few other bystanders have filtered in—parents ready to pick up the JV kids, boyfriends or girlfriends of some runners, and a couple cheerleaders who finished their practice already.

"She is such a slut." Connor exhales. "I heard she's got nudes somewhere on the Internet."

One of my teammates, Billy, to my left: "I wouldn't touch that with a ten-foot pole. She's probably got a cheesy pussy."

And another, Jack: "I'd rub one out to her breasts. Look at them now! Perky little fuckers. Then douse my dick in Listerine after."

Connor: "Eh, Jess's tits are bigger. Hadlee *does* have a decent ass. But she posts some emo stuff on her blog."

Ahead, Teddy: "You read that shit, you fag? It's cringe-worthy. You heard she got Suzanne's Uncle thrown in prison? Like, she doesn't even care who she hurts as long as she gets credit for it."

Travis: "We don't use the F word here or anywhere else. I'll punch you in the dick if you say it again, T."

Teddy: "Shit, sorry, Trav. Won't happen again."

Travis: "But as for Hadlee, amen to that, bro. She's a stuck-up, bitch."

He and Connor fist bump.

I want to punch every single one of them until they bleed.

I say, just above a whisper, "She's better than all of you."

No one hears.

Behind me, Mark: "Did someone fart?"

Travis: "Yeah, that was me."

Mark: "Jesus-FUCK that's terrible."

Travis: "Then move your asses so we can finish this and I can shit my brains out in the locker room."

And then rotten eggs waft into my nose, and I recoil slightly.

Damn, that's awful.

Connor: "Smells like something crawled up your ass and died."

Travis: "Yeah, it was your mom."

Travis shoves Connor, who bumps into Billy, who then head-butts Mark behind him. But somehow, we all keep running in a tight formation.

Connor: "I got a bad case of swamp ass right now."

To the right, Toby: "My balls are swinging like a goddamn pendulum over here."

As we pass the sprinters, Connor shouts: "Bunch of lazy assholes."

A sprinter: "Love you too, baby."

We all get flipped off, and even I laugh.

Travis: "ONE-MINUTE SPRINT!"

As we round a corner, I move to the inside, in line right behind Travis. But I do the one thing I know I shouldn't: I look to my right at Hadlee. Her camera is poised, but then she raises her head and stands up straight. She must know I'm watching her, because without anyone noticing, she smiles. And my heart jumps out of my chest.

Mr. Day is drenched in blood behind her, blood dripping from his canine-teeth. A hand reaches out to me, beckoning me. I shake the thought away as if it was an Etch-a-Sketch.

My shoulder knocks Travis in the back and forces him to stumble, his arms flailing, before ultimately face-planting. And then I trip over him and soar in the air before landing on my shoulders and tumbling over.

Coach Odis from afar: "EYES ON THE TRACK, LANDRY! HOW MANY TIMES DO I HAVE TO SAY IT? EYES ON THE GODDAMN TRACK, NOT THE STANDS!"

And once again, I'm a fool in front of Hadlee.

Fan-freaking-tastic.

Some of our team stops to help both of us, and Travis's watch beeps to let us know the hour is up. But as we all catch our breaths, my tank top logged with sweat, Travis shoves me in the chest. I stumble back.

"Watch where you're going."

Seeing things, Dev?

He has a scrape on his chin, and once again, I have some scrapes on my elbows. A little blood oozes to the surface.

Travis shoves me again, but then stops when Coach yells at us, storming over.

"Stay out of my way," Travis says, whispering. "I'll shatter your ankle next time."

"Both of you shake hands, walk it off, hit the showers," Coach orders, not hearing. "I don't want to hear another peep, or you can both stay and run an extra mile."

"Coach." Travis grits his teeth. "He bumped into m—"

"Not another word, Weathers. You're the captain. Shake, walk, shower."

The other runners on the team stop what they're doing. Sweat drips from my nose onto my lip, and it's salty when I lick it off.

"I'm sorry," I say.

Travis shakes his head and we slap hands. By the stands, Aiden has already gathered his books and is making his way to the exit. Hadlee just stands there, the expression on her face unreadable.

I make my way off the track, past the fence, and to the walkway leading to the school's back entrance. Aiden joins me.

"You really did resemble Superman back there. Twice in one week."

I sigh. "That must make Hadlee my Lois Lane."

"She could be your Jimmy Olson, if you wanted to change teams."

I look back, but Hadlee is nowhere to be seen.

"C'mon," I say, picking up my pace. "We'll be late for the late bus."

Aiden trots along. "Can you be late for a late bus?"

On the ride home, sore from the fall, I hold my phone and think about different ways to text Hadlee:

> *hey u*
> *wuts up*
> *guess who*
> *(random emojis)*

I settle on:

ME

i think ur a bad luck charm :-0

Almost instantaneously:

HADLEE

Are you okay?

ME

more embarrassed really

HADLEE

Stop. It wasn't embarrassing.

ME

i bet

so wut r u doing now?

HADLEE

Can I text you later? Can't really talk now.

ME

yeah, sure.

sorry

didnt mean 2 bother u if ur busy

want 2 just txt me when ur done?

I don't get a response. And after the bus drops us off at Aiden's and I walk home, I still don't get one.

Maybe last night was a fluke. Maybe she doesn't really want to be close again.

I try to put the thought out of my head, but when I go to log on at night during her regular time on her website, it shows that she's offline, and after an hour, I log off too.

By the time I go to bed in Room 13, she still hasn't responded.

CHAPTER 15

There's an empty desk in fourth period ELA on Tuesday. Hadlee's. It's two rows over and one back from mine. Mr. Jeffries stands in front of the room to start writing notes on the whiteboard. We each have a copy of *To Kill a Mockingbird* on our desks. None of what's said registers, because the unattended desk, the one without Hadlee sitting in it, serves as a beacon. My eyes are drawn to it.

As I sit here now, I can feel it. There's a stark coldness in the room, and I think everyone else can feel it too, because the class is quiet. No one speaks up or raises a hand to deliver answers. Mr. Jeffries must call on us individually to discuss the end of Harper Lee's book.

The blinds have been lowered, but rain patters against the window. Every now and then, thunder booms and lightning flashes from the cracks in the blinds, but it's mostly out-of-sight-out-of-mind. A dreary day to match my dreary mood. You can sense it in the air——the storm. The smell. The taste. It doesn't help that it's muggy, which means everyone's been sweating all day.

Ruby Reynolds sits at the desk in front of Hadlee's vacant

one. Head cheerleader, all-around pleasant person, countless friends, junior class president, one of Travis's many ex-girlfriends, and cute. Her blonde hair is tied in a ponytail, and she has on a yellow blouse with black skinny jeans and sunflower sandals. The top pushes on her breasts, making them perkier than they already are. They're glistening in the heat. She chews on gum and has her arms folded across her stomach. She must sense my eyes, because she rubs her cheek on her shoulder as if to get an itch, but cranes her neck until her gaze meets mine.

For some reason, I feel like she's too exposed. Like she needs to cover up. Too much skin.

I peel my eyes away and try to write down notes on a blank sheet in my ELA binder, but her eyes are still directed my way. It feels like forever before they focus on the whiteboard.

I sneak a look at my phone below the desk when the teacher's back is turned to see if Hadlee has called or texted, but then curse myself. Because why would she text me? It's not like we're dating after one day spent in a motel room. I'm worried, so I try again:

ME

r u ok?

is something wrong?

HADLEE

Following a lead! I'm so so so sorry, Dev! I promise I'll explain tomorrow.

ME

wut lead?

Radio silence.

Aiden and I usually sit by ourselves at a lunch table during sixth period. Most of the students eat in the courtyard outside the cafeteria when the weather is nice. Outside lunch is reserved for upperclassmen, so no one bothers us for a seat inside. Today, however, the higher-ups closed off the courtyard because of the rain, so everyone is crammed together. Aiden and I share a table with a trio of sophomores, though we don't acknowledge them. No one makes eye contact with anyone else.

A lunch monitor hovers a few tables down with his arms crossed over his chest, looking bored. Another one on the opposite side talks to a lunch lady as she carries a packet of buns. The room is bustling with voices and hushed whispers. Everywhere I look people are scrolling on their phones. Lunch today is a quiet type of chaos.

Hadlee has to be okay. I saw her less than twenty-four hours ago. There's no way she can be in any serious danger. Right?

What lead is she talking about?

Aiden dips a smiley fry into a glob of ketchup and munches on it. I stare down at my cheeseburger, but my appetite died several periods ago. It feels like freshman year all over again.

Hadlee is like a drug, and I can't kick the habit.

I force myself to drink some water.

"Don't you just love the taste of clogged arteries?" Aiden jokes. "Nothing like shedding a few extra days off my sad, nerdy little life with each bite." He picks up another smiley fry and sticks his finger into one of the eyeholes to wear it like a ring. He nibbles on it until all that's left is a thin strip of potato flesh. "You aren't eating?"

"Not really hungry."

Aiden clears his throat. "Mmm, yes. I see it. That pensive stare, the brooding look, and the stoic face. You'd make an excellent troubled teenaged heartthrob in every single teen soap ever created."

"Right."

Aiden chews off the remainder of the potato ring. "Alright, you're clearly not in the joking mood, so let's just get it out there." He wipes his hands on a napkin and takes a swig of his chocolate milk.

"It's just... did I do something wrong?"

Aiden shakes his head. "You said she was putting together some kind of collage of photos, right? Maybe she's just caught up in another one of her photography contests."

"I guess that could be true."

"It probably is."

"Am I freaking out for no reason?"

He puts a hand on my shoulder. "Listen here. I never knew her like you did, because that beautiful bitch, and I mean that in an endearing way, is all over the place. If any girl can take care of herself, I'd put my money on Hadlee. As for you, my neurotic best friend, you need to chill."

"You're right."

"Do I need to worry about this? She'll come back, and she'll be safe. Don't let this get to you, okay? I don't want to be thinking about you at the motel all alone and sad."

"I'll be fine."

"You know what they say about the word *fine*, right?"

"What?"

Aiden dips a smiley into his ketchup and pops it into his mouth. "Freaked-out, insecure, neurotic, and emotional."

A small smile spreads across my face, even if the last thing I feel is happy. Leave it to Aiden.

"I just don't want to screw things up again."

Aiden picks up his milk, thinks twice, and then puts it down. "You didn't screw anything up. It was her decision to leave, not yours."

I bite my fingernail. "It feels like there's more to it than that."

"Can I just ask why you still care, without me sounding like a jerk?"

I don't answer him, because I know he's not really looking for one.

"I get it, Dev. You were best friends for years and years. Did everything together. You had a crush, and I can forgive you for that. But she left you. Just high-tailed it Barry Allen style and never looked back. Never acknowledged you existed in that time."

"You don't understand."

"No, I do. It's you that doesn't get it." He picks up a smiley and squeezes it until potato gushes out. "She crushed you. Years ago. Ancient years ago. Unless she has a damn good reason, I really don't care *what* she has to say."

I must have a look on my face that shows my annoyance at trash-talking Hadlee because he softens his tone.

"Look, all I'm saying is, you don't need her like you think you do. You're my best friend, you're cute, lack any kind of muscle definition whatsoever, but you're good. Why else would I waste time with you?"

I smile. "So, I waste your time?"

"I'm going to be honest and say I thought you were gay when we first met."

"I know."

"But then you didn't respond to any of my flirtations."

"Which you were lousy at."

"I was a virgin in those days."

"You've had a sexual awakening in the past three years."

"You make it sound like a bad thing."

We both smirk, and the kids on the opposite end of the table look at us in disgust. One of them is about to open his mouth before Aiden shuts him down.

"What? You've never seen two men talk about the art of analingus before?"

One of the sophomores with a pimple above his lip says, "Ana-what?"

Just like that, I die laughing, water shooting out of my nose.

"That's the money shot right there." Aiden points to the mess I've made. "Giving gay men false hopes all over the world."

I reach over and grab his last smiley and shove it into my mouth, wiping away liquid from my chin. "No, just you."

Aiden blinks repeatedly for effect before shoving my arm. "Tease."

It's still raining after school, so Coach Odis tries to get us into the weight room to do some lifting, but because the football coach has most of the team in there to prepare for the upcoming season, we settle on stair training. The football kids, not to mention the entire school district and parents, think track is miniscule compared to football. Really, it's a bunch of bull.

Coach has us run up and down every single set of stairs in the building three times before allowing us a water break. It doesn't help that it's still muggy in the school, especially when they try and cut costs after hours and turn off the AC. One of the JV sprinters runs into the men's bathroom to throw up.

I hear Travis whisper to Connor, "He had milk and a cheese stick for lunch."

To which Connor responds, "Amateurs."

It's a good thing they're never around to see what YOU consume.

After we catch our breaths, Coach O'Donnell takes most of

the team to the gymnasium, which we have to split with the cheerleaders, to practice short distances. The long-distance runners stay in the hall and do more stairs running.

I'm in the middle of doing some stretches when Travis walks over. He folds his arms over his chest so the veins in his biceps and forearms bulge.

Honestly, his machismo is boring and annoying. I don't get what people see in him.

"Had an interesting talk with Coach before practice."

I don't look up. "Oh, yeah?"

He leans down. "He's putting us in all the same heats for our meet on Friday."

Now I look up, because besides the 3200m, we've never been matched in any other event. I'm not good enough to be at his talent level. "What are you talking about?"

He rolls his eyes. "Apparently, it's to motivate you to run faster. I think it's a waste, but, whatever."

I let out a breath and clear my throat. "Why do you hate me so much?"

"Cause you're a freak that doesn't belong on this team. You're not an athlete. You're a damn klutz."

"I'm sorry."

Don't apologize.

"You're lazy, Landry. You've always been lazy. You being here is a fluke, and you have no drive or heart in this, unlike some of the other guys on the team. I don't hate you, but I sure as hell don't like you. And for some reason, Coach just keeps giving you breaks and pep talks that no one else gets. It's bullshit. There's nothing special about you."

"You're an asshole."

He raises an eyebrow. "Well, look who grew a pair! Ha. You're right. I am. But hey, want to prove me wrong? Don't suck on Friday. Whether it's a 2A school or not, I want us to make it to State next year before we graduate." He puts his arms down by his sides, puffing up his chest more than seems natural. "Now try and keep up on the stairs, loser. You're our weakest link right now, despite what Coach thinks."

Travis starts to walk away, but for some reason, I can't just let him go. Can't let him just say whatever he wants and get away with it. It pisses me off. Him and his stupid undercut hair. Just because his mom is an attorney, he thinks he's above it all. He's not.

"You should stop harassing Hadlee."

He pauses. "What are you talking about?"

"You and everyone else that makes fun of her. None of you even know her."

He blinks. "And do you know her, Landry? Like, seriously. What is one single thing about her life now that you know so much better than any of us at school? She's a loner. She talks to no one. She's a snitch. No one trusts her. That's why no one likes her."

I try to think of a response but find none. He's right. I know nothing about her life now, only what her life was years ago. But that doesn't mean she's a snitch.

She couldn't have changed that much, could she?

I try to save myself. "If you do it again, I'll—"

"You'll what?"

"You'll regret it. Stay away from her or I'll hurt you."

He grins and sets the timer on his watch. "If you want to threaten me, do it on the track. You don't want to throw down with me. I'll kill you." He blows a kiss. "We'll see how tough you are then, little bitch."

From down the hall, we all line up in a single file as Travis leads the group. But as we ascend the first set of stairs, Coach looks at me, squinting his eyes. I can't tell what he's thinking, because he doesn't say anything.

Whatever it is, he's not happy.

When I get home from practice, Rosa is waiting for me in the front office with her haircut kit, as promised. I'd forgotten all about it. She must sense something is wrong, because right away she ushers me past Dad who leans against the front counter, looking over some documents. A fan is blowing in his face—he's sweaty and flushed.

I stop briefly and look at today's newspaper that's hanging off the counter ledge. The front story is of the drug bust that was on the news yesterday morning, and the photos on the story are various shots of the arrest and the culprits. I see Hadlee's name underneath given credit for the pictures.

Never ceases to be the justice seeker even in danger, does she?

Does this make her a snitch?

Mom is in the kitchen getting a glass of water, and she looks up as Rosa escorts me into our small bathroom.

"What are you up to?" she asks, stepping to the threshold.

"Giving Dev proper haircut. It getting shaggy. *Sí*, Mrs. Landry?"

"I *need* a haircut," I add.

Mom ignores Rosa and glances down at me, runs her fingers through my curls. "Your beautiful hair though, Dev. Do you really want to cut it yourself?"

"It's getting too long, Mom."

I want nothing more than for her to go away so Rosa and I can be alone. For some reason, she's not letting us do that. We've been doing this for years, to save money for how expensive going to a barber or salon is. I even do it for Dad, thanks to watching Rosa at work.

"Can I join you at least? Sounds fun, just, not too short." She points to me. "Your curls really are your best feature, you know?"

Rosa smiles after a pause. "Of course, Mrs.——"

"You can't," I say. "An artist needs her privacy." I force a laugh. "Maybe another time?"

She cocks her head at me.

I beg for her to get the hint. It must register at some point because she scrunches her forehead, exhales, and heads back to stand next to Dad. Rosa and I close the door behind us. A chair from the kitchen has already been pulled onto the tiles that face the vanity mirror above the sink. Rosa wraps me in a purple barber's gown/blanket and runs my head under the water faucet. When I sit back down, Rosa has a pair of scissors in hand and starts snipping away——using a finger to measure the length.

"*Tú madre*, she misses you."

I know what Rosa is going to say next, and she'll be right. So, I don't respond, which is all the confirmation Rosa needs. Each time she cuts some of my hair, I get chills that run down the back of my neck. It always feels good to have someone else cut your hair.

"Tell me what bothering you, *mijo*."

I tell her about what Coach and Travis each said to me and finally catch her up on everything Hadlee related. I know I can trust her.

Rosa does a sign of the cross. "*Ay Dios mío!* Now there is name I no hear in forever." She takes a comb through my hair and starts chopping the excess that sticks out the other end. "*Mi* Gabriella showed me pictures. *Chica con mucho talento.* Very talented."

"Is it weird for me to feel so bad?"

She tugs a clump of hair. "What you mean?"

"Just, you know, 'cause we haven't been friends in so long.

Does that make me a weird person that I'm upset over her forgetting about me, but then as soon as she comes back, I expect us to go back to how things were? That's not normal."

Rosa stops what she's doing and kneels next to me, brushing wet hair back from my forehead. She cups my chin. "You no bad person. You have a *corazon hermosa*. Beautiful heart. Look at everything you do for *tus padres*. What you do for me *los sábados. Tú corazon es* exactly where it should be." She touches a finger to my chest. "*Hermosa.*"

"I just feel like a hypocrite, I guess."

"*Escucha.* People fall apart every day. Friends, family, couples. Every day. The real tragedy *es* not caring. You do. It what make you special. It what make you *bueno.* That bond... it no go bye-bye. It always there." She stands straight. "That why you still care. Why you have to. Don't let that go. Not everyone *es* lucky to have it. *Bueno?*"

I try to smile, but I must be frowning, 'cause Rosa reaches into one of her pockets and produces a single Kiss. Out of habit, she places it onto my open palm, and I tear off the wrapper and pop it into my mouth. But all I can think about is if Rosa meant a bond like a friendship or something more.

"*Bueno?*"

"Only you, Rosa, would carry around a single Kiss."

"Like I said, boys... very easy to please. Just go for stomach every time. *Nunca falla.*"

"Huh?"

"Never fails."

"Gotcha. Is that how your, um, how do you say husband?"

"*Esposo.*"

"Right. Um. Is that how you married your *esposo?*"

"*Ya te dije.* Why you want to hear it again?"

"I like hearing it."

Rosa sighs and starts to cut my hair. "Short version, okay?" But she doesn't allow me to answer before continuing. "*Mi* Luis was a shy, quiet boy. *Mi madre* and *padre* worked for his *familia*. Big house—fancy fancy." She makes a wide gesture with her hands for emphasis. "I work with them on weekends outside of schooling."

"Like us, right?"

Rosa stops what she's doing and smiles in the mirror. "*Sí.* When I see him first time, I know I loved him. His short hair, dark eyes. Strong, hm... *jawline.* How he hunch when walk. He never came up to me. You see, back then, it was *malo* to talk with help, you see. His *padres* never approve of us. But I always knew he liked me. He follow me around house. Offer to help when his *familia* no around."

"So, you started leaving him chocolates?"

"*Sí.*"

"And then he came around?"

"Then he leave me long love notes in places only he knew I look. So, I leave him food."

"*Comida?* Food."

"*Sí. Comida.*" She takes a breath. "And he start buying me these sexy clothes——"

"Rosa!"

"*Qué?*"

I laugh, despite a very disturbing image coming to my mind. "True love."

"*Sí.* True love, *mijo.*"

Rosa kisses the top of my head and spits a few strands of my hair that get stuck to her lips. I laugh, which causes her to as well.

"And then you guys ran away together?"

Rosa catches her breath and gets back to work. "Back then, all we had was secret. It was shame to his *familia*, and *mis padres* would never approve. When we old enough, we ran away together."

"*Juntos?* Together."

"*Sí. Juntos.*"

"And your parents never spoke to you again?"

"No. His *padres* cut him off. Mine... well." She looks at me with somber eyes. Always the same expression when this comes up. I don't know why I ask. "*Tus padres* love you. Don't forget that. This life *es* no perfect, and *es* no what I want for you if you were *mi hijo*. But *tus padres* do everything they do for you."

"Did your parents want this life for you, Rosa?"

She clears her throat and busies herself. "No."

It gets quiet—the few times Rosa doesn't have anything to say. I go to apologize, but Rosa changes the subject.

"You remember what I told you last week when I gave you Kiss?"

It takes me a moment to remember what she's talking about, but then it comes back. "Secrets?" There's a knot in my stomach.

"You tell me if something wrong. *Sí?*"

I force myself to swallow saliva. "Of course." I don't usually lie to Rosa. Never, in fact. It's not something I like, that feels comfortable. I still haven't told her that I woke up in the woods again on Saturday night. For some reason, I just know only bad will come if I bring it up.

"You won't tell Mom or Dad, will you?"

"You think I want lose job?"

We both laugh. She pretends to zip her lip and throw away a key.

"*Hermosa*," I say.

"*Qué?*"

"Hadlee. She's *hermosa*."

"*Sí.*" She smiles, almost pityingly. "*Muy hermosa.*"

"I just don't understand why they hate her so much."

She gets still. "You ask. Maybe they tell."

"Why, what do you know?"

We lock eyes in the mirror.

"Head straight before I cut ear off." She takes a deep breath. "*Tus padres* don't tell me nothing. But I hear things here and there. Thin walls." She pounds on the wall for emphasis. "You come to *mi casa*, talk to *mi* Gabriella. She make you enchilada."

I roll my eyes. "I love you, Rosa."

What does she know, Dev?

"*Te quiero.*" She stares at me for a while before peeling her eyes away. "She come back home. That girl always look for trouble. Always look where shouldn't be."

"Hadlee was?"

"*Sí.* I loved Hadlee. Very sweet, but she type that will always find herself in middle of trouble." She mutters under her breath in Spanish. "And you, *chamaco*, were always there to help. Weren't you?"

It's awkward for a while.

We finish the rest of the haircut in silence. But the message is clear.

Rosa is telling me to be careful.

CHAPTER 16

Hadlee hasn't posted anything new on her website, which is bizarre. There's always new content, even if only once per day, but nothing new since Sunday night. No webcam either. My phone is playing "Tossin' and Turnin'" by Bobby Lewis when I lay down for bed in Room 13. But I can't sleep, like my phone just knows the perfect song each time I'm in this place.

My pillow isn't fluffy enough.

My sheets are too hot and too cold at the same time.

The red light outside my window that blinks on and off is both distracting and not.

The clock reads 9:37 p.m. and Already Tired-Past-Death, simultaneously.

I want to roll over on my stomach, but I can't sleep face-down ever since the accident. It always makes me really dizzy, so I'm forced to sleep on my back every night.

Pacing doesn't help, so I hop to the floor to do some crunches and pushups, but realize how much I hate doing both, and rip the buds out of my ears and toss my phone on the bed.

My breaths are heavy. I'm sweating.

The black sweatpants on my floor still look relatively fresh, so I take off my shorts and put them on. It's a cool night, so I also grab my green Asics and a yellow hoodie from track and sneak outside the bathroom window.

I need to run.

My breath condenses in the chilly June air. I make my way around the back of the building where the laundry shack is, take a running start, and catapult myself over the wooden fence to the outside. There's no destination in mind. No objective. I just run, heading west.

I pass run-down houses on either side—past a few vacant lots, the looted gas station, and the trailer parks. The image of Hadlee bending down to find the bruise marks on Sadie's neck from that day flash in my mind. The girl probably never sold lemonade again after that. I haven't seen her since. Like she just disappeared.

Past the trailers is the dirt trail that leads behind the lot to the opening of the woods. I stop, catching my breath. Rooted in place, there's something evil about it. Going inside, you might never come back out.

"Down the rabbit hole we go."

The scar on the back of my head seems to tighten and recoil. My legs decide it's time to go, so they make their way east, past our motel and past Aiden's house. They keep going faster and faster. Picking up speed. The faster I run, the better I feel. The air burns my lungs and rips through my new hair. My feet pummel the pavement below as I follow the white lines marking my path, count my strides and how often my feet strike the ground.

Coach Odis's voice:

"It's about facing obstacles head on."

Hadlee's:

"What do you remember?"

Rosa's:

"Always find herself in middle of trouble."

I have no clue how fast I'm running, but my hamstrings are on fire. There's no food in my stomach. Nausea. Vision blur. Arms pump back and forth.

The dark thing is behind me again. From the woods. I can't look back. To do so is to invite it in. I run harder to leave it behind, the nothingness.

Faster. Faster. Faster.

1 2 gauge
Broken glass
Olive-green pill

Faster. Faster. Fasterfasterfaster.

My insides are rotted, gutted. Empty. So empty. Unclean.

You deserve this.

My entire head feels like it's about to crack, and I think I'm crying, but I can't be sure. I can't stop. I don't know how. If I just keep pushing....

"Hold her down."
"Let her go!"
"Hadlee RUN!"

A piercing ring shatters the inside of my skull. My thumb has been scratching the scar raw, and before I know it, my pace slows, knees jerk, and I come to a light jog before dropping down to rest. My eyes burn as I cry and attempt to recover my breath at the same time. Oxygen can't get to my blood, and before I know it, I'm throwing up on the side of the road.

Down the neighborhood, a cat screeches. Around me are middle-class houses. Hadlee's neighborhood. I hadn't realized I'd come this far; it's a thirty-five-minute run.

What the hell was that?

I spit out leftover acid from the vomit, dry-heave twice, and stand up on shaky legs. Hadlee's house is four down on the left. Past the house with the uprooted tree stump, the one with the basketball hoop and rotted chain net, the one with the freaky lawn gnomes, and the one with a pile of chopped firewood by the garage door.

Some things never change.

And then it's like my feet are rooted to the ground. I can't move.

Dev, what the hell is wrong with you?

It takes a moment to gather myself again, but I do.

Hadlee's house is next. The front porch light is on, and there are four cars in the driveway. Everyone is home. The grass has been cut recently. There are three black garbage bags full of the cuttings on the side of the porch.

A thought comes into my mind to run into her backyard and climb up the American sycamore to her balcony, like we used to do in middle school. I'm in her backyard before I even realize I'd made a decision. It's dark, and I have no flashlight, so I edge along the siding of the house for support. The cat from down the street screeches again followed by a barking dog. My hair is matted to my face, so it feels nice when a gust of wind cools my flushed cheeks.

I can't make out much in the dark as my eyes try to acclimate, but there's the outline of the shed in the back-right corner behind the trampoline. Though I can't see it, her mom's garden is still there. I can smell the spicy, sweet tang of her oregano plants.

The American sycamore is right below Hadlee's window. The light is off.

It's now or never. Make a choice.

The tree has a few low-hanging branches that I'll need to climb up before jumping onto the balcony for her window. I've done it so many times, it's child's play. Some things, no matter how long it's been, just never go away.

Taking one last look around the backyard and the neighboring houses to make sure no one is watching, I leap and grab hold of a branch. I hoist myself up with my elbows and use my feet to walk up the trunk until I'm slung over the branch. I do it again to the next branch, and the next one, occasionally stopping when the branch quivers too much with the weight. It's not long before I'm high enough to touch the bottom of the balcony on the second story. I try to climb one branch higher and wrap my legs around the base. I hug it from the bottom and start to shimmy across it, like a monkey, until I grab hold of a few rungs of the balcony.

When I feel confident, I get enough momentum to swing my body over the top of the branch, steady myself, and slowly stand up. The branch quivers, and a few rogue leaves fall to their demise below. But I don't feel any fear or trepidation. Just excitement. The thrill of it all.

Sucking in air, I lean into the balcony and hoist myself on the railing until I flip over and land on my hands. Brushing myself off and standing to my feet, I look down at the lawn, like I'd do on many summer days and nights before high school. The tree and the dark obscure any view to my left, but from up here, I can see the tops of a few houses, and the in-ground pool of the next-door neighbor's. No one is outside, the pool cover is off, and I can hear the filter click on.

Like nothing ever changed at all.

I reach into the pockets of my sweats to pull out my phone to text Hadlee but realize it's still at the motel.

Genius, Dev. Truly brilliant planning on your part.

Even though it's beyond creepy, my heart pounding, I attempt to open the white door. It's unlocked. The door doesn't creek on its hinges, but a white curtain billows as the wind rushes in. Her room inside is dark. I place one foot inside, past the threshold.

Congratulations. You're now breaking and entering.

"Hadlee?" I whisper. "You awake?"

There's no response.

"Haddy?"

Still nothing. I take a step further into her room when something hard bashes me on my left knee. Pain instantly shoots up my thigh and down my shin. My leg crumbles to the ground as something else bashes me on the nose. There are stars followed by little black dots. When the bedroom lights flick on, it's like I've seen light for the first time. Everything blurs out of focus, and my eyes shut on instinct. It burns.

Some unintelligible words escape my mouth, but a coppery liquid drips on my tongue. I must be bleeding from somewhere.

It hurts so damn bad.

"Who the fu—?" Silence. "Dev?"

More guttural sounds. More blood drips into my mouth. It's coming from my nose.

"Jesus, Dev. What the hell are you doing?"

I feel her hands cup my cheeks. There's a ruffling sound and then a tissue is pressed to my nose, catching the blood.

Brilliant. You fool.

"Tip your head back. Did I hurt you? Are you okay?"

"Ust erfect." I give a thumbs up and open my eyes. Wait for them to adjust.

The room comes back into focus, and Hadlee closes the balcony door behind me, locking it. She proceeds to her bedroom door and creaks it open, pokes her head out to look either way down the hall, then closes and locks it. The end of the tissue is soaked with blood, so I pull it out and crumple up a clean end.

"Do you know what time it is?" she asks.

"No. I left my own at the otel."

She shakes her head, scrunches her forehead, which makes her eyes sad. "You sound silly with that up your nose."

"I ink you oak it."

"Take it out and talk normal please." There's an amused tone in her voice.

I do what she says. "I said I think you broke it."

"Let me take a look."

She sits down on the floor next to me. She's in bee-stripped sweats and an oversized tie-dye shirt that contrasts the bright yellow of her pants. Her hair is in a ponytail.

Around the room, it's both just like how I remembered and yet not at all the same. Her bed, which once faced out from the left wall, now rests alongside the right. She has two tall dressers against the wall next to the bedroom door that are topped with various trinkets and stuffed animals that have been there since we were kids. The carpet is still the same cream color, but the walls are different. Once light blue, they're now black. The walls are adorned with photography. Different pictures. Some I recognize from her website, some I don't. Some are hand-sketched drawings. Through all the nights staring at her with the grainy resolution on the cheap Wi-Fi at the motel, I never noticed how much it had changed.

Her iMac rests on a desk across the room from her bed. There is also a MacBook there with what looks like some kind of lens kit for her camera. There are strewn clothes everywhere, printed photographs piling like junk on her computer desk and falling to the floor.

Hadlee takes the tissue out of my nose, not even caring about the blood, and inspects my head. Tilting it one way or another to catch the right angle of light. She goes to touch it, but I wince.

"I don't think it's broken," she says.

"What did you hit me with?"

She smirks. "Kicked you in the knee to debilitate you, then elbowed you in the nose to stun you."

"You didn't have to go all Chuck Norris on me."

"I thought you were breaking and entering!"

Oh hell! A laugh bubbles up. "Touché."

She lets out a single giggle, letting her hands drop to her lap. The pain has mostly subsided, but my knee and nose still throb. There's an awkward silence where we look everywhere but at each other.

I point around. "This is a lot different than I remember."

"A lot of things are now."

I tongue my gum-line. "Is everything okay? You kind of disappeared after Sunday."

She nods. "I figured we would do more chit-chat, honestly."

"I'm past small talk."

"Touché."

"Well?"

Hadlee sucks in air and holds it in her cheeks while she ponders. She stands up and motions for us to sit on her bed, so I do, even though walking hurts. I'm going to be screwed for tomorrow's track practice and the meet on Friday.

She scoots on the bed so we both have enough room to tuck our feet under our legs. I cringe.

"Did you run here?" she asks.

"Yeah."

Hadlee brushes some of my hair off my forehead.

Chills.

"You cut your hair." She breathes out through her nose, and I feel it graze my cheek.

"It was getting shaggy."

"I like it." She drops her hand.

"You do?"

"Mmhmm."

I clear my throat. "Stop changing the subject."

She grins. "Just wanted the small talk before we got down to it."

Hadlee's face turns serious.

"Do you remember the pictures I showed you last time?"

A cherry in a pit of plums.

"Of course."

"That's the lead I was following up on."

"I still don't understand. Is it for a school project or a new contest or something?"

Hadlee fidgets with her hands and looks at her lap. "Have you thought anymore about them? Looked at them since?"

"Once, after you updated your website."

"And?"

I shrug. "I don't know what I'm supposed to get."

She bites her lip, then slides off the bed and over to the pile of printed photos topped on her desk. She rifles through a few and walks back over, a scent of lilac coming with her.

"What about these two?"

I take the photographs from her, careful not to leave any thumbprints on the surfaces. One is a black and white voyeuristic shot of two hooded men in an alley in the midst of throwing punches. One has a jagged beer bottle in his hand, the other a handgun of some sort. But the alley doesn't look like any found in Brook Meadows. Not unless she traveled a town or two over.

It makes me shudder. Not just the thought of the man holding the gun, possibly ready to commit a crime, or the fact that Hadlee took this photo mere yards away. It's the broken beer bottle. How its jagged edges seem to catch a fraction of the light from an out-of-focus streetlamp behind them. Like the teeth of a piranha.

The second photo, the most disturbing 'cause I can't tell if it's real or staged, is a pair of eyes. There are green leaves around the eyes, and the outline of a head. But the light from the camera only highlights the two eyes. Open wide. Staring just past the lens as if seeing something horrible. Something macabre. They are dark brown and bloodshot. The person is hiding inside some kind of bush or shrub or something.

What are they looking at?

My scar throbs again, so I have to look away.

It's me. Like the eyes in the photo are somehow alive and sentient and searching for me.

I don't like to be watched.

"What do you think?"

I crack my neck to try and control the anxiety I feel coming on. I get off the bed and start pacing back and forth.

"They make me feel weird."

Hadlee gathers the photos in her arms and presses them to her chest. "Good."

"What do you mean good?"

"It means they're doing what they're supposed to."

"Giving me anxiety?"

"Think, Dev. What do you feel?"

"Down the rabbit hole we go."

I stop pacing, but the pain in my head feels worse. I'm dizzy, and Hadlee must sense this 'cause she takes my hands and squeezes them. Enough to level me a bit and drown out the pain. She massages my knuckles, and we sink to the floor until she's caressing my back, and my head is cradled on her shoulder.

My body stiffens.

"It's okay," she whispers. "I'm here."

Tears escape my eyes out of nowhere, so I wipe them on her shirt. "I'm sorry. I don't know why I'm being so pathetic right now."

"You're not pathetic."

"Yes, I am."

She cups my chin and raises my head.

"You're not."

My eyes drift to her lips. How smooth and supple they look. I can still remember how they felt and tasted when pressed against mine. It would be so easy to just lean in now and—

But that's how last time got so screwed up.

Hadlee scoots closer. "Are you happy, Dev?"

I remember she asked me the same thing Sunday night right before she left. For such a normal question, it seems so odd, yet intimate.

"Right now, yes."

Hadlee's lip twitches. I wish I had it in a constant loop on camera to replay how cute and perfect it was. We raise our hands in the air and interlock them. I get tingles all over my body.

Her voice is barely audible. "What do you remember?"

I push a lock of her chestnut hair behind her ear.

"I remember you."

My heartbeat increases, and somehow, I don't know how, I can sense that she's holding her breath. We don't look away, and the pulse in her palms quickens. I can tell 'cause they've moved to my cheeks. Heat emanates from them, making my entire body weak. I couldn't move from this position even if I wanted to, and I can tell that she can't either.

But then something happens. My hands make their way around to the back of her neck, massaging it, and she closes her eyes. Her lips part to release a breath, and I lean in closer. Hadlee's body quivers and she falls back, me with her, until we're lying on the floor. I don't know what's happened, but something just feels... *familiar*.

"Hadlee?" Breathless.

"Yeah?" Barely a whisper.

"That time we kissed in the woods...."

She swallows, trembles. "Yeah?"

"It was the first time I've ever kissed anyone." I'm so nervous, so erratic. I'm crazy. This is crazy. But I can't stop. "I haven't done it with anyone since."

She doesn't respond, and we both lie still. Her eyes closed, mine willing them to open and look at me. My heart is pounding so hard I'm afraid she can feel it. See how nervous I am. But I continue anyway.

"You were my first and last kiss."

When she opens her eyes, it's like everything stops. Everything. Neither of us does or says anything, and I'm not sure how she's taking it. We're stuck in this weird limbo where time might be speeding up and slowing down at the same time. Then her legs wrap around my waist and force my hips into hers.

We haven't even kissed yet. I'm almost afraid to. But her skin is so soft. So beautiful. I could look at her forever. I've wanted this forever. I never want to kiss anyone else ever again. I'd be content to let Hadlee claim it. Own it. I would be hers if she'd have me again.

Her hands travel up and down my back. We're stuck in some weird kind of foreplay, neither being the first one to initiate. Maybe she's afraid too. Then her hands travel under my shirt and touch the skin of my back.

I'm frozen again.

"No," she moans.

Then she stops. Hands drop. Legs fall. Feet tuck up and push against my chest. My body flies into the balcony door causing a loud *BANG.*

Pain shoots up my back, and when I open my eyes, Hadlee is crawling away from me until she's pressed to the closet door on the opposite side of the room. I don't move. Don't blink. Don't swallow. The hair on my neck stands on edge.

"No. Nonono."

Hadlee's knees tuck into her chest and palms press into her eyes until she starts crying. Sobbing. My stomach sinks. The worst feeling in the world.

What the hell is happening?

I've ruined it again.

I start to make my way to her, and she must hear it when my shoes scrape over the carpet.

In between her sobs: "Don't."

I freeze, swallow. "A-Are you——"

There's a knock on the door as the knob jiggles.

"Hadlee?" A gruff voice calls out. Her dad's. "What's going on in there?" More knocking. "Why is this door locked?"

Shit! Shitshit!

Hadlee drops her palms, just as freaked as me. Tears stream down her face, fumbling for words to say or things to do. We're both dead. *So* dead.

From outside: "What in the heavens?" Her mom's voice, dazed.

Mr. Morgan: "It's locked. She's not answering."

Mrs. Morgan: "What was that loud noise?"

Mr. Morgan: "I don't know. I——" Forceful jiggling and

knocking. "Enough of this, Hadlee Renee. You're being a brat, dammit. Say something or I'm kicking it down."

Hadlee springs into action, jumping from the floor to the balcony door and unlocking it for me. She doesn't have to say anything more for me to get the hint.

Mr. Morgan: "Is there someone in there?"

Mrs. Morgan: "I'm going back to bed."

Mr. Morgan: "You better open up this goddamn door right now. There better not be a boy in there. So help me God, I'll—"

"No, Daddy. Just a bad dream."

Despite the circumstances, hearing Hadlee still call Mr. Morgan "Daddy" strikes an odd chord with me.

Mr. Morgan: "Don't make me come in there, or you'll pay for a new door."

Mrs. Morgan: "Lower your voice, Mel. I'm going to sleep. Let her be."

Mr. Morgan: "You want to raise our daughter to be a slut?"

"I said I was having a bad dream, just shut up already!"

There's more words shouted between them, but I don't hear them, as I jump off the balcony and land on a branch of the tree, somehow hooking my arm on the thick end of it to avoid falling to the ground. I manage to shimmy back down in the same manner as I made my way up. When I reach the ground, her balcony door has already been shut, the curtains pulled. I don't stay long enough to see if we got away with it.

A light comes on in a window to their dining room, right below Hadlee's balcony. I freeze, terrified that I've been caught. But when hands pull back the blinds, I see a girl. She has straight chestnut hair down to her breasts, a small nose, and close-set eyes. Pale skin. A purple lily tucked behind her right ear. She's younger, and so familiar. And then I see the silver bracelet around her wrist. The one Hadlee gave her for her eighth birthday when we were at the roller rink.

Maggie Morgan.

Hadlee's little sister.

I'm hypnotized. I haven't seen Maggie in over three years. She looks so... grown up.

She just stares at me, blinks. I do the same. From outside, I can hear muffled shouts floating from Hadlee's room. It sounds bad. Really bad. Like nothing I remember at all.

A hall light turns on behind her. Maggie jerks her head over her shoulder and then back at me. She waves. I wave back. And there is an inherent sadness in her eyes I don't remember being there.

Fuck, Dev. What the hell has happened to this family?

Maggie motions for me to go, one palm pressed to the window. I don't need any more encouragement. My feet pound the pavement as I run back to the motel, back to the safe and familiar and normal. My knee is killing me.

I can't help the images of Hadlee recoiling back from me so fast, as if the sight or touch of me sickened her. Scared her.

It's not long before I'm out of breath and back to the outside lot. I hop over the wooden fence, making my way back to the Room 13 window. And then as I pass the pool, I hear it again:

"Landry!"

I turn—look up and down. No one.

Tightening up, I quicken my pace to crawl back through the window. Afraid someone will grab my ankles and pull me back out at the last minute.

Once I get settled in, I check my phone but see no new texts or calls from Hadlee. I fall back on the bed, trying to catch my breath.

First the weird images while I was running, then the disturbing pictures from Hadlee. How angry her dad was. How sad Maggie looked. It's too much. Like something I should know but don't.

I don't think I want to know.

But the thing that upsets me the most was how Hadlee scurried away so fast the moment our skin touched. Like it was something so taboo and disgusting and bad.

Of course.

I swallow a lump in my throat as it hits me.

Something bad *did* happen. To Hadlee. Maybe that's why I can't remember. Maybe that's what she's been trying to tell me all along. Why she can't seem to just say the words out loud herself. She's trying to get me to figure it out.

Something terrible happened.

And either I need to be the one to figure it out. Or....

I'm the one who caused it.

CHAPTER 17

I ATTEMPT TO LOG BACK ONTO HADLEE'S LIVESTREAM when I can't settle my mind or fall back asleep. It's 2:37 in the morning.

When her page loads for chat, an error comes up saying the URL is unable to be accessed or loaded.

After two more attempts, even re-loading her entire website and rebooting my MacBook, it's the same.

Her website must be temporarily down.

Or she disconnected her server.

CHAPTER 18

I wake up a half hour earlier than usual on Wednesday. My mind is still reeling from the night before—unsure what exactly to make of it. What this will mean for me and Hadlee when I see her again. *If* I do. Maybe she'll ignore me. Her page still isn't working in the morning.

I text Aiden and decide to head over to his house early to talk about it.

When I get inside my "fake" room and look at the mirror in my wardrobe, there's a faint bruise on my nose. I go to touch it, but it stings, and my knee is still sore, though not as painful as last night. I can't fully extend it without wincing, but it's not swollen which is good. Coach is still going to kill me.

If Mom and Dad see this, they're going to freak and keep me home. The last time I got a cut when I tripped in the parking lot, Dad kept me home for two days. He's insane.

After I throw on some clothes in my fake room, I walk to the front office and see Dad hunched over the front counter staring off to the left. He doesn't acknowledge me when I come in.

"Good morning, Dad."

Nothing.

Without waiting for him to question why I'm up earlier than usual, I exit the front doors, half jog and half limp across the lot, and make my way to Aiden's. Halfway there, I realize I forgot to get breakfast. I jog-limp back to the motel to get something from the vending machine. I haven't eaten since lunch at school yesterday. I'm starving.

Your knee is REALLY messed up.

Walking back into the front office, Dad is still staring off into space. Still hunched over the counter. He hasn't moved an inch. I stop in my tracks; a sense of unease permeates the air. Even now, with me here, he still doesn't acknowledge my presence.

"Dad, you okay?" He doesn't respond, so I step closer. "What's wrong?"

I force out the first thought that comes to mind, not willing to even consider it long enough to percolate in my head. I give him a tap on the arm, but when he doesn't move, I shake his shoulder as hard as I can. Dad jumps up as if I'd poked him with a lightsaber. He yelps and curses out loud, clutching his chest and breathing in shallow repetition. His face is red and sweating, which it wasn't doing before when he was, what? Asleep? In a trance?

My heart, like my mind, is soaring.

"Jesus, Dev! You scared me half to death, son."

"I-I'm sorry."

He breathes in, expanding his chest, and holds it before the exhale. "No, it's not your fault," he says, breathless, like he'd been running. "Just... don't do that ever again. Okay?" There's a sternness behind his words. Almost a finality. I can't do anything except nod and avert my eyes.

"Were you sleeping?"

Dad gives me such haunted eyes. I want to wrap him in a hug, but before I can do it, he embraces me first. Pulls me right into his body until my face presses into his chest. I wrap my arms around him.

"I love you, kid." He pulls back. "I adore you and your mother more than you guys can ever know."

For some reason, I'm nervous. "I love you too, Dad."

He pulls me closer one more time before breaking away, like what we're doing is taboo. "I think I need to use the—" He points to the bathroom. "Can you just—?"

"Sure."

He throws on a restrained smile. "I'll be back in a couple minutes."

Dad trudges over to the bathroom and closes the door. I don't realize my hand is shaking when I get the keys and open the vending machine.

What the heck just happened?

When I get out a packet of Pop Tarts for me and Aiden, I also grab cheese crackers. Even though they're terrible for you, they were always Dad's favorite. Maybe they'll calm him down. When I get a packet of the crackers, I walk behind the counter to place them and the keys on top of Dad's documents so he'll see. But when I take a closer look, they're not his taxes.

They're names. dates. Meeting locations. Rory's name is on here.

What the hell is this?

Then I notice it on a shelf below the front counter.

The prescription bottle. Addressed to Dad.

He is still in the bathroom, so I pick it up carefully and look at it.

Dofetilide.

I pull out my phone to snap a picture of the prescription and place the bottle back exactly where I found it.

When I'm on the bus, I look up the medication online, trying to find what the heck my Dad is taking that I don't know about. Why he has names and dates on a spreadsheet with Rory. I'm having trouble getting service, so I give up, cursing.

I try again when we get inside the school, but the service is too slow, and I don't see any pages related to the name that was on the bottle.

Aiden asks about last night as we walk to our lockers, but I don't tell him anything.

Hadlee freaking out when we touched. Dad taking medication. It's too much.

Too damn much.

I'm biting my nails, which is a habit I picked up when Hadlee first left three years ago. I was released from the hospital after waking up from the coma. According to my parents, I was depressed, and I didn't have any recollection of how, exactly, I'd hurt my head. I suffered night terrors, I bit my nails, and when Rosa found me in the old wardrobe in my room screaming my lungs out, my parents took me to a psychiatrist. I went on the pills, and I stopped having night terrors. Stopped the habitual nail biting.

The pills also made me numb to everything and everyone.

So, I eventually stopped those too.

And here I am nail biting again.

Hadlee is sitting next to me. It's fourth period ELA. My left leg is bouncing up and down, and there's a pop quiz on a book that I know I read but can't remember. I can't concentrate. Can't sit still. Can't look at the sheet of paper. She hasn't looked at me once the entire period, but I'm having trouble keeping eyes on my own quiz.

Dirty. Inside.

"Dev," Mr. Jeffries calls my name. The entire class looks up. "First and only warning. Eyes on your own paper, okay?"

I nod, but find my mouth too dry to form any words. I sneak a look at Hadlee, but she's diligently working on her quiz. A few kids have already turned them in up front. It's only ten multiple-choice questions. One bonus short answer question. I still can't remember the book at all.

It's like everyone, even our teacher, is in on some horrible joke. Is Dad sick? Is Hadlee okay? What was so bad that she had to quit talking to me for three damn years? Did something else happen in the woods besides us kissing? Why do her parents hate me?

Because it's what you deserve. It's your curse.

"Mr. Landry." Mr. Jeffries holds out his hand for my quiz sheet. "I gave you fair warning. I will not tolerate cheating in my classroom. You can gather your books and make your way to the principal's office. I'll let them know you're on your way."

I didn't even realize I was still looking at Hadlee. Like in some kind of daze, I gather my books and hand my quiz in.

He seems even more disappointed that I didn't even bother to fill in any answers, like I failed in the act of cheating properly.

Hadlee still hasn't looked at me as I head out of the room. She probably hates me. I don't know what I did, but I can't say I blame her.

I'm just the weird-o who lives at the motel with his broke(n) parents.

Right?

Because my "fake cheating" was a first-time offense, the principal lets me off with a very stern warning, although I will take a o for the quiz and spend one lunch in detention instead of after school.

Being on the track team can have its advantages.

When the bell rings to end the period, and before I report to my next class, I make my way to the computer lab near the science wing of the school. I log online and begin to search for whatever Dofetilide is. I'm still having trouble finding what I really need, especially because some of the sites have been blocked for security reasons on the school's servers. The more I search, the more anxious I get. The more I bite my nails.

But when I find what I'm looking for, it makes me feel worse. Much worse.

It's medication for irregular heart rhythms. To prevent people who have had or might be prone to heart attacks or strokes.

I bite my lip until I break skin, and I try to hide my face from other kids also in the computer lab. There is a window next to me facing the athletic fields. The football stadium is directly in back. Outside, the sky is gunmetal grey. It's going to storm again.

I feel my stomach churn and know I'm going to get sick. I quickly log off and run to the nearest bathroom and vomit into a toilet. But as I slump down and flush half-digested Pop Tart, I hold my hands out in front of me. They're shaking and bleeding from my thumbs.

Why is Dad taking pills for his heart? How long has he been on them? Does Mom know? Is Rory involved?

And more importantly:

Why didn't he tell me?

CHAPTER 19

Practice is a joke. It rained during seventh and eighth periods, but it's holding off for the time being. The backfields are too wet and muddy to run on, so we're all cramped on the track with everyone else. It's congested, and the team seems just as miserable. But my head isn't in it. Coach Odis can tell. Travis can tell. I keep falling behind because of my sore knee. It's not as bad as this morning, but my strides aren't even. It hurts to stretch my leg too straight.

Coach yells from the center field for me to get in the game, and Travis keeps having to slow down to match my speed and "encourage" me to pick up the pace before he runs ahead with the other guys, but usually it just ends in whispers of how terrible I am.

After our hour of running is up, I hunch over and vomit on the field, unable to make it to a trashcan. Because I haven't really eaten much, it's mostly water followed by an annoying amount of dry heaving. Throwing up, at this point, is getting really old. Coach comes over to me, and a few of my Varsity teammates help me stand up 'cause I'm having trouble doing it myself.

Aiden, who's been standing by the bleachers with an umbrella, walks onto the track to grab my arm. Hadlee isn't anywhere. I feel so helpless and pathetic.

"Can you two get him to the locker rooms?" Coach points to Travis and Aiden. "Make sure he hydrates and showers. I'll be there shortly."

Aiden nods. Travis seems annoyed but also agrees. They help me off the track until I can walk myself on wobbly legs. Maybe it's the lack of food. Maybe I need nutrients or something. But I can't stomach the thought of food right now.

Travis and Aiden help me into the locker room and fill up a bottle with water and make me drink it even when I don't want to. Travis is just standing there with his arms folded. Pissed.

I feel awkward showering, showing skin, so I take off my track clothes underneath a towel and put on my school ones instead.

"You don't have to stay here," I say.

Travis runs his hands over the stubble on his chin. "If I don't, I'll get chewed out by Coach. Don't flatter yourself."

"Well, I'm good." I trade looks with Aiden, and he seems just as annoyed as me.

"Cool the angsty attitude," Travis says. "Practice is over in a few anyways. And you were sucking hard out there. Not looking good for our meet on Friday." He nudges my sore knee with his foot. "Looks like you're injured. Have you iced it at all?"

I wince, swinging my leg away. I'm sick of hearing about this meet. About how bad I am. It's like Coach and Travis are broken records. That's all it is with them.

"I don't care, Travis."

"Excuse me?"

Aiden steps between us, holding up hands as if preventing a near-fight. "Alright you two, let's all play nice here."

"Beat it, Brumberg. You're not even on the team."

I stand up, feeling a little better, but still lightheaded. "You can't talk to him like that. Why are you such an asshole? It's like you got muscles and you're suddenly better than everyone else."

"I'm better than everyone?" Travis steps forward before Aiden holds him back. It surprises all three of us. "If I'm an asshole it's because I like this team. Our school. Our reputation. Wanting to get a scholarship out of this shit town. I care about people other than myself."

"You don't know anything about what I want or what I care about. Why do you care about a scholarship? Your mom can pay to send you to any school you want."

I don't know why I'm getting so worked up, but I can't seem to control it. I know I'm partially in the wrong, that I'm the one picking a fight. But I'm tired of being walked all over. Tired of being a punching bag for his insults.

Travis runs his hands over his face and lets out an exasperated laugh, like he's about to really whale on me. "First off, you don't know shit, Landry. Don't open your mouth until you know what the hell you're saying. Secondly, are you telling me you actually care about the team? You care about getting to know the other guys and coming to pasta dinners before meets and hanging out with people who aren't named Mom or Dad or Aiden? You'd leave that comfy motel of yours?"

"What's wrong with me?" Aiden says. "The nerdy best friend. Everyone loves that guy." He tries to alleviate some tension, but even he knows it's not working. He doesn't move from between us—still ready to take a punch if one of us throws first.

"Leave my parents out of this," I say.

"Okay, I'll leave your parents out of this if you leave mine out of it too." He shakes his head. "So, how about Hadlee

Morgan? You don't think we remember how close you guys were until she decided she was better than you?"

"Stop."

He takes a step closer, raising his voice and puffing out his chest. "I don't like you. I don't like you because you're weak, and you need to grow a pair. Coach is right. You're holding yourself back. Acting like a victim from whatever shit happened that got your head so fucked. Hadlee Morgan is a bitch, and everyone can see how pathetic you are pining after a girl that wouldn't think twice about screwing you over. She's fucked up. She's on her own personal agenda and she doesn't care who gets hurt in the process." He uses air quotations for the next part. "Her *art* is nothing but gothic, disturbing, and emo shit to get people's attention so they notice her. You think I have problems? She has problems. She talks to no one. Goes nowhere. Takes pictures of dead bodies. She's posted nudes, before her website was created. I have so many people claim they were real until she was forced to delete them. She put them out there. Why? Who knows. And she hasn't said a word about your *accident*." He taps his knuckle against one of the locker vents. "That's why people think she's weird and only in it for herself. And you chase after her. Everyone can see it."

There's no way that's real. I would've known about it.

Right?

"Don't ever say her name again, Weathers." I ball my hands into fists, spitting out his last name like it's toxic, like he does mine. "You think 'cause your dad got you buff and your mom can get you out of any trouble that you're invincible, but you're not. You're pathetic, not me."

He reaches for my shirt with his hand, his eyes burning, but I duck out of the way. "What the fuck did I say about bringing my parents into this? I'm trying to help you, like it or not."

"Guys," Aiden says, his voice tense. "Let's all cool it and

walk away. Okay? Everyone is running a little hot. We're saying things in the heat-of-the-moment we don't really mean."

"If you think we're all such terrible people and you're so righteous and innocent," Travis says, "then prove us all wrong. Show me up on the field. Prove to me that you're not a fucking freak that had to take medication."

We all stop, and even Aiden seems to take a moment to do a double-take. My past emotional issues are not something anyone talks about. Not the teachers, not Coach, not Aiden. No one. But everyone knows. Small towns.

Travis continues, proud of himself. "We just don't want you to go psycho with your psycho girlfriend and shoot up everyone in this school. That's why we don't want you here."

I push him in the chest, which doesn't really do much. "That's not cool. Don't joke about that stuff." I run my hands over my face, my anxiety flaring up. "I'm not *crazy*."

I think there's a hint of firewood in the air, which is impossible.

How could there be a bonfire here? In the middle of the day?

Aiden reaches into his pocket and pulls out his phone as a last-ditch effort. "Netflix is streaming *Firefly*. Best darn show to be canceled. And—oh hey!" Aiden lights up, waving his phone in my direction. "Max texted me back about our date!"

Max.

He gushes, but it still doesn't work.

I don't know what's been getting into me today.

Yes, you do.

"Congrats, Aiden," Travis rolls his eyes. "No one gives a shit about your love life."

Aiden holds up a hand for me to high-five. When I don't reciprocate, he takes my hand and does it for me. "Got you guys to stop fighting, didn't it?"

The sound of some of the team walking through the outside

door rings in the locker room. Immediately we all back away. Aiden and I grab our backpacks. Coach comes in to check on us, but I'm so fired up I can't even look at anyone.

Calm down, Dev. You're losing it.

"How is he?" Coach asks Travis.

I can feel it and know what's happening before I can stop it. Travis steps behind me and extends his hand. There's electricity in the air, like magnets, and the hairs on my head and forearms stand erect.

"Hold her down."

Travis's knuckles place themselves on the back of my head, his palm on my scar, and the air is sucked from my lungs. Everything around goes black. Silent. My heart stops, and my knees give out. It's like I'm dying all over again. Like I'll never know what sweet oxygen tastes like. Everything is numb, but my heart keeps jackhammering; I'm afraid I'm having a heart attack.

Crack goes my skull
Thin line of blood
Shoes dangling

Aiden is shaking me and, when I eventually come to, I'm in a fetal position. Everything that happens next goes so fast I can barely process it. I'm scared and humiliated and embarrassed. Everyone, Aiden included, is looking at me like I'm a freak. Like I will break at any moment. Maybe they're right. Maybe I am a psycho that will murder everyone.

I *do not* like being touched from behind.

Coach Odis rushes to me, helps me to my feet, and sits me on a bench. He yells for everyone to back up, which the team does.

"Landry, listen to me, look here." His voice is frantic. "I'm going to call an ambulance. You just fainted. What did you eat today? Might be from lack of food in your system."

No, it isn't.

"You could be dehydrated."

No, you're not.

But I play along with it anyway.

"I'm fine, Coach. Just dehydrated. Haven't eaten since breakfast. T-Think the exertion just took a lot out of me today."

Travis stands behind Coach and, maybe for the first time, looks guilty. Like it's his fault.

"I can't just let you go without calling an ambulance, Landry. You need to be checked out. You fainted on school premises. I'll have to call your parents too. What is their number?"

Aiden asks, "Should I go get the nurse if she's still here?"

I stand up. "I'm fine, Coach."

He tries to sit me back down, but I don't budge.

"Landry, easy. Just let me call your parents to make sure——"

Too much. Too damn much.

Before I realize what I'm doing, I'm booking it from the locker room. I hear Coach shouting from behind, some people coming after me. I run down various hallways until I get to the front doors and out to the main drop-off circle. I only glance behind my shoulder once and see Coach and Travis darting for the front doors, Aiden trailing behind. Coach's blue tracksuit swishes in the wind. Neither of them comes after me as I run past the late bus, past the parking lot, and turn onto the main road that leads back to the motel.

CHAPTER 20

The sky is almost black. Threatening. The wind howls, and raindrops begin to fall. It's going to be a nasty storm tonight.

I run the few miles to my house and enjoy the scenery as I pass, let it clear my head. It always works. Most of the area between the motel and the school is wooded. A rundown gas station sits a little way into a clearing. It's long been closed, and it's where we got the ice machine. Weeds sprout up through the cracked pavement. Past that, a single-story house resides where two kids play basketball in the driveway. They shout taunts to each other as I pass.

Before I know it, I'm running faster. Letting the air brush past my face and ears, touching my lips. I push through the burning in my thighs and calves. The motel comes by on my left, but I run past it. Not sure why or where I'm going, and then it starts sprinkling again. The wind blows my hair wild, and I have to steady myself as I'm nearly led off the road into a ditch. I'm passing dilapidated houses on either side, rundown stores that no longer operate. Heading in the direction of River Road and the trailer park. The woods.

I flash to the moment of the kiss in the clearing, and just as I do, a horn blares in front of me. Bright lights flood my eyes, and I hold up a hand in time to see a truck barreling my way. For a moment, I'm frozen in fear, wonder what would happen if I dart out in front of the truck and—

But then I shuffle my feet to jump out of the way, and in so doing, land right in a ditch.

Did you almost think of—

I get to my feet, and mud stains the front of my clothes. I cry out a little, flip off the skies as if someone were up there to see. Try to shake away the feeling in my chest and the tears I hold back.

You're cursed.

I fling clumps of mud off and start to pull myself up to the road, catching my breath. Rain patters onto the ground, blowing down in slants from the wind. Lightning crashes from beyond the tree line of the woods a little past the trailer park, and thunder claps shortly after. I inhale and get a whiff of freshly mowed grass. The rain hurts my skin, little giant balloons pummeling my body, so I run despite the pain. Back to the motel. Let the rain wash away the mud.

I turn into the motel lot and make straight for the entrance, but stop myself. I stand in an empty parking space and look into the sky, squinting to avoid getting any rain in my eye. I let the rain wash off all the dirt and let it engulf me. Consume me. I'm not sure why, it's just comforting.

Being consumed.

From the second story, Room 17, the blinds flutter, and a second later the door cracks open. Mr. Day. He peeks his head out to avoid the rain, just enough where I can see only his head and nothing behind him. He stares at me, I look away, my heart fluttering.

Like Hadlee's picture of the two eyes staring.

When I glance back, the door is shut and the curtains fully drawn. My knees shake.

Inside the lobby, Mom and Dad are sitting on the couch leaning over a deck of cards on the cheap, wooden table. Rory is sitting on his knees with a handful of cards in front of his face. A pang of jealousy. The lights are all off, but they have a few lit candles on the table. The power must be out. I stay outside in the rain for a long time, despite shivering when it gets too cold.

Maybe not too long, as Mom notices me standing there after a while and jumps to the door to call me inside. Reluctantly, I walk in.

Did Coach already call them?

My hair is completely flat, falling down to my ears thanks to Rosa's haircut. It would have been a sopping mess had I kept it longer. Mom and Dad trade looks like I'm out of my mind before she runs to the bathroom to get me a towel. Rory chuckles before playing a hand. Must be poker.

"What on Earth were you doing standing out in the rain?" Mom says, wrapping me up and rubbing my shoulders. "Are you feeling alright?" She places her hand to my forehead to feel my temperature.

"I'm fine, Mom. Just got caught in the rain running home from Aiden's."

"Why weren't you home directly after practice? The power went out, and we couldn't get service in the storm to call you."

"I'm sorry. Just got caught up at his house trying to wait out the storm." I fully expect them to call BS. They never do. And I know they'll never talk to Aiden's parents to confirm the story. 'Cause I never lie to my parents.

Never.

I feel terrible about it.

Mom either frowns or attempts to smile, I can't tell which. And Dad pushes the glasses up farther on his nose, putting down the cards in his hand. "You should've skipped practice and come home early if you were going to be late. You had your mother and me worried."

"That's just fucking stupid, Dad."

Oh no.

Dad's nose twitches. "Excuse me, young man?"

Dev! What did you just do?

"I'm sorry," I say. "I didn't mean—"

"What *did* you mean exactly?" He stands up. Full-on Pissed Off Parent mode.

Rory looks uncomfortable on the ground, so he puts his cards down and brushes his palms on the floor. He stands up and purses his lips. "Suppose I'll just head back to my room and find something to do. This sounds like a family thing, and I'm not really good with family things, you know, because then I'd feel like I was intruding and it's really none of my business, and then I'd feel bad, like maybe I was—"

"Rory?" My dad closes his eyes and sighs.

"Yes, Mr. Landry?"

Don't say his name. He's not your dad.

"No offense, son. But I think you should just keep the rest of what you're going to say to yourself and leave now." He opens his eyes. "You have an exam Friday morning if I'm correct."

Son? What?

"Correct as always." Rory snaps his fingers. "I'll just go." He points to the door before walking to it. "Catch ya later, Godfather."

Rory takes a breath and holds it in his chest before darting outside to get to his room. It's still pouring out. I'm left in the lobby with my dad's eyes burning into me.

The power outage must have prevented them from finding out.

"Apologize right now," Dad says.

"I'm sorry."

Mom shakes her head. "It's okay."

"No, it's not!" Dad storms over to the front counter. "We all have responsibilities around here. One of them is coming home on time after practice. The other is letting us know if you're going to be late. You're lucky we even let you join the track team."

"He's home now."

"That's not the point."

"It's only an hour late; it's not like he was out all night." She tightens her jaw. "Take a breath and calm down."

And I know she notices it too. This reaction from Dad. So strange and unprovoked. He usually doesn't say anything, not even when we do something wrong. Just a stern Resting Asshole Face expression and a few mumbled words. So why now, when I'm home an hour late and still in daylight, does it matter?

But that's not all that happened, Dev. Is it?

"Joanne, don't. This is how it starts. An hour late here, an hour late there. Soon he's off doing God-knows-what with God-knows-who at God-knows-where!"

Mom winces like Dad slapped her. I can tell he regrets saying what he did because they both look over at me. And it's happening again: my filter. Or lack of one.

On a roll today.

"You mean Hadlee?" I ask, barely above a whisper.

Mom and Dad do a double-take, like they can't believe they're hearing that name. In retrospect, I haven't uttered it in front of them since they put me on the pills three years ago.

"You're worried I'm going to start hanging out with Hadlee again, aren't you?"

Mom hugs herself like she's cold. "She hasn't tried to contact you. Has she, Dev?"

"Why do you hate her so much? What has she ever done to you guys? Why is her family so bad?"

A flash of lightning and a boom of thunder from outside.

Dad says, "Were you seeing that girl today? Is that why you're late?"

That girl.

"I don't understand why my falling and hitting my head means she's a bad person."

Mom's face scrunches up. "It's complicated."

"She was my best friend."

Mom looks away. "I know she was."

Dad clears his throat, but his voice is softer than I would have expected. "She hurt you, son. She's the reason you ended up in the hospital."

"She wouldn't do that," I say.

"Don't argue with me. She left you there, unconscious. Have you been talking to her?"

It's when I notice how red Dad's face has gotten. How his breaths are bigger and more rapid. I remember his heart medication. I quickly shake my head to let them know it's not true. Mom, once tense, relaxes a little, but Dad hasn't. She goes to him and rubs his arms up and down.

"Honey, look at me," Mom says. Dad does. "Breathe, relax." Mom inhales and exhales, and Dad copies her. They both do it again in sync.

He straightens his glasses. "I'm okay."

"He's home now," Mom says. "That's the important thing." She hugs me and brushes wet hair back from my forehead. She exchanges a look with Dad, and the tension leaves. Like always, she reins him in. Just like that.

He looks so adoringly at her.

"Just be careful next time," Mom says. "Have Aiden's parents drive you home if the weather is bad."

"And don't," Dad adds, "ever bring up that Morgan girl in this household. You understand, Dev? That family is dead to us, and that girl is a parasite. She was no good for you. Always looking for trouble, and look where you ended up! A coma for two weeks."

"Joe," Mom starts.

Rosa's words echo in my head. How she was always looking for trouble, and I was there to help.

Dad takes a deep breath. "I love you. I would die before I let anyone hurt you again."

You are the worst son in the history of sons everywhere.

"I'm sorry. It won't ever happen again."

Mom, floundering, adds, "To prove how upset we are, you're officially grounded."

I groan, but it could've been worse. "How long?"

Mom contemplates it before grinning timidly. "School tomorrow morning."

I grin with her. Typical Mom. Things back to normal. "You guys really are the worst."

"Terrible, strict parents. Not sure why you don't run away."

She wants me to laugh, so I hesitantly do. Mom looks to Dad for encouragement. He removes his glasses to clean the lenses.

"And you have to cook us breakfast this Saturday," he adds, grinning despite his face looking pained doing so.

I roll my eyes. "So unfair. You two are destroying my child-hood dreams right now."

Mom ruffles my hair and kisses my forehead. "Go take a shower, you smell like sewage."

"Thanks, Mom."

Dad puts his glasses back on, rolling his left shoulder as if to get out a kink. His eyelids droop a little. He just looks out of it. And I'm worried again. About what's going on I don't know.

Mom shrugs. "Maybe he should also learn how to take a

look at the pipes when there's flooding, so I can just tell him to go to a room instead of going myself?"

"Now you guys are getting carried away," I say.

"Oh, I like that." Dad rubs his palms together. "I think the drain in the shower could be cleaned out as well."

Mom suppresses a laugh. "We can make him Cuckoo Clark's personal assistant, so I don't have to bend to that man's every whim."

I shake my head. "This joke ceased being funny two suggestions ago."

Dad lets out a breathy laugh. "That won't happen. Clark won't let you go, honeybun."

"Dammit."

Dad beams. "I do, however, love the way you think, pretty lady."

Mom pats my shoulders while looking at Dad. They smile giddily like I'm not in the room. It gets awkward. They are *so* gross sometimes. I pretend to clear my throat, which knocks them back to the present moment. Mom sighs and lets go of me.

"Next time call us," Dad says. "Power outages pending. Got it?"

I nod.

Why are they pretending like nothing even happened? Like I never mentioned Hadlee at all?

After the power clicks back on, I shower, and then we eat dinner. I join them in cards—progressing from poker to Go Fish and re-inviting Rory to play with us for a few rounds. Mom heads off to bed. Rory announces he's going to bed too to get up early to have breakfast with a "cousin" of his. Probably his dealer. I walk Rory to the front door as Dad cleans up the cards.

What's he doing with Dad, though?

The power has been on and off most of the night. Still no calls from Coach. And when I get pockets of cell service, I respond to one of Aiden's million texts to let him know I'm okay.

"I thought I heard something earlier today when it was storming." Rory scans out the door.

It's still raining out. The parking lot is flooded, and the lights have been flickering on and off for hours.

"How could you hear anything with the thunder?"

Rory looks both ways, waiting for someone to jump from the shadows. It freaks me out.

"I don't know, man. Shit's creepy around here. Don't get me wrong, I wouldn't go anywhere else, but this place is fuckin' haunted, man."

I force a laugh. "You crack me up."

"I'm serious! Every time I stay here, I have nightmares and shit."

"No ghosts in your room. That's a promise. Rosa blesses the motel every now and then."

"Tell her to re-bless my room tomorrow. Will you?"

"Sure thing, Rory."

"You're good people." He smiles. "I might have Charlie coming over this weekend."

"That's awesome! So you talked to her?"

"Nope. Wishful thinking."

"Give her chocolates."

"Chocolates?"

"Chocolates." I nod. "Everybody loves chocolate."

"I hope she ain't allergic and shit. Wouldn't want her to, you know, die or whatever."

"Yeah, let's hope that's not the case. Maybe flowers or something?"

"Unless she's allergic to those too."

"Shouldn't you know these things?"

He squints his eyes. "I should. Damn. Ya see. Here I go, all prepared and whatnot to have over the girl of my dreams, and there you go bein' all Marlon Brando."

"I'm sorry."

"Nah, it's cool." He punches my shoulder. It hurts more than I care to admit. "You're good, dude." He raises his eyebrows, which makes me laugh for real. His eyes are bloodshot. "You got rid of those bedbugs, right?"

"Bedbug free." I hold my hand to my heart. "Swear it."

"Good. Say, who was that old guy talking to?"

"What old guy?"

Rory points to Room 17. "Saw him talking to someone earlier when you were in here. Weird shit, man. Conspiracy shit."

"Mr. Day was talking to someone in his room? Did you see who it was?"

Rory shrugs. "It was raining. Didn't really stay long enough to creep, yo."

What the hell? He NEVER has anyone over. EVER.

Rory nods and darts out of the lobby before I can respond again. I close the door against a gust of wind that nearly knocks me over, and I see Dad is back behind the counter. His face is red, and he's sweating.

I don't know if it's the situation with Hadlee, how her family was last night, or what happened at school or just now, but I won't just let this go. Not now. It's so out of character. So different. I never stand up to my father. Ever. I bite a nail and walk right up to him until I get his attention.

"Are you okay, Dad?"

He cocks his head like I've asked him a strange question. "Of course. Why?" He goes back to his papers.

Lightning flashes outside.

We're going to play this game, are we?

"So, there's nothing wrong?"

Dad scrunches his forehead. "Dev, I'm not in the mood to play a guessing game. Don't you have homework to do?"

I'm so nervous. I don't want to catch him in a lie. Don't want him to admit a truth I'm not prepared to handle. Is he sick? Dying?

Thunder rolls in the sky, and the lights flicker again.

I just close my eyes and come out with it.

"What's Dofetilide?"

Dad stops. A statue. My heart leaps into my throat. He doesn't look at me, like he can't face me. And there's so much tension in the room I don't know how to deal with it.

"What are you talking about?"

I take a breath and hold it in my chest. "The pills you're taking."

He raises his head, and there's something so different about his eyes that it scares me. He's terrified. Not just scared or regretful or guilty. My father is legitimately terrified.

I wish I'd never said anything. But I can't back away now.

"How did you—?"

"I found the pills." I point to the counter below. "You left them out here this morning."

He runs a hand over his face—out of words to say. The rain pattering against the roof answers for him.

"A-Are you sick, Dad?"

"Dev...."

Shit.

My mind runs with a million possibilities. "Are you dying?"

He jerks back. "What? No! I'm not!" He whips his head back, afraid we're being too loud. He leans closer and lowers his voice, tries to laugh it off. "It's nothing."

"Don't tell me it's nothing! You're taking heart medication."

"As a precaution."

"A precaution for what?"

He grits his teeth, and I feel terrible even making him tell me. But I *need* to know.

"I'm not sick, and I'm not dying. It's just stress."

"It's for heart attacks and seizures."

He blinks. "The one time you actually do your homework."

"Does Mom know?"

He doesn't respond.

"Does she?"

He whispers, "No."

"Are you going to tell her?"

He shakes his head. "Your mother has enough on her plate without having to worry about me. I'll be fine, Dev. I'm not going anywhere. It's just the upcoming summer season. You know it stresses me out with inspections and a lack of guests. I'll be back to normal and off them as soon as things pick up."

I don't like hiding things from Mom, not one bit. I could never keep something this big from her. I also don't believe him. It doesn't explain the documents with the names. "I don't think she would—"

"Promise me, Dev. You won't say anything to your mother. I'm going to be fine. Okay, kid? I love you. Come here." Dad reaches over the counter to wrap me in a hug.

I'm close to tears, but I can't cry in front of Dad. Not now. Hugging is weird enough as it is, and this might be the longest conversation we've had in as long as I can remember, but I don't want to let him go. The scent of his Calvin Klein aftershave wafts into my nose. I breathe him in and stay in his arms for a while, like it will be the last time.

"This is our secret. Just us. All right?"

We pull apart. He has one hand on my shoulder and is pleading me with his eyes. He drops his glasses to hang from his neck. And all I want in this moment is for him to tell the truth. To believe him. I just don't want to cause him more stress, and I can tell I'm doing that. If I tell Mom, and they get into a fight, and he gets more worked up, or if he thinks I betrayed him.... Plus, Mom has enough on her plate making sure the motel doesn't break, let alone Dad.

So, I do the last thing I ever want to do.

"I promise."

He forces a smile and squeezes my shoulder. "That's my man. I'll be okay. You don't have to worry about me, all right?"

"Okay." I force a smile.

I have more questions, but he won't give me the answers I need. He goes back to his papers like nothing ever happened, and I know this means that from here going forward, nothing ever did. So, unable to think clearly, I decide to go to my "fake" room and "pretend to head to bed early."

But on the way back, I can't help but think it's a bad idea. Keeping Rosa's chocolates a secret from Mom. Keeping the sleepwalking a secret from everyone. The panic and anxiety attacks. The nail biting. Hadlee's parents. How we promised not to tell anyone we were seeing each other. How Hadlee freaked out when we were together. Aiden's secret boyfriend. Keeping Dad's secret from Mom. Keeping Room 13 a secret from everyone. Mr. Day's unknown visitor. It's more than I can handle.

In a place where people come with secrets behind closed doors, why do I now have a closetful of my own?

We're all just staying in a temporary place with temporary secrets.

But that's the thing with motels: you can't stay forever.

And the thing with secrets is:

They don't stay secret forever either.

I'm not dead—

Still alive.

There is a pond here, in the clearing, where lines of shoes once dangled over.

The full moon is out, a coyote howls in the distance.

Silhouetted from the moonlight, hidden inside the underbrush

There are eyes—large, pleading. Brown.

I step up to the glimmering pond—

Lean over it—

Smell rot and sulfur—

A crunch and SNAP—

Someone calls my name—

I look into the pond to see my reflection—

Then it comes out of the water, rippling.

*A **hand** reaches out and grabs mine and pulls—*

Wish eyes would look away.

Stretching. Pain. Burning.

*The **hand** pulls me into the depths, my distorted image reflects back as I emerge—*

Disappear.

CHAPTER 21

White flash.

SNAP

Steady drip of rain onto my exposed flesh.

I awake with a jolt, as if landing from a fall. My body jerks upright, and I gasp for air. Choking.

I'm here again. The woods.

My skin is slimy. I'm sitting in some kind of muck, but something is off. Different. I'm freezing. I feel my body while my eyes adjust to the dark. My breaths are rapid and shallow.

Naked.

I'm completely naked.

I try to get up, but my ankles are caught in vines. When I fall, the sharp point of what might be a thorn or twig pierces my palm.

Tears burn my eyes. I don't even try to wipe them away as I untangle my ankles and stumble out of the mud.

When my sight adjusts, the trees are much, much thicker here. I don't recognize this place at all. When I rub my eyes, I get dirt in them, temporarily blinding me. I can't see. I'm lost. I'm alone. I'm naked. This has never happened before.

SNAP

There're crunching footsteps behind me.

They're coming for you, Dev.

Snot runs from my nose. I use the crook of my elbow to clean my face. In the distance, a coyote howls at a moon I can't see through the canopy of trees. The same footsteps from before echo and reverberate all around me. Bouncing off the tree trunks.

"Leave me alone!"

Out. I want out. I don't want this anymore. Normal. Why can't I be normal?

The footsteps suddenly stop, but then I hear breathing. Behind me. Another white flash that blinds me in the dark.

I try to run, but my feet are rooted like cement.

Here is where you die.

And then I hear it. A whisper:

"Dev."

It chills me to the bones.

I cover up my exposed parts, my skin, crying harder. "Please just leave me alone."

The thing behind me takes a few steps closer until hot breath coats the back of my neck. They step around me, coming into vision. I close my eyes, not wanting to see whatever evil has followed me out here. Because if this isn't a dream, then nothing good can be out in the woods this late at night.

Hands place themselves tenderly on each side of my face. Warm palms make my body shiver. Teeth chattering. But they're so tender. So soft and delicate. Breath exhales and melts my chilled face. There's a hint of lilac.

"It's okay," they whisper. "I'm here."

And I know that voice. I open my eyes and see her. The person who's been following me. Maybe she was there the last two times. Maybe more times than that. Maybe she never left.

"Hadlee?"

She's standing in front of me. Tears in her eyes, holding my face. She has on a spring jacket, her hood up. There is a blanket slung over her shoulder, and she wraps it around me. Covers me. Her camera is slung around her neck in a waterproof pouch.

I reach out to stroke her hands, her arms. Let them travel to her face. She closes her eyes and lets out a sigh. The rain on her pale skin makes her look almost luminescent.

I don't understand what's happening. How or why she's here. Why she brought a blanket like she knew I'd need one.

But she's here. For me. With me. I'm not alone.

Maybe I never was.

She wraps her arms around me. "Let's get you home," she whispers.

"I–I don't know where I am."

Hadlee holds out her hand for me, steps forward. "I'll keep you safe. Do you trust me?"

Without a second thought, I interlock my hand with hers. Squeeze tight.

"Forever."

I'll follow her wherever she'll take me. Traveling in the dark. Traveling toward light.

Traveling toward freedom. Together.

THINGS THAT HAPPEN BEHIND CLOSED DOORS

PART FOUR

SATURDAY, MAY 16TH - THREE YEARS PRIOR

MOM AND DAD ARE OUT IN THE LOBBY WATCHING TELEVISION together, and I'm just about to fall asleep when I hear it: a tap on my window. It jolts me awake, so I jump up on my knees and there Hadlee is, beaming at me through the glass. I unlatch and crack it open; the cool breeze makes me shiver. Hadlee leans in, letting her hair fall in front of her face, wearing a black school hoodie.

"Don't tell me you were sleeping," she says. "It's not even ten o'clock."

"I had a long day helping vacuum the rooms with Rosa. She finally let me help clean one, even though she just re-vacuumed after I was done."

She rolls her eyes, then grins. "Silly Rosa. I love her to death." She starts to hoist herself up. "I'm coming in, by the way."

"What if my parents—?"

"Just shut up and help me in, you goof."

She extends her hand to me, so I take it and pull until she's sitting with her legs crossed beneath her. I stiffen, because even after all these years as friends, being next to her feels so surreal. Like I'm not good enough.

She nudges my shoulder with her own. "Had to get out of the house."

"Did you bike here?"

"Yeah."

"Do you want to go somewhere?"

She tucks her loose hair behind her ear. "I already am somewhere."

Oh.

She inhales. "Dad's gone for the week on business, Maggie has a ballet friend over yet again, and Mom is, well, who knows where she is."

I close my eyes, swallow. Hadlee doesn't like to talk to me about her parents, so I know it must be bad. The Morgans were always nice when I was there, putting on a happy front, and Maggie always seemed too oblivious to really notice how their family was barely a family.

Hadlee is hurting, more today than normal. Enough for her to vent a couple sentences, which for her is well beyond normal. For as close as we are, she doesn't like to be vulnerable too often.

I grab her hand—squeeze it to let her know I'm with her without actually having to say anything.

Hadlee exhales, and I feel it on my skin. On the tiny hairs of my forearms. I wish I could kiss her. Wish I could just take the pain she tries to mask and shoulder it for her. I wish I could just be man enough to do something.

Hadlee squeezes my hand back. "Wanna go on an adventure?" Her voice is just above a whisper.

"Where to?"

We both turn to each other. A strand of her hair falls forward, so I push it behind her ear. She doesn't react at all, at least nothing noticeable. Just something we do. That we're comfortable with as friends.

"Do you still have access to your Dad's keys for the motel?"

"Of course."

She gets so excited she actually squeals, which makes me laugh, which in turn lets her release her trademark single giggle. Hadlee places a hand on my chest, and right away my lungs forget to work. I hate and love how she has this effect on me.

Her eyes light up. "Let's explore the other building."

"You know we can't. If my dad catches us—"

"Dev!" She cups my cheeks and mushes my face together. "I love how adorably by-the-book you are. But stop being a baby. I want to just have fun, forget some things for a change."

Forget about what?

I wiggle out of her grasp. "Can't we just stay here and talk?"

She rolls her eyes mockingly. "That's all you ever want to do."

I roll mine back. "False."

"What would we talk about?"

"You know... stuff."

She inches closer. "Stuff, huh?"

I clear my throat. "Yeah."

"What kinda stuff?"

Come on, just lean in and kiss her.

My voice comes out in a strange hoarse-squeak. "Whatever it is, um, you would want to talk about."

She inches forward again. She's so close I can practically taste the chocolate on her breath.

"What if I'm sick of just talking?"

Kiss her right now. Do it. If ever there was a moment....

I swallow what feels like sand. "W-We could playyyy a board game."

Hadlee stares at me a while. She closes her eyes and leans back.

"Board games."

"Or cards."

"Cards."

"Whatever you want."

Goddammit, Dev. You're pathetic.

Hadlee opens her eyes and scoots away. Whatever moment we could've had is gone.

"Dev."

"Hadlee."

She glares teasingly. "Devvy."

I glare back. "Haddy."

She stands and yanks me to my feet with her, suppressing what I think is amusement. Maybe frustration. "Keys. Window. Now!"

I shake my head and chuckle, letting her know she's won, like always. But as I'm about to hop off the bed to sneak away the keys from the front office, Hadlee grabs my wrist to stop me.

"You're a good friend, Dev."

Friend. Good friend.

"You know I'm always here for you, Hads."

She nods, looks out the window. She's still holding my wrist. "Have you ever thought of running away?"

There's something about the way she says it, almost detached. And how her voice drops a few octaves. I step closer and see the moonlight reflected on her face. How it makes her pale complexion creamy and smooth. Beautiful.

"What are you talking about?"

"Just like, getting away from all of this. Our families. This motel." She gestures widely. "We could go anywhere in the world."

I'm not sure if we're playing a game or not, but something tells me to play along. "Where would we go?"

She smiles. "Anywhere we want."

We.

"Just us?"

Hadlee is silent for a while. Doesn't answer my question. Just when I think I've ruined the moment, she lets go and hikes her legs out the window. When she jumps to the ground, she rests her elbows on the ledge and peers in.

"Let's just go now."

I laugh involuntarily, 'cause it catches me off guard. "Are you serious?"

"Yeah. Why not? We can see the whole world. Do you really want to stay at this motel forever?"

I don't know what to say. "I can't just abandon my parents."

"It wouldn't be abandoning them."

"What would you call it then?"

She rolls her eyes for real this time. "Can't you just pretend to be a rebellious teenager for my benefit?"

"Where is this coming from?"

"I'm just tired, Dev."

There's something off with her voice.

"Hadlee, talk to me. What's wrong?"

She shakes her head. "You don't get it."

"You're right, I don't. So tell me."

"I didn't come here to get 'talked' to." She puts the weight on the balls of her feet and rocks forward. "I just thought you'd understand."

"Understand what?"

She shifts her weight back, seems to contemplate something, and then presses close until her boobs push up onto the window ledge. Her eyes open wide, pleading, desperate. I beg myself not to let my eyes deter once, 'cause she will notice, and it will be embarrassing.

"Nothing. Just thinking that you're one of the good ones." She sticks her head in the window. "I know the boys at school pick on you because of this place." She indicates around us. "But I... I admire you, Dev. You're... you're different, you always have been.

Even now when I'm pressuring you into leaving, you're thinking about everyone else but yourself."

"Issss that a bad thing?"

She smirks. "Usually no, most of the time. But right now, kinda."

"Are you being sarcastic?"

"No. Not at all." She blinks twice in a row and flares her nostrils. "You're not getting it." She bites her lip, composes herself. "What do you want to do right here and right now?"

"I don't underst—"

"Yes, you do."

I close my eyes, suddenly feeling a headache coming on. My heart is hammering.

"I guess I just want to hang with you."

She nods as if waiting for me to continue. "Why?"

I don't know what she's asking or what she's trying to say. But suddenly I'm terrified that she knows. Maybe she's always known how I feel about her. And I want to tell her. So bad. I want to just tell her that everything I could ever want is standing right in front of me.

I want to tell her that I love her chestnut hair and russet eyes. I love how creamy her skin is, and how I've wanted to know the feel of it on mine. To know the taste of her breath, even her choco-late one. How I love the way her face scrunches when she's thinking or stressed. How she has the one single giggle, a tiny note, when she's feeling nervous or awkward.

Her lilac scent. Her boobs. How out of everyone else, she somehow still thinks I'm cool enough to hang with. How compassionate she is toward others. How I don't care about her messed up home life. There is not a single thing I would change about her. Flaws and all. Even when she gets frustrated with me.

How I wish, more than anything, that we could run away

together. Just pack up and go. There is nothing else. There is no one else.

There is only me and Hadlee Renee Morgan.

But, of course, I don't say any of that.

"I thought you wanted to do less talking and more exploring?"

Hadlee frowns, pulls back from the window, and something in her face changes. The gleam in her eyes is gone, and the smile falters. "You're right." She looks away. "Go get the keys. Let's just have some fun tonight."

I can't help but feel like I let her down. But what is she looking for? To really just pack up and go without telling anyone? No money or clothes or food to our names? And where is this even coming from?

"So, what exactly are we going to do in the abandoned rooms?"

She disappears around the side of the building but calls to me. "To see if they're really haunted. Hurry up!"

Just like that, it's as if nothing ever happened. There was no moment and no conversation. Just Hadlee and me up to the same old tricks.

Nothing ever changes.

Chicken-shit.

I sneak out of my room and grab my dad's keys without him or Mom noticing, as they're too distracted by the TV. I've gotten quite good at sneaking around lately without people seeing me. Taking things and returning them before anyone even knows they're gone. So, after I throw on a hoodie and hop out the window, I walk around the side of the building and find Hadlee standing in front of one of the rooms. There is a red light outside of it. She points, crosses her arms over her chest.

"Why this one?" I ask.

She shrugs. "I just have a feeling."

I flip for the right key, despite the fear kicking in. I hate being anywhere near this building. "Like what?" I watch as my breath condenses.

Hadlee whispers, "The sounds of dead people."

I stop and stare at her until she cracks.

"Bad joke."

"Dammit, Haddy."

"You're too silly."

"Give me a freaking heart attack over here."

"Oh, hush. Rosa is superstitious, and she has you buying into her crazy stories."

I hunch my shoulders. "Like you never got freaked out once all the times you'd sleep over."

She smiles. "She does know how to spin a good tale."

"I'm telling you, she has the best stories."

"Even if she tells them over and over again and forgets she did."

"That's what makes them legendary."

She lets out a single giggle and waits as I enter the key until it clicks and push open the door. We stare into the darkness, the door creaking on rusty hinges. A puff of cold air greets us from the threshold, so we take a deep breath and step in at the same time.

Right into Room 13.

CHAPTER 22

HADLEE HOLDS MY HAND AS WE WALK OUT OF THE WOODS, past the trailer parks, and along the edge of the road until we hit the motel parking lot. Dad is in the front office, staring off into space.

He's going to die—no, stop. It's Dad. He won't.

No cars are outside, but it's so chilly that our breaths fog in the air. Crickets chirp all around, and another coyote cries in the distance.

I'm shivering—the blanket not doing much besides shielding my naked flesh. Hadlee gestures at the wooden fence, and I nod.

What was she doing out there, Dev? Waiting for you?

Words are unspoken between us as she turns around and allows me to scale the fence in privacy. I'm more than a little nervous just free-balling it. All it takes is one wrong move and....

When I reach the other side, landing on my bare feet, I wrap the blanket around my torso just as Hadlee leaps over. She grabs my hand and walks us to the window to my "fake" room.

She motions for me to lean in and whispers, "I can go in and get you some clothes before you crawl through."

When I tremble in response, Hadlee must take that as a yes, because she raises the window and starts to crawl through before I catch her elbow. She jumps, startled, and comes back, her eyes wide.

"The other one," I whisper.

Her eyes focus on me before she looks over her shoulder toward the direction of Room 13. It must not take much to convince her, because once again she grabs my hand and leads me around the two buildings until we reach the back window. It's already cracked ajar.

"Do you have fresh clothes in there?"

I nod.

"Wait here."

"No," I step in front of her. "Let me do it."

My heart beats frantically in my chest. All the trinkets we've collected over the years. Everything is still here, and more, in the past three years.

What will she think? Freaked? Happy? Sad? Nostalgic? Terrified? Pathetic?

I force open the window, tie the blanket around my waist, and carefully ease myself into the window to avoid any unnecessary shows. Hadlee crawls slowly after and shuts the window. My boxers are on the floor in the bathroom, so I scoop them up and put them on under the blanket. My red mesh shorts are in the threshold to the outer room, so I put them on too and remove the blanket. Go to hand it back to Hadlee.

She shakes her head, holding back a smile. "Your junk was rubbing everywhere in that thing."

I'm not sure I should be smiling. Wondering why I'm not more freaked out about what happened in the woods. But I smile anyway.

"Touché."

We stare at each other in the dark of the bathroom, only the moonlight spilling in from the window and illuminating the dark in sharp silhouettes. We don't move, only stare. Let our breaths befriend the silence.

Hadlee takes both of my hands in hers. She rubs my knuckles, sending jolts of excitement up and down my arms. It warms my body, and she must sense it, 'cause she keeps doing it.

I close my eyes. "What were you doing out there?"

Hadlee exhales, and I feel hot breath on my chin. "Waiting for you."

"Waiting for me?"

I can't see it, but I can feel her move.

"Out in the woods. I waited for you to show up."

WTF!

"H-Hadlee—"

"I know it's weird."

"A little."

"I know I have a lot to explain to you."

I nod, and even though she probably can't see, I know she can feel me move too.

Finally, for the first time since she grabbed my hand in the woods, the question I've wanted to ask comes out: "Do you know what's wrong with me?"

Hadlee lets go of my hands and runs her fingers over my cheeks. It feels so good, so natural, so us. My entire body relaxes, now covered with goosebumps. I want her to keep tracing my skin with her fingertips until there's not an inch of me she hasn't marked.

No, that's not right.

She whispers, "There is nothing wrong with you." Takes a breath. "Is this—is it okay?"

"None of this is okay," I whisper back. "You and me are the only things that feel normal."

She drops her hands. "Get a shirt. We'll talk."

I can't help but feel a little panicked when she steps away, but I back out into the main motel room to put on my T-shirt that is in a crumpled mess on the floor. Hadlee is still in the bathroom. I take one last look around the room I created for her. For me. Us.

It's now or never, Dev. "You can come out now."

It feels like a lifetime before she hesitantly steps out into the dim light. She's in an oversized black hoodie and grey sweats. She lowers the hood, but her hair is wet, the shade a darker red than normal. The camera pouch is still around her neck.

At first nothing happens; there is no visible reaction. But then she looks around. Pausing on each wall before completing a circle. Then she stops. Unmoving. Unblinking. Not breathing.

I'm not sure how to take it. I've fantasized about this moment for years. The time Hadlee could see the collage we started—that I've kept going. My heart jumps into my throat until I cough, which breaks Hadlee out of her trance. Because she does something I wouldn't expect.

She cries.

On the wall opposite the bed are different trinkets pinned or tacked or taped up:

- Maps from different states
- Random photos of strangers found at garage sales
- Old Polaroids from the boys' dormitory before it shut down
- Pins
- Necklaces/chains
- Watches/stopwatches
- Wrappers from different foods or items
- A collage of torn/cut faces and landscapes Hadlee taped up that I never touched
- Some of Hadlee's early sketches

- Magazine covers
- Old 50s and 60s movie posters
- CD booklets
- Etc.

On the opposite side of the room outside the bathroom door:

- My old, red Schwinn bicycle I haven't used in three years
- An old music box
- Boxes full of clothes left behind from guests
- Trolls, original Barbie dolls, etc.
- A transistor radio that doesn't work
- A decoder ring
- Yo-yo
- A broken model airplane
- A few matchbox cars
- Baseball cards
- Parts of an Erector set
- Tinker Toys
- Lincoln Logs
- A Mickey Mouse guitar
- A rusted switchblade, *The Outsiders* style
- Etc.

Boxes upon boxes are stacked with overflowing objects found within the motel or around town in abandoned buildings/garage sales when Hadlee would drag me to them. But then above the headboard to my bed are more posters/photo collages Hadlee had started. Us; my parents; her parents; Rosa; Maggie; our old middle school; the motel; the town. There are a couple dreamcatchers hanging up. Hadlee always believed in them.

Two of the lost, in a room of the lost.

So many trinkets. So many memories. Sometimes I forget how overwhelming it can all be until Hadlee falls back on my bed and cries into her palms. I move to comfort her, but my ankle cracks as I approach, so she immediately jerks her head up and jumps across the room. Away from me. Like the threat of being close suddenly terrifies her.

What the hell happened to her, Dev?

"H-Hadlee?"

She sniffles, sucking up snot. Her voice is so soft I can barely make out her words. "You kept it. All of it."

I swallow. "Yeah."

Hadlee wipes her eyes, now bloodshot, and looks at me. Keeping her distance. I just want to run over, wrap her in a hug, kiss her lips and melt my skin into hers until they're one. She looks so... *overwhelmed.*

Her eyes widen, and she runs her hands through her damp hair, now matted in clumps on her shoulders. She hugs herself as if cold, but the room is perfectly comfortable. She walks to the far wall to stare at the hanging items. She runs her hands over the pocket watch, the one from the garage sale with the inscription to Sylvia. She looks back at me, her mouth open. A fresh tear rolls down her cheek.

And then I see that spring day as if it had just happened yesterday:

Hadlee browses the items on the foldout table in the drive-way. Rifling through a few used and overpriced shirts, she makes her way to the jewelry section and wades through cheap, plastic necklaces and bracelets before finally landing on a pocket watch with an 1800s locomotive etched onto the face. A gold-painted chain wraps around it like a snake. She turns it over in her hands, and it catches a glare from the fading sunlight.

"Dev," she calls. "Come here. Check this out."

I hurry over, and she unwraps the chain and opens the pocket watch before showing me. The hands don't work. Permanently stuck on 6:43.

"Whoa. That's cool."

"Right!?"

I turn it over in my hands and see there's something on the backside of the lid. It's an inscription. I point it out to Hadlee so we can both see.

Sylvia,
My platform when the tracks go dark
So you can count the days until I'm home

Love, Reggi

"This," Hadlee starts, "this is amazing. Who would ever sell this?"

"I have no idea."

Hadlee takes it back and inspects it further. Lets her hands glide over the etching inside and outside the lid. Holds it up to her ear as if to hear its inner-life. The imaginary ticks and tocks of the gears working their magic. Her eyes light up, and she smiles.

Something so beautiful in its simplicity. It's amazing to Hadlee and, hence, amazing to me. She just has a way of making everything larger than life.

She leans in close to whisper. "What do you think it means? The inscription."

I study it for a while, and I can sense Hadlee studying me in return. But I know nothing about watches or antiques. Then it takes shape, clear as day.

"I think a soldier during the Civil War. Maybe he gave it to

her before he left."

Hadlee cups the pocket watch in her palms and stares off into the purple horizon of the setting sun, closing her eyes and imagining it.

She whispers, "Tell me more."

You're so beautiful.

"Well." I flounder for words before they come. "It was love at first sight. The moment Reggi saw Sylvia, that was it. There was no one and nothing else. He would love her and protect her and provide for her."

Hadlee sways on her feet, clutching her palms to her chest. "And she believed that he would never leave. He'd always be there to support her. They'd go on adventures. He'd surprise her often just because. It didn't matter if their families didn't approve. They'd just go away somewhere together and start a family. Start new."

I stare at her. "Yeah." Clear my throat. "And he did. He built her a log house with his own bare hands. A secluded spot out in the middle of the woods. Just the two of them. And they wanted to have a baby."

"And she got pregnant."

She opens her eyes and turns to me. But there is something inside them. Her eyes so round and sincere. So desperate. I can't help but get lost in her.

"It was a baby boy," I whisper.

She pushes her shoulders into me. "He was everything they ever wanted."

"Everything they hoped for."

"It was perfect. Everything about their life was perfect."

"And then Reggi got the draft notice."

Hadlee's eyes drift away, and I'm so desperate to get them back I'll say just about anything. But she says it first, breaking our fiction.

"Don't leave me, Dev."

I'm slightly taken aback, unsure where this is coming from. I go to speak before Hadlee cuts me off.

"Do you ever feel suffocated here? Like there's this whole life you're supposed to be living but aren't?"

Whoa.

"That's kind of dark, Hadlee."

Why did you say that?

Her eyes seem to glaze over and she breathes in through her nose and points to the pocket watch, back to our fiction.

"Does he ever come back for her?"

And just like that, I'm back in the present.

"This was my favorite," she says.

I walk up to her, making sure it's okay to close the gap. She leans back, but doesn't move.

"Mine too."

We lock eyes.

"I think I always kind of knew this was still here."

"Really?"

Her lip twitches. "I think that's why I kept leaving you things at school that you'd pick up."

Of course, she did it on purpose.

I point out the gum wrapper from Friday. We smile.

"Dev, I—"

"I still have our old music collection."

I grab the milk crates full of vinyls and 45s and drag them over for Hadlee to scroll through. Most of my music is on my phone. We used to have a record player before it broke. I haven't listened to them in years.

- Chuck Berry
- Bo Diddley
- Etta James

- Ray Charles
- Fats Domino
- Bill Haley and the Comets
- The Beatles
- Little Richard
- Jerry Lee Lewis
- Buddy Holly
- Eddie Cochran
- The Champs
- The Coasters
- Hank Ballard and the Midnighters
- The Tokens
- Ben E. King
- Frankie Valli and the Four Seasons
- Frank Sinatra
- Etc.

Hadlee starts fingering through them, occasionally pulling a few out to admire the artwork. All of them are dusty, and her hands are covered in dark grime when she's done.

"Did you ever get a new record player?"

"No."

She frowns. "Why did you keep all this stuff?"

"They kept me company."

"Kept you company?"

"After you left."

"Oh."

"It's kind of like I still had you here with me, you know?"

Hadlee hugs her legs to her chest and rests her head on her knees. She chews on her lower lip. "I'm sorry."

"You don't have to be."

"I'm not a good person, Dev. It's my fault this happened."

What's your fault?

"You mean me hitting my head or you leaving?"

"My dad says all I do is fuck everything up."

"Hadlee—"

"He shouts, and Mom, when she's home, does nothing but hole up in her room. And poor Maggie has to listen to it every night."

"I didn't realize it was still that bad."

Another tear rolls down her cheek. I wipe it away with my thumb. Hadlee's warm breath exhales on my hand, which makes my entire body alight inside. I feel guilty for even getting excited by her proximity, but it's almost silly how every single thing she does still has this crazy effect on me.

"We should talk about what happened last night." She exhales. "When we were on the floor together."

"Why did you freak out on me? Is it because of your parents? Your dad?"

She freezes. "It was just too much."

"What was? You and me? Them?"

She fidgets her fingers on the carpet. "Are you happy, Dev?"

Jesus, this again? "Why do you keep asking that?"

"It's important."

"Is this a test?"

She frowns. "Are you happy?"

"I don't know how you want me to answer."

"The truth."

I try to measure her question, determine the right answer. I'm not sure if this is a trap or not. Hadlee must sense what I'm doing, 'cause she rephrases.

"Are you depressed?"

"I... I don't think so?" I lick my lips. "Are you?"

She runs her hands over her camera. "Do you love your parents?"

A chill shudders through my body.

"Hadlee, what the fuck?"

"Please, Dev. I'm not trying to beat around the bush."

"Of course, I love my parents, but what does that have to do with last night?"

She can't look me in the eyes—just holds the camera to her stomach. "Are you lonely?"

I sigh, frustrated. "I'm always lonely."

Finally, she acknowledges me, her eyes still bloodshot. There's something passing over her face, something I should know but don't.

"Me too," she whispers.

"What happened to you?"

She wipes at her nose. "Nothing happened to me."

"Bullshit nothing! You're freaking scaring me."

I want to believe her. I want to trust her. Part of me feels obligated to, but another, deeper part knows she isn't telling the whole truth. She was hurt. Really bad.

There is something very wrong here.

The scar on the back of my head pings.

The scent of firewood.

The room feels hot, unreasonably so. My vision blurs for a moment before lightheadedness kicks in. My skin is boiling. I close my eyes to shake away the terrible feeling of nausea. When I open them, Hadlee is staring at me with glistening irises. But behind her the wall is on fire. Flames dance and lick at the ceiling as if trying to swallow us whole. A life of their own. And Hadlee is so close, I'm terrified it's going to consume her.

I stand up and grab her shoulder to jerk her back so hard she falls into the night table. She cries out, and in that moment when I blink again, it's gone. There is no fire. My skin is not burning. It's just us.

I point to the wall, speechless. My heart raging. I can't seem to move a single muscle in my entire body.

"What just happened?" she asks, terrified. "What's going on?" She scrambles to her feet, staring toward the wall with me, trying to find what I'm fixated on. Rubbing her elbows and wincing.

Seeing things again, Dev. It's getting bad like last time. You just hurt her.

I shake my head to clear my thoughts and finally find the courage to breathe. The fire is not there. It never was.

"S-Sorry," I utter. "Just thought I saw a... spider."

Hadlee raises her eyebrows. "Spider?"

I nod.

She frowns.

If anyone finds out, they'll put you back on the medication.

I point to where she's hurt, but she shrugs it away, keeping her distance.

"I think I just need sleep," I say. "It's been a long day."

"Oh. Okay."

Are you going crazy? Is Travis right?

"I believe you, Hadlee. That nothing happened to you."

"You—you do?"

No. Yes. What's even real anymore?

I nod, swallow. "I just need sleep right now."

"I understand." She pivots awkwardly, hugging her camera still. "I'm going to stay with you if that's okay."

Oh shit.

"Stay wi—"

"In this room. Yes. I don't think you should be alone."

If this were any other normal teenage situation with a girl in a room, she would be asking to stay for a very different reason.

For some reason, that thought makes my stomach turn.

"You don't—"

"I do." She furrows her brows, which makes her nose and forehead scrunch. "I don't want to be alone tonight." She looks up, almost begging. "I just want to stay here with you."

My heart skips. "S-Sure." I look around, not even knowing how abstract concepts such as sentences or words or letters are even comprehensible. "I can sleep on the floor. You can take the bed. Is that okay?"

"Can you sleep in the bed?"

"I'm not having you sleep on the floor, Hads."

She combs her fingers through her damp hair, puffing out her cheeks. She forces an awkward laugh. "I meant with me."

"Oh."

I open my mouth and close it several times. Settle on nodding and making some guttural throat noise to indicate my approval.

Of course, the moment Hadlee wants to share a bed is the same night she finds you sleepwalking naked in the woods and hallucinating things. Brilliant.

I'm not sure how this works, what's supposed to be said or done next. I don't think Hadlee does either. And even though I try not to picture what any other alternative of this scene could be, I do. I'd take off my clothes. She'd take off hers. We'd stare at each other awkwardly, *The Notebook* style, she'd run to me, jump in my arms, and I'd twirl her around, my mouth on hers as I lay her gently on the bed and climb on top. And the rest is... well....

But somewhere in between real life and my imagined one, Hadlee begins to take off her wet clothes, putting her camera safely on the night table next to where I sleep. We stare at each other. Normally, I sleep shirtless, but I'm thinking better of it.

Too much exposed skin.

Hadlee looks at her wet clothes. And I get why she's hesitating.

"I don't keep extra clothes in here," I say, like I've broken some kind of promise.

"I don't want to get your bed wet."

Heh-heh. Wet.

I chastise myself. "You should wear my shirt, I don't need it." I start to take it off before she shakes her head.

"I can just, um, sleep in my underwear."

"Oh."

My mind goes right back to her white lace panties from Sunday.

Jesus-freaking-Christ.

"I don't want you to be uncomfortable." I start to lift my shirt again, but she stops me.

"Really, Dev. I'm okay. It will help me dry off faster."

I nod, my mouth too dry to form words. She stares at me until I get the hint, shake my head, and turn around. I can hear a zipper, cloth rubbing against skin before landing in a *PLOP* on the carpet. Before I know it, the bed groans and creaks, and the sheets are ruffling.

My heart is pounding.

"Okay, you're good," she says.

I turn slowly, making sure she isn't messing with me and is secretly naked, but even that thought honestly makes zero sense. I make zero sense. This whole night is a big, giant, senseless zero.

Hadlee stares, waiting for me to do something, so I shuffle my feet and slowly climb in next to her, as close to the edge as possible. My body is as rigid as a board. I pull the covers up to my chin like a kid.

"I don't have cooties, Dev."

Weren't you the one that freaked out last time we were close?

"I'm—I'm good."

"Are you sure?"

Don't come closer.

"Yup."

A single giggle. "I want to say this doesn't have to be awkward, but this is totally awkward, isn't it?"

I still can't move like a normal person. My heart is in my throat. My joints are locked so tight it hurts, and I can't seem to loosen them up. I'm sweating. "Not awkward at all."

What the hell?

She moves around, trying to get comfortable, and I slowly pivot so I'm lying on my side, making sure my back isn't to her. It feels safer somehow to face her, to see where she is at all times. I don't like the thought of her lying behind me, out of sight.

"This is kind of scary, isn't it?" she asks.

I huff. "Sure is."

"If you really need me to, like, go or...."

"No!" I shout, making Hadlee jump. I cover my mouth with my hand until we both chuckle. "Can we just direct the conversation somewhere where I'm not going to make a complete fool of myself?"

"You're not a fool."

"Then you're a fool too."

"Am I?"

I purse my lips and curse. "I don't know why I said that. Jiminy Cricket."

It takes a moment, but after a few seconds, Hadlee bursts out laughing, making the bed vibrate. I'm mortified by the realization of what came out of my mouth.

"You did *not* just say that."

I cover my eyes with my hands as she calms down. "Please just shut me up. I'm on a roll of stupidity tonight." I uncover my eyes. "Do you see what you do to me here? I'm unmoored."

"I like this Dev." She pokes my pillow. "I think you shouldn't be ashamed of who you are."

Mixed signals.

"Like when I tripped over the hurdle last Friday in gym?"

She grins and pulls the covers tighter around her body. In all the time I've seen her since Saturday when she came by the motel, this is the most at peace she's been. The most normal. The most like the old Hadlee. Almost girl-like in an innocence I haven't seen for a long time. Like there's this glowing aura around her.

She is so beautiful.

I can't help but think that there's this darkness surrounding her too. Consuming her. Her sudden change of appearance freshman year, the website, the obsession with her camera everywhere she goes. Like she's somehow vulnerable without it.

Why was she asking all those dark things?

"Do you want to skip school tomorrow?" she asks.

"Yeah." I adjust my pillow. *Any excuse to spend more time with you.* "Why?"

She fluffs her pillow and repositions her head to angle it better my way. "I just want to spend the day together. No school, no teachers, no parents."

"Like old times?"

She nibbles on her lower lip, the bra strap on her bare shoulders exposed. And I notice a faint, pink line that trails from her left shoulder to the top of her breast. So faint I almost couldn't see it until this close. A scar.

When the hell did she get that? WTF?

"Exactly like it."

"I'd love that."

She smiles. "Me too."

We stare at each other for a while. Something we've gotten pretty good at over the past few days. I don't know why, but I get the urge to lift my hand to move her bangs behind her ears. Her nose twitches when I do.

"Goodnight, Haddy."

She presses her cheek into my fingers before I pull my hand away. Her skin is hot.

"Goodnight, Devvy."

Neither one of us wants to be the first to close our eyes, but at some point, it must happen, because soon I'm drifting off to sleep.

Next to the only person in the world I ever want to fall asleep beside.

CHAPTER 23

There is a noise coming from the attic. A *THUMP*. A *CRASH*. And a *SCREECH*.

Something is banging on the floor, making the ceiling shake and spit dust. I fling the covers off my sweating body and walk out into the hallway, hugging my arms around my torso. It's unreasonably cold. The walls are all a slate grey. Down the narrow hallway, the stairs leading up to the attic have been pulled down. A red light flickers inside. Phosphorescent.

My feet creak along the wooden floorboards, groaning with each step. I reach the staircase leading up into the dark attic. Shadows appear to dance on the ceiling as if a fire were orchestrating a symphony inside. But something is pulling me up into the attic. Some unseen force out of my control. My body moves separately from my mind.

And then I hear it: the voice. A whisper, really. But layered. As if a group of people were whispering at once, but their words coming from a single mouth. The whispers rise and fall in pitch and crescendo. Something vibrates the closer I get. And just through the noise, there's a voice. Unintelligible words. Desperation. Fear. I must get to it.

I look behind me to see how far I've come. The staircase seems to keep going forever and ever. But when I look behind me, it's nothingness. I've come from nowhere. I'm heading to absence.

Finally, I reach the attic landing, but I don't want to be here. The whispers stop, and the shadows dancing on the ceiling suddenly fall into one another, become a wiggling mass of obstruction. They come together, growing, and a low hum emanates from the walls. Oozing from them like some forsaken monstrosity.

Dev.

I turn my head to the sound of my name. The voice calling me. But no one is there. No one is anywhere. That's when I see it: the well. A perfect circle burrowed into the attic floor. The phosphorescent glow from before pulsates down below, bright red.

The palms of my hands are sweating, and even though I know that going toward it is the last thing I should do, once again my actions are not mine. I'm not in control.

Please.

The voice again. Coming from everywhere and nowhere. Goosebumps rise on my flesh, and the wiggling mass of shadows above forms into a ball before plummeting into the well. The *WHOOSH* knocks me back, and a cold gust of wind slices so hard that the skin of my face cracks wide open. I'm bleeding.

See.

The room becomes so cold I can't stand. My joints are frozen stiff. The snot in my nose icicles. I want out. I want to run away screaming and crying. But I'm crawling on my hands and knees—the bitter, death-grip of cold splitting the skin of my knuckles until they reveal the white bone beneath. The only escape is the well. There is heat emanating from inside. Sucking down anything above its circumference like a blackhole.

"Fucking look at me!"

Not coming from outside, no. Inside. It's inside my head. Only....

It's from a voice that's not mine.

I reach the edge of the well and look down, heat pummeling my face until it boils. I fall on my stomach, my shoulders hanging over. It's just blackness. An endless tunnel of hopelessness leading into the den of nothingness.

DOWN Down down down down down down down down down down

Something *CRASHES* behind me. I jump up, my joints in full swing, and see a grey trunk sitting in the middle of the room. A light shining down on it from somewhere above, where no light fixtures hang. But the crate is moving. Sliding back and forth—left and right. Jiggling.

Something is trying to get out. Break free.

It pounds on the inside. There are muffled cries. From behind me, the cacophony of unintelligible whispers. And from inside my head, the voice that's not mine beckons to me. Calls to me from inside the well.

Something is at the bottom, waiting. But something else is in the trunk, desperate.

"Where do you think you're going?"

I want to open my mouth to speak, to ask what it is I'm supposed to do. But blood pours out of my mouth. The trunk rises out of the ground a foot before plopping back down, causing the floorboards beneath to split open.

And from the well, deep inside, an echoing cackle.

Deep, resonant, inhuman.

An endless cycle of cackling slowly rising in pitch the closer it gets to the surface. The phosphorescent glow pulsating with a frantic purpose.

Coming for me. Something is coming for me. And the

shouts from inside the trunk become desperate pleas. Screams so curdling my teeth shatter.

The humming from beneath the floorboards becomes so loud I have to cover my ears, but not even that stops the voice inside my head.

"See what you made me do?"

The room shakes around me, the cackle now a resonating maniacal laughter. Abhorrent. I'm pretty sure my bladder releases, and I'm crying blood tears. I don't understand. This doesn't make sense. But as the pulsating red light grows brighter and brighter, and the room shakes more and more, the laughter gets louder.

The whispering becomes a chorus of moans. The trunk keeps rising and falling before it hovers in midair and stops. My senses are on overdrive. My skin bleeding and cracked. Then the locks come undone, latches open, and the top rises slowly. Creaking.

"Why did you have to fucking get inside my head?"

Everything stops. Everything. No red light, no whispers or laughter. No shaking. But as the trunk lowers steadily to the ground, even the shouting stops. I'm terrified to look inside. Horrified at what evil lies dormant.

Just as I'm about to peek into the trunk, I hear a voice calling to me from the well. Echoing off the stones. I can't make out what they are saying, but it's afraid. The voice almost tiny, in hiding. Begging me to come closer. I shuffle to the well and look down. An echoing chorus of screams rises around me. Hundreds of voices all wailing at once. The red, pulsating glow is back, illuminating a figure in the cavernous pit below. The well is dry; there is no water.

The figure looks up to me with an extended hand and—

I awake with a jolt. Sweat mats my hair across my forehead and ears. The sheets around me are soaked, and the bed is moving. At first, I'm not sure what's going on until my hands dart to my ears as the piercing screams invade my head.

No, not screams. Scream. Singular. Hadlee's.

I fumble for the lamp on the night table and hop out of the bed, bashing my knee against a sharp corner of the table. Nearly knocking her camera over, I catch it in time and look up to see Hadlee thrashing around wildly. Her hands claw at the sheets as if fighting off an intruder. Her head jerks back and forth so forcefully, I'm afraid she's going to break her neck.

Her back arches until her torso is off the mattress, and then she crumbles back into herself. My heart is beating so madly that I'm having trouble breathing. Like Hadlee is sucking all the air out of the room. Her eyes are closed—face dripping. Her legs and feet kick the air.

Fuck. Oh, fuck.

I cover my ears again—terrified that Rory or Mr. Day or my parents will hear it and dash over thinking someone is being murdered. She's screaming as if someone is being murdered. I call her name to get her attention, but it's not working. When I try to wake her up, her palm collides with my cheek, a nail digging into my chin and drawing blood.

I glance to the front door, and still no one comes. I try to grasp her shoulders and shake her awake, but she thrashes around, sitting up and screaming herself raw, shredding her vocal cords. Another nail finds my forehead and makes a gash. But I don't let go. I pull her close and hug her as her body fights me off.

I plead for her to wake up. Beg her to. I whisper anything I can but have no idea what to do or say. She's having a night terror. Am I supposed to wake her up? Let her get out of it alone? Do I comfort her? Talk to her? Use force? Is there a right or wrong way?

"Hadlee, I'm here," I say breathless. "I'm with you. I'm not going anywhere."

I hug her tighter and press her head into my shoulder. Tears fall down my hot cheeks, and her body calms a little, so I keep murmuring anything that comes to mind. Anything that will get her to stop. Anything to let her know I'm not letting her go. And soon enough she stops, her body stills its convulsions, and her mouth closes on incoherent mumblings.

When I pull her head back, her chest is heaving. Sweat has matted her hair over her blue bra. Her mouth and nose twitch—eyelids flutter open and eventually find mine. I'm still cradling her against me, and she's holding on for dear life, maybe afraid of falling into the abyss of her mind.

"D-Dev?" she asks foggy, half-asleep.

"Hey." I stroke her damp hair with one hand and hold her lower back with my other. "I'm here. I got you."

Hadlee's eyes open wide, taking in her surroundings as if she can't remember where she is or why. When realization spans her face, her hands clutch the back of my shirt, and she pulls me into another hug. Her breasts press into my chest. I can feel them through the wet fabric.

"Dev...."

"It's okay. You're okay." I'm still breathless. "You scared me there."

She pulls back, but we still hold each other. "What happened?"

"You don't remember?"

She shakes her head. I brush away a few damp strands of hair clinging to her forehead.

"You were having a night terror."

Hadlee seems to chew on the thought before she trembles. She notices my cuts and touches them. "Did I hurt you?"

"I'm fine."

She looks down at our position, how she's only wearing her bra and underwear. She scoots back against the headboard and out of my hands, running her fingers through her hair and parting it in clumps. She brings a few loose strands to her mouth and chews on them. A nervous habit she never did grow out of.

"I'm sorry. I'm sorry I'm sorry I'm sorry."

"Don't apologize." I raise my hands in a gesture to ask if it's okay to come closer, but she shakes her head no, so I stay put. "I couldn't wake you up. You were just screaming and thrashing everywhere. Wouldn't calm down until I hugged you."

"Must have been being here with you that did it. Sleeping in the same bed."

"What are you talking about?"

She rubs her temples. "Night terrors. I used to get them a lot. They're more sporadic now. Being here with you must have triggered it."

I cock my head. "Why would being here cause you night terrors? I—I didn't hurt you, did I?" I scoot back, worried. "Wait. This has happened before? I don't remember you ever having nightmares this bad."

She nods, stares at me for a while before continuing. "After your coma. I had these for a while before I started to grow out of them."

I'm still so confused. This doesn't make any sense. "Why would you have night terrors because of my coma?"

Hadlee looks away, and it's then that I know she's keeping something else from me yet again. New style, dropping me and any other friends she knew, her website and disturbed photography, these secrets she can't seem to open up about, how she freaked out when we got close the other night, and how she doesn't like when I get too physically close. Too intimate.

But you can't seem to say it out loud, not even to yourself. Can you?

Hadlee must see my mind working, because she pulls the sheets up her half-naked body, covering up the faint scar above her breast. "I'm fine, Dev. Night terrors are normal."

Seriously?

"Hadlee, there is *nothing* normal about *any* of this."

She leans her head against the wall. "I meant that people have night terrors. I'm okay. It's just being here again, finding you in the woods, this room... it was too much."

"What were you dreaming about?"

"That I was being chased and couldn't escape. Trying to go somewhere but never being able to reach it." She watches me. Almost studying me. "What about you?"

"What about me *what?*" I fold my legs underneath me and rub my palms on my shorts.

"Did you have any dreams?"

I shake my head, like it's cloudy. "I don't dream."

She squints. "Everybody dreams."

"I don't."

Why does it feel like you're lying to her?

She sits up. "That's impossible."

"If I do, I don't remember them. I haven't had a dream since the coma."

"Isn't that impossible? Never a dream? Not a single one?"

Holy shit. How have you never thought this was a problem until now?

"Never."

What's wrong with you?

Hadlee falls back against the headboard. "That's crazy."

I cock an eyebrow. "Crazier than having night terrors?"

"No, I mean, you sleepwalk. It makes sense you don't remember your dreams. That's why you sleepwalk. Your unconscious mind is trying to tell you something. Since you can't remember your dreams, you go out to the woods." She mumbles to herself. "Of course."

"I don't understand."

Hadlee clasps her hands together. "You wouldn't. It's your unconscious mind at work trying to send you a message."

She may actually have lost her mind.

"This is going over my head."

Hadlee scoots over to me until our knees touch. The blood warms in my veins.

"You don't think it's odd that the same night you sleepwalk in the woods, I have a night terror when I haven't had one in *months?*"

I frown. "I guess."

She somehow manages a weak smile, her face still glistening from the sweat. "The collective unconscious. Your mind must have transferred whatever you were feeling while out in the woods into my mind."

Play along. See where this goes.

"Let's say I understand for just a second what you're saying." I clear my throat. "That means I go out into the woods because I'm dreaming of being chased?"

"No, not necessarily." She bounces up, excited. "But whatever feeling you had, maybe it somehow made an impression on me, and those feelings reminded me of being chased. Or my mind is trying to make sense of what you were feeling. I don't know. I'm not a dream guru, Dev."

I contemplate the thought, mulling it over. Even if I still don't really understand, it makes a weird kind of flawed sense.

"That's really out there."

"Yeah," she agrees. "I guess we're both really messed up. Aren't we? One of us sleepwalks, the other has night terrors."

She smiles almost pathetically, enough to flash her white teeth. I can't help but do the same. Even if the thought is a little too "woo-woo" and creepy for me to fully agree with or like.

Is it though?

I make a gesture again to come closer and she nods slowly. We both scoot up against the headboard, our shoulders touching. We breathe in and out in sync, stare down into our laps.

"How long have you been following me in the woods?"

It's silent for a while before she murmurs her response, ashamed. "Almost two years."

It's like a punch in the gut before I recover. "Are you serious?"

That's embarrassing. Invasive too. Maybe?

"I told you I had a lot of explaining to do."

"Yes, you do."

She yawns. "Tomorrow. Still skipping school, right?"

I yawn back. "Right."

"You know yawning when someone else does means you're empathetic to others."

I look over at her. She's gesturing to her neck as if to cradle her camera, but it's not there. Her hands shake.

"I've never heard that before."

Hadlee nudges my shoulder with her own. "I didn't need you yawning to know that though."

I nudge back. "We're talking tomorrow. About everything. No secrets. Okay?"

Please, just say yes.

She brings a few strands of hair back to her mouth and mumbles a yes. I don't feel totally convinced, but I'm too tired to argue.

"Do you think anyone heard me?"

I reach over to turn the light back off. "We would've heard someone outside if anyone had. This building must somehow mask the sounds. I don't know how."

We both scooch onto our backs, the covers off. The room has suddenly grown way too hot. My waterlogged pillow feels disgusting on the back of my neck.

Why the hell is your pillow covered in sweat?

"Maybe it's the ghosts?"

"Dammit, Hadlee."

"What?"

"Go to sleep."

"Still terrified of that story Rosa told?"

I flip over my pillow to the side that's not wet. "I told you before. She's Mexican. And religious. Her stories are terrifying."

Hadlee turns over to face me. I can tell because her hot breath tickles the peach fuzz on my chest.

"I know I'm not how you thought I was going to be," she whispers. "I know I probably disappoint you."

I turn over too, confused. "You don't disappoint me, Hadlee."

"Yes, I do."

"It's just weird, you know? After all these years, it's like one moment it's the old us, and the next there's all these secrets where I feel like we're two completely different people."

"Yeah, I feel that too. Like we're not the same people as before." She moves again. "Does that upset you?"

I think about it. "It's just different."

She moves closer. "Sometimes I feel like I don't even know who I am anymore. Like I'm living this life. Going to school, being a daughter and a big sister. I feel like an imposter in my own life." She sniffles. She might be crying again. "I feel like I'm only myself when I'm on my website."

And I don't know why I ask what I do, but it just comes out

anyway: "Did you really post nudes on the internet like the guys on track said?" I hate myself immediately for even asking. It's none of my business.

Hadlee stops. I'm afraid she fell asleep before she breathes a response. "Yes."

An urge comes over me to go to my computer and find any trace and delete them from every server I can find. I want to roam the school and punch every single person that has ever seen or talked about the photos. I want to shout at her, at myself.

Why would she do that to herself? Exposed? All that skin?

"I deleted them," she answers for me. "The school received a tip. Local police too, and social services, 'cause I'm still under-age." Another pause. "You remember Mr. Pleck? Algebra teacher?"

"Yeah. He was fired and arrested after you posted those photos of him propositioning those teenaged girls."

She nods. "I was one of them."

Everything stops. Throat dries up. Words escape. Mind blanks. Scar pings.

"Is it okay if we don't talk about this right now?" She clears her throat. "It was a stupid thing to do, and I'm not in the right mood to tell you the details."

I reach out until I find her hand and squeeze it. She inter-locks her fingers in mine. It's so warm that my heart skips a beat. I just want to hold her and never let go. Take away all her pain.

Maybe this is enough.

She smiles and squeezes my hand.

"Why didn't you come to me sooner, Hads? After the coma."

"I couldn't. If either of our parents found out, it would've been over."

"Yeah. I mentioned you to my parents today after track practice."

She stiffens. "You did?"

"Just your name. Not that we were hanging out. I don't think I've seen my parents more upset."

She sighs. "After you left my house, my dad was sure you'd been over."

"Really?"

I feel her nod. "I'm not allowed to lock my doors. Not ever. He was so mad, Dev. I've never seen him so mad." She takes a breath. "Mom just went to bed like nothing mattered, like she always does. Just me up to no-good. And poor Maggie." She moans. "I just wish I could get her out of that house."

I'm almost afraid to ask the question, but hesitantly do anyway. "Have you ever—does your dad—Hadlee, you're not...." *Goddammit.* "Does he hurt you?"

"No." She jumps a little. "No, nothing like that." She scoots closer, eyes dart anxiously. Tears fall from her eyes. "Sometimes, I mean...." She mumbles under her breath. "Mom couldn't care less either way."

I'll fucking kill him.

"Why haven't you said something? Gone to someone? Like, are you okay? Is your sister okay? Why are you pretending like this isn't bad?"

"I mean, I can't really complain. A lot of people have it worse than me or Maggie do. But... it just hasn't been the same. We haven't really been a family in a long time."

"I'm sorry." I squeeze her hand. "You don't deserve any of this."

"Maybe I do."

"Stop saying that. You don't." I feel like running down to her house and beating the shit out of her dad. "Any father who abuses his own kids is a fucking coward." I rub her shoulder, wiping tears from my eyes. "I'm so sorry I haven't been there for you. I had no i—"

"It's the price I pay to reveal the truth." She lets my hand go. "I've hurt people with the pictures I take. I hear what people say. What my dad says. That's why everyone stays far away."

"We really need to talk about this now. Fuck waiting. Three years, Hads. Stop playing this cryptic game where you're keeping secrets and acting like what's happened is acceptable."

Hadlee breathes out on my chest before turning over, away from me, and letting go of my hand. "Tomorrow, Dev. I promise. I know I haven't given you many reasons why you should, but please believe with all your heart that I'll tell you every single thing I know tomorrow. You just have to promise things between us won't change, okay?"

Something tells me not to press the issue, despite how badly I want to. Instead, I reach out one final time and stroke the back of her hair, still damp. She pushes her head back into my palm and seems to relax a little.

"I don't care what you've done or haven't done. To me, you're still my best friend. You always have been, and nothing is going to change that." A pause. "And I will never, ever hurt you."

When Hadlee doesn't respond, her back rising and falling from breathing, I snuggle into my semi-dry pillow and close my eyes. Letting myself drift off to sleep, hoping for all the answers tomorrow.

CHAPTER 24

The alarm on my phone wakes me up earlier than usual on Thursday. I shut it off quickly, careful to let Hadlee sleep a little longer. She murmurs something in her sleep and stirs before snoring quietly. It's actually really cute. Hadlee is shivering a little, so I take the sheets that were kicked off the bed during the night and tuck her in.

Without wasting time, I climb out the bathroom window and sneak around to my "fake" room. I climb through the window and roll across my bed until I land on my feet. Different ideas of how exactly I can skip school come to mind: fake sick, pretend to leave then come back, say I hurt my foot at track practice to stay home.

Before I even really decide on a plan, I'm already walking out my door and into the kitchen just as Mom is relieving Dad at the front desk. They kiss on the lips, and Dad taps her lightly on the butt—

So. Much. Ew.

—before heading to his room. He stops when he sees me. "Morning, son."

Just do it. Don't think. Just whatever comes to mind.

"I'm not going to school today."

Well, shit, Dev. That was blunt.

Dad stops and looks at me. Blinks his eyes. Mom pops up from behind the counter and raises her hands in a 'Say what?' gesture. I nod, stomp my foot down for emphasis. I feel like such a poser. I wouldn't even be intimidated by me.

"Are you feeling okay?" Mom asks. "Joe, did our son just say he wasn't going to school?"

Dad frowns, clearly too exhausted to do much else. "It appears so, dear."

Mom rushes to me and places her hand on my forehead to check my temperature. I shove her hand away, trying not to laugh.

"I'm skipping school. I'm allowed to if I want. This is America."

Mom guffaws. "Who are you and what have you done with our son?"

Dad rubs his eyes. "Like hell you're skipping. Get dressed, Dev."

Mom rests her elbow on his shoulder and leans. "Fun Mom is intrigued by this."

I roll my eyes. "Not this morning, please. You're gonna ruin the effect I'm going for."

Dad straightens his glasses. "Honey, we can't just let him skip school."

"I think it'll be good for him."

"This is how it starts; you remember?"

Something tells me that was not a comment for my ears, because she hits him on the arm as if to scold. They both look at me.

"Can we call it a mental health day?" I force as much innocence into my voice as I can. I'm not usually like this. It's new for me.

Mom laughs. "Our son, the delinquent and self-care enthusiast. I'm so proud."

Dad sighs as Mom massages his shoulders, trying to butter him up.

"You show up late last night and now you're skipping school to——"

Mom nudges Dad in the back. He straightens his glasses again, but his brow furrows, and I can see him mask the pain.

Stop, Mom.

"Just this once, Dev. And you'll be doing nothing but homework, understood?"

"Yes, sir."

He gives a curt nod. "Then, The Law rests."

We exchange a look, and there's a mutual understanding. I won't make him regret this as long as Mom doesn't find out about his heart. It seems like such an unfair agreement, but Mom can't know. It would destroy her. It would destroy them both.

We stand there awkwardly before I retreat to my room, muttering something about a project I have to do and, hence, can't have interruptions. At least this way I'll be able to walk around without getting caught, especially when Hadlee gets hungry.

When I step up to the wardrobe and open it to look in the mirror, ignoring the chill that eases down my spine, I stare at myself and do a happy dance. Because now I get to spend all day with Hadlee. Just like old times.

And it. Feels. Awesome.

ME

wont be in school

AIDEN

What! Why? You okay?

ME

hadlee stayed the night

AIDEN

I smell some bologna.

Does this have to do with what happened in the locker room? Are you okay? You scared us all.

ME

u smell nothing. dont wait up 4 me, ill explain later

but yes im fine. it was nothing, just dehydration

AIDEN

Sureeeeee.

So I take it you guys made up, and yet, you didn't tell me???

I'm keeping record, boy.

:-/

ME

still working on it

she said she will tell me everything

AIDEN

Hmm... Maybe I should skip too?

ME

no

AIDEN

No? Did you just say NOOOOOOOO to MEEEEEE!?!?!?!!!?!!?

ME

isnt that self-evident in my original no?

AIDEN

Okay, smartass. Sarcasm noted.

ME

luv ya!

AIDEN

I don't accept your love. Not this time. There's
only so much rejection a guy can take... :'-(

ME

im ceasing txting after ur next response

AIDEN

How dare you!

I'm hurt.

You've wounded me.

ME

and communication is ceased. ttyl!

AIDEN

I'll keep texting you.

Over and over.

Until.

You.

Respond.

Get it?

I can keep going...

...

...

...

I have excellent stamina. And I last for hours.

:-p <3

On the plus side, Max and I are going out again tomorrow night. He's taking me to the shelter he volunteers at for the homeless a few towns over.

Isn't he SO sweet?!?!?!

Soooo excited.

Lkehrjnjrnoifelfnsjkfndjq;wewgjejnklv

That's how I feel ^^^^^^^

So wait, did you guys, like, hook up?

Are you no longer a virgin?!?!?!

Did Hadlee steal away my virgin sacrifice to the D&D Gods?!?!?!

Answer me.

ANSWER ME!!!

DUDES 'N DICKS DEMANDS YOUR VIRGINITY

ME

bsgina

bsgina**

vagina**

WTF!

AIDEN

Ew. GoodBYE!

ME

b careful with that guy. Max? he might be a creeper. 4 ur sake I hope not. lemme kno!

AIDEN

Thanks, boo!

ME

<3

When I sneak back to Room 1 3 with a fresh pair of my clothes for Hadlee to wear, she is on the bed with her camera around her neck. She takes photos of the room around us. Her clothes from last night are still a crumpled, damp mess on the floor. She has my bed sheet wrapped around her body, leaving only her exposed shoulders and feet uncovered. The mysterious scar above her breast is visible.

What about the scar above her belly button, Dev? What happened out in the woods?

I try to take my eyes away, but I can't. She's so beautiful, so sexy. But I don't like how her skin is exposed. Like it's wrong on her somehow.

She posted nudes online and was propositioned by that pedo, man. Fuck.

She lowers the camera from her face and smiles at me. As if the vulnerable girl from last night was a shell she crawled out from. This Hadlee is the one from the hallway I see every day in school. Like the second the camera is in her hands, she's in control and calling the shots.

"Successfully got my parents to let me skip school." I beam.

"Your mom convinced your dad, right?"

"Yup." I put my hands on my hips as if posing for a hero shot. Hadlee snaps my picture, which makes my arm twitch. "What about you? Did you call your parents or something?"

"Nope. They won't even notice or care."

I'm not really sure how to respond. Hadlee was never this blunt before. Her indirectness was a comfort when I never knew what to say to her. Now I can't really figure out what her intention is.

Attention?

She drops the camera so it dangles from her neck "So, what do you think we should do today?" She sees the bundled-up sweats and blue T-shirt. "Did you get those for me?"

"Yeah, they are." I throw them to her. "Do you want to stay here and hide out or try and sneak off somewhere?"

"Go out. There are a few things I want to show you." She picks through the clothes. "You didn't have to do this, Dev. Really." The corners of her eyes crinkle. "You're the best."

"That's what friends are for." I nod and put my hands inside the pockets of my shorts. "Cool?"

She smirks. "Cool." It seems like she's waiting for something.

I smirk too. "What?" Then she indicates the clothes, and I smack my forehead. "Why does this keep happening?" I whirl around to give her privacy.

"You're such a dork sometimes."

"Thanks."

"It's a compliment. It always has been, you know."

Don't just stand there with your back turned awkwardly. Compliment her, you fool!

"I really like your...." I look around at the walls and try to find something simple to compliment that's not too obvious but also unique. "Feet."

"My feet?"

Jesus, man. JeSUS!

"Nope."

"So, you don't like my feet? You can turn around now."

Hadlee sits up on her knees as I do, toying with me now. "You really know how to make a girl feel special."

"Oh, shut up."

She single giggles, looking adorable in my grey sweats and shirt, the perfect fit seeing as we're the same height. There's just something about seeing a girl in your own clothes that—

"Can we move past this awkward small talk, please?" I ask.

"You really hate your small talk."

"I really do."

"Down to business, then?"

"Absolutely."

When Hadlee hops the fence by the pool, I tell Mom I'm going for a jog. Thankfully, she's nowhere near as strict as Dad, so she's okay with it as long as I'm not gone long, and I promise to take my phone. I head back to my "fake" room and throw on my running attire for show, but just as I'm about to head out, she stops me. She's got her toolbox on the counter, ready to dive into one thing or another that's broken at this motel.

"Your father and I never wanted this life, Dev." She pulls out one of her tools and starts wiping it with a rag, polishing the metallic sheen of a hammer. Concentrating on what's in her hands instead of at me. Maybe the tools, like Hadlee's camera, are her shields. "I wanted to be an engineer, but your dad wanted to run a business. I supported him for years, saving up some money for school before we had you." She puts down the hammer and pulls out some kind of wrench. "I love your father. I've always loved him." She puts the wrench down and looks up.

I'm suddenly terrified of what she's about to say.

"This was never supposed to be our lives. You were never

supposed to be stuck here." A pause. "I was never supposed to be stuck here."

No. This is not happening. Not today.

"I'm not stuck, Mom." My voice is weaker than I'd like it to be. "Neither are you. I would never want to be anywhere else except here with you guys."

She looks at me with such... pity. Like I'm not getting a point she's making. Her shoulders heave when she breathes.

"I love the three of us, but I think this life is finally catching up, especially to your father." She frowns. "Has he said anything to you lately? Like, being stressed or unhappy? About our finances?"

"What do you mean?"

"He just hasn't been himself, has he? Is it just me?"

It occurs to me that I can do one of two things: I can tell her the truth and betray Dad, maybe make his heart worse if he gets upset. Or I can lie to Mom and save both of my parents the pain of getting hurt. I know what the right thing to do is, but I also know it's not that simple, and I hate my parents for putting me in this situation.

"No, Mom. He seems fine to me." And for added effect: "Maybe he's just overtired?"

That's not technically untrue.

"Maybe. What about you?"

"What about me *what?*"

"Last night, when you mentioned Hadlee."

Oh my God. Not now. I don't have time for this.

"I'm sorry I freaked out like that."

"You can trust me. I won't tell your father. Has she tried to contact you at all?"

What the heck is this? Mom wants to keep secrets now too?

"She hasn't." My legs bounce as I get antsy. "I really need to run."

She picks up the measuring tape. "How's your head been?"

Does she know about the sleepwalking? The hallucinations? Shit.

"It's fine." My arms can't stay still. "I really need to go."

Pleasebuyit. Pleasebuyit. Pleasebuyit.

Still frowning, she resumes polishing her tools as I let the moment dissolve and walk out the front doors, guilty. Rosa is on the second story sweeping the walkway. She waves to me with a confused look, probably wondering why I'm not in school. Even though I know she knows the exact reason. I wave back. Then I round a corner and find Hadlee waiting, taking a picture of a butterfly in motion. The wings spread wide, her camera capturing their beauty.

I grab her hand, and we head in whatever direction fate will take us.

We walk down the road toward town. I have a pit in my stomach, but I try to ignore it. We stick fairly close to the side of the road by the woods, angling our bodies away so people driving by can hopefully not spot our faces. We're mostly silent, stopping every now and then so Hadlee can snap a picture of a bird or a squirrel or trash on the side of the road. Every now and then, she points the camera at me, ignoring my complaining, and snaps photos.

It's not until a half hour has passed that I realize Hadlee is taking me to her house. When I ask, she admits to it.

"Maggie will be at school, and my parents won't be home. Trust me."

You and Hadlee home alone in her house. If only this were any other normal teenage scenario where girl invites boy....

When we reach her street, Hadlee and I both sneak like

ninjas into her backyard and climb the tree to her balcony. Hadlee leads the way, some rogue leaves tickling my cheeks as they fall to the ground. Nothing is left untouched when it comes to her.

When I reach the base of her balcony, Hadlee extends a sweaty hand and helps hoist me over the railing. We look out at the peaceful neighborhood, most everyone either at school or work. Hadlee extends her hands, embracing the humid air, so I do the same.

There's a hint of fresh soil and mowed grass with the breeze, birds chirping from the treetops, and the revving of a motorcycle from a few blocks over.

"I love coming out here and just looking down at the world," she says. "Seeing everyone from afar. How they act when they think no one is watching. You really get to see inside the hearts of people when they think they're alone."

I look out with her, understanding exactly what she means. "That's how I feel about guests at our motel."

Hadlee positions herself against the railing to snap a few pictures of a middle-aged woman in an orange sweatband walking her dog down the street, unaware she's being watched.

"Mrs. Carmichael. Gorgeous, too. All the neighborhood boys adore her. Moved here earlier this year from a few towns over. Her husband passed away from a heart attack."

"That's really sad."

"I like to think maybe she moved here to start new, start fresh."

I can't help myself from taking the bait. "Is that what you still want to do?"

She lowers the camera and rubs her chin on her shoulder to scratch an itch. "I know that people have it worse than I do, Dev. I see it every day at school, in this neighborhood, on TV. I'm not delusional enough to think my pain is worse than everyone else's." She takes a breath. "Do you remember that used to be our dream? Starting fresh somewhere new."

"It was always yours." I clear my throat and lean on the railing with her. "I would've followed you anywhere you told me to go."

She slides closer to me. "But is that what you wanted?"

Wanted. I'm not sure what I wanted. What I still want.

Just you.

"It doesn't matter what I want. My parents need me. Their motel will sink if I'm not there to help. They'll worry about me constantly. They'd be homeless."

Hadlee chews on her lower lip. "That's not your problem. It's theirs."

"You don't understand."

"Don't I?" She stands straight. "I was at the motel day and night with you for years. I know how amazing your dad's cooking is, how badass your mom is with a monkey wrench and a screwdriver, and how Rosa had a fetish for scaring little kids with ghost stories and eating chocolate. And how creepy Mr. Day was when he'd come back from hunting. I know you better than anyone. I can tell when you're lying to me. I've always known."

"Yeah, you were always good at that." I stand up straight too.

"Where are you going to apply to college?"

I hesitate before answering, embarrassed. "I'm not."

She steps back like she didn't hear me correctly. "What are you talking about?"

"We can't afford it. I'm not smart enough for scholarships. I'm not good enough at track for a scholarship. I don't even know what I want to do. That motel is all I've ever known."

"You—you can't just not go to college. This is your life, not theirs."

"I don't know what my life is outside of the motel. It's all I have." I look her in the eyes. "I don't even have you anymore."

Hadlee curses under her breath. The door to her bedroom is unlocked, so she enters and stops midway through.

"You need to stand up and start doing things for yourself and not others. I love how selfless you are. It's one of your best traits. But there's so much in you that you can share with the world. Maybe so much you don't even know. But I see it. In the halls at school, when you're on the track field. I see who you really are."

She places her hand over my heart and it starts beating faster. She places my hand over hers. It's beating just as fast.

"Do you feel that?"

I nod, choking on my words. Melting.

"You're *alive*. We both are." She pushes her palm harder into my chest. "Don't be scared of the world, Dev. *Embrace* it."

We stand there holding our hearts. I want nothing more than to gather the courage to lean in and kiss her. Take her in my arms and let her wet kisses consume my own. Breathe her into me. Have her chestnut hair blanket my face. Maybe part of her wants me to, maybe expects me to. Maybe it's the opposite of what she wants. Something deep down is telling me, despite the circumstances, it's not the right moment to kiss her.

Not yet.

She walks all the way into her room, and I follow, closing the door behind her and drawing the curtains. Her room is the same as before, maybe more chaotic. Printed photos and sketches now lie on the floor and the unmade bed. Like it's the den of some manic stalker. She leads me to her bed where her MacBook is and types in her password, Mag0022—our nickname for Maggie that we called her when she was little.

I chastise myself for creeping on her password—turn on her bedroom light and walk around the room to take a closer look at all the pictures and sketches I never got a chance to view last time.

Most of the pictures are similar, if not exact replicas, of the ones on her website. Some dangle from strings pinned to her ceiling. Just moments. All just seemingly random. All dark and disturbing. One that stands out is a grown man leaning against a tree in a park in mid-cry. Another one shows a father grabbing the wrist of a little boy who fights against the strong grip. Another one shows a girl sitting by herself in the window to a coffee shop, a scarf around her neck as Hadlee focuses on her red-rimmed eyes.

Another one is the image of a graffitied wall: a red rose with a green stem. Above it is the illuminati symbol. The eye in the triangle. And below it are the bolded words:

THIS STATEMENT IS FALSE

Odd.

There are sketches of the woods, of the boy in the shorts I know too well. The boy is me. And on her desk is a half-written poem on a napkin:

> *She stays quiet*
> *to save grace*
> *"There is no cure for loneliness."*
> *Her hands*

> *weave butterflies*
> *Sometimes caterpillars*
> *die too*

Maybe last week I would've let it go. But we're both past that now. I hold it up.

"What's this?"

Hadlee looks up from her MacBook, closing the lid and putting it on her pillow. "It's just a poem."

I read it again and continue holding it up. "Is it, though?"

She gets up and walks to me, grabbing the napkin and reading it over.

"You remember how you said earlier you know me? It's a two-way street. So why don't you start telling me the truth like you promised." I wait for her to respond, but she doesn't. "You said you were lonely. You said your parents hate you. Hate me too. Are you...." I'm having trouble finding the words, hating that I have to ask. "Have you...."

"I haven't tried to hurt myself if that's what you think."

Thank God.

I nod, swallowing a lump in my throat. "So, you're not—?"

"I'm not suicidal." Her voice is quiet. "I just hate how fake it is."

"How fake *what* is?"

"The world. The people." She puts the napkin back on her desk and points to all the pictures. "People lie. My camera doesn't."

Who lies?

"Is that why you're always with your camera?"

"Partly, yeah. There's something naked and vulnerable in photography. It captures moments. It captures beauty. The world can't hide from the lens. People can't either. The smallest tick in their mouth or crinkle of their eyes, the hunch of their shoulders, the direction of their hips... it tells a story. Everything tells a story. Every story tells a truth."

She fumbles through a stack of photos on her desk and pulls one out. It's of a girl sitting on a bench staring at a boy walking his dog. He is focused on the golden retriever while she looks at him, adoration and longing in her eyes while hunched forward, pretending to be reading a book.

"What do you see here?" she asks. "What does this say?"

"That she's in love with him."

"Exactly!" She jumps. "And the guy?"

I study him, how his body is angled in her direction. "He's watching her?"

She smiles, proud. "If you were to go up to them in the park, it would be nothing more than a guy walking his dog and a girl reading her book. But from here," she points to the picture, "their story. Their truth." She hands it to me. "He goes there every Sunday to the exact same spot to walk his dog. She goes there to read. Do you know why?"

I look up into Hadlee's eyes, and I think I'm finally starting to understand.

"It's because he goes there for her."

She nods. "They go there for each other, but neither can admit it out loud. But in that" — she points again—"they can't lie."

I can't help but fall more in love with her as she continues to speak. So much passion and energy. As she talks about her photography, there's a spark behind her eyes that I've never seen before. I don't want it to ever go away.

"Can I ask you something?"

She nods.

"The other night when you freaked out, when we got close."

"Yeah."

"Was there a reason?"

She nods again, slowly.

I'm afraid to ask the next part. Terrified that I'll never be able to find the words. But then I go over the facts in my head once again: new style, no friends, obsession with dark things, how being close or touched irks her, the night terrors. My coma from being hit on the head.

"The day in the woods before I blacked out," I say. "I remember following you into the clearing; I remember chasing you around and falling down and kissing you."

I hold my breath, afraid to train my eyes up at her. I don't want to see her face for the next part. Don't want to know what the truth in her story is.

"You freaked out, and I remember there was clapping. Then...."

Hadlee holds both of my hands. "Dev, listen. You—"

"Did something bad happen to you out in those woods?"

I look anywhere but at her. My eyes land on her trashcan by the desk. Inside are some tissues, but on top is a juice box. Exactly like the ones we used to drink after school when I'd come over to play. Just like the ones Hadlee brought for us on that day in the woods.

Silence. Pins and needles. Heart hammering. Blood pumping. Hairs rising. Goosebumps showing. Ears ringing. Scar throbbing.

The scent of firewood.

There's this sense of heat against the side of my face, and the room around me becomes fuzzy. I feel like I'm going to vomit. And then:

I'm holding the jagged end of a beer bottle in front of me with one hand; the other is shoving Hadlee away. In front of me, a bonfire rages.

"Hadlee, run!"

"I can't leave y—"

"I'll be right behind you. Juuuust get out of here!"

Then a figure approaches, but my strength is weakening and my vision blurring. All I want to do is lie down, but I can't. I mustn't. Not until she's safe.

I'll die before they touch her.

He laughs. "You don't have the balls to do something with that, little boy."

I swing it but lose my balance and almost fall over before righting myself. Something is wrong. Something is very wrong.

"Hadleeeeee," I slur. "Get outta hereee. Get helllf."

"Get her!"

"I don't think this is a good——"

"Grab the bitch!"

"Lookit the lil' guy droolin'."

Thoughts aren't coming. Thoughts aren't come. Thoughts aren't.

Fuck. No. Noooooooo.

"Where do you think you're going?"

I blink several times in a row to shake away the dizziness and fatigue, but all it does is make my eyelids heavier and my functions slower.

I stumble. "Hallleeeeeeeeeee."

"Hadleeeeeeee," he mocks.

And then just like that, I'm back here, in the real world. Except I'm not in Hadlee's bedroom. I'm lying in a bathtub as it slowly engulfs me in ice-cold water. The faucet is running, and Hadlee is kneeling next to me with a damp cloth pressed to my forehead. Hadlee's face is scared, devastated, and guilty all at once.

When I gather the strength, my joints are too stiff to move, so I plead for Hadlee to pull me out with chattering teeth. My clothes are matted to my skin, constricting me, and my body is convulsing so bad.

What the hell just happened? Why are you submerged in ice water?

Hadlee hoists me out with all the strength she can muster, and then when I flop onto the tiles of her floor, she wraps a few blankets around to warm me up before cradling me to her. Rocking me back and forth. But the wet clothes on my skin keep emitting harsh waves of cold. The blankets do nothing.

You're fucking insane. You're sick. Maybe you do need the pills again.

"It's okay," she says, crying. "It's going to be okay." She hugs me tighter, and I hold on as if she were my anchor. "I'm going to make this okay. I have to. I have to. I have to."

She repeats it over and over like a skipping track. She keeps repeating it even after I warm up. But the cold won't leave my bones. It latches onto me like a parasite.

How can you make it right, Hads?

I think....

I think you were raped in the woods.

CHAPTER 25

I'M NOT SURE HOW LONG WE'RE ON THE FLOOR TOGETHER; my mind swirls with questions. It was a vision, a memory. Definitely a memory. Unlike any I've ever had before. Every now and then, I'd get these moments where some recollection leaks onto the surface of my mind, but this is the first time it's been a full-blown vision.

How could you have forgotten it, Dev? What else did you forget?

I'm freaked out, still unable to move or process the information, somehow comforted yet uncomfortable as Hadlee cradles me, rocks me like a baby. Her hands run through my curls, but she doesn't say anything. Neither do I. But I should be the one comforting her. The one telling her things will be okay.

Right?

I stare up, but her eyes seem glazed over. She's fixed on one of the shower walls. My gaze travels down the scar from her left shoulder to her breast. Before I know what I'm doing, my finger reaches up and traces it. She finally looks down, but she doesn't remove my fingers.

"Tell me."

Hadlee stops running her hands through my hair, so I slowly sit up, still shaky and freezing. She grabs a few strands of her hair to chew on, but I stop her.

"It's a bad habit."

She points to my bitten-off fingernails. "So is that."

I retract my hands, ashamed. She pulls up her knees to her chest and hugs her legs—rests her chin on them. But then I think about my vision again, and I'm forced to look away, like I'm somehow committing a cruel act by staring. Like I played a part in what happened to her.

She was... no. She can't... no. You would've known. She would've said something. Her parents would've said something. The police. The hospital. They would have arrested whoever did it. Right, Dev? There's no way. No way. No... way?

"What happened to you?" she asks, quiet.

Fuck. You have to tell her. You HAVE to. She's questioning what happened 'cause you've been acting so different lately. This is about her, not you. But you can't just ask her that. How do you just ask her if she was raped? How? How!

I make some kind of guttural noise with my throat, but Hadlee's gaze is so hot it burns. Like she's branding my soul, marking it. So many different things go through my head, but my mouth won't work. I can't even pick up my head to look at her. I can't speak. Can't think.

No. No. Nononononononono.

"Please say something."

That must be why she posted the nude photos. Right? Was it, like, her acting out?

I'm reeled back to the present moment. Hadlee's eyes are large and pleading. I don't know what to say, how to react. Nothing has changed between us. I'm still me, and she is still herself, but EVERYTHING feels different.

She's still Hadlee. She's lived her life. Don't be a dick, Dev. You know it changes nothing.

My eyes burn. I need some air. But before I can force my legs to work, the front door to her house opens and slams shut with a vibration that rattles the tile beneath us. Hadlee jumps up, bashing her head onto a corner of the porcelain sink. It shakes, causing a loud *BANG* that's enough to make me cringe. She cries out and falls to the ground, her hands darting to the top of her head. Her mouth opens into an O as she silently cries, her vocal cords not finding the right pitch yet.

I'm sliding across the floor and over to her before I even have time to contemplate what's going on. Her eyes water, and her lower lip trembles. I just want to take the pain away. When I pull her hand away to view the damage, a few trickles of blood are smeared on her palm. Before I can do or say anything, Hadlee points a shaky arm in the direction of her room across the hall—both doors are open.

From below: "HADLEE!" Her dad. "I got a call from the school. You better not be home!"

"Room," Hadlee chokes out, a tear falling out of her eye. "Don't leave." She winces, too weak to get up. "Please stay."

I'll never leave you again. Never.

I open my mouth to protest, but she points to the room again. Footsteps ascend the stairs, making my stomach drop, so I jump out of the bathroom, fly across the hall, and tuck my feet underneath me so I somersault into her room. It helps that her little sister Maggie showed us a few ballet and gymnastics moves when she was younger.

When I roll up onto my feet, I pivot my hips and silently force the door shut. My heart feels like it's ready to explode and sweat falls from my hairline. I'm going to die. Hadlee is hurt, may even need stitches if it's bad. And now Mr. Morgan is home, and I can't do anything to help her.

You weren't there for her in the woods. You weren't there over the past three years. You still can't be there 'cause you're a selfish asshole, Dev. Maybe that's why you sleepwalk, because you know it's true. You know it happened. Maybe a blow to the head made you forget. It happens—head trauma impacting memory.

From outside the door, I hear their muffled voices. I press my ear to listen, like a play:

Mr. Morgan: "Hadlee, where are y—why are—what happened?"

Hadlee: "I'm fine."

Mr. Morgan: "You're bleeding. Jesus Christ, it's always something."

Hadlee: "What are you doing here?"

(There is sniffling followed by feet shuffling. The echo of an ankle cracking as movement sounds through the door)

Mr. Morgan: "The school called. You didn't show up twice this week. I don't even know what to say anymore."

Hadlee: "Don't say any—ow! Don't touch it!"

Mr. Morgan: "You're hurt. This wouldn't have happened if you'd went to school. Goddammit, Hadlee. You never learn. No wonder your mother's never home."

Hadlee: (pause) "I'm sorry."

Mr. Morgan: (clears throat) "You're making me nervous. Let me ta—"

Hadlee: "Stop fucking touching it; I'm fine. I never asked you to come home."

Mr. Morgan: "Watch your mouth, young lady.

You're in my house, living off my dime. You will respect me, or I'll take away those cameras you love and sell them."

Hadlee: "I said I'm sorry."

Mr. Morgan: "No, you're not. It doesn't matter what we do, you'll just go off and do whatever you want with whoever you want. I'm done, kid. I don't know how to get through to you anymore." (pause) "Maybe the doctor was right. Maybe boarding school would do you good." (pause) "Do I need to take you to the hospital?"

Doctor? Does he mean a medical doctor or for therapy? Shit. Did they make her take pills too?

I pull my ear away from the door, feeling sick to my stomach. Heat courses through my body despite my hairs standing on edge. I'm filled with so much anger. So much hatred toward her dad, a man I used to look up to when I was little. She's lived like this the entire time. Our entire high school careers alone, like this, with a terrible secret. Let alone anytime her dad has laid a fucking finger on her.

There is no way I'd ever allow them to send her away. Or let her dad hurt her any more than he already has.

You have to make it right.

I move to open the door and storm out, punch her father right in the mouth. But then what? Run off with Hadlee? No. I can't. Not like this. There's a better way. I look around her room, my emotions soaring from guilt to disgust to anger. I don't know what to do, so I start pacing, praying that he doesn't walk into her room but hoping he does so I can lunge at him.

This anger is so sudden I'm not sure what it means or what to do. I'm biting on another fingernail until it snaps off between my teeth. I need to take a breath, sweating profusely now, and I sit on her bed. Her MacBook slides off the pillow, and without thinking, I open it. It requires her password: Magoo22, and before I know it, her desktop is pulled up.

Did you just hack her computer?

There's a picture of me and her when we were nine years old as we planted vegetables with Hadlee's mom in their back-yard. Mrs. Morgan is hunched down with a packet of seeds. Hadlee and I look up into the camera, shielding our eyes from the sun, beaming. Dirt smeared on our chins. Our arms are interlocked. Her in a polka-dotted one-piece bathing suit and me in just my swimming trunks. In the background is a slip-n-slide.

I touch the screen, thinking somehow I can get to the little kids in that photo that were untouched by whatever's happened between then and now, but I can't reach them.

Before I know what I'm doing, there's a blue folder marked:

Cherry in a Pit of Plums

I click on it, unable to stop myself but knowing it's beyond an invasion of her privacy. I start scrolling through some pictures.

Mr. Morgan: (raising his voice) "Let me help you."

Hadlee: (mumbles a response)

Mr. Morgan: "One more word and—"

Hadlee: (unrecognized response)

Mr. Morgan: "I'm done, Hadlee. That's enough of this routine. Bandage yourself up and then get downstairs. You're going back to school."

Hadlee: "I never asked you to leave work and come here. I'm not going back."

Mr. Morgan: "You ARE! Either by walking out or being dragged." (silence) "I'm your father. It's not my job to get you to like me."

Hadlee: "Stop. You're hurting me."

So many photos: bonfires, the police raid she showed me before, the couple sitting on the bench, the woods, the man in the dark lighting a cigarette, etc. It's all the same. But then farther down there are photos of a figure in the woods, taken from afar, only seeing the figure's backside. Right away, I know it's me. It looks like it was taken months ago. Who knows how many of these there are. Suddenly, snooping around on her computer feels fair, but I hate that I even try to justify what I'm doing.

There is a loud noise, a creak in the hallway, and my stomach leaps into my throat. I freeze, a statue, waiting for the door to swing open, but it doesn't.

There's another folder, zipped, in the middle of what appears to be hundreds of photos uploaded from her digital camera. It's labeled:

Bloodletting

I click on it, confused and creeped out. But when I do, it prompts for a password.

Shit. What the heck is this?

Mr. Morgan: "What are you wearing? Those look like a boy's clothes." (silence) "Did you—" (silence) "Are you kidding me?"

Hadlee: "It's not—"

Mr. Morgan: "Where the fuck is he?"

Hadlee: "Stoppit. I said you're hurting me."

Shit, Dev! Shit!

Before I know what I'm doing, I close the MacBook, hug it to my chest, and run to the closet across the room and hide inside. Before I catch a breath, I hear the door to her room open, but I can't see anything in the dark. Only a faint line of light underneath the door. Different outfits press into my back, and one of my curls gets caught on a zipper to a jacket, making me wince as I try to untangle myself. The closet, like Hadlee, smells of lilac.

Mr. Morgan: "You've really outdone yourself this time, kid."

Hadlee: "Dev's not in here. I told you we don't talk anymore."

Mr. Morgan: "Do you think I'm stupid? I've seen you wear some outrageous things, but that's clearly a boy's outfit. And you don't own any shirts like that."

Hadlee: (quiet) "I'm surprised you noticed."

Mr. Morgan: "I notice everything about you. *Everything.*"

Hadlee: "Just take me to school. Please."

Mr. Morgan: "Did he sneak out the window? Were you two having sex?"

Hadlee: "Please stop."

Mr. Morgan: "The Landries are trash; you know how we feel about them. But if I find that you've been seeing that boy behind my back...."

Hadlee: "His name is Dev."

Mr. Morgan: (angry) "Should I go visit his parents with my lawyer?"

Hadlee: "Daddy, no! Stop."

And it's there again, the *daddy* that just doesn't feel right.

Mr. Morgan: "After everything we did to protect you from this, if you waste it all on that Landry boy, then you won't be welcome in this house anymore. He's trouble. Understood?"

Hadlee: (mumbled response)

Mr. Morgan: "I'm sorry, what did you say?"

Hadlee: "I'll go back to school; just let me change my clothes."

Mr. Morgan: (sounds of things falling to the ground, papers being shuffled, bed sheets ruffled) "Why couldn't you be more like your little sister?"

Asshole.

And I smell it again, seemingly stuck to her clothes in the closet. Firewood.

There's a muffled sound like a scuffle followed by a very loud *THUMP* that vibrates the ground.

Oh shit.

Before I know it, the closet door swings open, and her dad is there with gritted teeth. He grabs me by the collar and rips me out of the closet.

The outside light is so sharp, I have to squint. It hurts.

"Just going to hide in there while I degrade my daughter? Is that the type of man you are?"

Hadlee is lying face down on the carpet, the left side of her face red. I don't remember her being slapped. She's begging for me to help her, extending a hand my way. Her dad shakes me so hard my head spins.

"Did you help my daughter when she was being violated in the woods? Or did you forget because you were the one that caused it?"

"No. No!" I shout. "I didn't—"

"Bullshit!" He shakes me again. "Maybe you did it yourself.

Maybe you were tired of being the best friend and thought why not fuck her right in the woods. IS THAT IT!?"

"NO!"

Hadlee is crying behind him, and I can't reach her. I can't reach her. I can't.

Her dad shakes me again, lifting me in the air by my collar like I'm nothing more than a paperweight. "It wasn't her that left, Dev. It was you. You left my little girl alone the past three years to deal with this. YOU did this. YOU are the reason everything is messed up."

"I-I'm sorry," I cry. "I didn't mean to."

Hadlee screams until her voice goes raw. Screams so loud it pierces my eardrums. And then she opens her eyes and calls to me:

"Dev. Dev. Dev. Dev. Dev."

The sharp light blinks out.

And just like that, I'm back in the closet. The door is open, and Hadlee is staring at me with a freaked look. I'm still holding her computer in my hands, but she doesn't seem to notice. Her eyes dart behind her, but her dad is gone.

"What the hell is going on with you?" she whispers.

My mouth is too dry to answer. I don't understand what's happening. Hadlee doesn't wait for me to respond before grabbing my shoulder and yanking me out of the closet.

Her dad isn't here. Her face has no red mark. The light isn't sharp.

WTF?!

"Wait until we drive down the street and go back to the motel. I'll come find you." she whispers, still not noticing her MacBook in my arms.

She reaches into the closet and pulls out a random owl-print T-shirt and a pair of red leggings. It makes no sense fashion wise, but Hadlee makes it work. It occurs to me now that neither one of us has showered since yesterday.

"I'm so sorry, Dev. Just... you'll be okay, right?"

OhmyGodohmyGodohmyGodohmyGod.

I don't respond before she leans in and kisses me on the cheek, furrows her brows, and dashes into the hallway and down the stairs where her dad must be waiting.

I'm not sure how long I stand there after they must have driven off.

I'm not sure how I got home when I find myself standing in Room 13, wearing the same clothes and realizing for the first time how rancid I smell when I lift my arms.

Was that all in your head?

And I'm definitely not sure when I made the decision to take Hadlee's MacBook Pro without telling her.

It's open, on my bed, with the locked folder files. I'm not even sure what the password could possibly be. Not sure if I really want to know. Not even if I have the guts to break into her personal space.

I close the lid to the Mac, resisting the temptation despite jonesing for whatever version of Hadlee that is hidden away, locked up, and keeping me at arm's length.

If it's true, if what I think's happened really did, then it makes sense. Her changing. My coma. Why my parents were freaked out. But not why everyone hates each other.

I just hope it's not true.

But I also can't help but worry. The sleepwalking was one thing, but with Hadlee's night terror, my nail biting, and now three times I've hallucinated in the span of less than twenty-four hours....

You will NEVER go back on those meds. Never.

What's happening to me? Why can't I stop it?

More importantly:

What will it all mean when I uncover the full truth?

BUTTERFLY TRAPPED IN A BELL JAR

PART FIVE

CHAPTER 26

Her computer tempts me so badly that I can't stand to be around it anymore. I find a way to make it outside the front door of Room 13 without anyone noticing. Rosa is busy vacuuming inside Room 4, Mr. Day hasn't opened his door to creep me out yet, and Rory is standing just outside the front office with his back turned. The sun hangs high in the sky, and it's just after noon. My armpits immediately become slick, and sweat beads the back of my neck.

I bring my thumb to my mouth to chew on a nail but see it's already bitten practically to the cuticle. The exposed skin raw and swollen. Dried blood on the surface, yet I don't feel any pain.

Rory must hear me approach because he faces me and waves. He's got on a cheap pair of sunglasses——wearing a black T-shirt with holes below his chest. He smiles, flashing the gap between his two front teeth.

"Godfather! Just who I was lookin' for."

"What's up, Rory?" My mouth says the words, but I don't remember thinking them.

He slaps me on the back when I'm close enough, wrapping

his arm around my damp neck. I shield my eyes from the sun. I don't want him touching me.

"Had a crazy dream last night, man." He squeezes my shoulder with more force than is wanted or necessary. "Sounded like someone was gettin' murdered. A girl. Woke up in sweats and shit. I was gonna run to the front office to get your dad to check it out."

Don't you dare try and break into her files, Dev. That's beyond a dick move.

"But," Rory continues, "too scared. 'Cause then I got to thinkin', what if I get outta bed and these claws just reach out and pull me under? Then I'll be dragged into some shit, bro. That's fucked. This motel is just messin' with me." He digs his nails into my shoulder. "But I did what you said the other day and just chilled the eff out."

"Sounds good," I mumble.

She needs help, Dev. Help her. Don't betray her. TALK to Hadlee.

"You all right?" he asks. "You're gettin' all silent on me." His bloodshot eyes go wide. "Was that shit real? Fuck. I don't even know anymore."

I can't take Rory, not today.

"You dreamed it, Rory. Stop freaking out." I shake off his hands. "Lay off the drugs, because you're starting to sound like a cliché."

That was an asshole thing to say.

Rory backs up. "Whoa. Easy there, killer. You look tired. You get any sleep last night?"

I don't know why I don't just let it go. Rory has no way of knowing the truth, and there's no way I can tell him. He's just trying to be a friend, but I can't stop what comes out of my mouth.

"I'm sorry, just, can we please talk later? I'm kind of busy right now and you're being annoying."

Rory, for a moment, doesn't react at all. If he does his sunglasses mask it. But then he steps back with his hands up.

"Sorry. I'll just go back to my room, Godfather."

"No, it's fine. It's ju—"

The light outside gets sharp, blindingly so. I have to shield my eyes, caught off guard.

"S'all good. You know best, Don Landry." He flashes a mischievous smile. "Bet she opened up like a flower in the woods."

My heart skips a beat, and I rub my eyes, catching a breath I didn't know I missed. "W–what was that?"

The sharp light blinks out.

Rory stares at me with a straight face, his nose scrunched. "I said I hope you feel better."

When I don't respond, he skulks away, and I feel terrible. I shake my head and slap my face.

"Get it together, Dev," I tell myself. "You're losing it."

I'm not ready to face anyone else yet, and before I realize it, I'm walking up the stairs to find Rosa. She's in her Secret Keeper uniform, still vacuuming. She turns it off when she sees me approach and raises her hands in the air questioningly.

"Why you *no en* school?"

"Mental health day."

She puffs up a breath to move a few strands of hair off her nose. "What wrong?" She motions to the bed, so I close the door behind me and walk over to sit.

I'm not sure where to start or what to share. I can't tell her the full truth about Hadlee, not until I figure it out myself. So, I tell her how she slept over last night, leaving out the details of the sleepwalking and my vision of the woods. I even tell her about Hadlee's night terror. Rosa listens, doesn't interrupt.

When I'm done, she reaches over to her cart and hands me the whole pack of Kisses.

"You need all the chocolate, *hijo*."

"*Gracias*."

"*De nada*."

I unwrap a few of the tiny candies and pop a handful into my mouth, let the milk chocolate warm and melt over my tongue. My mouth waters as it liquefies, and I swallow it down. I reach in for more. Rosa does too.

"You tell *tus padres*?"

"What would I tell them, Rosa?"

"Her *padre*, he hurt her?"

I wait until I swallow, some chocolate leaking onto my chin. I wipe it away. "I think so. Hadlee never really came out and specifically said yes, but she damn near implied it."

Rosa looks really sad. Helpless, even. "You feel guilty?"

"I wasn't there for her, Rosa. In the three years, I've been here cooped up in this motel—and I love my parents and I love you. But now she's back and saying that it wasn't her choice for us to be apart." I feel my eyes water and get up to pace the room. "Three years wasted."

"No."

"We could've been friends. We could've, I don't know, maybe been together."

"*Hijo*."

"And now everything is just different and so messed up."

"*Chamaco. Escucha.* Listen."

"I mean, this is my fault, right? Hadlee was physically hurt back then, like me. Maybe emotionally hurt. Her relationship with her family is toxic, abusive. She is keeping some secret from me. And she can't tell me because I left her. I did something I shouldn't have, or didn't do something I should have. Or someone else did something they shouldn't have."

"Stop."

"And now she doesn't trust me. Her parents hate me. My parents hate her. I shouldn't have kissed her, shouldn't have freaked her out. But I can't remember, Rosa." I grab my hair and start to pull. "I can't remember a goddamn thing because I'm broken inside."

Rosa immediately grabs my arms and pins them by my sides and hugs me so tightly I can't breathe. My eyes water again, so I wipe them on Rosa's uniform. She massages my back and guides me to sit back down on the bed.

"Story time, *sí?*"

I nod. "*Sí.*"

Rosa places a hand on my shoulder, contemplates something, and then exhales. "You remember, hmm, *camion de bomberos?*"

"Fire truck?"

"*Sí!* Fire truck." She smiles, furrows her brow. "You remember fire truck you got for *Navidad cuando tenías seis?*"

"When I was six? No."

"No surprised." She pats my shoulder and reaches for a Kiss to pop in her mouth. "*Tu abuela* sent it to you." She motions with the object with her hands. "Came in big, red box. Sat under tree for *una semana. Y cada día* you go down and look at it, hug it, wonder what inside." She shakes an imaginary box. "Drove you *loco*. Crazy." She touches her temple.

Rosa gets up to hand me a duster from her cart. I take one, and together we start dusting the dressers and lamps around the room while she continues.

"Morning of *Navidad* came, *y* you asked only for that *presente*." She smiles to herself, seemingly lost in the memory. "After you open, you put truck aside and play with box all day long. *Tu madre no* believe it. The box drove you *loco* wondering what inside, it even drove *tu madre loca también*."

We put away the dusters and work together to change the bedding.

"Then you find out what it was, yet you still love box more than what inside." She stops momentarily to point to my chest. "*Dentro*." She wipes more hair out of her face. "*Tú entiendes?*"

I shake my head. "Not really, no." I don't even remember my grandma sending me a fire truck.

She frowns, but then strokes her lip with a finger before continuing. "Sometimes we drive ourselves *loco* worrying about wrong things. Maybe *es no* what inside. Maybe *es* what you see *cada día*. Every day." She smiles, hopeful. "*Sí?*"

I shake my head, still not understanding the connection. We finish making the bed. Rosa comes up to me and places both hands on my shoulders.

"You too focused on what the *presente* was that it was *no* exciting for you. It was mystery of what *tu abuela* sent that drove you *loco*." She waits, and I think I'm starting to understand now. "Maybe *es no* what Hadlee *es* keeping from you. Maybe *es* why." She motions a box with her hands. "Packaging *no es* everything. We give power to things in dark. Only see true value when brought in light." Rosa touches my chin with her thumb, ruffles my hair, and pats my back. "No more long face. Very handsome. *Sí?*"

Rosa walks away from me to continue her vacuuming. I'm left standing there for another moment, contemplating what just happened. How it makes so much sense now. If Hadlee really was sexually assaulted, then why didn't she say anything? Maybe Rosa is right. Maybe it's not what happened, but why she still can't say it.

Maybe you're not the only person who lost their memory, Dev.

When Rosa realizes that my mind has wandered and has prevented me from cleaning efficiently, she sends me away, muttering in Spanish. I attempt to go to my "fake" room and do some homework for class, but can't concentrate. Dad is still sleeping, so I manage the front desk for a while when Mom leaves to go fix the washing machine that's on the fritz. So far, the only other guest actually staying with us is Mr. Day. It's pointless to even pretend to be doing work.

It's never been this dead before. Not ever. Not that I can remember.

Then I get a text:

HADLEE

Hey.

> ME
>
> hey

HADLEE

How are you doing?

> ME
>
> im ok

HADLEE

I didn't mean to just leave you like that.

> ME
>
> r u ok?

HADLEE

Not really. I'm worried about you.

> ME
>
> dont b
>
> hows ur head?

HADLEE

It stopped bleeding.

ME

can i ask u something?

HADLEE

He didn't hit me, if that's what you were wondering.

I would tell you if he did. He just kept squeezing my arm really hard.

ME

ok. but does he always treat you like that?

HADLEE

Yeah.

I don't realize I'm biting my tongue until a sharp pain pings in my mouth and I get the coppery taste of blood. I pound my fist on the front counter.

ME

i need 2 c u again

HADLEE

I was just thinking the same thing.

ME

can u skip school?

HADLEE

No.

If they call my dad again I'm going to be in SO much trouble.

I wish I could though. I really want to see you.

My heart skips.

ME

maybe i could just go 2 u

i mean my mom is fixing the washer

> but when shes done...

HADLEE

You can't just show up at school after skipping.
But we can meet after school is over. Do you
want me to go to you, or do you want to meet
somewhere else?

ME

> ill c u there

> we can go wherever

The front door to the office opens, but I don't look up to see who it is when I get the next text.

HADLEE

I'll meet you out by the road, past the entrance.
Okay?

ME

> sounds good

> c u then

HADLEE

Be careful, Dev.

And PLEASE text me if anything happens,
okay?

ME

> wut do u mean?

> wut else would happen?

Radio silence.

I must be in a daze, because the silver bell on the front counter is rung by the person who walked into the front office, and I look up and see a girl waiting. A customer.

"S-Sorry," I utter. "Welcome to Brooke Meadows Inn. How many days do you need a room for?"

The girl stares at me with a blank expression, blinks once, and doesn't say a word. She's one of those types of girls that just looking at her intimidates you. She's not dressed like anyone that goes to our school, kind of goth/emo/punk rolled into one, but she looks my age, maybe a year or two older. She wears some kind of combat boots, I think, with fishnet over nylon leggings. A red plaid mini-skirt. Fingerless gloves that travel up to her elbow.

All she has with her is a backpack about to burst at the seams. Clearly, she's been traveling for a while, as some of her hair clings to the side of her face, the top of her nose glistening. Her clothes look used in a haven't-been-washed-in-a-few-days-look. There's no car or taxi outside, so she's been traveling on foot. Hitchhiker.

She's either running from something or searching for something. I've seen her type before.

I swallow saliva. "Are you looking for a room?"

She stares at me again, expressionless. I'm afraid she's going to jump over the counter and throttle me. And then I see the hoop nose piercing and immediately think of Hadlee's septum piercing.

She puffs up her red bangs. Her brunette hair is highlighted red, hanging over her shoulders in a just-rolled-out-of-bed way. The color kind of reminds me of Hadlee's hair.

Hadlee's prettier.

"How much?" Her voice is raspy and hoarse.

I tell her the price just as Dad walks out of his bedroom door. He looks at the girl as if she were a mirage, like us getting a customer is a figment of his imagination. I nod to him to let him know I can take care of her. Normally, he would take over, but for some reason he doesn't. He just nods back, attempts a smile, buttoning up a striped shirt. His face looks pale, almost ashen.

It freaks me out.

"Tell your mother I'll be back soon," he huffs.

"Where are you going?"

"Just need to take care of a few things for the motel."

He doesn't look back at me as he says it. But he does smile and wave to the girl before he walks out the front. He stands outside the door waiting for something. I'm about to walk to him and see what's up before I realize the girl is still waiting.

"One night." As if someone were silently scolding her, she begrudgingly adds, "Thanks." Her stomach growls.

She hands me the cash and her driver's license. I take it and enter her information into the computer, copy down all I need, and then cash her out, giving her the change. As she holds out her hand, each middle finger painted black, I look up and see Rory's truck pull up to Dad. He gets in, and the two drive off and out of sight.

What the hell?

The girl clears her throat, so I finish handing her the change and her room key; my eyes pass over a seashell necklace around her neck. I almost wish I could take it from her—it seems like something Hadlee would love.

"That's a really beautiful necklace."

Right away, I regret saying anything, because she clasps the necklace in her hand as if I'm about to steal it. Once again, I'm clueless when it comes to paying any kind of compliment to anyone ever.

Why does Hadlee even tolerate you?

But then she says, "It is." A pause. "Thanks. Again. Or whatever." Another stomach growl.

I think her eyes glaze over, but I can't be sure, because she hums some kind of tune and straightens her backpack. I hand her back her license and cringe at what I'm about to say next.

"Enjoy your stay at Brooke Meadows. Where our family is your family. The one-stop pit-stop for your hospitality needs."

It takes a moment, but then she smirks, and I notice she has one single dimple.

"Dude."

"My parents make me say it."

"Relax. It's cute."

"Really?"

"Fuck no. It's terrible." She pauses. "And don't apologize for being yourself. Ever."

I like this girl, despite being terrified of her. "Yeah... it is terrible."

She puts away her license and twirls around, her stomach once again growling. But I can't take it anymore. I hop around the front counter, grabbing the vending machine key, and walk to open it up. Most of the stuff in here is terrible, even outdated. The cheese crackers my dad loves and the Pop-Tarts are really the only edible things, so I reach in and throw her a strawberry package. She catches it, despite me not warning her I was doing so. But she doesn't change her sour expression, just holds the food. I close and lock the vending machine and make my way back around the counter.

"Don't tell anyone I did that for you." Still nothing, so I add: "My parents will make me pay interest on it." Again, no response, and I feel like a fool.

She walks to the front door before turning back to face me. She squints her eyes and cocks her head, studying me. I shiver a little. It's weird.

"Thanks," she says, again, strained. Like it's taking all she has. Like she's made some kind of promise to someone to be this way.

I can't help but feel she's a very sad girl inside.

"For what?" I ask.

"Being nice. Small towns and I don't tend to mesh."

"Um, you're welcome?"

"Don't phrase your sentences like questions. It's very passive and unattractive." She straightens up. "What's your name?"

"Dev. And you're right. It is passive. I'm working on it." I inhale and exhale. "What's your name?" Even though I already know what it is from her license, it feels like the polite thing to do.

She opens up the Pop-Tarts and breaks off a piece to put in her mouth. Then spits it into her hand and chucks it outside the door. "Fuck, these are terrible. Are these death?" She looks at the package. "Expired a year ago." She frowns. "Sadly, this was better than my last meal."

My face gets hot. "I-I'm sorry."

"Stop apologizing." A pause. "It's Aubrey." She grins again. "You remind me of someone."

Now I cock my head. Maybe she did go to our school, in which case, I'm a terrible person for never noticing. "Who?"

But she doesn't respond, she just studies me again, touching her necklace, and her eyes seem to glaze over. She salutes good-bye, holds up the pastries in acknowledgment despite knowing full well she won't finish eating them, and walks out the front door to her room.

I curse myself for being so awkward. But that feeling is gone as soon as I remember that Dad went somewhere with Rory.

Why would they leave together? Where could they be going? What could Dad be doing with a stoner/dealer? Does this have something to do with the spreadsheet of names and dates?

It leaves a very bad taste in my mouth, and when Mom comes back and asks where Dad went when she finds him gone, I lie and tell her he went for a brief walk, which is a terrible lie, because Dad *never* goes for walks. And I can tell Mom doesn't buy it, but she doesn't say anything. Just looks sad, like things are falling apart right before her eyes and she can't do anything to make all the pieces fit together again.

Our life can't be fixed by her toolbox.

It's like we're all living in a house of cards right now. Sooner or later, it's all going to come toppling down with the slightest push.

I don't want to be there when it eventually does.

CHAPTER 27

After I manage to shower and dress in fresh clothes, I tell Mom I'm going to track practice. She's so concerned about Dad, who still hasn't come home, that she doesn't even really give more than a hum before I walk toward the school. It's too humid out to run, and really, I'm just not in the mood. The walk itself takes over an hour, and by then it's a little after three in the afternoon. The regular buses have already left; only a few cars remain in the parking lot from leftover faculty and the upperclassmen who stay for extracurricular activities.

I hide behind some shrubbery on the side of the road, fully aware that anyone driving by can see me. Hadlee is pacing along the right side of the school building, so I make my way over to her. Her camera dangles from her neck. She sees me, and together we make our way to the shade of the building to hide out. When we press our backs to the brick siding, a wave of her body odor comes my way, and I recoil a little. Not on purpose, but she notices just the same, and I feel terrible.

"I haven't showered, okay?" she says defensively.

I wave my hand to shoo the comment away. "We can't stay here."

She agrees, and we edge along the building until we reach a patch of open gravel before the soccer field. On the left side of the field are the bleachers dividing this field from the track. The girls' volleyball team is out in the middle of the soccer field, so we crouch down low, around a large lawnmower, and dart to a nearby tree and hide behind the bark. I press my back to the trunk, Hadlee stepping into me until her breasts are pressed to my chest and I can feel them—

OHMYGAWD HER BREASTS!

—squish beneath her bra. The seam of the jeans I'm wearing becomes taut, and I have to close my eyes and will myself to think of anything besides how soft her boobs feel. I don't even care that her un-showered odor surrounds us. Nothing can ruin the physical contact. I could lean in and kiss her right now and—

What if she really was raped, Dev?

Right away, any sexual tension just deflates like a tire. The heat is gone, and the closeness suddenly makes me feel like some kind of predator, and I get uncomfortable. Hadlee must sense the change, because she backs up, putting an invisible barrier between our skin.

We don't talk, but there's this fear in her eyes. Maybe she knows something is up. Starting to suspect I know her secret. There's an unspoken understanding as we hold our breaths and run as fast as we can across the open field in hopes none of the volleyball team sees us. We run until we reach the open area of a thin patch of woods. Part of the cross-country trail moves past here, so we can safely hide on the path without anyone coming. Coach never has us run the cross-country trail the day before a track meet.

And then I remember that tomorrow is a meet and I didn't even go to practice.

He's going to have my balls for dinner.

We stop to catch our breaths, her hands on her knees. She's not used to this as much as I am. I give her a second to recoup before we do anything else.

Hadlee stands straight and runs her hands through her hair. "About what you heard earlier in the closet—"

"I had no idea it was that bad."

"That's because it's not."

"It is, though."

Hadlee turns, her back to me, fumbling with her camera. "I don't want your pity, or anyone else's. Maybe I deserve to be treated the way I am."

So, her dad confronting you was a hallucination then....

I walk up and stand next to her. "No, *you don't*, Hads." I turn her around to face me. "He's your dad. He should never talk to you like that, no matter what. How could you possibly think you deserve that?"

"I only have to put up with it until college, then none of this will matter."

"And your mom doesn't say or do anything?"

Hadlee doesn't look me in the eye. "Can we talk about what happened in my room before you passed out?"

I freeze, panicked. Not sure how to ask her what I want to ask her. Not sure if I even want to. "I can't really explain it...."

Hadlee backs up and paces around, attempts to put strands of hair into her mouth, thinks better of it, and stops. I look at my own hands for a clean nail but find only my left pinkie that's not bitten raw. I nibble until I tear away a nice chunk.

Hadlee watches, wincing and pacing. "I put you in cold water 'cause you were muttering something, and you were burning up. I was going to call the police, but I wanted you to wake up. A cold bath seemed like a smart idea in the moment."

"I think it worked?"

"What did you see?" She stops pacing.

Now or never, bud.

"I... I think I saw a vision from that day in the woods."

She stops, waiting on edge for me to continue. I think I can feel the anxiety emanating from her, and it makes me anxious too. So, I continue cautiously, short of breath throughout.

"We were by a fire, I was yelling at you to run, and... I...."

Hadlee starts to walk to me but stops herself and creates distance. The camera is clutched so tightly in her hands, I'm afraid she's going to crush it. Her knuckles are white.

"You didn't see anything else?"

I can't do this. I can't. How can I possibly ask Hadlee if she was assaulted? What person can ask another person that? How do I even start?

"T-These guys were taunting you."

"Okay."

"They were making fun of me."

"Right."

"I was yelling at you to run and get help."

"Dev."

"Hadlee."

She finally closes the gap and takes my hands in hers. They're sweaty and shaking. Goosebumps rise on her flesh. It makes goosebumps rise on my own.

"Were—was—um...."

Hadlee squeezes my hands tighter and nods for me to go on. Her lower lip trembles. I just want to suck her lip into my mouth and take her into me. I want all of her right in this second. It's disgusting that in such a tough moment I just want her, like somehow it will make everything better. I hate that we're skirting around sexual assault, and I'm here sexualizing it.

What kind of fucking asshole does that even make me?

"Dev, listen—"

"Were you raped?"

My stomach is in my eyes—my heart in my toes. There is the hollow nothingness that bounces from me to her. It seems as if the sounds of the outside world stop; we're in a bubble. She stops shaking, and she doesn't blink or move or twitch. Just. Nothing.

Terrible mistake. I've made a terrible, horrible mistake. Maybe she'll laugh it off. Hopefully she does. But the more the time passes, the more I think I've made some fatal error.

This is going to destroy us. Whatever version of us that is left. Then it happens:

Hadlee laughs.

Not a light cry or a shrill hiss of air. Not even a grunt of frustration or annoyance. It's a full-on hysterical laugh that slowly morphs into just plain hysterics, bordering on screaming. If I wasn't here with her, I'd be afraid she was being attacked. Just like when she was having the night terror.

Immediately, my feet backpedal from her—hands rise in the air as if to fend off some feral intruder. My feet manage to trip over a twig, and I fall back onto my butt. I don't even notice the pain as Hadlee balls her hands into fists, bends over, and laugh-cries into her palms. At me. Trying so desperately to silence her pain.

Did I say the wrong thing?

"Oh, Dev." She shakes her head, looking up at me but avoiding my eye contact at the same time. "Fuckfuckfuckfuckfuckfuck."

Tears stream out of my eyes, and I hate myself. Hate what I've done. Wish I could take it all back. Wish I could go back and never let her stay in my motel last Saturday night when she showed up. Maybe if I turned her away, she wouldn't be here in this state. Maybe she wouldn't be in so much pain.

It's there again. Firewood. A sharp, blinding light.

Hadlee is crying now, snot coming from her nose. She stops like it was nothing, her scream carrying on the wind and echoing around us. If no one knew we were here before, they will now. I scramble to get up. Hadlee stares at me, her eyes like daggers. But there's no hate there. Just the opposite. It's so contradictory. So pure and raw.

I raise my hands and inch towards her in a peace offering. "H––Ha––Had––"

She stands at an unnaturally odd angle. The tears from before suddenly cut like she turned off the nozzle to her sadness. She wipes snot away on the back of her hand.

"I'm sorry," I say. "I'm so sorry."

She blinks in response. There is something wrong about this. Something terribly wrong. My head starts to feel heavy, so I shake it away. My eyes dart around for signs of people approaching. It could be any second now.

"We have to go," I say. "Someone is going to come. We have to––"

Hadlee blinks again. She's not responding.

Why isn't she responding?

"Please." My right foot is prepared for flight, my left planted in place. At war within myself. "I'm sorry. Whatever I did, whatever I didn't do, just please come with me. I don't care what happened to you, Hadlee. I wasn't there for you, but let me make it right. Just come with me. Please."

My head feels heavy again, and I close my eyes to shake it away. When I open them Hadlee is wearing the same clothes that she was in in the woods three years ago. Her shoes are tied together from the laces with a knot, and her shirt is torn at the shoulder and abdomen. Her scars are fresh, oozing blood down into her breasts and waist.

Her pants are around her ankles, and her knees are muddy. Her inner thighs are bruised, jaundiced. The right side of her face has a gigantic, bright red handprint, as if someone was holding her face to the ground. But when I shake my head again, everything is back to normal and I'm in the now. Hadlee's eyes are wide, still in the same position as before.

But then she opens her mouth in a whisper. "Maybe you raped me, Dev. Maybe you're the one who did this to me."

"No!" I shout back at her. "No, I didn't!"

Hadlee doesn't respond.

I slap myself in the face, but she's still there, staring at me with her accusing eyes. I can't even tell anymore if I'm imagining this or not. Am I even really here in the woods? Is Hadlee really here with me? Is this another hallucination?

"I would've been there for you!" I shout again before controlling myself. "If I would've known, I could've helped you through this." I step toward her, but she steps back, so I stop. Then her voice in my head from the day at the garage sale when we found the pocket watch:

"Don't leave me, Dev."

"I'm never going to leave you again," I whisper.

"Can you keep a secret?"

The blinding light blinks out. The only scent that lingers is pine.

Hadlee is suddenly right in front of me, less than inches apart. A single tear falls from her eye, so I wipe it away with my thumb. She falls into me, her arms wrapping around my waist, and her head presses into my chest. I wrap my arms around her and rest my chin on the top of her head, feel her body expand and contract with each breath she takes.

No.

Then she says, "Are you having visions?" Hadlee must take my silence as admission because she hugs me tighter. "You've been hallucinating?"

Not again.

"H-How did you—"

"You were screaming, Dev." Even tighter, followed by a whisper, "I don't want this to destroy you."

You weren't screaming. SHE was screaming. What is she talking about?

Before I can respond, there is a ruffle of branches from down the path. A few girls call out, asking if anybody is here or needs help.

She screamed.

Without wasting time, I grab Hadlee's hand to book it, but her feet are planted to the ground. She shakes her head, refusing to go.

"What are you doing? We need to—"

"Go," she says. "I'll find you later."

"But—"

"Are you going to be okay to make it to the motel safely?"

I panic, looking both ways, debating whether to stay or run. Hadlee shouldn't be left alone, not now after that breakdown that may or may not have been in my head. I try to grab her hand, but she pulls it away.

SHE was the one who screamed. Not you.

She shoos me. "Get out of here. I'll handle the volleyball team. Just leave, Dev. Please. I'll fix this for you. I'll fix you. I promise."

Fix me?

There's not an opportunity to argue, because as soon as I see the shape of bodies down the path, I curse and sprint to the end of the woods. Without looking to make sure no one is outside in the open, I jump out of a patch of trees and look behind me to see if Hadlee changed her mind, but she's not coming. Just as I turn my head to look forward, I see Coach Odis standing with his clipboard by his hip. He points to me, and right away I stop, like he sucked the life right out of me.

"Landry!"

"C-Coach?"

He looks around, some of the volleyball team and the track team are huddled in big groups down both sides of the field. Hadlee's scream or laugh or whatever must have sounded worse than I thought.

Not yours.

"What the hell are you doing?"

"I-uh, I—"

He stomps over to me. "We almost called the police."

"Y-You what?"

He stops, menacing. "Did I stutter, Landry?" He looks behind me for some explanation. "Are you hurt? Is somebody else hurt?"

I shake my head.

"Someone was screaming. Was it you?"

"I...." Looking behind me, a few of the girls' volleyball players exit the path, bewildered. Hadlee isn't with them. She must've gotten away. "I...."

Coach Odis calls to the volleyball coach down the field, "Nothing?"

I look and see a few girls shake their heads. When Coach looks at the girls, who just exited nearest to us, they shrug and glare.

"Come with me."

"I can exp—"

"Now. Not a question, Landry."

We walk to the school's back entrance, past the track team

as they all stand in a horde by the bleachers. Travis folds his arms over his chest.

"Weathers," Coach calls. "Go to school security and tell them a student was screaming. I want to make sure that area is looked at. Get them out here." He shouts to the entire field, "Everyone else stay together."

Travis runs off toward the direction of the school police, his eyes not leaving mine.

Coach leads me past the boys' locker room and into his small office, complete with a desk, an outdated PC, and a three-tier filing cabinet that's dented in the middle. It smells like musty gym socks in here. Coach Odis points to a rusty metallic chair, so I sit.

It couldn't have been you screaming.

He paces the two feet behind his desk before sitting down and leaning with his elbows. "I don't know where to even start." He sighs obnoxiously and leans back. His chair creaks as he does. "You weren't in school today. You ran off after practice yesterday. Now you're in the woods around school, and we hear someone scream." He leans forward again, the chair replying. "Was anyone else with you?"

I shake my head. "No, Coach."

He stares at me, and I have to look away.

"Are you hurt?"

"No."

"What were you doing in the woods?"

What were you doing?

"Shhhh, stop moving."

"I—I heard the scream too."

"You heard someone else? Not yourself?"

I nod and shake my head at the same time, unsure what

Coach makes of it. "I went in to look same as you guys, but didn't find anyone."

"What are you doing here? You weren't in my gym class. Travis says you never showed for your others. Talk to me. What's going on with you?"

My hands fidget in my lap, and one of my legs bounces up and down. Different explanations form in my head, both the truth and several lies. Deciding which tactic will be best.

"My parents needed me at the motel today. I couldn't leave."

Coach looks at his watch and mumbles something. "After running out on us yesterday, I'm benching you, Landry."

I start to speak up, but Coach silences me.

"You're out of the meet tomorrow. That's it. We'll have someone else take your place."

I nod, silent, afraid of digging myself into a deeper hole. It's just not fair. The one thing, maybe the only thing that feels safe, and now I can't do it.

All because of Hadlee.

I shake away the thought.

No. No, that's not right. You brought this upon yourself.

Coach studies me before speaking again. "How did you get here? I don't suppose your parents drove you."

"Walked, Coach." I'm so ashamed, I can't look him in the eye.

"Tried to call the motel last night. Was the power out with the storm?"

"Yes."

"I'm driving you home, and we're having a talk with your parents."

I start to object, but he silences me again.

"I don't care, Landry. If you won't talk to me, then we'll talk to your parents. I'm worried about you. I need you healthy, both physically and mentally. Let's go." He stands up, his chair crying out. "I can't very well let you run tomorrow after fainting yesterday." He leads me out into the locker room. "Strike one, Landry. Three strikes and I'll bench you for the first half of next season. Understood?"

"Yes, Coach."

We don't say anything else as he leads me out of the school and into the parking lot. There's no getting away from it now. Mom and Dad will know something more is going on.

A few of the track guys head toward the parking lot to take the late bus or drive home. Coach is parked next to Travis's car. Travis is on his phone. I can't make out a majority of what he's saying, but I can't help overhearing either.

"You said that the past three weeks, Mom." Travis listens. "Two more meets, and if we make State, then I might be able to—" He's cut off, listens, nods impatiently.

Coach unlocks his Buick and steps to the driver's side. I step to the passenger door and open it.

"I can tape the next for y—" More nodding. "No." Pause. "Yes." Pause. "Fine. See you when I see you, then. Whatever." He hangs up, cursing.

I'm not sure Coach heard, being on the opposite side, but Travis and I lock eyes. His face turns sour, and he flips me off before throwing himself in the car. Clearly, I heard something I wasn't meant to hear.

Coach clears his throat and backs out of the parking lot to take me home.

Are you ready for the fallout?

CHAPTER 28

Coach decides to go shortly after telling my parents about practice yesterday and earlier today. Dad is back, and he's sitting down on a stool behind the desk, looking haggard. Mom rubs his back tenderly, unable to do anything except sigh and point her chin. Rosa is already gone, and Rory isn't anywhere near the front office.

What have you been doing with him, Dad?

Coach leaves awkwardly, tells me he'll see me at the meet tomorrow, where I will definitely be benched. When he's gone, and I'm left alone, Mom and Dad let out a shared breath. They don't acknowledge me, not right away at least.

Outside, the sun starts to set, and a glare reflects off the windows, casting a slanted line that travels across the carpet and up the counter. I have to squint.

The tension is boiling in the room. Mom and Dad don't speak, don't yell or cry or argue or scold or throw a tantrum. No Angry Parent mode. Nothing. My back is still turned to them.

An ice cream truck passes by outside, the muffled jingle finding its way through the windows. And then I see her again, Sadie, from that day before we rode into the woods:

"Maybe you can come back when the ice cream man comes?"

There's a ringing in my ears, so I blink and rub my ears to get rid of it.

"Dev," Mom says. "Turn around and face us."

It's the last thing I want to do; even the thought of it hurts. But I do anyway.

"Is it true? Did you faint in school?"

Dad still can't focus on anything. His eyes are bloodshot and his breathing heavy. He looks terrible, worse than I've ever seen him. I'm suddenly terrified for some reason I can't really figure out.

You're making him sick.

"Answer me," Mom says. "Is it happening again?" Her eyes glisten.

I'm about to argue, but really there's no use. The jig is up, so I nod.

"How long has this been going on?" Mom does all the talking, as Dad can't even lift his head to look at me.

"Just yesterday."

Mom reaches out her hand then retracts it. She doesn't leave Dad's side. "Why didn't you tell us?" Her lip trembles. "We're supposed to be honest with each other. We don't keep secrets."

Dad's eyes flicker to mine for a moment before he looks away. Once again, the choice is between honoring one and betraying the other. I hate lying to either of them.

"It's fine, Mom," I say. "I'd tell you if you guys had anything to worry about."

Mom slouches, deflates. "Is that why you didn't want to go back to school?"

I don't answer her.

Then Dad speaks up, his voice barely audible. "Are you still getting the headaches?" Before I have a chance to respond, he jumps in with another question, defeated. "Are you seeing things again?"

Mom tries but fails to compose herself. Dad's shoulders shake, and I realize before long he's crying. Tears stream down his face. I haven't even answered his question, but somehow, he knows. They both know. One thing my parents are not is dumb. They can see right through me.

Mom wraps Dad in a hug, and I'm worried for his heart. Scared that it's causing too much strain. I need to stop it, need to agree to whatever it is that will ease their mind.

I can't let anything bad happen to him. It will kill Mom. It will kill us all.

And it will be my fault.

"You don't need to worry about me." My voice is weaker than I want it to be, but I can't find any conviction behind my words, 'cause not even I believe them.

"You're going back to see Vanessa," Dad says through clenched teeth. "We're making an appointment first thing in the morning for you to start your treatment again." Exasperated sigh. "She told us not to stop your therapy."

"I don't need to see her. I'll be fine."

"After that, you're going back on your medication." He grabs Mom's hand and squeezes. "Doesn't he still have his prescription here? Do we need to book a session with Dr. McMahon as well?"

Mom shakes her head. "No, it's outdated. We can't afford a new one without health insurance, Joe." Mom wipes away a tear. "How are we going to pay for his sessions again?"

I never see her cry, not since the day I woke up in the hospital. I hate it—all of it.

Maybe it would just be better if you weren't here anymore.

Dad rubs his eyes. "If our son needs help, then I'll get it for him."

"I'll be fine." Mom and Dad don't hear me. "I don't need the sessions or the pills." I whisper, "I can stay home from now on and just help run the front desk. Okay? I can get a job to help pay the bills."

They must not be paying attention to me, 'cause they argue as if I'm not even here.

Mom: (to Dad) "How do you expect to do that? We're barely scraping by with the place as it is."

Dad: "I'll take care of it, Joanne."

Mom: "How? You can barely keep this place standing."

Dad: "We'll make do. We always make do, honey."

Mom: "What does that mean? Where have you been the past few days?"

Dad: "What are you talking about?"

Mom: "You disappear and come back without a word to anyone."

Dad attempts to reach out and stroke Mom's hair, but she shoves his hand away.

This is how it ends.

Dad: "It's nothing that you have to worry about."

Mom: "Bullshit. Lately, you're everywhere but here with us." Mom cries. "This was not the life I wanted, Joe." She steps away from him and sways. "I gave up my entire life for you and this goddamn place. And while I'm here trying to make sure it doesn't fall apart every goddamn day, you're out God-knows-where doing God-knows what." She stops crying and composes herself—remembers I'm in the room.

"Did you just say you were leaving school?"

"He said what?" Dad says.

"Dev, no. We're not even entertaining that idea. Not even Fun Mom."

"Entertain *WHAT* idea?" Dad raises his voice, irritated.

I don't know what to do or say, how to react. I've never

heard them argue like this. Not ever. Not in front of me. Maybe behind closed doors I'd hear them argue, but I never thought it was anything this bad.

How have you never noticed your parents fighting like this before?

How long have you been hallucinating?

Have they always been unhappy?

The ringing becomes so loud it's painful, and I have to cover my ears to drown out the sound that's nowhere but in my head. Mom and Dad say something to me, but I can't hear them. The ringing is too deafening, so I close my eyes. Firewood.

Jesus, not again.

Then a voice inside my head:

"Feels weird, right? Like you can't move or think straight."
"Your friend is an ugly cunt."
"Shhhhh. No one can hear you both out here."

When I open my eyes, I'm facing the windows to the parking lot. But something is wrong, off. Out of place.

Hadlee is standing outside the front door, looking in.

This isn't real. This isn't real. Mom and Dad will snap you out of it when they notice.

I blink, but Hadlee doesn't go away. I rub my eyes, the ringing slowly fading away, but still she remains. Mom and Dad are arguing behind me, asking me questions, but none of it registers as the Hadlee Hallucination pounds on the door with bloodied fists. Mom and Dad don't notice, so I know for a fact it's not real.

Eventually, the ringing fades completely, and the entire world around me mutes. Even Hadlee's pounding is quiet. Her fists are nothing but bloody pulp, but the glass never once cracks.

I twirl around to get my bearings, but Mom and Dad are gone, and now it's just Hadlee in front of me. Light dances in shadows on her cheeks, as if from a fire, but there is none in sight. She doesn't open her mouth to talk—yet still I hear her voice in my head:

"You need to remember."

"Remember what?"

"What happened."

"I'm trying."

"We're in danger, both of us."

"Why? In danger from what?"

"Not what. Who."

"What?"

"He's back."

"Who's back?"

The Hadlee Hallucination reaches out and grabs my hand. I think I can feel it, some warmth that travels through my knuckles and up my arm. It's not real, but it feels like it is. Again, her inner voice:

"There's no going back once you see."

She's so real. So real and beautiful and terrifying. I both want and don't want to see it. See what really happened to Hadlee. What I did or didn't do. But when I blink and open my eyes, Hadlee is gone and Mom and Dad are still arguing with each other. The world's volume slowly reverts to its normal setting, and I'm staring outside. There is no blood. No bonfire scent.

You're dangerous, Dev. You need to figure this out before it gets worse and you hurt yourself, or somebody else.

I tell my parents I'm going back to my room to rest, but they still don't see or hear me.

How could they not tell you were hallucinating? Do they hate each other that much? Have they always hated each other and were just putting on a show?

My breaths are short, and my heart is pounding. I can't get it to stop or settle down, and my head feels light, like maybe I might pass out.

They love each other, Dev. You know they do.

Inside my "fake" room, there is an unopened bag of Hershey's Kisses on my bed. I know they're from Rosa. I close the door behind me and open the bag to shove two in my mouth and start to feel better. From the door, their muffled voices:

Mom: "He's *my* son too. Not just yours."

Dad: "I'm trying to protect him."

Mom: "And you think I don't want to? Our son has no life, no friends, and he never opens up to us. Don't you think that's a problem?"

Dad: "If he's here, he's safe. He's alive. He's not out lying in those woods alone and nearly freezing or bleeding to death."

Mom: "You sheltering him is killing him inside. It's killing me, too."

Dad: (a whisper) "You made me promise back then to do whatever I could to keep our son safe."

Mom: "He was in a coma, Joe. He was in critical condition. I was scared."

Dad: "Well, I'm scared every day."

And it's the words again, about protecting me, the same thing Hadlee's Dad said to her when I was hiding in the closet. I just want to go out there and hug them and tell them I'll never leave or disappoint them. I'll never hurt them. I didn't realize how scared they must have been before I woke up, not knowing if I would ever wake up.

What if Hadlee was the one in the coma instead of you? How do you think you'd act? Do anything to protect her from ever getting hurt again?

But another part of me feels so sick again. Mom and Dad are

supposed to be the strong ones. They're supposed to be the ones looking out for me and having all the answers. So, why does it feel like I'm the one who needs to keep them safe? Why does it feel so wrong that they're just as clueless as me?

Mom and Dad try to come in the room, but I've locked it. They knock several times, even threaten to get the master keys and open it up, but I tell them I need to sleep, that I'm not feeling well. Eventually, they let it go and let me rest. As long as they think I'm in this room, they won't think I'm up to no good or in danger. They've always been predictable like that.

I remember Hadlee's MacBook with the locked folder is still in Room 13. So I check the lock and then climb out the window. When I hop on the concrete, that Aubrey girl is behind the iron gate to the empty pool, sitting on the concrete and swinging her legs over the opening. She's smoking a cigarette, puffing a plume of smoke. She sees me, and I freeze. We lock eyes, and I know this girl's just heard everything. I'm almost embarrassed enough to climb back inside, but without saying anything, she mimes zipping her lips and throwing away a key. I nod and make my way to the other building, grateful for a stranger's secrecy.

What are our parents trying to protect us from?

Then I hear the Hadlee Hallucination's warning again, and I feel nauseated.

"He's back."

Who are our parents trying to protect us from?

CHAPTER 29

I TEXT AIDEN TO LET ME KNOW WHEN HE'S BACK FROM HIS date, so we can hang out. I need him to either help convince me not to break into Hadlee's files or help me figure out how to do just that. In the meantime, I don't want to be anywhere around this motel or Mom or Dad or Rory.

I don't know why, after all these years I do it now, but after I pack her MacBook into a backpack, I get the rusted red Schwinn from the corner of the room. After I wipe off dust and cobwebs, I realize the tires are flat. I sneak out back to the laundry shack, where Mom keeps some tools, and I find an old tire pump.

There's a fear, and I know it's not realistic, but it's there. Like this bike ride is just another step into a journey I won't be coming back from. Like I'll be one step closer to the truth of that night with Hadlee, and one step further from the person I used to be.

Will I still like who I am, who Hadlee is, when I reach the other side?

I can't sneak out with the bike via the fence in back, so I plan to bike as quickly as I can through the parking lot. It's a little after six, and dusk makes everything glow in a dim light. The sky above is a fiery pink that Hadlee loves. At least, she used to. Maybe she still does.

"Going somewhere, Little Landry?" A voice from above.

It startles me so bad my head jerks up, and Mr. Day is leaning out his bathroom window, which faces the back walkway. He doesn't say anything, just patiently waits for a response.

He looks freshly shaven. A nick just below his chin where blood has dried.

I stutter to find words, terrified, but none come. And his staring sends me over the edge. I just can't deal with it. Not anymore.

"What's your problem, Mr. Day?" My voice is a little breathless, but not as bad as I feared. It's firm enough to take my stand, despite my heart pounding erratically. "You act like you hate us, but you almost never leave."

He stares, not amused. "What makes you think I hate you?"

"D-Don't you?"

He leans farther on his elbows and points to the bike. "You're starting to remember, aren't you?" He studies me. "Your head injury acts up when memories come back, doesn't it?"

WHAT?

He doesn't allow me to answer before cracking his neck. "It'll do that. Anything that triggers you. Very inconvenient, but a side effect nonetheless." He scratches his neck. "Carry on, if you must. Just be prepared for what you'll find if you go galli-vanting down Memory Lane."

I'm so confused.

"Do you know what happened before I was in the coma?"

"I'll be here, when you're equipped. After it comes back." He offers a small smile that is anything but friendly. "Tell Miss

Morgan, when you encounter her tonight, that I very much appreciated her visit, however brief."

Her visit?

Before I can formulate a response that resembles something coherent, he ducks back inside and shuts the window.

What the hell is going on?

I walk around the second building and pedal as fast as I can past the front office, putting behind whatever that conversation was about.

I glance over my shoulder twice. Once to see that Mom and Dad are still talking in the front office, unaware I'm leaving. The second time is because Mr. Day is outside his door, a rare occurrence when not hunting, and watching me pedal away. He's back in his camo gear and boots, the 12 gauge in his hand as he waves at me.

I'm in the street and heading in the direction of school—toward Hadlee and Aiden's houses, where I can't see Cuckoo Clark or the freaking gun anymore.

I *REALLY* don't like that gun.

CHAPTER 30

Hadlee still hasn't gotten back to me by the time Aiden texts me a little after seven. I convince myself to wait for her to come to me, so I just ride around, letting the cool air run over my clothes and hair. It feels good, and I'm surprised at how natural it is. Some things never change.

The sun has dipped well below the tree line, so only a faint glint of light remains—quickly fading fast as a tenebrous darkness veils us all. The air still carries a scent of petrichor, like the ground after a hard rain. The smell of spring, of summer, of new beginnings.

I ride up and down streets and blocks. Bike my way around paths Hadlee and I used to take. Sometimes, I can still hear our tires treading over the gravel if I close my eyes. I can see how young both of us were. Innocent.

It's bittersweet in a way, doing this alone.

Mom and Dad have called me six times already and texted a bunch more. I do feel bad, but I just can't deal with them right now. Figuring out what I forgot, and where Hadlee ran off to, is more important.

It's close to eight when I make my way to Aiden's house. He is at the end of a cul-de-sac. The roofs on this street are all a slanted red slate, with beige shingle sidings and concrete leading down to blacktops. Aiden's three-story house is the only one without a basketball net. His mom's blue Prius and his dad's black BMW are in the driveway. They come from decent money.

I hitch my bike up against the garage and step along the walkway to his front door; the outside lights are on to greet me. I shoo away moths and mosquitos, and to my right, a bug fries in the zapper. I don't even knock or ring, just open the door and walk right in, because this is normal behavior.

His parents are in the living room to the left, watching some show together, their bodies facing my way. I take off my shoes, and my socks slide over the paneled wooden floorboards. A bright chandelier hangs from the ceiling via a bedazzled cable.

Must be nice to live in luxury.

"Hello there, Dev," Mrs. Brumberg says, while reaching into a shared bowl of popcorn. "We haven't seen you around here in a while."

"Yeah, I've been busy with end-of-year essays."

Their dog, a tiny Yorkshire Terrier, bounds up to me, emitting squeak-barks that sound so adorable. I pick her up, FuFu, as she attempts to maul my face in kisses, wagging her little tail. She jumps on my chest and shoulders, trying to climb atop my head before thinking better of it and wanting down, so I lower her to the ground, where she proceeds to run in circles by my feet, sniff my socks, and paw at my shins.

"And with the track team," his dad says, sipping from a can of Budweiser. "Two more meets this season, right?" His dad always cared about how I was doing with the team, like it could be my ticket out of Brooke Meadows.

"Yeah. Just resting today for the meet tomorrow."

Until you got yourself benched.

FuFu eventually gets bored and bounds over to the smell of buttery popcorn and attempts to hop on the couch before Mr. Brumberg yells at her to get off.

"Well, tell your parents that we miss them," Mrs. Brumberg says when she's done chewing. "The other moms miss her being at book club."

I forgot she used to do that. Years ago. Ancient years ago.

I miss that version of my mom. Badass Tool Wielder by day, Book Club Reader Mom by night.

We have more small talk before Aiden hops down the stairs, smelling like a gigolo with all the body spray, but with a grin plastered across his face. He's in a wrinkled *Buffy* T-shirt.

"We'll be upstairs in my room and up to no good, probably looking at porn," he calls as I follow him up the stairs.

His dad calls back, "Sounds good. Just delete the browser history, you two."

His mom calls up, "Don't listen to your father. He's a pig."

He says, "I hate it when you chew the kernels."

Aiden rolls his eyes and leads me past family portraits and photographs, past framed school photos of him—back during the year he suffered terrible acne—and into his large bedroom, cluttered with clothes everywhere. FuFu follows behind us and gets into the room. Not that I'm one to stereotype anyone, let alone Aiden, but he might be the messiest gay person I know.

On his dresser nearest the door is a picture taken last year when his parents took him to New York City for the Gay Pride parade. All three of them arm-in-arm with a mass of bodies around in fuzzy distortion. I'm a little envious of it.

"My parents just love you," he says.

"Can you blame them?"

He bites his lip. "All right, cocky, I'm home." He goes to

pinch my nipple, but I get to his first. A weird thing we do from time to time. He sighs. "Damn you, Obi-Wan." He picks up FuFu, who wiggles her tail and licks his face. He adopts baby talk. "Yeah, girl, yeah, little girl, whose breath smells terrible? Yours does! That's whose. Your breath smells like old farts. Like Darth Vader's farts after being singed with hot lava." FuFu barks in his face, jumps out of his arms, runs in circles by his feet, and then runs out the door and into the hallway.

"She is so neurotic sometimes," he says.

I shake my head and laugh. "How was your date?" We sit on his unmade bed together.

His room is adorned with posters of video games and movies: *Indiana Jones, Star Wars, Star Trek, Buffy, Angel, Dungeons & Dragons, The Terminator, Alien, Predator*, everything *Marvel* that's possible, *Call of Duty, Grand Theft Auto, Mario Kart*, etc.

Aiden lights up, one leg hanging off the bed and the other folded underneath his butt. "Max. He is *so* gorgeous, Dev." He beams. "He is so nice. Has a great smile. Very much a gentleman, kind of soft spoken, and timid, but very sweet. Scrawny build like you. He still hasn't tried to kiss me. He said he didn't want to rush anything. I think he comes from a rough upbringing. But here I am, like, let's fuck already, ya know?"

"So, no catfish?"

"No catfish. Just blue balls and smelly, heterosexual men who beg to come over 'cause there's an emergency."

I put my hand on his shoulder. "I'm happy for you, but just be careful." I'm not sure why, but it still seems off to me. Aiden is seventeen, Max is twenty-six. It just feels wrong, but I don't tell him, because it won't make a difference with Aiden.

He slaps my knee. "Your turn, mister. I don't take it you summoned me to my humble abode to lure me into the taking of your virginity?"

I shake my head. "Do you still have the bed swing?"

He pouts then winks. "We can make one."

"Then it's a solid no."

"Alas, I shall convert you soon enough."

"You can try."

"And I will succeed." He raises his hands as if to the heavens, gathering bravado in his voice. "Dudes 'n Dicks shall soon be knee deep in scrotum!" He pauses, lowers his hands. "Scroti? Scrota?" He taps a finger on his chin, purposefully drawing out the joke. "Scroat the Goat!"

I shove him, giggling. "Hadlee, motherfucker."

His eyes go wide. "Ummm, hanging around Rory much? Sounds like something that Neanderthal would say."

Screw Rory.

I ignore the comment. "Hadlee."

"Of course." He gets up. "What else is new?"

"I need to show you something."

I reach into my backpack and take out Hadlee's MacBook and proceed to tell him most of the story. Not about what might have happened in the woods, or my hallucinations, because that's not my story to tell, but everything else I can say that won't betray her or make me seem crazy. Aiden waits patiently until I'm done. Despite our jokes, Aiden always knows when it's time to get serious. He and Rosa are the same in that way: always here to lend an ear and offer advice.

He watches as I enter in Magoo22 for the Mac, and I double click on the zipped file folder, prompting for another password. "That's creepy." He flops on his bed and shuts the lid to her Mac. "Bloodletting?"

"I know."

"Do you even know what that means?"

"Not really."

He reaches out and squishes my cheeks with his palms, so I laugh while pushing him away.

"It was, like, a common practice forever ago where doctors thought that draining a person of their blood could cure any illness."

"What the hell?"

"I know! Max can drain me of blood as long as it's followed by fellatio and assless chaps."

"You have a problem."

"I know! I'm obsessed with sex. Sue me. I'm a teenage boy."

"This still doesn't answer my question or help me out at all."

"I know!" He pushes the computer away from him as if it were contaminated. "Why does she have a folder called that on her computer?"

"That's what I'm trying to figure out. The answers could be in that folder. Why encrypt it otherwise?"

"This is wrong, Dev." He sits up, his eyes scolding me like a child. "Why did you steal this from her? You think that, excuse my language here, but that crazy, beautiful bitch would somehow overlook the fact you stole her computer and dug around into stuff you had no business digging around in?"

"Can you help me or not?"

He shakes his head. "No. This is wrong. I love you, but this is beyond screwed up." He bites his lip. "It is weird that she keeps a password lock on a folder...."

"Exactly."

I can tell he's curious. Part of me hopes he tells me no again, 'cause I'll leave it alone if he does. But the other part hopes he's just as intrigued.

"I love you and hate you at the same time."

I shrug. "It's a gift."

"Are you sure you're not even bi-curious?"

"If I was, it wouldn't be for you."

He scowls. "Now that was just mean."

"Still love you."

He blows me a kiss. "I'm out of your league anyway."

I shake my head. "So're we doing this?"

Aiden goes to crack his knuckles, but nothing happens, and the moment is gone before it even arrives.

"Well, that was an epic fail."

"Yeah," I say. "Very anticlimactic."

"Like the *Episode I* of all things useless."

"*The Phantom Menace* again?"

"Like, no, George Lucas. No!" He slaps his pointer finger as if scolding it. "Bad. Naughty. Little. Lucas!"

"I've heard this argument before, you know."

"Like, Midichlorians as The Force? What even—I can't even—" He grunts. "Ew."

"You done now?"

"Yeah, I'm good."

We try several different passwords, but none of them work: Hadlee, Maggie, Magoo22, Brooke Meadows, Rosa, Dev, Devon, kisses, hersheykisses, motel, photography, NightRunner13, MalevolentBeauty, bloodletting, Room13, RoomThirteen, pocketwatch, locomotive, Sylvia, Reggie, woods, etc. I even try the names of some bands we like and other items at the motel. Nothing works. We stop after a while to take a snack break. Aiden even says distraction might help, so I let him try and teach me about D&D, but I just can't see how it serves anything but to satisfy his sick need to get me to play with Greg and Davey and be their fourth player.

I think back to that day with Hadlee in the woods and wrack my brain for any other details. Try to think of what else it could be. Then I remember: lemonade, cherry, popsicle, icecream, Sadie.

Bam. The folder unlocks and opens up.

Sadie. I wonder if Hadlee knows what happened to her.

My lungs stop, and my nerves are on fire. My heart thumps so fast I'm afraid it's going to burst through my chest. I have to remind myself to breathe. Even Aiden stills. A separate window opens a series of Word documents and photos. Suddenly, I'm terrified this is a bad idea. I'd hate it if Aiden or Rosa or Mom and Dad went through my stuff. I wouldn't mind if Hadlee did because I have nothing I'd want to hide from her.

Before I control the conflicting thoughts, the guilt, the shame, Aiden is clicking on a few photos. None of them are labeled, so it's all random. I tell Aiden to sort them by date modified. He does, and on top are a few separate file folders. One is labeled:

The One That Left the Nest

We click on that, and some are photos so grainy or dark we can't make them out. But then I see the outline of an older woman with hair that looks like Hadlee's, but a darker, cherry red. Wide hips and a pointed chin, slender jaw. It's Mrs. Morgan, Hadlee's mom. As we click through the photos, I feel very ill. One after another after another. I can't stand to look at it anymore. But to think Hadlee just stayed there and took picture after picture after picture. The dates go back days, weeks, months, over a year ago.

"Ho-ly rutabaga," Aiden mumbles. "Is this real?"

I go to swallow, but my mouth is dry. "I think so."

We stop on a picture of Hadlee's mom in the backseat of a car, the windows fogged, a ball gag in her mouth. A hand is pressed to the back passenger side window. From the same car but a different angle. A man is above her, hair matted to his neck. A riding crop in one hand.

The man is not Mr. Morgan.

"Jesus," Aiden says. "This goes back a couple years. She's been snapping her mom having an affair for years. A kinky one. Dude...."

I close my eyes, my stomach churning. I'm about to get sick, but Aiden doesn't notice. He just goes on.

"I knew she was a weird girl, but Dev... this is... this is *sick*."

"She's not sick."

"No?" He flips around the computer so I can see and clicks to a new one. It's from a different night, but Hadlee's camera is pointed up at some kind of hotel. There are outlines of two people deep in the window, a woman who appears hogtied. Right away I know it's her mom and someone that is not her dad. "This is SO messed up. She's stalking her mom. And what the hell is her mom into? Was this going on when you two were friends?"

I shake my head, my mouth too dry for words.

Aiden pulls up one more. It's an image taken from a really odd angle. I almost can't make it out at first. I've never seen something like it before, but I can only assume it's her mom. It's a body, vacuum sealed with some pipe extending out, like a breathing apparatus.

Chills.

She said her mom doesn't even care anymore.

I know I should stop, should put an end to this. But my curiosity gets the better of me, as does my need to know the truth about what happened. If Hadlee won't tell me, then it must be on here. We exit out of that folder and find another one.

Those Who Walk at Night

I'm pretty sure I already know this one will be about me, and I'm about to stop Aiden from clicking on it, but he opens it up and double clicks to enlarge a picture before I get a chance.

This one looks like it was from Saturday night, after she first showed up at the motel. I'm in only my mesh shorts. It's from behind. Aiden studies it for a while before I slam the lid down on the Mac.

"That's enough."

"Was that... no. Was that?"

"I should go," I say. I try to shove the Mac into my backpack, but Aiden grabs my wrist.

"Was that you?"

"No."

"You're lying."

I shake off his grip and sling the backpack around my shoulders. "I need to go see her."

"What the heck were you doing shirtless in the woods, and why was she filming it?"

"It's nothing, Aiden. Drop it."

"Anakin started lying to his best friend. Look how that ended up."

"This isn't *Revenge of the Sith*."

"Villains are born when they start to lie to their best friends."

"Life isn't a movie, okay?" Like a switch, I flip on him. I don't want to; it isn't right. But I can't stop myself. "You're the weird one. All you do is wear weird shirts, quote nerdy stuff, and talk about sex all the time. What are you even doing with a twenty-six-year-old? It's weird and creepy. If Hadlee were still my friend freshman year—" I stop myself by covering my mouth.

WTF, Dev? WHAT THE FUCK?

Aiden stands up, his expression hurt. "If she was still your friend, you'd *what*?"

Asshole. First Rory and now Aiden. Maybe it's you. Maybe you're the one Hadlee needs protecting from.

"I didn't mean—"

"That you never would've been my friend if Hadlee was still talking to you?" I think he wipes at his eyes, but I can't be sure. 'Cause when he looks at me again, all I see is hurt and anger. "I know I'm weird, Dev. I'm a nerd. I play Dungeons and Dragons with three heterosexual men in one of our basements. I have no job and no car, I wear logoed shirts, and I'm gay. Which pretty much already makes me a target at school." He wipes at his eyes again. "But I'm me. I've always been me, and I couldn't care less what people think. You're so focused on Hadlee this or Hadlee that, that honestly, it's lame. Who are you, Dev? Besides Hadlee's ex-best friend, besides a victim? Besides a cute boy who lives in a motel with his parents? You're nothing outside of her or your parents. They define your very existence."

"No, they don't."

"I just don't get what you see in her. Hadlee is such a cliché. Honestly."

"Shut up."

His lip trembles. "I'm not perfect, but at least I like who I am most days. Can you say the same?"

I'm gutted. Hollow. Because he's right. I don't want to believe it, but who am I without Hadlee? Without my parents or Rosa? What do I want? It's nothing but emptiness.

You're cursed, remember? Rotten to the core.

It makes me hate myself so much that I don't know what to do. My head is pounding, and everything around me becomes so hot I get antsy. One minute I'm standing next to Aiden, the next moment he's on the ground and I'm above him. His hand is pressed to his eye and my right fist is clenched. I don't feel the sting of the punch right away. It takes a second for the pain to register, but when it does, I cry out and curse, pin my fist in between my knees to somehow squeeze away the pain.

Aiden is crying. I try to apologize, to tell him I didn't mean to do it. Must have blacked out. I'm not even sure where it came from. I didn't want to hit him before. I would never want to. But Aiden kicks and sobs at me to get out. I attempt to help him up, but he kicks at me again and screams for me to leave his house.

From below, I hear footsteps ascend the stairs, so with one more look at him, Aiden scoots away from me. I feel like crying, but before I do, his mom knocks and opens the door.

"What on Earth are you two doing up here?"

When she sees Aiden on the floor covering his eye, me standing above him, she screams and pushes me away. Kneels down next to Aiden to inspect his face.

I grab the MacBook and backpack and leave. Just run out into the hallway, down the stairs, grab my shoes, and without putting them on, blow out the door to bike away before they can follow me.

He'll hate you forever. His parents will hate you forever. Congratulations. You've now lost the only friend you have.

I'm crying and pedaling as fast as I can down a random street until I reach another cul-de-sac. I stop to catch my breath and fall off the bike. It's all falling apart. I'm falling apart. I don't know what's wrong with me or how to stop it from happening. Like every time I try and do the right thing, it all comes out wrong.

Maybe it would be better if you just lay down in the street and waited for a car to—

No. No. That's NOT the answer.

"I can fix this," I tell myself, still lying in the middle of the open street at night. There are no cars on the road, no one outside. Crickets answer my declaration. A cat screeches from somewhere far off. "I will fix this. I'll get well, I'll apologize to Rory and Aiden. I'll fix things with Coach and the team. I'll fix Hadlee. I'll fix my parents. I'll fix Dad." I can't stop crying now. "I'll fix myself."

Just as I'm about to have a meltdown in the street, my phone vibrates in my pocket. I think it's Aiden, so I pick it up without checking.

"I'm sorry. I didn't mean to hit you."

"What are you talking about? Hit who?" It's a voice I'm not expecting on the other end.

"H-Hadlee?"

"Are you okay, what happened?"

I sit up and wipe my nose. "I'm fine. Where are you? What happened after you ran away at school?"

I can hear her breathing on the other end of the line, followed by the static of wind. She must be outside.

"That's not important right now. But what is important is that you need to stay away from the motel. Don't come back for a few hours, wherever you are."

I think the worst. Dad. Something happened to Dad.

"What happened?" I don't really want to know, though.

"My dad. He's heading down to your motel right now."

"WHAT?!"

"My dad was convinced you were at the house earlier today and Tuesday night too. He said he was going to talk to your parents once and for all to end this."

"No."

It'll destroy them if they find out about me and Hadlee.

"I-I don't know what—"

"Just stay away. It'll only be bad if you come back. I'll text you when it's safe."

I'm already on my bike and pedaling before she says the last thing.

"And Dev?"

"Yeah."

"For whatever happens when I get there...I'm sorry."

"Sorry for what?"

But she hangs up, and the line goes dead.

And despite her warnings, I pedal toward the motel anyway. If everyone is going to be there, then I will be too.

It's time to end this, once and for all.

If no one else wants to tell me, then I'm going to find out the truth myself.

CHAPTER 31

My feet are shoeless, so they must still be in the street from when I fell. The bike strains against me as it gets harder to pedal, and I hear chains scraping and snapping. The chain must completely snap, because before I know it, my legs pump nothing but air. I jerk the handlebars left and right to try and compensate, and the momentum of my body sends me flying over the bike until my face breaks my fall, the bike landing on top of me.

I can't move, not even sure if I want to. The pain comes in slow waves, and there's the coppery taste of blood in my mouth. I'm so terrified I've chipped or lost a tooth, but a quick scan with my tongue reassures me I haven't. But I'm definitely bleeding.

All that matters is getting back to the motel, to Mom and Dad, to Hadlee. I just need the secrets and the lies and the darkness to end. I gather the strength to push the bike off me and roll over onto my back in the street. I never should have taken it out. There was a reason why I never rode it until now.

After some finagling, I shakily stand up. My arms and legs are sore, pretty sure they're all scraped up. There's a small gash on my forehead, skin torn from my chin, and my nose might be bleeding, though I can't find a mirror to be sure. I can taste blood in the back of my throat. The phone in my pocket is cracked, the touch screen completely inoperable. I curse, but it hurts to make big gestures. Thankfully, Hadlee's MacBook is undamaged in my backpack.

I pick up the bike and attempt to walk it back, but it won't move. I leave it in the middle of the street. We can get it later tonight with the car.

If there *is* a later tonight.

The motel is only a mile down the road, but half-limping/half-jogging makes it seem farther. My nose might be broken, and my ankle might be sprained. But the fear and adrenaline work as a numbing agent to the physical pain.

It's late when the motel comes into view. Not sure what time it is, so sore that tears are mixed with blood on my face, I drop to the ground to rest a moment and catch my breath. My eyes close, suddenly tired, but before I know it, hands are around me and lifting me up. Maybe I fell asleep, I can't really tell anymore. But when I look at my savior, it's Rory.

"Like damn, Godfather." He helps me walk to the parking lot from the side of the road. He reeks of weed—wears blue sweats and a white V-neck that's two sizes too big. "You all right?

"I—I'm fine."

"Shit man, you look all jacked up. Someone jack you up? I'll go knock on doors. No one hurts my friends and shit."

I'm a little touched that he cares so much—to the point I temporarily forget how he's been sneaking off with my dad. Then I get annoyed all over again.

"I'll be okay, thank you though."

I really won't be.

"Seriously, what happened, bro?" He readjusts my weight,

but we both sway. "I'm so messed up right now." He giggles lightly. "You look terrible."

"It feels just as bad as it looks."

"I bet." He takes more of my weight on him. "It's hostile in there." He indicates the front office, which is rapidly approaching. "You wanna chill in my room?"

Now I really feel bad about how I acted before, like I had better things to do. This is where it starts. Rory is easy. I'll fix Rory first.

I don't know why, after everything, I feel the need to do this. I just do.

"I'm sorry about before when I sort of freaked out on you earlier. I was just stressed out, but it wasn't your fault."

He contemplates the thought like he doesn't remember, then it registers, and he has a wide grin on his face. He leans in close as if I can't hear him. The weed on his breath is disgusting. "No worries, Don Landry. You're the tits. You just remember that. You are the tits, and the tits are you."

I nod, because it makes no sense to me but all the sense to him.

Well, that was easy.

The answers for what's going on with him and my dad will have to wait.

When we step into the parking lot, there are four bodies huddled in the main office. Mom and Dad behind the counter. Hadlee and her dad in front of it, their backs turned. My dread expands the closer we get, at what Hadlee meant. What could she possibly be sorry about? What could happen? That her being assaulted is out in the open? That I'll know?

As soon as I'm in view, Mom and Dad see me from the window. It's the succession of events on their faces: the curiosity, the thought, the realization, the confusion, the surprise, the slow creep of horror, and the fear. Mom pushes herself from behind the counter so fast I can barely process the move before she's gone. She's outside in less than three steps and taking me in her arms. Rory is forced off me while he tries to explain how he found me like this. Dad shuffles out, limping.

Hadlee tries to get near me, but her dad pulls her back, and my dad yells at them both to get away. His voice is weak, frail. It's chaos. Mom protecting me as she tries to inspect my wounds only to cause me pain. She starts to walk me back inside.

Hadlee looks so betrayed. A promise broken.

I'm sorry, Hads. I tell her with my eyes. This is where it ends.

Rory steps next to me. "Is there anything I can—"

"Go back to your room, Rory!" Mom shouts.

"Okay. S-Sorry."

I don't see him trudge away, but I can feel the movement in the air. I'm ushered inside and laid on the couch. Mom runs back toward the bathroom, while Hadlee fills a cup of water from the water jug. I take it from her and sip. We lock eyes, and I just want to kiss her, I want to hold her so bad. Like only she can take away the hurt. She must somehow sense this, because she wipes away the hair matted to my forehead, some blood on her palm.

Jesus, how bad is it really?

Hadlee is suddenly ripped away by her dad. She yelps, as she's practically thrown to the other side of the office.

"You trespassed on my property," Mr. Morgan seethes, pointing to me. "Stay away from my daughter, or I'll press charges so fast your head will spin."

"W-What are you talking about? D-Dev has never stepped foot on your property." Dad hand-fans himself, sweating and pale, ghostly. He's never angry like this. Not ever. "You came here and accused our son of something he never did."

Mr. Morgan pokes my dad in the shoulder as Mom comes rushing back with washcloths, cotton balls, and peroxide. I try not to pay attention to the sting, the sizzle, as it works its magic on my wounds. Tears well in my eyes.

Mr. Morgan hunches over Dad. His salt and pepper hair is thinning, like Dad's, but kept short enough to look natural. He has Hadlee's thin shoulders and milky complexion. A few freckles dot his nose and below his eyes. His cheeks are caved in, cheekbones jutting out, making his face look elongated. He looks much older than I remember. More weathered, maybe.

Mr. Morgan points to me. "Then why the hell was she wearing his clothes?" He points to a bag of clothes that's been placed on the counter from when I lent them to her this morning. "These are your son's, right?"

Mom and Dad look from me to the clothes, and I don't know what they're thinking, but they don't defend me. We all know they're mine.

Caught. Red-handed.

"Our son would have had nothing to do with your d-daughter," Dad says. "Maybe she trespassed on our property and stole them." There is no conviction behind the words Dad speaks. Just trying to save face.

"Every time Hadlee is in trouble, your son is never far behind, Joe," Mr. Morgan says. "Where was he just now?" He turns to me. "Where? In my house again?"

Dad places his hand on Mom's shoulder to steady himself. He closes his eyes and takes a few deep breaths. "You've always been a bully, Mel." He leans in close and lowers his voice. "Get off my property before I call the police."

Hadlee eyes me and speaks up, "Dev is hurt. Can this not wait until later?"

"Enough," Mr. Morgan says. "Just wait until we get home, little girl. You just wait."

I really hate him. So much.

I just want to save Hadlee. I just want to hold her hand and run off and kiss her, hug her, stroke her hair. I want us to build that cabin in the woods and start a family, start new. Like we talked about at that garage sale when we found the pocket watch. Even if back then it was just a story.

It's a story that could be ours.

And then it all happens as if in a play. I'm merely a spectator as Mom cleans my wounds.

Hadlee: "Can we please leave?"

Mr. Morgan: "Oh, we're going home, all right. After I make sure this is never going to happen again, from either of you."

Dad: "I won't tell you again… get OUT of my motel, Mel."

Mom: (to me) "Who did this to you? Did someone hurt you? (tear falls) Were you attacked?"

Dad: "What's he saying, Joanne?"

Mom: (to me) "You can tell me, honey."

Mr. Morgan: "Tell your son to stay away from my daughter. I warned you before, and we had an agreement about their relationship. Your son broke it."

Mom: "No, we told your daughter to stay away from our son. How do you know she never approached him first?"

Hadlee: "Daddy, please. He's hurt. This can wai—"

That "Daddy" again….

Mr. Morgan: (almost raising a hand) "You're in just as much trouble. Don't think you're off the hook, you selfish little bitch."

Dad: "Your daughter was the one that always wanted to go off exploring areas she knew were off limits, dragging our son with her."

Mr. Morgan: "Put him on a tighter leash."

Dad: "Put her on one."

(Staring at each other as if in a western standoff)

Mr. Morgan: "I want a restraining order, so this doesn't happen again, from either of them."

Hadlee: "What?"

Mom: (standing up and letting Dad take over with me) "How about we file one against your daughter? She was the one who was sitting out there and did nothing to try and get help. My Devon would never have known about such a foul place if it weren't for your rebellious daughter trying to get away from you. It's a big wonder why."

Mr. Morgan: "You're all delusional. My daughter's life was threatened, and she was drugged, and you're upset because she didn't have the sense to come back here and get you two after everything she went through?"

Mom: "That's not what I'm saying."

Mr. Morgan: "Hadlee knows everything she's done that's wrong. I've told her often. But don't go acting like your son was innocent in all this."

Mom: "So our son deserved to be in that coma, is that what you're saying?

Mr. Morgan: "Don't go twisting my words,

Joanne. You did that shit in high school. You're not doing it again now. You're not nearly as pretty as you were back then."

Hadlee: (crying) "I'm sorry."

Mom: (trying not to look hurt, deflecting) "Please leave. Our son hasn't been to see your daughter at all since the coma. And I'm offended that you think, just because your daughter misbehaves, that Devon has anything to do with it."

Mr. Morgan: (listing each off on a finger) "I told you. She's been sneaking out all hours of the night and skipping school. She's been locking doors when she knows it's forbidden. And there was a boy over at the house a couple nights ago! Now I find her wearing your son's clothes. How *convenient*."

Mom: "Oh, so you're saying your daughter is a whore? In high school, wasn't your wife jerking off all the varsity footba—"

Dad: "Joanne." (cringes, sweat dripping from his nose, trembling) "Not now." (to me) "Who hurt you?"

Me: "No one."

Dad & Mom: "What?"

Me: "What happened three years ago?"

Hadlee: (pushing her dad away to come closer) "He needs to know the truth."

(Silence)

Dad: "The truth about how he got so cut up just now. I agree."

Me: "From in the woods."

(Silence)

Mr. Morgan: "What's going on here?"

Mom: "Stop it."

Hadlee: "Look at him! He deserves to know!"

Dad: (to me) "Don't listen to her." (turning) "She's lying."

Mr. Morgan: "You haven't told him?"

Mom: "Told him what? That while our son was unconscious in the woods, your daughter was just sitting there next to him, doing nothing but waiting for him to wake up?

Me: "What?"

What was she doing?

Mr. Morgan: "This is not cute, Joanne. You're being unrealistic and petty."

Mom: "You're being insufferable."

Dad: "Joanne. Not now. Please." (he squeezes my hand)

Hadlee: "They're lying to you, Dev."

Me: "I know."

I do.

Hadlee: "Why do you think you've been sleepwalking?"

(Silence)

Dad: "You've been sleepwalking again?"

Mom: (covers her mouth) "No."

Dad: "Is this true?"

I don't answer, shocked and pissed at Hadlee.

Why did she do that?!?!?

Mom: "You two need to leave. You're scaring our son."

Hadlee: "He's scared because he has no idea what's going on."

Me: "What really happened to us in the woods?"

Mr. Morgan: (after a moment) "Unbelievable."

Dad: "Don't listen to her, son. We're your family. Would we lie to you?" (his right arm shakes, so he clenches his hand into a fist) "I love you." (strokes my hair with his free hand) "I l-l-looove you."

Mr. Morgan: "You guys have been lying to your son about that night, yet I'm the asshole?" (snickers) "No wonder your son's a fucking basket case. He has no idea. And you all keep filling his head with crazy stories of things that never happened. You're all going to hell." (snickers again, points to me) "Look at him. He's barely a man anymore. Didn't really have much to learn from though. Did he? Not enough to defend himself like a man."

The play is broken when Mom launches at Mr. Morgan. She slaps him across the face so hard, I feel it in my bones. The sound echoes long after she stops. Mr. Morgan stumbles back into the glass door to outside, holding his face. No one does or says anything. Hadlee doesn't even go to him. His eyes dart around, processing what just happened.

Mom's chest heaves up and down. "Get the fuck out of here, you asshole. I'll call the police if I even see you driving past this place. And if you don't leave, I'll knock your teeth out with my socket wrench." She grabs his shirt and shoves him with a strength I've never seen Mom have. Ever. "You don't ever speak to my husband or my son like that again. Understand, *Melvin?*"

Mr. Morgan straightens himself out, still in shock, maybe even a little frightened. His voice lacks conviction. "You'll be hearing from my lawyer about that restraining order." He starts to walk out the front door. "Now, Hadlee!"

She shakes her head. "I'm not going with you." Her voice is so tiny, she's just as shocked and disgusted, maybe even impressed, that someone stood up to her father.

"If you don't come with me right now, then you can find somewhere else to stay, because the locks *will* be changed first thing in the morning, little girl."

Hadlee stiffens, seems to go numb. Maybe trying hard not to get emotional. "Goodbye, Daddy."

Mr. Morgan scoffs. Mutters under his breath, and shoves open the door harder than is necessary. He gets into a truck and peels out of the parking lot. After he's done, it's so quiet that we can hear the laundry room mid-cycle from way out back. Finally, Hadlee clears her throat to awkwardly speak up.

"I'm sorry about my dad."

Mom and Dad ignore her.

"You can stay here as long as you need to," I say.

"Not under my roof," Dad grumbles, not looking at her. Never once. "I'll call the police if I ever see you heeeeeeere again." He stops to catch his breath, straining.

Dad?

"Honey, what's wrong?" Mom goes up to him and rubs his back.

Dad is still kneeled by me. "I'm fine." His fist is still clenched.

She feels his forehead. "You're burning up, Joe."

Dad closes his eyes. "I'mmm fine."

I sit up quickly and ignore my body screaming at me. Dad needs help, the doctors, the hospital, something. But he glances up at me through one eye and shakes his head so slightly only I can see.

Why? Why not?

No. It all ends tonight. No more secrets.

"Mom, I have to te—"

"I'm fine, son." He blocks my path to Hadlee, points to her accusingly. "You're not allowed to be here."

Hadlee frowns, shuffles her feet, and looks away. "I know."

Dad sucks in a breath. "Please leave."

"Dad, she's not going."

He whips his head around. "What did I tell you the other day? I'm trying to protect you." He gets anxious. "She is the reason you were out in the woods. She is the reason you hit your head and that you were in a coma."

Mom covers her mouth again and blinks tears.

Hadlee stands there, looking ashamed. "You know that's not what happened."

Dad reaches down to the coffee table and pounds his unclenched fist on it. "He's *MY* son. He's *MY* baby boy. He almost *died*."

Before Hadlee can speak, Dad cuts her off.

"No. NO. When you're a parent, maybe you'll understand the horror of almost losing a child. But I hope to *God* you never do."

"I would never do anything to hurt Dev." She walks forward, but my dad blocks her. "You're doing him more harm than good. He's at this motel day and night for you." She points to Mom. "And you, Mrs. Landry. Did you know that he doesn't even want to go to college because he thinks he has to stay here to take care of you two?"

"Hadlee?" I say, hurt. Betrayed. Why would she say that to my parents? That was told in secret.

Mom lets out a moan, tears falling, looking at me. "Is this true?"

"You think you're protecting him by keeping him here, but you're hurting him. He's not living."

Mom doesn't respond, just keeps quiet, and then nods. "I knew this would happen."

"Not this again," Dad says. "We've discussed this."

"No, you did." Mom rubs her forehead. "I told you that I don't like it anymore."

"Like what?" I say.

What the hell is everyone talking about?

"Nothing." Dad chokes, turns to Mom. "I won't do this, Joanne. He's my son. He is MY son."

"He's *OUR* son."

"You're not doing this. You can't do this."

"We can't keep him here forever."

Dad gets flustered, stuttering. "We're a family."

"This is not our life, Joe." Mom runs her hands through her hair. "This was your life."

"Oh, so now I'm the bad guy?"

"I did this for you because I loved you. But we're not happy here anymore."

"Joanne—"

"You're not even happy here."

Dad shakes his head. "I made a promise to you to protect our son and our family."

Mom gives him such a pitiful look that I can't stand to face either of them anymore, so I watch Hadlee.

Mom lowers her voice. "You don't need to keep that promise anymore. I was scared, and I didn't know if he would ever wake up."

Hadlee adds, "It's the right thing to do."

"What the fuck is everyone talking about?" I shout. "I'm right here. I can hear you all. What are you keeping from me?" I look at Hadlee. "Is it about what happened to you in the woods when I was unconscious? About my time in the coma?"

Mom's eyes go wide. "Do you know what happened?"

Hadlee shakes her head, brings strands of hair to her mouth. "He...." She gets uncomfortable, tries to compose herself while her lower lip trembles. "He's starting to remember."

Dad advances on Hadlee, hunched over, swaying a little. His face is so red, I'm afraid he's going to explode. "You're a liar just like your father." He raises his arms as if he is about to push her, which drives Hadlee to trip backward and fall. But he must realize the horror of what he's about to do, because he stands rigid, his arms drop, and he looks so confused, so lost, so ashamed.

"Joe!"

"Dad!"

I run past him to help Hadlee up. It's getting out of control, nothing makes sense. None of it. I'm sick of being lied to. Sick of the half-truths and cover-ups.

Dad points. "Leave my family alone! Lea—"

"Tell me the truth," I say.

Dad looks perplexed.

"Tell me right now, or I'll run away with Hadlee and I'll never come back."

She was assaulted. Hadlee was assaulted, and I caused it. Just admit it.

Dad tries to get past me and to Hadlee, but I hold him off. He's so weak, it's not hard at all. He's acting so deranged and crazy. I'm terrified he'll break. He's hurting Hadlee, hurting me. Hurting himself.

"Get out of my way, son."

"Joe!" Mom runs over and tugs on his shoulder. "Joe, you're acting ridiculous. You're scaring them."

"I wasn't raped," Hadlee whispers.

I have to process the words before they sink in.

"What?" I ask.

"I wasn't raped."

No. No, I saw it.

"What do you mean?"

Hadlee grabs my hands. Behind me, Dad is pleading, he's begging for me to get away from her, but he's too weak and Mom is holding him back. I glance over my shoulder, and Mom places her hands on each side of his face, pulling him close and whispering to him. Dad closes his eyes, tears falling.

So soft my Dad might not even have said it: "He's our baby boy."

When I turn back to Hadlee, her eyes glisten. I don't understand what's happening. This makes no sense. It's so surreal. Just when I think everyone is going to leave me in the dark again, Hadlee looks past me to my parents. She nods.

Then from my mom: "We love you. We only wanted to protect you."

Protect me from what?

Hadlee whispers, "Are you happy?"

She rubs her thumbs over my knuckles so tenderly that I get chills. I don't answer her. My heartbeat jacks into overdrive. The scar on the back of my head starts to throb, the room heats up. Firewood scent. As if from somewhere near, a bonfire rages, but there is no fire. For just a split second, behind Hadlee, three-years-ago her and me. Standing outside the glass doors waving, perched on their bicycles. Not smiling, no emotion. Just waving. Maybe saying hello, maybe saying goodbye. Then her voice in my head:

"Don't ever leave me, Dev."

And then:
"Does he ever come back for her?"
And finally:
"But isn't it amazing here?"

"Shhhhh, stop moving, little boy."
Broken beer bottle
12 gauge
Olive-green pill
Dangling shoes
"You made me do this."

And then I see it, that night from three years ago. Not faces, but fuzzy shapes.

"Halllleeeeeeeeeeee," I cry, my vision blurring. "G-Get hhhheeeellllllllfff."

"Hadleeeeeeeeeeee," he mocks. "Feels weird, right? Like you can't move or think straight?"

No. No. No. No. I can't. I can't. I can... I... I... N... O....

I fall to the ground, face first into the dirt. My eyelids don't close; I can't make them. If I blink, it's beyond my comprehension. I will my arms or legs to function, but it's like I'm melting into the earth. I can't consciously breathe, yet I must be doing it. The fire is right in front of me, and he stands by it, cursing.

"Ohhhhh FUCK! I didn't want to do this. You made me do this. You and the slut friend of yours." He swigs from his bottle of beer before chucking it into the woods. "You think the others will find her?" He bends down to try and meet me at eye level. "I'm a fucking man. You're not taking that away from me." He pounds the ground. "People like you and her and my dad are all the same. Fuck you all."

I can't even talk. My tongue melts into me, which is melted with the earth. I am nothing but thoughts.

Tears fall from his eyes, so he rubs them raw. "I just need it out of my head, man." *He slaps the side of his face repeatedly.* "Why did you have to fucking get inside my head?"

Please. Please. Just make sure she's safe. Just make sure—

"Just like him." He squats on the heels of his feet, grazes a finger against my cheek. "How do you think we should teach you a lesson, little boy?"

And I'm back in the present. Back with Hadlee. Her eyes are wide. She knows I've seen something. But I don't remember it. I saw it, but I don't remember it. Like it's not really me but someone pretending to be me. Or someone else's memories. Not mine. Not mine. Not fucking mine.

"It wasn't me that was raped, Dev."

She wraps me in a hug, holding me so tight. But all the heat drains from my body. Everything just goes cold and numb. Because she says the next words that rock my world.

She says the next words that kill me.

The words that betray me.

I close my eyes and wait for darkness. My curse. I can feel Hadlee's tears—feel her body tremble.

Then she whispers it:

"It was you."

Devastation.

> *Abomination.*

>> *Self-destruction.*

Mutilation.

Absolution.

Skull cracked.

Wet.

Pain.

Stretching.

Burning.

*Extended **hands**.*

Disappear

> *Disappear*

Disappear

Disappear

Disappear

From afar she calls my name. Hadlee. Calls to me.
I am not here. Not here. Not. Here.

Not here anymore.

WHEN THE LEVEE BREAKS

PART SIX

FRIDAY, AUGUST 8TH - THREE YEARS PRIOR

Everything hurts. My mouth is so dry, but I can't move. They won't give me water—won't let me drink anything. My throat hurts, my head hurts, my legs hurt, my stomach and back and neck hurt.

Everything is in pain, and I have IVs and machines attached to me.

No one is telling me anything. I woke up a couple days ago.

I just want to go home.

Mom and Dad don't really go home. They sleep here, in the hospital. Alternating who goes back to shower. I wish I could shower.

No one will tell me what's going on. Why I'm here. What happened.

It's just so fuzzy.

Hadlee... I want Hadlee.

Where is she?

Why isn't she with me?

Was she hurt too?

I can feel the drugs kicking in again—the ones that make me

sleepy. And everything starts to feel soooooooooo empty. I can't bear it.

Like a void.

Fight to keep my eyes open. Mom and Dad are perched awkwardly in hospital chairs, snoring. Mom has tissues bundled in her hand. Dad has a large coffee cup.

Was Hadlee hurt? Is she home or in the hospital?

Try to remember, but the drugs, whatever these are, drag me away.

Pull me underneath the surface.

My tongue like sandpaper. Throat like a cheese grater.

Something is watching me, out of my vision. I can feel the eyes, all the eyes.

So. Many. Eyes.

Sleep is....

Sleep....

Haddy....

Where did you go?

Where am I?

I'm about to sleep, but I hope they covered me up good. So cold. Don't want any skin exposed. Not any.

Is that a figure? There. At the foot of your bed. See it?

Don't want to be watched. Need to stay awake, stay alert. Need to lie face-up.

What do you think it is? It's so dark, like a curse.

But sleep looks so good.

CHAPTER 32

My heart stops. Lungs close. Mouth dries up. Eyes burn. Body sweats but shivers at the same time.

You're hallucinating again, clearly. 'Cause what she said makes no sense.

Hadlee pulls back, but I don't move. My feet are planted to the ground and my joints are locked in like the Tin Man. My mind races with visions. Of what happened just now, what happened earlier in her room. About the scar on the back of my head, the sleepwalking, the amnesia from whatever happened to cause my coma. How Hadlee pushed me away when we got too close earlier this week.

No. You're hallucinating... no. No.

I lock eyes with Hadlee, her beautiful russet eyes. Her milky, pale complexion, her chestnut hair. I take it in, take it all in. Nothing is said; she just nods. She. Just. Nods.

No. It DID happen.

She's... known? But Mom and Dad—

It's a joke. You're hallucinating.

No... think, Dev. THINK. What do you know?

Hadlee's voice in my head:

"What do you remember?"

Then from my dad, his voice wrecked, weak, sobbing, "You were only thirteen...."

It's true.

I open and close my mouth once. Twice. Three times. Hadlee looks down and away from me. Ashamed? I can't tell.

"Is this a joke?" I ask, my voice stronger than I thought it would be. And I turn to face my parents, finding something inside that wills me forward. "A-Are you all messing with me?"

Mom and Dad don't look, not right away, and when they do, it devastates me. There's nothing remotely humorous. Nothing that can be mistaken for misjudgment.

You were raped.

"I'm so sorry," Hadlee says from behind. "I wanted to tell you." She looks so distraught. "But you forgot after you woke up."

I whip around, but she still can't look at me. How long has she lived with this truth? How long has she known?

Too exposed. Feel like all my skin is exposed outside in the middle of a blizzard. I shiver and hug my body. Need to cover up, get warm.

"I don't understand," I say, a headache coming on. "This entire time?"

She nods again, ashamed, tears falling. Suddenly, I'm annoyed. Like she doesn't have a right to be upset.

I turn back to face my parents. "The story about hitting my head?"

Mom steps back from Dad and tries to come toward me, but I back up. She stops, hurt. "You didn't remember."

"No." I close my eyes and shake my head. "No."

The darkness, right there, bubbling up from the depths.

"You were in a coma."

"I woke up."

"You had no memory of what happened. Your father and I had no idea if you would remember or not."

I pound my fist against the side of my head. Maybe for clarity. Maybe to wake myself up if this is a dream. But it doesn't work, and I start pacing back and forth.

Void.

"Just tell me the truth."

"We were——"

"I don't care what you were! I just want the fucking truth!"

Silence.

Migraine coming on.

"Why did you have to fucking get inside my head?"

I flinch, punch at the air. Pound my palm against the side of my head. Out, out. I want it *OUT*.

It happened.

Rotted, empty insides.

From behind: "You could've been so happy." Hadlee sobs. "I just didn't want you to have to live with it." Her hands move to her chest as if to grab her camera that's not there. "You just——I just...."

Jesus Christ, what happened to her?

I reach back and grab her wrists and pull her forward, shake her. It still doesn't make sense. The memories are there, but implanted in my brain. Like it was my mind in someone else's body, or my body with someone else's mind. Even now it doesn't add up. How could I forget?

"You were working with my parents?"

"No."

"Were you ever going to say anything?"

"Of course."

"I... I don't...."

"I was still there when it happened."

No.

She hugs herself, shaking her head back and forth, snot dripping from her nose. "I heard it all, Dev." She reaches out a hand for me to grab, but as much as I want to, I don't hold it. "I'm so sorry." She breathes heavily, unable to compose herself, fanning her face. "I'm so sorry I left you. I—"

And then I remember Hadlee's picture of the two eyes staring in horror out from the bush. The one she staged, the sketch she drew that burned into my mind from the other night.

No. Nonononononononono.

Tears fall from her face so fast it smears some of the light makeup she wears around her eyes. Part of me wants to comfort her and tell her that I understand, that I'm sorry, but the other part just wants her to get the hell away from me. I can't process this. It's too much. It's too much at once.

There is a steak knife in the kitchen if you just wanted to cut your—

But then I think about how much she's changed. The hipster clothing, the septum piercing, the dark, disturbing photography, her website, how she dropped every single friend she ever had and started taking pictures of everything. The nude photos. Her whole life, uprooted.

And then there's Dad. He's crying—everyone is. There are so many tears it makes me sick. Physically sick. I feel bad, but I don't want to. I shouldn't feel bad. How long have they been keeping it from me? Three years? Were they ever going to tell me? Did they think it would just go away, and I'd live my life without knowing the truth?

The truth. I don't even know what the truth is.

It's your curse.

Mom falls back into the counter and her shoulders shake, crumbling into herself.

Dad has his hand over his chest, rubbing at it, his one hand still clenched in a fist, straight out by his side. He's cringing and craning his neck.

You don't get to win, Dad.

I point to him. "Is that why I'm not allowed to leave the motel? Why you never let me go anywhere without checking in?"

He struggles to respond, his entire face starting to turn red. He gasps for breath, uses a free hand to rub his chest and air out his shirt. "You don't understand."

"Explain it to me." A pause. "Or should I explain to Mom about how you've been taking—"

Hadlee puts a hand on my shoulder from behind. "Dev, calm down."

I shake her off, paranoid. The hairs on the back of my neck stand up, and I feel lightheaded. "Don't touch me. I don't like it when—"

—when people touch you from behind.

"You were just out in the woods," Dad continues. "You were—" He almost chokes saying it. "They burned your clothes." He stops to gather himself.

I don't want to think about it. It can't be me if I don't think about it.

"We didn't know what happened until Cuckoo Clark carried you in here unconscious," Mom says.

"Mr. Day?" I ask. "He was there?"

Hadlee: "He's the one that found us, Dev." She closes her eyes, as if to remember the moment. "I didn't know what to do. I was still in shock."

Dad: "Bullshit."

Hadlee: "He's the reason we both made it back safe."

"I'll be here when you're equipped. After it comes back."

Holy shit.

Then Dad: "I would... I'd...." He coughs and looks down at his arm. It's shaking.

"Mr. Landry?" Hadlee asks.

Stop this, Dev. Stop this. He can't handle it. Dad can't handle it.

I look to Mom. "Something's wrong with D—"

"I-I-I was so scared." He sways and tries to walk forward but stops. "I—"

"Joe?" Mom looks up. Rushing to him.

"You're my—" He swallows. "I messed up s-so much in my life. I've done wrong in so many ways. I'm a failure." He cringes. "I've run us into the ground, I made your mother resent this life. I jus—" His breaths become staccato. He rubs his chest again. "Christ, it's so hot in here." He clears his throat. "I didn't want that, that thing, to define who you were and how people would judge you."

"You lied to me."

"I wasn't going to lose you and your mother." He looks at Mom. "I'm nothing without you two in my life. I'm no one."

He's so broken. So much so that looking at him physically hurts.

Mom kisses his forehead. "We would never leave you. I love you. Listen to me." She kisses his lips. "I married you, and I would never trade you or our son for the world. You hear me?" Another kiss. "I. Love. You." She looks to me. "Both of you."

Dad closes his eyes, breathes out. "I love you too." He holds his hand out in my direction, his eyes begging for me to take it. "We will get through this as a family."

And Dad cries so hard, makes such an unusual sound that it terrifies me. It's so high pitched and scratchy, so defeated and tragic. Mom can't calm him down, and Hadlee fidgets from behind.

There's something about seeing a parent cry that just shakes you to the core. My dad, a man I looked up to, who I thought would never lie and would always protect me, a man I thought invincible, is just like me.

Human. Flawed. Confused. Scared of the world.

I don't know what to do, and he's begging for me to grab hold, but no matter how hard I want to, I just can't bring myself to do it. My mind and my heart and my body all tell me different things to do. Neither knows what is right.

"Please forgive me." Dad closes his eyes and repeats it under his breath. His entire arm shakes. He rolls a shoulder until it locks in place in an unnatural position.

Me: "We need to tell them."

Mom: "Tell us what?"

Dad: "I'd die before I let anyone hurt you."

He again holds out his hand, asking for me to grab on. Mom waits for me to. Hadlee, I can sense, waits for me too.

But I just can't do it. He's so desperate to bring us together. The three of us, a family like we always were, like we still are. And I want desperately for it to be true, but I just don't know if we can be.

I close my eyes and breathe in and out real slow to gather my thoughts. And then I see it:

Me when I was six years old, lying on the blacktop of the parking lot outside, a scrape on my knee after falling on my rollerblades. Dad looks so young, so thin. A full head of hair and a smile as wide as I can remember.

The sign to the motel is still lit up and beautiful. The pool out back is still operational and full of motel guests. The parking lot is packed. Mom stands off down the road talking to a group of walking mothers, complete with fanny packs and sun visors. This was one of the last seasons when the motel was still popular.

The scent of cotton candy finds its way to me from some-where, and Dad kneels on one knee to apply a Spider-Man Band-

Aid. He presses it on, me wincing, and ruffles my hair. He is so carefree, so... happy.

He says, "Now, would Peter Parker stay down when he was kicked, or would he get up and keep on fighting?" He squats down low so we're the same level. "I'll tell you a secret." He cups his hands over my ear to whisper. "Pain helps make us feel real. Sometimes the strongest thing you can do is ask for help when you need it most, and then keep on fighting." He holds out his hand. "Grab my hand, son." I don't do it right away, hesitate from the pain of getting up, afraid I'll fall again. So, he leans in close to again whisper in my ear. "Do you want to know what it feels like to soar, champ?"

He pulls me up and puts me on his shoulders, running around the parking lot while I have my arms out to the sides, pretending like I'm flying. Dad is making the cockpit noises of an airplane, signaling traffic control. Eventually Mom joins in, and Dad runs us right out back and jumps with me into the pool. Mom is standing off, laughing and clapping her hands as Dad splashes water up at her. Eventually, he gets out, grabs her by the waist, and flings her in.

We just play in the pool. And I remember it so vividly. Hadlee is here. In the pool with me. Mom and Dad swimming off to the side, and Hadlee is giggling. Her smile... even then her smile was magical, something to behold. Something to cherish.

Such a different, happy time.

Back in the now, Dad's so pale and out of shape, dark rings around his eyes. And he looks so sick, like a cancer patient. I don't remember the last time I've seen him smile outside. I just can't stand to look at this shell of him.

Mom is so broken and unhappy, like the life she could've had is gone forever, stuck with us in this motel.

Hadlee—so different from the girl who found the pocket watch with me.

And me—I don't even know who I am. Am I the same? Different?

Am I broken too?

"I'm a fucking man."

"I love you, kid," Dad says.

He tries to signal we can get past this. He wants me to fight. To soar despite falling.

And for just a split second, I see the life we had, the man Dad used to be. How he used to dream of this grand life for us, how he would flash Mom that smile that made her miss a step. How strong and powerful he used to seem. How it felt like with him and Mom in my life, nothing and no one could ever hurt me.

Not ever.

But that split second is gone, and it makes me want to cry.

I don't grab his hand.

I can't.

I want to.

And then he must see it, my hesitation, my fear, and his face just shatters like ceramic.

He gasps, freezes.

"Joe?"

"Mr. Landry?"

Dad's face contorts, his body as rigid as a board, and then without word or warning, he collapses. Falls to the ground and lands on his face. Lands with a *THUMP*. The motel floor vibrates with the impact. And the world stops.

"I'm going to be fine. Okay, kid?"

Mom cries out and drops on her knees, rolls him over. Dad's eyes are so wide, they're practically bulging out of their sockets.

His body spasms and jerks, his right arm stiff to his side, his left hand pressed to his chest, over his heart.

No.

Mom's hands hover above him, don't know where to go. She's calling his name, trying to get him to sit up or shake it off. But I can't focus on anything except her hands. So desperate, so frantic. Looking for someplace to go or something to do but unable to find it. They just hover above him, like a guillotine blade waiting to drop.

Hadlee pushes past me to go to him. She pulls out a phone and dials a number before placing it to her ear. Mom tries CPR.

I can't move, can't breathe, can't feel. The world is muted and numb.

Stuck. My body won't allow me to exit. I'm trapped.

"How do you think we should teach you a lesson, little boy?"

He'll get up; he'll be okay. 'Cause he's my dad, 'cause my parents are always supposed to be okay. They're always supposed to be there to help guide me and heal me and protect me. I'm supposed to learn from that. I'm supposed to——

(Running in the woods from nothingness)

I still can't move as Mom and Hadlee call me, ask me questions in a language I can't seem to understand. Not even when the ambulance arrives and EMTs rush in, Dad still on the ground, his eyes rolled back into his head, his entire body twitching. Not when a police officer comes in to ask questions. Not even when they roll in the stretcher and load Dad's body onto it.

The only things I remember are Mom's lonely, desperate

hands. Her begging and pleading for Dad to answer her. And how he never grabbed them. Never got up.

(Trapped in a closet with a predator)

When Mom follows the paramedics outside and into the ambulance, the red and blue flashing lights silhouette everything outside, she fights with a paramedic who tries to keep her from getting in. But after a while, they let her aboard. Hadlee walks with me to the parking lot, but I'm a zombie. They say we can follow in our car.

Rory is out there, Aubrey too. Mr. Day is leaning over his balcony, watching. A breeze picks up and cools me. It's so sudden that I get the urge to vomit, so I lean over and do.

(Reflection distorted in pond)

Hadlee grabs my hands and then my face. She says things, but there is no sound. Her mouth moves. *Heart attack. Stroke. Are you okay?* I think this is what she says.

You were raped.

Your parents lied to you.

Hadlee lied to you.

Dad had a heart condition.

You lied to them.

Now he's....

He'll be okay. Dad will be fine. He will be—

(Stuck in the bottomless pit of a well)

Hadlee looks at me and interlocks her fingers in mine. She's crying. It takes the breeze blowing against my face to realize I have been too. She's still here, with me, next to me. It's all happening so fast, yet not fast enough. Mom and the paramedics are in the parked ambulance. She's holding Dad's hand and crying. Talking to him. She hasn't even acknowledged me. I don't blame her because I did this. I caused this.

I never said anything when I should've.

They never said anything when they should've.

And it's all a circle.

Secrets. So many secrets.

So many revealed. How many more are there still to come to light?

(Not here anymore)

"I'm here for you," Hadlee whispers, getting closer. "I'm not going anywhere this time."

"Don't ever leave me, Dev."

She gets so close that our shoulders touch. She wraps her arms around my waist and holds me. Doesn't let go.

I just want to run to the ambulance. I want to jump in and wrap my dad in a hug and tell him I love him, and I forgive him. I want to rewind time and go back to when I was like a little kid, back when he was still happy.

Maybe if I'd noticed the signs earlier....

Maybe if I'd told Mom sooner....

Maybe if I'd never let Hadlee stay with us last Saturday....

Mom doesn't ask me to go with them to the hospital—doesn't tell me to stay. The doors to the ambulance are still open, the paramedics hooking up machines to him, chaos surrounding the inside as the police officer gets back in his cruiser to follow the ambulance.

He can't die. He won't die. That doesn't happen to your parents, only other people's parents, right? Right?

If he dies, it's because of you.

Hadlee's entire life changed because of you.

You were raped because of you.

From the distance, a dog barks on repeat, the sounds of a trashcan being knocked over. The scent of a bonfire from afar wafts in the air. It makes me sick to my stomach, but I don't throw up, not again.

Behind me, the motel and all I've ever known.

Out past the parking lot is a world I've been kept from, protected against. Some terrible past I still can't fully recollect. Is it even real if I don't remember living it?

"We'll figure this out. I'll help you remember. We'll talk to someone." She squeezes my hand, but I still can't bear to face her, not yet.

She whispers, "I love you."

My knees lose all their strength, and I fall to the ground, Hadlee guiding me all the way. We sit in the parking lot. The words I've always wanted to hear, the ones I've wanted to say back, and I can't. I don't even know how to.

Who am I? Who are we?

We can't ever be the same. We can't ever go back to before. Not to three years ago, not even to last night.

In my head, I say the words back. I say that I love her, that I need her, that I'm so mad at her. That I understand her. That I forgive her.

But I just don't know if any of it is true.

Hadlee. Hadlee Renee Morgan. My best friend; my first crush. The first girl I ever loved. The first girl I ever kissed.

No longer just the girl in the bleachers I'd watch from afar.

No longer just MalevolentBeauty.

No longer perfect.

Hadlee hugs me again, sitting next to me in silence. Looking out into the unknown with me, the lights from inside the lobby shining on us from the window. The first time Mom and Dad will ever leave the motel together. The first time they'll ever leave me behind.

One of them might never be coming back.

And I don't know why I don't feel more. Why I'm not as hysterical as Mom is.

Why I'm so numb.

Hadlee's lilac scent reaches to me with the breeze. I close my eyes—remember happier times. Listening to old records at the motel, jumping on the beds. Her trampoline in the summer. Her sister Maggie's ballet recitals. Her mom's garden. The petunia incident. Dad's omelets. Cleaning rooms with Rosa. Her scary stories. Watching Mom fix the Ford Pickup we had to sell for money. Running track. *Star Wars* marathons with Aiden. Room 13 with Hadlee. Bike rides at dusk. Exploring new places and things. Finding gems at garage sales. Card games with Mom and Dad during thunderstorms in the motel. I used to be terrified of the rumbling skies when I was little.

"Just means it's a bowler's strike," Dad used to say.

Something comes over me. They close the doors, and one of the paramedics hops into the vehicle and pulls from the parking lot. They're taking him away, and I'm off after it. Pumping my legs and my arms, ignoring the pain in my face and my sides. Running faster as the ambulance picks up speed. I extend my hand and open my fingers wide, calling out for them to stop, to let me in. To let me be with him, with both of them. I just want to be together. I want to be there for him like he was there for me.

But, of course, I can't. Because I'm still sitting here with Hadlee. Frozen. Sitting here in this vacant parking lot of this vacant motel as the red and blue flashing lights fade away, and the sirens echo into the distant night.

Not man enough to do anything, like Mr. Morgan said. 'Cause real men wouldn't let this happen to them.

Right?

"Is there anything I can do?" she asks, her voice soft. "Do you want me to get Rory to drive us to the hospital?"

Who are you now? What does this make you?

I finally look at her, and she locks bloodshot eyes with mine.

You were raped.

For the first time in what feels like years, I whisper:

"What am I supposed to do?"

Her eyes wide, pitying me. Such a weak, embarrassing look.

Maybe one I'll have to get used to from now on.

She eventually looks ahead with me, interlocking her fingers in mine. Allowing us to stay still, to stay silent. A breeze blows through my hair and gives me the sensation of running.

Soon, we'll go to the hospital, deal with the reality of my choices. The secrets I kept to protect Mom and Dad. Where Hadlee and I stand. After that, the reality of what happened in the clearing in the woods.

But for right now, we sit. We think. We wait.

From behind, I feel it. My darkness. Beckoning me to join it. I close my eyes and count down, will it to go away.

What the hell do we do now?

TWENTY-FOUR HOURS EARLIER

HADLEE

Clark Day opens his door after being sure no one is watching. At this point, I know how to be somewhere without really being there, seeing as I've been practicing for years at home.

When he lets me in, I close the door behind me and wrap him in a hug. He stiffens because it's awkward for him and me as well. Maybe I shouldn't be doing this, but it's too late now. I owe him my life.

He doesn't say anything before he breaks away and reaches on the bed to a manila folder. I don't need to open it to know it's the files I requested, so I tuck it under my arm and shift the weight on my feet, as I anticipate getting out of here. Dev is going to need me soon.

"I don't suppose I can convince you to contact the authorities about this," he states, even though he means it as a question.

"Not really, no." I bring a strand of hair to my mouth and chew on the tips. Daddy always used to tell me not to do it when I was a little girl. It's a bad habit for bad girls. But he's not around to tell me to stop. Soon, I won't be either.

"What are you planning on doing with those?" He points to

the folder before walking to his night table to sip from a glass of red wine. He swallows it, eyes me as he does.

I nod and breathe in deep. I sent him all the photos I had, and he contacted a friend to help. Hopefully, it will be everything we need.

Without thinking, I hug him again as he tries to balance his wine. "Thank you."

He pats my back lightly. "I'm indebted to you kids. You know that."

I nod again and disentangle us. When I step back, I can see Clark like the perfect canvas. The bathroom light is silhouetted behind him, giving a warm, albeit eerie, glow that lights up half the side of his face. Clark at once in the light and the dark. He's like the uncle I never had.

We don't waste time when we get together, so I smile and head to the front door to sneak out. No one is outside, so I can get back across the lot easily without being spotted. I'm wearing my black hoodie that I use on stakeouts. I zip it up to the very top and put the hood up, my Olympus E-M10 hanging from my neck in a waterproof protection bag.

I hold on to it because I need to hold on to it.

"What are you going to accomplish with it, Little Morgan?" He takes another sip of wine.

I shrug and head out of the room, making my way to the street and in the direction of the woods before I overstay my welcome.

PRESENT DAY

Dev isn't moving or saying anything; he's sitting here staring off into blank space. I hate myself so much. Why couldn't I have told him sooner?

I love him, and I think I always have, even back when we were kids. He was always there, always someone I could talk to and count on and have fun with. But I took him for granted and let our parents choose for us. We should have taken off long ago.

When he still doesn't move, I lean into him and rest my head on his shoulder, which he lets me do, but he doesn't acknowledge it.

I really do love you, Dev.

When he's ready, I'll be with him when he wants to see his Dad. I'll be with him when he's ready to talk about what happened and how Clark fits into all of this. I'll be with him when he's ready, like I am, to take control.

Gosh, I really want my camera right now.

There are things I wish I could tell him:

How they never caught the guy who did it, and that's why his parents kept it a secret. He just vanished without a trace, and I've been trying so hard to track him down for both of us. I can't remember the look of his face, but I won't give up.

He is the dark thing.

It's taken me three years, Dev, and I am SO close to finding him.

He won't get away with what he's taken away from you; he will pay. We will find him and make him wish he never did those things he did. Our parents can go around pretending it never happened, but I was there with you.

I watched it happen.

We've been in the dark place ever since.

There are so many things I would have done differently between us back then, but I need to make them right now. It's time I'm there for you in all the ways you were there for me.

I'll keep you safe.

He doesn't know that I've been looking, but I have. I know his truth.

I think he's back here, Dev, in Brooke Meadows.

And we're going to find him.

Our monster.

TO BE CONTINUED

ACKNOWLEDGMENTS

I truly don't know where to begin with this one. This project had been shelved for eight years before I dusted it off as my follow-up to *Aubrey Fisher*. None of this would have been possible without dozens upon dozens of people behind it. More people than I can fit in this section, but we'll try, like before.

Thank you once again to the people from Seton Hill University that really saw the potential in this story and helped shape it from a vastly different genre to what it is now. Also, again, to my graduating class: Glorious Writer's Republic of Cat Herd. You still know if you know.

My mentor on this book: Lee Tobin McClain. Following up my debut with this was a departure for both of us, and you were there championing it every step of the way.

My critique partners: Effie Rose and Melanie Bates, the Trifecta of Cat Herd forever.

My other critique partners: Mark Hoff, Mario Moreno, Derek McElfresh, and K. Parr. You saw some UGLY first drafts for this project and helped me realize I was trying too hard to make a bigger spectacle out of what should have been a personal narrative. You never got to see what it became then, but you will now.

My editors who worked their glorious magic: Mike Dell, Kat Nics, and Effie Rose. If you like how smooth this reads, it's because of them.

My beta readers, then and now: Elvi, Henry Haisch, Jesika, J.L. Gribble, Kate Cunningham Martel, Kristin Molnar, Mason

Carlisle, Matt Andrew, Nina Fedak, and Shelby. May you all forever live in these pages.

To Jacob Baugher, for the hours we talked about running and photography. I hope I got it right.

Thanks again to my absolutely stunning cover designer: Nicole Hower. She brings my vision to life.

My audiobook narrator and collaborator: Eric Altheide. You get it right every single time. We are now two for two. More to come?

Also, thanks to my OGBBB (you know if you know): Bethany Taylor, Courtney Ricigliano, Julie Ann Cordero, and Tiffany Schaffer.

To my parents and my brother, for continuing to put up with me.

To my friends, who at this point should have ceased talking to me a long time ago.

And to Victor T. Cypert, who was (partially) the inspirations behind Aiden. If it reads like nonfiction, it probably is.

I said before that writing a book is hard, but it's also emotional. This was written in 2016 and shelved. It was a follow-up to my debut. It was a departure for me, and it was ambitious. I knew it would challenge reader expectations, and it would ask very complex questions without any answers. It's not a "crowd-pleasing" story like my debut might have been. This is book one of what is a two-book narrative. It's a reverse narrative arc, meaning the characters end in worse places than where they started, and more questions are asked than what the plot originally asked.

It also deals with very heavy topics, even for an upper-YA audience. But one thing I have never been is afraid to push boundaries and challenge societal norms.

This is not a true story. But like *Aubrey Fisher*, there is a lot of truth in it. Dev is another representation of me put under a microscope. The various side characters are loosely based on real people in my life, and the emotions the characters feel are based in reality. Everything in this book was researched and fed through professionals/sensitivity readers. If I got anything wrong, it is no one's fault except my own.

When I wrote this book, Me Too wasn't yet a thing, but I knew that there was a stigma, especially for young boys and adult men. Toxic masculinity is a real problem that affects too many men from a young age. Men are supposed to be strong and in control and the "foundation." They aren't supposed to show emotion. They especially are not supposed to be weak. Ever. This was a misconception I carried with me through a lot of my adolescence.

We devote too much of media to showcasing these alpha males that perpetuate this idea that men are only desirable if they act a certain way, and it has wreaked havoc for far too long. Glorifying toxic men in toxic relationships perpetuates rape culture, and it leads young men to grow up thinking that certain things are acceptable. We do not need any more men like that in our society.

Not fucking one more.

Because of this stigma, young men feel ashamed when they themselves are survivors of sexual violence. It's not assault if it's a man—because he enjoyed it, right? 1 out of every 10 survivors of rape are men. Since 1998, 2.78 million men have survived an attempted or completed rape (if reported). And college men aged 18-24 are the most at-risk. This is not even considering women or transgender people or marginalized communities. Or those that go unreported every day.

Every sixty-eight seconds, an American is sexually assaulted.

We live in a society where silence is encouraged and rewarded. Where survivors are afraid to speak up. Of not being believed. Of being ostracized. Of being criticized. Having their experiences invalidated. Especially women. And it needs to stop.

Another theme I find myself coming back to time and time again is the masks we wear. The versions of ourselves we curate. The "us" we present for work, for family, for friends, for social media, etc. The things we choose to say and the things we don't. It fascinates me, and it's a theme I will continue to explore in future projects.

We all lie, and I'm no exception. Sometimes I do it to protect the ones I love. Sometimes, selfishly, I do it for self-preservation. Sometimes I do it out of fear of repercussions. It's a coping mechanism. And this book, like in *Aubrey Fisher*, deals with characters keeping secrets that they feel unable to share. In both of these books, it always ends the same. With pain, and heartbreak, and maybe even relief.

While I am not a perfect person, and I have made plenty of mistakes and will continue to make more, my hope is that, if anything, this helps others out there to be honest. Open up. Speak your truth. Like Dev says, secrets don't stay secret forever.

We never know what someone is struggling with. We never get to see the version that they sit with when alone at the end of the day. The most authentic version of a person is the one they are when alone.

I wrote this story because it was immensely personal to me. And the subject matter keeps me up at night. Yet I didn't feel I had the right to tell it initially, which is why it remained shelved for eight years. Thankfully, a few beta readers convinced me otherwise. And my hope is that this will open up a dialogue. Offer hope to anyone out there who feels silenced. Who feels alone. Who feels like they are screaming and no one is listening.

I hear you.

I see you.

I wasn't there for someone when I should have been, and I will never forgive myself for that. But it's not too late. It's never too late.

This was written as a way to process what I was feeling. To try and understand something that happened to someone I loved very much. I only hope that it can help others out there.

Hope. Maybe the single most important thing we can all have.

If you or anyone you know is suffering with thoughts of suicide or self-harm, please seek a professional as soon as possible. Or call or text 988, the Suicide and Crisis Lifeline.

If you or anyone you know has survived any act of sexual violence, please visit https://www.rainn.org/. Or call the 24/7 hotline at 800-656-HOPE (4673).

As always, I will keep writing stories for the voiceless. For the ones who feel unseen and unheard. For the neurodivergent.

It's because of all of you I get to live out my dream of bringing stories of hope and redemption. To spread awareness and positivity in a world that is so dark. If you keep reading, I will keep writing. And even if you stop reading, I'll keep writing anyway.

All it takes is one person. Just one to make a difference.

You are never alone. You are never too far gone.

Just give me your hand, and I will hold it until you can stand again.

Remember to be kind to yourself, always.

Let's be each other's platforms when it gets too dark and we're unable to see.

And I'll keep you here, with me.

Whenever you're ready to come back home.

SIGN UP TO BE A MALEVOLENTBEAUTY!!!

Like this book? Want to keep up with Hadlee and Dev's whereabouts? Or news about future projects? Maybe receive exclusive content and behind-the-scenes extras for book two? (Yes, there WILL be book two very soon!)

Consider signing up for my newsletter—The **Malevolent-Beauties**. Our little fan club.

I promise not to spam you and will only send content once or twice a month unless I have an upcoming release or giveaway.

Sign up on my website or the link below!

christophermtantillo.com

subscribepage.io/OdzKko

Join my discord, "The Aubreyverse," where you can chat directly with me and other readers! You may also get early access to future projects. Link below!

https://discord.gg/2rhHXqTsdt

Hadlee Needs Your Help...

If you enjoyed this, she asks if you would kindly consider leaving a review on your platform of choice. Not only would it make her extremely happy, but it would help others find this book, like yourself. More reviews means the different retailers will help show this book to more readers, meaning we can grow our **MalevolentBeauties** Club.

I spent seven years trying to get traditionally published and almost just as long thinking I needed validation from others. It took nearly giving up my dream for good, believing I didn't have the talent, before I took the steps to release my first book myself in 2023. As an independent author, I don't have as much access to market or promote my book as a major publisher would.

This means that you can help with a review! So, don't do it for me. Do it for Hadlee.

Use the link below to get to your chosen retailer.

https://books2read.com/keep-you

IF YOU LIKED KEEP YOU...

The Night I Spent with Aubrey Fisher

A boy determined to die. A girl determined to save his life.

After the death of his little brother, Grayson's guilt spirals his life into chaos; it's all his fault. He wants to rewind that night back. To erase the pain he's caused.

So he's decided; in twenty-four hours, he'll kill himself.

Then mysterious and reckless Aubrey shows up with a proposition: A "literally insane" all-night adventure that will show him the beauty in the mundane.

Grayson doesn't know why the foster girl with the piercings, crimson locks, and fishnet leggings is helping, especially when he finds out Aubrey harbors dark secrets of her own. Yet as they spend his last night learning to let go of pain, Grayson may have a new choice to make.

But can he ever really be happy again?

Told in a heartfelt and poignant style interspersed with quirky humor, *The Night I Spent with Aubrey Fisher* is a coming-of-age romance about two people who need to get lost in order to find each other.

Turn the page for an exclusive sneak peek!

THE NIGHT I SPENT WITH AUBREY FISHER

SNEAK PEEK

A STORM IS COMING, AND BLOOD FROM THE OCEAN WRAPS around my ankles. I'm planted on the beach; my feet stuck in wet sand that glues me in place like cement. There is no one around. No sound. No breeze. No atmosphere. The skies above are overcast and gunmetal gray. Ominous. A half-constructed sandcastle to my right remains unattended.

And he's out there. The boy. Out in the blood-waves as the swell crashes into the rocky shore. I try to reach him, to call out to him, but I can't. My voice won't work, no matter how hard I scream. My legs can't break free of the sand. Blood-water stains the entire beach.

Tears fall down my cheeks, and I'm suffocating. The waves get higher. Blood-mist sprays my face, and the boy keeps getting carried out farther with the tide.

From somewhere beyond, two faint glowing lights race closer, toward me, from out past the boy. Two round lights that force me to squint my eyes.

I scream as loud as I can, but my voice won't work, like the entire world is muted. Only the sounds of the little boy screaming out my name over and over.

I can't reach him, but the sky gets darker, the blood redder, and the waves bigger.

The two round lights closer.

But I just can't reach——

PRE

FRIDAY, 6:29 AM

Sometimes it's hard just to wake up.

I love lying awake in bed, one arm bent underneath the nape of my neck and the other extended as I wave it in and out of the prisms of light that seep in through the cracks of my blinds. Trying to catch the dust. This moment, the quiet signaling the pre-dawn in the mornings before school, is blissful. These are the moments I look forward to. It's the one time when I can hold my breath, stare up at the blank ceiling in the dark, and just sink, hiding from the world. It won't last long. But maybe it will be just long enough.

I roll over in preparation for my alarm clock that's about to blare its ugly trumpet. I'm ready for it; I never give it the satisfaction of getting out more than a squeak before bashing it on the head like a whack-a-mole.

BEEP.

Roll.

BANG.

I swing my legs over the bed and hop down, stand on the balls of my feet until my ankles crack, and then move forward over the carpet. Before I touch the knob, I press my ear to the door and listen to the muffled buzzing of Dad's electric shaver from the bathroom down the hall. I can hear the feathery slap of my mom shuffling a deck of cards in the kitchen downstairs, and I imagine her blue night robe draped around her as the tea boils on the stove.

It's their morning ritual, and it never changes.

It's been like this every morning for six months.

I peer over my shoulder at the last beam of light shining in and extend my hand, bathing in the golden ray. The particles seem to hover, almost trapped. They belong to the pre-dawn— just another thing that unnerves me about opening the door. The beauty will no longer belong to me. I won't be able to control it in the real world.

My hands tremble as I flick on the light, shielding my eyes from the piercing white. I grab my phone from the nearby dresser and see a new text:

UNKNOWN

i kno a secret about u...

liar

Chills.

I've never gotten a text like this before.

But they're right.

After I clear away the screen, confused, the picture on my background comes into focus—me with an arm wrapped around my brother in a headlock. He is wearing the seashell necklace. We are in the tree house we built in the woods. My breath catches in my throat until I cough and throw the phone on my bed.

Goosebumps.

My heart pings and I clutch at my chest. A bead of sweat rolls down my forehead, and I undress for my shower. I suppose, my last shower. And that's when it strikes me for the first time today:

My last shower.

I take off my shirt and stare at the purple bruise below my left rib cage. Run my hand over the bumpy surface and wince at the pain, but push harder to feel the pain deeper. It's the only thing that feels normal. It's exactly what I deserve.

With one last deep breath, inhaling the memory of my room, I place a hand on the brass knob of my bedroom door. It's cool under my sweaty palm. Inside my head, the sirens' wail echo their approach. Even today, months after everything, it tells me this is the only way.

I step into the dim hallway and jiggle the knob to another bedroom door on my left.

Still locked.

Breathe in.

Anybody in there?

Breathe out.

You can come out now.

My name is Grayson Falconi, but most people call me Gray.

I'm seventeen years old.

And today I'm going to die.

ABOUT THE AUTHOR

Christopher M. Tantillo earned his MFA in Writing Popular Fiction from Seton Hill University. He enjoys witty banter, awkward conversations, tarot, tea, and has an unhealthy obsession with pizza and gelato. You can find him, and his doggo Benji (Benito), on their own adventures in Niagara Falls, New York, where he grew up. He hopes to spread mental health awareness and advocacy with his writing. He wrote the poetry trilogy, *things i never got to tell you, things you never got to hear,* and *things we never got to share.* He is also the author of *The Night I Spent with Aubrey Fisher* and *Keep You.*

You can find him online at christophermtantillo.com.

www.ingramcontent.com/pod-product-compliance
Lightning Source LLC
Chambersburg PA
CBHW031241310726
48971CB00004B/1115